THE PALMA FOUNDATION

Pete Davies

Copyright © 2023 Pete Davies

Revised Edition September 2023
All rights reserved

The characters and events portrayed in this book are fictitious, with the exception of those people who have given their expression permission to be included in these books. Any similarity to real persons, living or dead, is otherwise coincidental and not intended by the author.

Every appropriate effort has been made to obtain the necessary permissions with reference to copyright material, both illustrative and quoted. I apologise for any ommissions in this respect and will be pleased to make any necessary acknowledgements in any future editions.
No part of this book may be reproduced, or stored in a retrieval system, or transmitted in any form or by any means, electronic, mechanical, photocopying, recording, or otherwise, without express written permission of the author.

e-book - ASIN B0C6FZPJ8W
Paperback - ISBN 9798396321199
Hardcopy - ISBN 9798396329638

A copy of The Palma Foundation will be deposited with The British Library in accordance with the Legal Deposit Libraries Act 2003 in due course.

Cover Design by: Brian Tarr
(brian-tarr.pixels.com)

All Rights Reserved

*To all my amazing supporters of my books.
You continue to inspire me everyday with your
stories of how my writing has given you enjoyment
and a continued interest in my work.*

ABOUT MY BOOKS

This is the 4th book in the 3R International series and I believe they are best read in order.

My stories are complex and interwoven and to help you keep track, you will find a list of characters at the back of the book.

Occasionally I get a request from readers to include their name as one of the characters. I love doing this, although I hasten to add, the characters do not reflect the reader's character traits!

In this book, Hannah Luisa Lopez's name comes courtesy of Hannah Louise López, who I met whilst at Restaurante Bar Coral. Hannah runs Mallorca SUP if you're looking for a paddleboard company in Puerto Pollensa.

If you would like your name to be included as one of the characters, please email me on petedavies01@hotmail.co.uk and I'll see what I can do!

1

She was smiling. It was the first time Sam had really seen any sign of happiness in her face since Simon had died.

Then he found himself gripping the car seat again as Terri dropped the old Porsche down into second gear, before accelerating hard towards the next corner.

They were on their way down from Santuari de Cura, once a monastery and now a hotel. It was right in the middle of the island on top of the Puig de Randa, a mountain perhaps best known for something that looked like a huge golf ball, although it was actually a communications centre, which was situated at the top of the puig, close to the sanctuary.

They'd stopped for a quick coffee at the hotel, one of the time trial stops of the Mallorca Classic Car Rally they were taking part in. But now Terri wasn't hanging around to admire the scenery, drifting the car serenely around the tight corners and then keeping her foot firmly down on the pedal, urging the Porsche down the short straights towards the next bend.

"You do remember that this isn't a race?" said Sam.

"Stop gripping the seat and man up, Bro!" she laughed.

She'd called him her brother almost from the time

they'd first met and she'd discovered Sam Martínez was her half-brother.

"I'm just saying, because we'll get penalty points if we turn up early. That's why they call it a time trial," said Sam.

She had been really pushing the car hard coming down the mountain road and despite the fact it was no doubt a well-built car in its day, he wasn't now quite so sure the brakes on the 1958 Porsche would be up to the workout she was putting it through as they headed back towards Reco de Randa.

It didn't help that there was nothing between him and the very steep sides to the edge of the road, plus he knew she'd caught him glancing across at the speedometer.

She laughed and gave him one of her looks. The one when she'd tilt her head to one side, make her eyes go cross-eyed and do a sad clown look with her mouth. He called it her 'monkey-face.' He smiled at the sparkle he saw in her eyes, because he hadn't seen much of it since the horrific events of six months ago, when the man she'd loved, Simon Barnes, had been shot and murdered by Diego Sanchez.

"Ah, so it's the time trial you're worried about and not my driving?" she said, as she set up for the next corner, another sharp left hander.

Now it was his turn to laugh, but as he did Terri pulled the handbrake up and expertly flicked the steering wheel hard to the left, putting the Porsche into a half-spin. This forced the old fashioned tyres, desperately narrow by modern standards, to fail miserably as they tried to find some grip, before she brought the car back under control, coming to a screeching halt in a run-off area at the next bend.

"There, now we can stop for a moment and not risk the wrath of the marshals. Happy?" she grinned.

He hadn't realised he had grabbed hold of the sides of his seat again, but he started laughing, as he slowly released his fingers from the vice-like grip he'd had on the leather upholstery.

"Sis, you're officially, absolutely nuts!"

*****

They sat in the car for about five minutes, just chatting and taking in the amazing scenery on what was a beautiful Mallorcan spring day. Sam checked his watch.

"As long as you keep to the speed limits, we'll still have plenty of time," said Sam, returning a wave to the driver of a blue 1975 Mercedes 450SL convertible that was going up the hill towards the Sanctuary.

"Who was that?"

The way she said it made him realise it wasn't a general inquiry.

'Was that 'interest' in her voice?'

"Marcos Ramírez."

"Nice."

"Him, or the car?"

She gave him another look.

He grinned.

"I'll introduce you if you like when we get to Bodegas Angel." He didn't wait for her response. "Now, come on, you might actually have to put your foot down again to make up a bit of time now!"

She didn't wait for a second invitation.

"Got it!"

He tried not to, but as she put the old classic convertible into first and accelerated off down the road, Sam felt his fingers going back to the same impressions in the seat where they'd been before.

*****

They had started out earlier that day on a two day classic car rally around the island. Sam had been invited to join in the week before by Andres Gelabert, a friend he'd known for about ten years, almost since the time Andres had set up Bodegas Angel, a vineyard in Santa Maria del Camí, in the Binissalem wine region.

"Someone's had to drop out at the last minute, Sam, so it'll really help us out. It starts and finishes at Belver Castle and I won't spoil the surprise, but we have a beautiful car already set up for you. It'll be great fun and hey, maybe you could get Terri to join in with you," Andres paused, "seeing as you haven't got a girlfriend, again."

Sam winced at the word 'again.' He still wasn't managing to hang on to any sort of long term relationship. He didn't know if it was the PTSD from the shooting when he was back in the Met, or whether he was just crap at keeping hold of someone he might care for.

"Your point, although perhaps a little blunt amigo, is taken in the spirit I think you intended…"

"Good," interrupted Andres. "Because I've already entered you both."

"Well, I'm okay doing it, but I don't know about Terri. I mean, she's still barely going out, except for work, or to socialise with me or Lily."

"Look my friend," Andres's voice softened, "we can't keep creeping around her with kid gloves, can we? I mean, it's not exactly worked with you, has it?" grinned Andres.

Sam smiled.

"You're right, Andres. She loves driving and it will give her something new to focus on."

"Great, so get Terri onside, and then get yourselves into Palma and up to the Castle for nine o'clock next Saturday morning for the team briefing, and then the rally starts at ten."

*****

She hadn't exactly jumped at the idea when he'd first suggested it. But then Sam had roped Lily in, who'd arranged a meal the following night at Bar Coral in Puerto Pollensa, where he tried getting Terri interested again.

"Sounds like it's something right down your street, girl," said Lily, who had become a close friend of Terri's after they'd been kidnapped the previous year, before being subsequently rescued by Simon and Sam.

But Terri still wasn't going for it, so Sam called in reinforcements.

"What do you think, Aina?" asked Sam. "Do you think Terri should come on a classic car rally with me this weekend?"

Aina, the third, or was it the fourth generation to own and run Bar Coral beamed at him, "Si, but of course, Sam. Terri, you must do this! You are a superb driver and besides, you can't leave poor Sam on his own, especially because he has no girlfriend at the moment."

Terri took a deep breath and a half-smile appeared on her face, but it still lacked the energy and life Sam had seen in her the first time he had met her.

"Well, seeing as you say that, Aina, then I think you're right. We can't have him sitting in the car all on his own, can we?"

"Look, will you guys lay off me!" Sam joked, although inwardly he grimaced. He knew the reality was less about their concern about his lack of a girlfriend, but much more about how he was doing long term with coping generally. "If it's not my mother, or Greg, then I'm getting it in the neck from you guys," he grinned at Lily and Terri. "And Aina, now you're joining in!"

"It's only because we love you," said Aina, as she hugged him, whispering, "and care for you amigo."

"Gracias, amiga," he whispered back.

Seeing the attention Sam was getting on his love life, or rather lack of it, seemed to give Terri a reason for her to do the rally with him.

"Well then," laughed Sam, "I'll gratefully accept your kind offer to keep this apparently sad and loveless man company, especially as it's all in aid of charity."

*****

It was 8.30am the following Saturday when Sam and Terri got out of a taxi at Belver Castle, the start point of the rally. The spring sunshine hadn't yet brought its warmth, but the sky was bright blue as they both looked around the throngs of people and the rows of classic cars lined up in the car park.

Sam saw her smile return.

"Glad you came?" asked Sam.

"Yes, mate and what an amazing view," said Terri, looking out across the Bay of Palma below them, seeing La Seu, the famous Palma Cathedral in the distance. "Can't believe I've never been up here before?" said Terri.

"I think we need to check in over there," said Sam, pointing towards a set of gazebos on the other side of the car park that had rally banners hanging from them.

One of the rally administrators met them as they approached and took their names.

"Ah, buenas dias, Señor Martínez y Señorita Anderson. Thank you so much for helping out and stepping in to take the empty spot we had." He gave them a briefing pack, before adding, "Now we have a beautiful car for you. Here, please let me show you." As he walked them across the car park he said, "I think this is your first time in the rally?"

"Si, Señor," smiled Terri. "Any top tips?"

"Just remember it's a rally and not a race, Señorita. The local police take a dim view of anyone speeding."

"All noted, Señor," she grinned back at him.

The administrator stopped by a gleaming silver coloured two door convertible.

"Is this it?" said Terri. Sam saw her passing her hand across the soft lines of the car before them.

"Si, Señorita. You approve?"

"Oh yes, it's beautiful, Señor. Late 50's, or maybe early 60's?" she asked.

"1958, it's a Porsche...."

"356, 1600 Speedster," Terri interjected. "Is it the 60, or 70bhp model?"

The administrator smiled. The beautiful young woman clearly knew her cars. "It's the seventy, Senorita."

"Ooh, even better," said Terri.

They completed the rest of the paperwork and then he took them to the drivers' briefing. Sam couldn't help but notice the change in Terri as she listened and took notes. She was literally beaming, her eyes alive with excitement and anticipation.

"Glad you came, Sis?"

She gave him a friendly punch on the arm.

"Yes, mate." She smiled warmly at him. "And Sam? Thank you."

*****

After a few words of encouragement from the chair of the rally committee, the participants rose and made their way back out to the car park. Without asking, Terri took the driving seat and held her hand out for the keys. Sam didn't argue and handed them over.

Terri checked the pedals. They were quite close together and offset to the left, making her have to shift her driving position. Then she twisted and pulled the chrome choke lever out, then turned the key in the ignition and heard the Porsche burst into life. She listened, just for a moment, taking in the sound of the engine, then pushed the clutch in. It felt a bit spongy and she had to push it all the way to the floor before she could engage first gear. Then she blipped the throttle a couple of times, grinned at Sam and eased the car out of the parking space, negotiated a path through the other cars before setting off down the curving access road to the city below.

He noticed she was taking it easy at first, especially going down the road back into Palma, feeling the way the car reacted to the corners and checking the steering and brakes as she went.

"No power steering and they're drum brakes."

"But she seems to handle pretty well?" said Sam.

"Yes, pretty amazing considering they didn't really get into proper suspension on cars until a good few years later."

"You really are a petrol head, aren't you, Sis?"

"Just a bit," she laughed.

As they drove along the Passeig Marítim, the main road through Palma, they passed the marina where the roadside was lined with people. They were waving and cheering, and Sam and Terri could hear the other cars sounding their horns as the procession of classic cars made its way along the seafront.

"I didn't know it was such a big deal?" said Terri, pushing the horn button on the Porsche.

"To be honest, Sis, neither did I, but looking at the cars and some of the people taking part, there's a lot of money here, so I guess I shouldn't be too surprised at all of this."

They joined in with the other drivers and co-drivers, smiling and waving back as the crowds stretched as far along as La Seu. Then just beyond the Portixol exit, where Terri lived, the road merged into the Ma19 motorway. As the speed limit increased, she eased the Porsche up to 120kph, once again checking the car's stability with a few gentle flicks of the steering wheel from side to side, before lifting her hands just off the steering wheel to feel if the car was pulling one way or the other.

"Seems to ride well?" said Sam.

"Yes, it's beautiful, Sam. It sits really well on the road and the tracking is perfect. Pretty responsive too! With that she gently pushed down on the accelerator and even though it clearly wouldn't be any sort of a match for a modern day supercar, Sam still felt the car surge forward as the power eased in.

"Not bad given it's only a 1600," said Sam.

"It's so light, Sam!" her face lighting up with a smile.

As they continued on the motorway, the convoy of classics gradually started to spread out as the drivers adopted their own driving speed. Terri kept the Porsche at 120kph and it wasn't long before she flipped the indicator, coming off at the Llucmajor junction.

She slowed as she approached the town and then turned left onto the by-pass road. Because of Sam taking her to Contrabando, his favourite tapas restaurant, she knew the roads around the town. Making her way along the by-pass she followed the road and then headed left towards Santuari de Curi, the old monastery. As the road started to climb up through the hills, she really started to take the old car through its paces on the sweeping road up to the first time trial stop.

Sam had done enough driving courses, whilst in the Met Police, to be able to recognise when someone could handle a car. He hadn't often seen her driving first hand, at least not driving fast, but he quickly realised she was a really skilled driver.

They had just passed the little village of Randa when he said, "You're really going to enjoy it when we get to Sa Calobra. It's pretty much a driver's paradise."

"I've heard of it, Bro, but never driven it before, so it should be fun."

Again, he could see she was smiling.

"Good decision," he said.

"What was that?" she said.

He hadn't realised he'd spoken aloud. But so far, it had been a really good decision to get her involved with the rally, as he was seeing much more of the old Terri Anderson he knew. He found himself watching her again. She was enjoying her driving and perhaps just maybe, it had been something of a helpful distraction to allow her some temporary respite from her grief.

"Nothing," said Sam. "Now come on, I'm looking forward to a coffee at our first stop, so show me what this old bucket has still got under the bonnet!"

He sat back, admiring the effortless way she handled the old Porsche and actually found himself relaxing as the countryside flew by under the beautiful Mallorcan sun-filled sky.

*****

A journey that had taken Sam about half an hour, last time he'd been up to the Santuari de Cura from Llucmajor, took only twenty minutes with Terri at the wheel.

As they sat having coffee in the café at the former monastery, they watched the planes on their final approach path into the airport.

"The puig is only just over 500 metres high, but it's still an amazing thing to see those planes on their glide path," said Sam.

His half-sister nodded, "It's almost a bit surreal. We're usually looking up at them, aren't we? Rather than seeing them below our eye line." She looked at her watch. "Come on, we should think about heading off, I want to see if she handles as well going downhill, as she did coming up."

*****

After seeing Marcos Ramírez coming up the hill in his Mercedes 450SL, Terri had set off down the puig, heading towards Bodegas Angel, the next time stop, with Sam once again gripping the sides of his seat for all he was worth.

She was keeping up quite a pace even though the Porsche had been built in the fifties, thought Sam. But he could see Terri was super smooth with her driving and the lines she was taking around the corners were straight out of an advanced driver manual.

He slowly found himself breathing a little easier and he even managed to release the death hold he'd had on his seat.

"You've let go then?" said Terri.

"I might have," he said, a little sheepishly. "It was the heights! I'm not great with them."

"Ah, okay and there's me thinking it was my driving!"

She laughed in a way he'd not heard from her in quite a while.

*****

They passed slowly through the sleepy village of Santa Eugènia and it wasn't long before they joined the Ma3030. Terri gently eased her foot off the accelerator, as she spotted the sign for Bodegas Angel. Turning left, she then drove slowly up the entrance lane and into the vineyard, where she brought the convertible to a halt alongside a row of the participants' cars.

Andres was there to meet them.

"Amigos, good to see you both."

"Good to see you too, Andres," said Sam, but he saw his friend seemed distracted. "What's up?"

Andres frowned. "There's been a report that a car's gone off the road."

"What do you mean it's gone off the road? Is the

driver alright?"

Andres was silent for a moment.

"It's not looking good, Sam. One of the drivers saw smoke coming from down in the ravine. They stopped to see if they could see anything."

"And?"

"He thinks it's a blue Merc convertible."

They all knew whose car they were talking about.

"Marcos?" said Sam.

Andres nodded.

"And we can't get hold of him!"

*****

2

The job had gone smoothly, just as he'd planned it. Jaime Ortiz always approached every job in the same way, with in-depth research and careful preparation. He prided himself on his professionalism, something he knew put him in a different league to other people in the same line of work.

He had scoped out the route of the rally and calculated how and when he would do it, all well in advance of the actual day.

Setting up early that morning on the Puig de Randa, he was there a good hour before the classic car rally had even started off from Belver Castle.

Ortiz had waited patiently, parked up in a van. Just off the main road, he was hidden from view, but where he could still see the whole road through some trees. He knew this was one of the timed trials within the rally. Designed to discourage the cars from racing on the public highway, the drivers had to complete the journey time within a minimum and maximum time allowance.

He watched as the cars went past on their way to the Santuari de Cura, crossing each one off on his list, then adding in a time to help calculate the gap between each car once he saw them come back down.

It was clear that all the drivers were keeping to their time schedules, except an old Porsche soft top that he heard before he saw it coming back down the hill. He'd seen it earlier on its way up, the driver catching his eye as she was a very attractive blonde. As the Porsche passed him again, he saw the young woman was still driving. She was smiling as she pushed the car hard around the winding road, whilst her co-driver, a man, looked decidedly less happy.

A few minutes later he saw the car he'd been waiting for. The blue Mercedes 450SL, driven by Marcos Ramírez, passed him on its way to the Sanctuary. Ortiz knew he then had twenty five minutes before he'd see it as it came back down the road after the time trial check. He set his watch with a five minute alert and then sat back in his seat and closed his eyes.

When his watch alarm went off, he started some breathing exercises, preparing himself for what lay ahead.

Almost to the second, the blue Mercedes 450SL passed him on the way back down towards Randa. Ortiz already had the engine running and he eased the big van out onto the road and accelerated hard. Whilst he knew he'd lose out to the big Merc in a straight line race, the van's modern two litre turbo engine had more than enough power to keep up for the length of time he needed to get the job done.

He was soon close up behind the old Mercedes. He saw Ramírez clock him in his rear-view mirror and smiled, as Ramírez actually slowed and waved at him to pass. But Ortiz ignored him, moving the van even closer up behind the Mercedes.

Ramírez waved at him again. This time Ortiz could see the driver was starting to get annoyed, especially as the van was now almost touching his rear bumper and clearly couldn't understand either where the van had come from, or why the driver wasn't trying to pass him.

Deciding he needed to create some distance between him and the van, Martínez pushed hard down on the Merc's accelerator. He breathed a sigh of relief as he started to pull away from the van, not realising that he'd unwittingly given Ortiz exactly what he wanted. Momentum.

Ortiz needed the Mercedes to be going fast enough so as to maximise the effect of the impact and it worked perfectly. With the point in the road, that he'd chosen, fast approaching, Ortiz changed down to second gear and accelerated hard, aiming the van at the left rear corner of the Mercedes.

Ramírez felt the car shudder as he felt the van hit him.

"What are you doing?" he yelled.

It was an instinctive reaction, because with the speed they were going, there was no likelihood of the van driver actually hearing him. He felt another jolt. Only this time it was harder and Ramírez felt the Mercedes rocking. It was a big solid car, so at first it only weaved a little, but then there was almost a ripple effect as the suspension, a little soft after so many years, started reacting to the impact and suddenly, as well as weaving, the car was bouncing, just as Ortiz had anticipated.

Ramírez was struggling to retain control, but rather than try to steady the car by driving it through the rippling effect, he turned to gesticulate at the van driver.

Ortiz saw him turn back towards him. Ramírez was waving angrily. It was another reaction Ortiz had considered might happen, leaving Ramírez with just one hand on the steering wheel. Ortiz accelerated even harder this time and rammed the Mercedes again. He hit the car with such ferocity that the car started to twitch and weave from side to side before the Mercedes went into a full spin.

Ortiz eased his foot off the Renault's accelerator, watching the almost slow motion effect of Ramírez losing control of the Mercedes. Seeing the look on Ramirez's face, he smiled. Had it been fear, or maybe Ramírez had recognised him?

Everything seemed strangely quiet, but then Ortiz heard the tyres squealing as they fought for traction before they gave up and the Mercedes careered towards the edge of the road.

It seemed to stop momentarily, as though balanced on a fulcrum, the rear wheels hanging over the side of the road. Ortiz realised Ramírez must have his foot hard down on the accelerator as the rear wheels were spinning uselessly in mid-air.

Ortiz moved the van forward, so that it was touching the front nearside of the Mercedes. Ramírez was shouting at him, but he ignored him, smiling instead as he started to rev the van's engine, before letting the clutch out. He saw the look of horror on Ramírez's face as he saw what was happening, but the driver's door was partly over the ravine, so he tried to undo his seat belt, but it hadn't released by the time Ortiz had let out the clutch on the van and it had moved forward, nudging the Mercedes just enough to send it over the edge and down into the ravine below.

Ortiz checked his watch. He had at least five minutes before the next car would be passing him. He got out of the van and looked down at the wreckage he could see about eighty metres below him. He knew there was a small risk that Ramírez might walk away from all of this. But this was about sending a message. That's what she'd said. So going over the edge had been how she'd wanted it to happen and whether Ramírez actually survived, or not, had been less of a concern to her.

He couldn't see any movement from inside the car. He wondered if Ramírez might actually get out, but then the petrol tank exploded and the car was soon engulfed in flames. Ortiz watched without emotion, knowing Marcos Ramírez would be dead within minutes, if nothing else from smoke inhalation.

He checked his watch again. Two minutes. Then he saw some movement from below, down to his right. Someone had come out from a finca down in the ravine. Ortiz stepped back, getting out of the line of sight. They must have heard the explosion and seeing the car on fire, Ortiz knew they'd be ringing the emergency services.

It was time to go.

*****

Given the location, the police and fire service had got to the scene really quickly. It was possibly because of the seriousness of the accident, or it could have been because the person in the finca had been able to describe the car as an old Mercedes and someone at the rally control had soon put two and two together and realised it was Marcos Ramírez, the son of one of the oldest and also the richest families on the island.

The full fire report would later say that as a result of the Mercedes 450SL convertible coming off the road and careering down the rocky hillside, it had spontaneously combusted after coming to rest. It was determined that the fire had started because the brake pipes, damaged as the car went down the hillside, had spilled out fluid that had then ignited from the heat of either the engine, or the exhaust manifold.

The post mortem would then conclude that Marcos Ramírez died primarily from smoke inhalation, with secondary burns being a contributory factor. Therefore, he had been alive when the car left the road and went down into the ravine.

However, the police officer in charge, the one who initially attended the scene, had enough experience to know that the driver of the burned out Mercedes was clearly dead. He checked with the race organisers if Ramírez had been with a co-driver and finding out he'd been alone in the car, the officer got on with securing the removal of the vehicle, or what was left of it, for it to be taken to the vehicle forensic team for them to determine what caused it to leave the road.

The accident led to the temporary suspension of the rally and as the remaining cars arrived at Bodegas Angel, the drivers, many of them in shock, were milling around in the mini piazza at the vineyard.

The rally organisers were gathered in a room, considering whether to continue with the rally. Some thought it would be disrespectful to the Ramírez family, whilst others felt the significant benefit to the chosen charities would be lost if they discontinued it, something they thought the family would understand, as they had been the major sponsor and supporter of the event for many years.

It didn't take long to reach a simple and practical consensus. They needed to contact Rafael, the remaining son, to tell him the tragic news and to seek his views. The decision made, one of the organisers went out to speak to the drivers and advise them that there would be a delay and that lunch would be provided by Andres for those who might want it.

Terri had been watching her half-brother as they'd listened to the spokesman. Sam seemed to be deep in thought. She was about to say something when a couple of other drivers came across to talk about the accident.

When they were alone again, she spoke, "Was he a friend?"

"More of an acquaintance really, but he seemed like a really good guy and we'd talked a bit about us both losing our dads during the last year," said Sam.

Sam had lost his adoptive father, Luis, to cancer over a year ago now and Marcos's father, Ramon, had died suddenly after a massive and unexpected heart attack six months ago.

She could see he was thinking about something.

"What's up? Something's niggling you."

"I don't know. It's probably nothing."

"You thinking something doesn't add up?" she asked quietly.

There was something nagging away at Sam, but he couldn't put his finger on it.

"Look, maybe it's my copper's nose, but it's definitely twitching a bit. I've got nothing to suggest there's anything untoward. But that said, it just seems one hell of a coincidence that first his father dies and now the new head of the family is dead."

Sam thought for a moment, then shook his head.

"Maybe I'm seeing connections that aren't there. I think I need to wind my neck in, Terri and stop thinking like a copper when I've left all that stuff behind. Come on, let's go and find Andres and get some lunch."

*****

Parked just up from the entrance to Bodegas Angel, just off the main road, was a rented grey Ford Fiesta. The driver was taking photographs on her phone of the column of classic cars as they pulled into the vineyard, ticking them off against a list of participants.

Kat Reyes looked at her list again. One was missing, the blue 450SL of Marcos Ramírez. She craned her neck, looking behind her, back up the road towards the

Sanctuary. There was no sight of the car, but what was that? In the sky? Black smoke was starting to float high up into the clouds above the Puig de Randa.

"Oh my god! Surely they haven't? Is there nothing these people won't do?"

*****

3

'*Watch the news.*'

Standing at the edge of the cliff side just down from Cala Pi, Jaime Ortiz sent his boss the text via a burner phone, one he'd got a young kid to go and buy for cash from a back street shop in Palma the day before. Without waiting for a reply, he took the battery out and dropped the phone on the floor and stamped on it hard, before picking up the pieces and casually dropping it down into the deep water below.

He walked back to where he'd left the stolen Renault van. It had been a simple enough job to find a suitable vehicle to steal the night before. He just needed somewhere with no prying CCTV cameras and Ortiz had found the Renault down a side road and it had been more than big and powerful enough to do the job.

He knew it would only be a matter of time before the police found the van and any half decent investigator might even make the connection between the van and the Mercedes. However, Ortiz had never been even close to being caught for anything because he had always been extremely careful, especially when it came to negating any opportunity for forensic evidence.

He started a complete wipe down of every surface

on the vehicle, to make sure they'd find nothing to connect him to the van. It took him well over an hour before he was satisfied and then for good measure, he set it alight and watched from a safe distance as the fire took hold, feeling no sense of emotion, or guilt, that just a few hours before, he'd taken a man's life.

Then, leaving behind the smouldering wreck of the stolen Renault, he pushed the ignition button on the hired Seat he'd previously left in situ and headed back towards the airport.

*****

She had seen his text come through on one of the phones he'd given her. With a nod of satisfaction, Hannah Luisa Lopez then walked across to the other side of her office, pushed a hidden button and waited as the secret cupboard door popped open. Removing the battery from the phone, she then put on a heavy duty glove and took the security lid off a container in the cupboard, before very carefully lowering the phone and battery into a yellow liquid.

The fluoroantimonic acid quickly went to work, the so-called superacid effectively 'eating' the phone and battery.

"Another problem removed," she smiled, without a trace of humour in the smile.

*****

Rafael Ramírez, Rafa to his friends, was sitting on his boat, a large cabin cruiser, off the coast of Monte Carlo. His phone rang and he recognised the caller's name.

"Señor Verdi, what an unexpected surprise. What can I do for you?"

José Verdi, the chair of the Foundation's Classic Car Rally organising committee, broke the news to the new head of the Ramírez business empire and waited.

Rafa was stunned. He and his brother were like

polar opposites, but they'd always had a brilliant relationship, even though their lives had taken very different pathways. He'd only spoken to Marcos that morning to wish him good luck with the rally. He was stunned. First their father dying suddenly, when the old man was as tough as old boots, still running a couple of miles a day and keeping his two personal trainers on their toes and now, his brother was dead.

"How did it happen, Señor?" he asked quietly.

He listened as Verdi briefly explained what they knew from the police and fire services.

"Christ, Verdi, how could that happen? He's driven it so many times, he must have known it like the back of his hand."

Verdi waited, not being sure what to say, or how to broach the subject of whether to continue with the rally.

"Does my mother know?"

"No, Señor, we thought…"

"Yes, quite right, better it comes from me. Look, what are you going to do about the rally? It was my brother's thing, but I know he really cared about the charities."

"Si, Señor, but we wondered if you might think, given the circumstances, that it might be more appropriate to cancel the rally?"

Rafa thought for a moment. Verdi was looking for a decision. He knew how important the rally was to Marcos. His brother had set it up over a decade ago and since then it had raised an enormous amount of money for so many charities across the island.

"José, how much money were you likely to raise this year?"

Verdi felt a note of pride that Ramírez had used his first name.

"About five million euros, Señor."

Rafa didn't hesitate.

"Right, cancel the rally. I think the drivers will understand and I'll make sure the money is covered so the charities don't miss out."

Verdi was slightly taken aback. He'd had very few dealings with Marcos's younger brother over the years and as far as he knew, he had little involvement in the day to day running of the Ramírez family business. But the decision had been quick and decisive. Maybe Rafa had something more about him than the reputation he seemed to have with the press, because this was nothing like the reaction he'd expected.

"Señor, if I may say, I think this is the best decision and I can only thank you for your generosity."

"It's what my brother would have wanted, José. Now, what's the vibe like with the drivers you've got out there?"

Verdi looked out of the window, onto the small piazza below.

"I think they're all stunned by what's happened, Señor. Most of the drivers, other than a few new ones, are people who have been supporting your brother's charity rally for many years, so I know they'll understand, but there's obviously an overwhelming sense of shock at losing your brother."

"Listen, are you okay with telling the drivers, José?"

"Si, Señor."

"I appreciate you doing that, thank you. Now please can you text me the details of the other sponsors? I'll call them and let them know what's happening, and José?" A pause. "If you need anything and I mean anything, call me, but in the meantime, I'll be leaving shortly and flying back to be with my mother, so I'll be in Mallorca later today."

Once again, his response left José Verdi surprised, not only at Rafa's decisiveness, but also by the level of empathy the younger brother had shown.

*****

Rafa Ramírez was stunned, but knew he had to call his mother and he needed to do so quickly. It was far from ideal to break the news to her over the phone, but the last thing he wanted was the press getting hold of this and putting a cold call into the family.

Of course she'd be shocked, but she was no shrinking violet. Since she'd met and married Eduardo Ramírez, Rafa knew she'd been the mainstay of the family and helped his father take the floundering family business and turn it into what it was today, a multi-national, billion euro corporation.

Christina Ramírez heard her mobile ring and saw her youngest son's name on the screen.

"Rafa, what a surprise. Has your boat run out of fuel, my darling?"

He ignored her tease and gently broke the news to his mother as best he could.

She went quiet and he let the silence hang, knowing she would be trying to take in what he'd just told her.

"Do we know how it happened?"

He heard just the slightest quiver in her voice. He knew her heart must be bursting as she'd only recently lost his father, Eduardo, and now she was having to deal with this.

He gave her the detail of what he knew about the accident and then said, "Mama, I'm leaving now. I'll be home by late afternoon."

"Gracias, my boy."

She'd held it together whilst on the phone, but then collapsed into a chair, tears streaming down her cheeks.

*****

He'd never fought the playboy tag he'd been given. It was just easier to let people think what they wanted.

Yes, he enjoyed himself, and he had a higher public profile than his brother, but Rafa Ramírez was no fool.

Despite his father and brother's encouragement, he'd always resisted taking up any sort of formal position in the family business. However, he still regularly attended the board meetings and always ensured he read all the briefing notes. This enabled him to, at the very least, positively contribute to the discussions of the family business. A business that had given him, and continued to give him, the wherewithal for his real passion of conservation, and in particular, the conservation of the seas and oceans, which was why he spent so much time on his boat.

He called his PA, a young Italian woman, who was outside on the deck checking out water samples.

"Martina?"

Her beaming smile appeared through the door, until she saw the look on his face.

"What's wrong?"

"I need to get home and quickly!"

Within half an hour he was on the heli-pad by the marina waiting for the short transfer flight to Nice airport.

*****

4

Some of the drivers owned the vehicles they were in, whilst others, like Sam, had been allocated a car from those supplied by one of the supporters of the rally. However, they were all united in the decision to cancel the rally and the cars were soon rolling back out of the vineyard.

"Sam, I'm not sure I've properly thanked you, but it was a good call to get me in on this, even though it's ended on such a sad note," said Terri.

"I know, but I'm pleased you came, Terri because I thought you'd enjoy it and I'm really glad you did. I didn't know Marcos particularly well, but it's still a hell of a shock."

"What now then? I suppose we'd better get this thing back to its owner," said Terri.

Sam smiled, "Yes, we better had, before you go getting any ideas about keeping it!"

"Aw, I was thinking we could just take it for a spin before we give it back?"

"No!" he laughed.

"Maybe I should buy it then? I mean I have been thinking about getting a little runabout?" she grinned.

"Well, if you've got the odd two hundred and fifty thousand lying about, for this little runabout as you call it, then maybe the buyer could be persuaded."

"Ha! There was me hoping it might just be a really good replica."

"Nope," he grinned again. "It's definitely the real thing."

"Best we make the most of it then."

He heard Terri laugh again, as she accelerated hard away from the vineyard.

She would have enjoyed the drive back to Palma more if the circumstances had been different, but it didn't stop her getting a sense that she had also started feeling a little different in herself.

As she parked the Porsche in a temperature controlled private underground garage complex, alongside another half a dozen luxury and rare cars, in the centre of Palma, she took a deep breath.

"You okay?" said Sam.

"I don't know. I guess I'm feeling just a bit guilty that I enjoyed that."

"What? Guilty because of Marcos? Or is it, maybe Simon?"

She thought for a moment.

"I don't know," she said quietly.

"Hmm, I know, let's go for a drink," suggested Sam.

*****

Minutes later, they were walking up Carrer de Sant Feliu, passing one of Terri's favourite shops, Rialto Living, before they stepped through the door to Bar 13%, dropping down the steps into the wine bar.

A young woman with bright purple hair looked up from behind the bar and beamed at them.

"Sam, good to see you!"

"Hola, Paula, ¿Que tal? How are you?"

"Muy bien, amigo."

"Paula, this is my sister, Terri."

"Ah, Terri, encantada. What can I get you?"

Moments later they were sat on bar stools, at an old wine barrel table, each with a glass of rosado.

Sam looked into his wine glass, thinking about how to respond.

"It's very normal, you know? The guilt, I mean," said Sam.

"I know."

He barely heard her as she spoke with a whisper. He knew all he had to know about the 'guilt thing.' As even now, it still flooded over him. That perhaps he could have done something more, or done something differently that might have prevented what had happened to his best friend Jimmy, who had been shot by Frankie Walker during a police operation to stop an armed robbery.

"I don't think it actually ever goes away either," said Sam. "I think we just get better at dealing with it."

Terri had often talked to him about his PTSD, and with her own experience as a combat soldier in Iraq, he knew she understood what he was living with. But when he'd spoken to her about what had happened to Simon, she hadn't necessarily thought she was suffering from PTSD, even though that's what the therapist had told her.

What she did know was that whether it was grief, or PTSD, didn't really matter to her. She hadn't actually seen Diego Sanchez shoot Simon, but she had been there moments later, trying to stem the blood from his chest wound and had been with him when he'd died. Whilst she had dealt with death many times before of comrades in Iraq, some of whom were close friends, this was of course, something very different.

This had been the man she'd fallen in love with and losing him, so soon after they'd both finally opened up about how they felt about each other, had somehow made it hurt even more.

"I'll be okay, mate. Sad as though it is about Marcos, I think we both know that it's more about me trying to get my head together about Simon and allowing myself to smile and…."

As she hesitated, he helped finish her sentence.

"…. get on with your life?"

A half smile, as she said, "Yes, something like that. And yes, I know, he'd want me to get on with it, as he'd hate the thought of me moping around the place." Another slight pause. "But it's hard, really bloody hard."

"I know, Sis. I didn't actually lose Jimmy, but I still find it hard to deal with the fact that I think it was my fault. You know? That he ended up in a wheelchair and will be in it for the rest of his life."

"But what does he keep telling you, Sam? It wasn't your bloody fault, mate. It was Walker's, even though we did maybe see a different side to him when he stood up to Sanchez and tried to help save Simon."

"Yes, that was a surprise," said Sam.

"Anyway, I think it's time we ended this little therapy session," said Terri, raising her glass. "So, a toast." She took a deep breath. "To Simon."

He gently chinked his glass against hers.

"Simon."

As she put her glass down, she took in another deep breath, as though turning a page in a book. Then turned and looked at Sam.

"So, have you had any more twitching?" asked Terri.

Sam looked at her, then as she touched the end of her nose, he realised what she was getting at.

"Ah, my now former copper's nose you mean?"

She grinned and nodded.

"When I was in the Met, crime investigation was all about making connections based on the intel you had before you. Now I don't know much about what happened to Marcos Ramírez's father, nor do I know how the accident occurred, but two unexpected deaths? In less than six months? That all sounds more than just a bit of bad luck."

"But you're still calling it an accident, Sam, so is that what it still is?"

"Quite possibly and I might be looking for things that aren't there. Or, maybe the old nose is just a bit rusty, as it has been out of the business for a while," he grinned.

"Hmmm, I'm not so sure," said Terri with a wink. "Once a copper, always a copper."

*****

5

Lori Garcia had seen the news on the TV.
"Nino!" she called out.
"Yes, Boss?"

She smiled. They'd worked together for three, or was it four years now and even in private, he still rarely called her Lori.

"You've seen the news? Marcos Ramírez?"

"Yes, I've sent for the accident report. The basic outline should be with us any minute," said Nino.

"Good. I want us to take a closer look."

Traffic accidents were not the everyday business of the GEO, the Grupo Especial de Operaciones, one of the elite Spanish police tactical units, however, Lori Garcia had a deeper interest in the Ramírez family.

"Too much of a coincidence?"

"Hmm, maybe Nino, but if it wasn't for the fact that we've been looking at them, then this accident wouldn't even be on our radar."

"Maybe not so much of a coincidence then?" said Nino.

"Let's see what the report says first."

*****

Less than an hour later she'd seen the preliminary accident investigator's report.

"Nino, get your bag. We're on the next flight to Palma."

He nodded. The team carried a national responsibility and as such, they all kept an overnight bag ready in the office as they often had to deploy at short notice.

"You're thinking it's suspicious?" he asked.

"Looks a strong possibility. Especially as the report mentions 'unexplained damage.'"

She showed him the electronic file. It was only the initial findings, but the first impressions of the accident investigator were quite clear. Even with the effects of the fire, there was unexplained damage, especially to the rear of the Mercedes that wasn't caused by the slide down the hillside, or by the subsequent fire.

"What about it being old damage? After all, it's a pretty old motor, Boss."

"If it wasn't a classic car rally, then I might be inclined to agree with you Nino, but I reckon the people putting cars into this sort of rally would have had them shined up to the nines and in the very best condition they could."

"Fair point."

"And let's not forget, those old 450SLs from the 70's were big old beasts, so it would have taken quite a shove, or more likely, quite a few of them to force it off the road."

"You don't think this was an accident, do you?" said Nino.

"Doesn't look like it and it certainly doesn't feel like it," said Lori, pulling her overnight bag out from under her desk.

*****

As she and Nino sat waiting to be called for their flight, Lori thought about the unexpected call she'd had the previous week.

"Good morning, DI Garcia, my name is Mendez, Cesar Mendez and I'm with the CNI."

"Good morning, Señor. What can I do for you?"

"Inspectora, we look after…."

"I know what the CNI do, Señor."

The Centro Nacional de Inteligencia provided the country's President with the national intelligence assessment, a document that covered anything that might threaten the independence, or territorial integrity of Spain.

"Of course. Okay, I'll get to why I've asked you here, DI Garcia. I'd like you to look into something for me."

He waited for her to respond.

"Señor, my first thought is to ask why this is not coming down through the usual channels?"

"Yes, good point. Can we meet this afternoon?"

Lori had just finished putting his name through the GEO database.

"I'm assuming you've just checked my name out, Inspectora?"

She smiled. He'd obviously expected her to check him out.

"Si, Señor Mendez. When and where would you like to meet?"

Three hours later, she was sat in a coffee shop, just off the main shopping area in Madrid.

She had been surprised at his choice of such a public location to meet, but he soon explained why.

"What I'm about to tell you is highly confidential. That might sound odd, seeing as we're meeting in a café, but there's no signing in and out here."

"And therefore, no record of our meeting, Señor?"

"No, is that a problem for you, Inspectora?"

She ignored the question.

"So, is this official, Señor?" said Lori, who was

starting to feel just a little uncomfortable at Mendez's cloak and dagger antics.

"Yes, and no."

"I liked your first answer better, so you'd better explain what you mean, otherwise this might be a very short meeting."

"I'd heard you would be direct and straight to the point Lori. Forgive me, I can call you Lori?"

She nodded.

"Please call me Cesar by the way. We don't have specific ranks, or anything like that in the CNI."

She nodded again. She knew the CNI weren't operational, at least they didn't put their people in the 'field,' but they still operated in the murky world of intelligence.

"Okay, Cesar, can we focus on the 'No'? Which bit of this isn't official?"

"I will, but might it help if I tell you first, that this is sanctioned at the very highest level of the Government?"

He saw her give the faintest of nods.

"Perhaps, so go on."

"I want you to investigate an organisation that we think is responsible for political and economic corruption at a national and regional level."

Allegations of corruption within politics and business wasn't anything new to her, although it didn't as such fall into the GEO's remit.

"Power corrupts and absolute power corrupts absolutely," said Lori.

This time it was his turn to nod. "I see you know your quotations, Lori. The 19th century British politician wasn't it, Lord Acton?"

"Yes, it was, but I'm still not sure this is something my boss will sanction, but if, as you say, it comes from the President's Office, then what precisely do you want me to do? And can I ask, why me?" said Lori.

"Let me be clear, Inspectora, this is not from his Office. It is from the President himself."

Mendez's friendly smile had quickly been replaced by a much more earnest look.

"Okay," she said slowly, trying to digest what Mendez had just said.

His smile returned.

"Let me deal with your second question first. I'm asking you, because I've been watching you for some time and feel I can trust you."

He saw she was taken aback by what he'd just said.

"Don't worry, Lori, we watch a lot of people. It's our job."

He smiled again. It was like a trademark, she thought.

She didn't smile back. Whilst he might trust her, she really wasn't sure if she could trust him.

Whether he was anticipating this response, or he might just have seen the doubt in her eyes, he took an envelope from his inside pocket.

"Here, take a look at this."

It was a letter with the Spanish President's crest on it.

"Open it."

"Whatever it is, this could be a forgery."

"Yes, it could," he said.

She heard something in his voice. Was that frustration or irritation?

"Please, just read it."

She broke the seal on the envelope and took out a single sheet of paper and read it. Was she surprised that it was addressed to her personally? Perhaps not. If it was a forgery, then why not address it to her? But the content was clear. And it was a handwritten note from the President of Spain asking her to co-operate fully with the man sitting before her.

"I feel I need to ask you again. Is this official?" asked Lori.

Mendez held his hand up to his mouth, as though in thought as to how to answer her question.

"I think it's probably perhaps best described as semi-official."

"You're talking in riddles, Señor. Can't you just give me a simple yes, or no?"

He paused.

"No, as in no I can't."

He saw her eyes flash. A temper, as she tried to control her response? He knew she was starting to get even more annoyed with him.

"Please let me explain, Señora. However, first, I need to take you into my confidence, because once you know, you may also become a target and you will need to be careful."

"A target? Who for? And what do you mean, careful?"

Mendez took a long slow look around the café before answering.

"Have you heard of La Fundación de Palma?"

"Aren't they a pretty big charity, based out of Mallorca?"

"Yes, that's what they purport to be."

"Purport to be?" queried Lori.

"The Ramírez family were major players in the original set up back in the seventies," said Mendez.

"Okay, now you've got my interest, Señor," said Lori, "and I'm guessing you're going to tell me the highly confidential bit now?"

"But first a little bit of background. Which I think may help," he said. "The Palma Foundation was set up in the late 70s by Eduardo Ramírez and three other partners, who all lived in Mallorca. It came after they held a secret meeting up at Belver Castle. You know it, Lori? It's just on the hillside above the city."

She nodded. Not quite as iconic as La Seu, the Gothic cathedral, but the castle was still one of the standout images around Palma de Mallorca, sitting high above the city with a commanding view out across the bay.

"It all sounds a bit melodramatic, that the meeting was held at the castle," continued Mendez, "but there were many less visitors to the castle back then and the four of them had a much better chance of spotting one of Franco's spies."

"So, this was around the time the Franco regime was ending and a new democratic government was coming to power?" said Lori.

"Yes, and there were still a lot of Franco's spies about who were only too willing to give information to his secret police."

"I know from my parents just how bad things were, even when we were supposedly moving to a more democratic form of government," said Lori.

"Exactly, so they couldn't afford to be seen to be effectively plotting."

"What were they doing then?"

"Okay, let's start with Ramírez senior. He was from an old and originally, a wealthy Mallorquin family. However, their business was failing, partly due to bad business decisions, but also because he was from 'old' money and he had little support from the new Balearics politicos. Ramírez knew he needed to do something and he decided to join forces with three other guys from the island. They were people who he'd crossed paths with at some stage in the previous five years, or so and most importantly, who he saw as ideal partners for his new venture."

"Partners for what though, the Foundation?"

"Yes, exactly. He wanted to create a business and

political network to benefit them as they sought to take advantage of the economic freedoms he saw could be gained following the Franco era."

"What do you mean by benefit? In what way?" asked Lori.

"Business and trade in general under the Franco regime had been almost entirely state controlled, with little or no opportunity for local entrepreneurs to build, or grow, their business at the speed they liked."

"So how did this Foundation fit in with this then?"

"It gave them a vehicle to influence and persuade. But before you ask, the Palma Foundation wasn't about corruption, at least not then. In fact, it was more about fighting the very corruption they'd all encountered during the Franco era. When they decided to set it up, the Foundation I mean, it was because each of them was looking for ways to expand their business by pulling their networks together and not just across the island either, as they developed and extended them over on to the mainland as well."

"Okay, so it wasn't corrupt, at least not when it started. Who were the other three guys then?"

He could see he was getting her interest.

"Let's stick with Eduardo Ramírez, just to start with. It was actually his idea from the outset. He was from, let's call it 'old money.' Born into a traditional and well-established Mallorquin family, but with a business that was going badly downhill.

Then there was Manuel, or Manny Lopez, a black marketeer, who also ran a profitable protection racket up until around 2008, or 2009, when he suddenly stopped. We don't know why, but it might just have been because the Autoparts side of things was really taking off. Then there's Enrique Fernandez, would-be entrepreneur and finally, Juan Rodriguez, who at the time was an up and coming young lawyer, with aspirations to go into politics."

"I've heard of Rodriguez," she said, who despite his advancing years, was still a high profile political figure.

"He's got a strong following in Government and is a thorn in the side of the current President."

"In that case, are you sure this isn't just you and now potentially me, being used as pawns in some sort of political power struggle?"

"It might look like that, Lori, but the more I've looked at this, the more I've seen the dots starting to join up."

"But why now? Why is the president bringing this to you now, when you say the Foundation has been going for nearly fifty years or more?"

"Two reasons. The first being the election of the new president two years ago and the access that gave him to certain information to confirm his suspicions over recent years. The second was the death of Eduardo Ramírez. He seems to have been someone who has, at least to some extent, kept a lid on the lengths to which the Foundation will go."

"The lengths to do what though? What is it the Palma Foundation actually does?"

"Where do I start?" said Mendez. "It's like an old boys' and old girls' network. Where, if you scratch my back, I'll scratch yours. But over the years, it's gone from lining up new suppliers, for instance, for the likes of helping Manny Lopez and his back street black market racketeering and protection racket, to helping him fund and build new premises all over Europe for his multi-national, multi-million euro business that is Lopez Autoparts."

"He's Lopez Autoparts?" She gave a low whistle. "They're…"

"Huge." He finished her sentence.

"And you think they've been achieving things like

the funding and arranging licences for new premises through corrupt practice?"

"Yes, although of course it's not every deal, which is what makes it difficult to determine which ones are genuine and which ones are bent."

"Who is the third partner?" asked Lori.

"Enrique Fernandez. He started off selling beach towels and straw mats on the beach. Now, think all things holiday. You've probably been in one of his hotels, Enfern Hotels, or sat on one of his sunbeds, or under one of his beach umbrellas."

"Yes, I've heard of Enfern. But I've never realised where the En and the Fern came from. They're middle to upmarket quality, aren't they?"

"Yes, there's a big one in Madrid."

"The Foundation is therefore not merely the benevolent benefactor it makes itself out to be then?" said Lori.

"Well that certainly doesn't seem to be the primary reason. However, they have supported a considerable number of charities and donated millions of euros, but I think I can safely say that the majority of it has been for less than charitable reasons."

"Meaning, it's given them a front for the real reason behind the Foundation?"

"Yes. It's much more about them having created one hell of a powerful network."

"That they use to effect influence, which benefits the four founding members?" said Lori.

"Yes, and it's not just them. It's a membership that's been steadily growing since its formation, with new members paying annual fees. This is what has given them the wherewithal to make the often significant donations to charity."

"But you're saying that much of their individual success that has resulted from the Foundation has been achieved through corruption, Cesar? That's a pretty serious statement given the levels these guys operate at, especially Rodriguez. I mean, the guy ran for President a few years back!"

"Yes, and almost got in. But to be fair to the original founder, Eduardo Ramírez, I think he did perhaps originally see the Foundation as being much more about influence and persuasion. The corruption element seems to have come about more from the other three and then it looks like it's just continued, perhaps even more so, as some of the founders' offspring have joined the Foundation during the last decade."

"Why do you think that is?" said Lori.

"We know that some of their businesses have been subject to increased competition and that seems to have been the catalyst for an escalation in not just financial backhanders, but also in violence."

"Violence? But no one has gone to the police?" asked Lori.

"No, probably because once the Foundation has its claws in you, then you are going to have a difficult job explaining away why you suddenly want them off your back when things get sticky," said Mendez.

"Sounds about right, but what's been causing the economic downturn for some of them then?"

Cesar knew he pretty much had her attention now as she was asking more and more questions.

"Our intel suggests it's because of increasing pressure from the foreign competition, especially from Russia."

"I'm still not happy about this cloak and dagger stuff, Cesar. Why haven't you just gone through my boss? I mean we deal with high level investigations all the time and they're all on a need to know basis."

"Inspector Jefe Flores is being moved," said Mendez.

She looked at him, her eyes narrowing and her forehead furrowing into a deep frown.

"Why?"

"Because he's vulnerable."

"Vulnerable? Look, I know Flores can be a pain in the arse and he can't make a decision to save his life, but I can't see him being in any way vulnerable to corruption."

Mendez looked at her. It was always going to be a bit of a leap of faith, both from him in trusting her, but also from her to believe what he was telling her. He made his mind up and took a deep breath.

"I'm sure you're aware, Lori, that corruption can take many forms and isn't just about someone getting paid off."

"Yes, I get that, but he's…"

"He's what? Innocent? Maybe, but he has a sick mother who he couldn't get into the care home his family desperately wanted her to go in. That is, until one of the main shareholders of the care home made a personal call to Flores to tell him his mother now had a place."

"Major shareholder?"

"Hannah Luisa Lopez, Manny's daughter."

"But why would they want Flores? Unless…"

"What? Unless the Foundation have some sort of connection with organised crime?" asked Mendez, raising an eyebrow.

"Well, yes, but that's a bit of a stretch isn't it, Cesar?"

"You might think that Lori, but here's a question for you. How many times did you see a prosecution for the Sanchez family collapse?" he slowly asked.

She looked at him. Stunned at what he was insinuating.

"Too many," she said quietly. She'd been trying to get something on the Sanchez organised crime gang for over two years and until recently she'd seen every prosecution case fail because of witness interference.

"We think he was feeding details of the key prosecution witnesses to someone in the Foundation," said Cesar.

"But why would he do that? Even though he may have made a mistake in accepting the place for his mother in some care home, surely he can just take her out?"

"These people are ruthless, Lori. Once they've got into you, they then slowly turn the screw, either with more favours or, if that doesn't work, they resort to, well let's call them old fashioned threats, shall we? Which is what we think they did with Flores about his mother."

She realised straight away what Mendez was saying.

"It wasn't going to be him they were threatening to harm, was it? But for god's sake, Cesar, we're the GEO! If we can't protect our own, then what bloody chance does anyone else stand?"

"And we think that's what Flores thought, but we'll know more soon when he's put into a full debrief."

"But what about the Foundation? Won't they suspect something? What about his mother?"

"We've been waiting to make our move."

"So why now?" she asked.

"Señora Flores passed away last night."

The realisation hit her straight away.

"When you rang me?"

"Correct. As of this moment, Inspectora Jefe, Chief Inspector, you are now head of your unit."

"What? No promotion process?"

"That won't be necessary, Lori. Remember, you now have friends in not just high places, but very high places."

She thought for a moment. She wasn't sure she

could believe what she'd just heard, both about Flores and that she was now head of her unit.

He watched her absorbing what he'd just told her. He'd spent a long time researching her background, both before her husband was murdered, and then her subsequent career. She was tough, professional and had shown herself committed to her job.

"Well?" he said eventually.

She looked at him. She'd need people she could trust around her.

"Can I keep my current team? And choose my replacement?"

"Yes, and presumably you mean someone like Nino Castilla?"

Nino had been her Detective Sergeant for a couple of years now and she trusted him implicitly.

"You've already checked him out?"

"Of course, Lori. I'd assumed you'd want to keep him close-by."

"You've certainly done your homework, Cesar."

"Yes, but make no mistake, Lori, so will the Foundation if, or rather when, they discover you are looking at them."

*****

6

After the plane touched down at Son San Joan airport in Palma de Mallorca, Lori and Nino were met at the gate by one of the local police officers.

Lori had met her before and smiled as she greeted her.

"Detective Delgado, Sofi, thank you for meeting us. Do you remember Nino Castilla?"

"Si, Inspectora Jefe and she nodded towards Nino, "Es un placer volver a verlo, Inspector Castilla. It's a pleasure to see you again, Inspector Castilla. Many congratulations on your promotion."

Nino smiled. If Lori had been surprised at her promotion in the field to Chief Inspector, then he was even more taken aback. He'd taken and passed his Inspector's exam, very much with Lori's support, if not insistence, but he'd expected to have to go through the usual selection process and then probably move to another role in another part of the organisation. Instead, he'd heard first from Lori, and then through a follow up confirmation letter from Human Resources, that he was taking over the helm from Lori with immediate effect.

"Gracias y es un placer volver verla, Sofi. Thank you

and it's a pleasure to see you again, Sofi."

"My boss has laid on an office for you. It's the same as last time and he's happy to release me to you if you need any help."

"I appreciate that, Sofi and that would be really helpful. Can I ask, do you know why we're here?" asked Lori.

"No, Inspectora, I'm sorry, I mean, Inspectora Jefe, I don't. My boss just said he'd had a call from on high and that we should help out as best we could."

"Okay, so I'll brief you properly later, but for now, Sofi, please can you get us to the hotel? And can you also get us a car? An unmarked one please."

"Yes, of course."

Sofia Delgado had no idea what was going on, but it was pretty obvious that she wasn't going to be told anything by the GEO officers until she needed to know, so she changed the subject.

"How's Sam?" she asked casually.

A smile slowly appeared across Lori Garcia's face. She'd thought she'd seen something in how Sofi had dealt with Sam the first time she'd come into contact with him when he'd been arrested on suspicion of assault. Sofi had dealt with the investigation and it had actually been his alleged victim who had been in the wrong, when he had tried to attack Greg's daughter, Terri, when they'd been working on what had turned out to be a kidnap job up in Puerto Pollensa three, or four months before.

"He's fine, Sofi. Should I tell him you were asking after him?" she teased.

"Oh no, well, maybe just tell him, I said, hello."

"I'll be sure to do that. Now, Sofi, we're here, so drop us off and can you please let me know as soon as you've arranged a car for me?"

Sofi recognised it was more of a statement, than a

request.

"Si, of course, Inspectora Jefe."

As they stood watching the young detective drive away, Nino looked across at Lori.

"From what I remember, Boss, I think she might be a good one to think about recruiting."

"You might be right there, Nino," she nodded. "Now, once we get the car, we need to get out to the accident site, and I'd like the accident investigator to meet us there."

"I'll call them now."

*****

The early June sun was still high in the sky, even at five o'clock when Lori Garcia and Nino Castilla saw the marked police car parked at the side of the road on the way up to Santuari de Cura.

"Thank you for coming back out here," said Lori, after the introductions were over.

The accident investigator hadn't had much choice when an Inspector from the GEO had phoned to ask him to meet him, and his Detective Chief Inspector, at the Ramírez accident scene, but he nodded his appreciation at the thanks.

"It's no problem. Presumably you wanted me here because you've seen my preliminary report? I'm not sure I can tell you much more, at least not until I've fully examined the car?"

"I appreciate that, but I'd still be grateful for your early thoughts on what you make of the accident scene."

Nino smiled to himself. She had such a great way with people and they almost always went the extra mile to help her if they could, primarily because she made them feel that she genuinely valued their contribution to the investigation.

"Well, I was going to leave all this to the final report,

but you might as well have this now. Can you see the skid marks here, here and here?"

As he spoke, he walked them both back up the road, pointing out the marks as he went.

"If Ramírez had merely been going too fast and had been breaking hard, then the likelihood is that we'd be seeing tyre marks much nearer the corner."

"Whereas, these are some way from the corner," said Nino.

"Si, Inspector."

"Any other possible explanation, other than he was being rammed?" asked Lori.

"Maybe if his brakes were faulty. But I've had a quick look at them. The brake pads themselves had been damaged in the fire, but the discs were still in one piece, and I couldn't see any specific damage that suggested anything was wrong with the brakes before the car left the road."

By now they were standing where the Mercedes had left the road, looking over the edge at where, until a few hours before, the wreckage of the Mercedes would have been. Lori walked around the scene. Backwards, then forwards and then back again.

"There are no skid marks indicating where the car left the road?" she asked.

The scene investigator shook his head. "No, you're right. And there would be, at least if the car had gone over because the driver was just going too fast and we assume they would have been braking hard, trying to stop."

"So?"

"I think the Merc went into a spin for some reason. Then, and this is partly supposition, I think it tipped over the edge and slid down the hillside gathering a fair old pace before it slammed into the bottom."

"And which way was it facing, Señor? When it

stopped at the bottom of the ravine?"

"The front of the car was facing back up the hillside, but it's hard to tell if it had been in a further spin on its way down, although I can say one thing for sure. It didn't roll, because we'd have seen a lot more damage to the windscreen."

"You got the vehicle moved very quickly, Señor. Is that usual over here?" asked Lori.

"We'd done all we needed to here at the scene, Señora and I thought it would just be a matter of time before the press arrived and I didn't want them getting too many pictures and coming up with their own assumptions. We were lucky that there's an access road down to the bottom and we were able to get the lifting gear in there pretty easily."

"You've been very thorough, Señor, including your preliminary report findings. We really appreciate your contribution to the investigation," said Nino.

"Gracias, Inspector," the accident investigator said, feeling a glow of pride.

Lori smiled at seeing Nino's people skills coming to the fore.

"Yes, excellent work, gracias," said Lori, before slowly adding, "One last question. You don't think this was an accident, do you, Señor?"

He didn't hesitate.

"Not in a million years, Inspectora Jefe."

*****

'Another Ramírez out of the way,' thought Hannah Lopez.

He'd been getting too close and asking too many questions. The same questions his stupid old man had kept asking, which was why she had decided Eduardo had to go. Making it look like a heart attack had been easy enough and given his age and workload, it had been simple enough to deceive the doctor who'd attended the sudden death.

Marcos had been a different matter. Getting rid of him needed to look more like an unfortunate accident, because she needed to avert any suspicion, given his father had only died six months before.

The Foundation's annual classic car rally in Mallorca had seemed like the perfect opportunity and Ortiz had done a good job, albeit she knew that such a big story might still create its own conspiracy theories within certain areas of the press.

However, all things being well, the police should accept that it was simply an 'accident' and things would quieten down soon enough in the press. Whilst she'd grown up with Marcos Ramírez and liked him well enough, he had become too much of a thorn in first her father's and now her side, with his constant demands for answers, especially when they were answers he wouldn't like.

She remembered Marcos storming into her office demanding to see the records of payments around a building development for a new Fernandez hotel complex.

He'd made it abundantly clear to her. He wouldn't hesitate to go public if he found anything linking the Foundation to the corruption allegations that had plagued them for years, but which had become even more open to gossip, since Rodriguez had made his fool-hardy attempt for the Presidency.

Since Marcos had been on his crusade, Lopez couldn't rely on him not finding anything, because if he did, she knew it would destroy the Foundation, the life work of her father since he'd effectively taken over the main role from that old fool Ramírez.

'No,' Hannah Luisa Lopez had said to herself, *'that is something I'm never going to allow to happen.'*

It was a decision that cost Marcos Ramírez his life.

*****

7

As they drove back from what was now a crime scene, Lori and Nino talked through the next steps of the investigation. It wasn't long before they got to the issue of jurisdiction.

"You think we should take this over, don't you?" said Nino.

"Yes, I do. I know the locals might not like it, but then again, not having the responsibility for such a high-profile case might make the local police commander sleep a bit easier," she grinned.

"Should we be thinking of looking at the alleged heart attack that Eduardo Ramírez had then?"

"I think that's now got to be a given. Taken individually, we could look at the two things as separate incidents, but with what the accident investigator is now telling us, the likelihood of both deaths being an unfortunate coincidence just took a back turn."

"Agreed, Boss. I'll get the medical papers requested and start looking into another PM."

"Go carefully, Nino. The family aren't likely to be in the mood to hear that we want to exhume Eduardo's body for another post mortem, but we can cover that when we go and speak to the family."

"I'll see if I can set up a meeting with them when we're back on the mainland."

"Good," said Lori, whose phone suddenly rang.

"Inspectora Jefe Garcia?"

A voice she didn't recognise.

"Si, who is speaking?"

"Rafa Ramírez."

She was about to ask not only how he had got her number, but also how he knew she was now a chief inspector. But she stopped herself. He was from one of the wealthiest families in Spain and through great wealth usually comes power, influence and access to knowledge.

"I'm very sorry for your loss, Señor Ramirez."

"Thank you, that's very kind of you. I hope you don't mind me calling you direct, but I understand you are in Mallorca looking into my brother's accident?"

This also wasn't the time for her to challenge him as to how he knew what she was doing, she thought.

"You're probably wondering how I know this, Inspectora Jefe and…."

She interrupted him. He might be from one of the wealthiest families in Mallorca, if not the whole of Spain, but that didn't mean he and his family could simply bypass every single process, just by having enough clout.

"I am, Señor, so please tell me how you came about this confidential information."

Rafael Ramírez thought for a moment, then decided it was perhaps unwise to open up what might become a hornet's nest for the person concerned.

"Let's just say, they're a concerned friend who wanted me to speak to the right person."

It wasn't going to help the situation by pushing him to find out how he knew she was in Mallorca looking at how his brother had died.

"Okay, we'll leave that for now, Señor, but to answer your question, yes, I am looking into the circumstances surrounding your brother's death."

She'd already decided not to hide the fact as to what she was doing. She had enough experience to know that the press would soon sniff the story out and he was after all, Marcos's brother and deserved to find out from her, rather than some journalist.

Rafa had accepted the fact that Marcos had died in an accident, so had been a little surprised when his contact had given him the name and number of a GEO officer. They weren't the traffic division, so why were they interested? Now she had said they were looking into 'the circumstances,' with no mention of it being an accident.

She waited for him to speak again, but then the silence made her think he may have been cut off.

"Señor Ramírez?"

"Yes, sorry, I was just thinking. You said, 'circumstances,' Chief Inspector?"

She knew he'd picked up on what she'd said. *'No point hiding any of this,'* she thought.

"We're looking into the possibility that your brother's death wasn't an accident, Señor."

"And?" he said slowly.

"I'll know more later, after a full examination of the car your brother was driving. But it seems highly unlikely that his car left the road as a result of an accident."

"You're saying he was murdered then!"

"I'm sorry to have to break this news to you over the phone, but yes, that's what we're currently looking at. I will come and see you and your mother, to explain more of what we know, Señor, but for now, can I ask if Marcos had any enemies that you were aware of."

Rafa swore.

"I'm sorry, Señora, forgive me. I don't know if it's connected, but he told me recently that he was worried about something he'd found out about the Foundation. I've been in Monaco for a while and he said he wanted to talk to me about it, but face to face. I told him I could come home, but he told me it could wait."

"Did he give you any more detail as to what it was about?"

"No, just that it was to do with the Foundation and that our father had been worried about it too, before his heart attack. But I don't know how any of this can be connected to what's happened to Marcos."

"It's very early in the investigation, Señor, but I will keep you updated on how things develop." said Lori.

'And there's probably going to be a whole lot more you're going to find out before very long,' she thought.

*****

Later that evening, Lori drove the short distance from Palma down to Illetas to have dinner with Anna Martínez at her villa.

The two women hugged. It had been a while since they'd seen each other. To some it might have looked like a complicated relationship between the two women, but they were happy in each other's company, knowing how they both fitted into their own periods of Greg's life.

Lori was now with Greg Chambers, although she still didn't really know what to call him. He was her… what? She still wasn't sure what the right term was. Her boyfriend? She felt a bit old to have a boyfriend, but as they didn't live together, she didn't think partner sounded right either.

Anna's connection to Greg had started over thirty years ago. They'd both been in the British Secret Intelligence Service, MI6 and Anna's son, Sam, was the result of a short-lived relationship between the two of them, although Greg had only found out about Sam being his biological son following a chance encounter with Anna during the last year.

"Come in, come in," said Anna, as she ushered Lori in through the main doors. "And many congratulations on your promotion Lori! You must be really pleased, but why the sudden trip to Mallorca? Or can't you tell me now you're a chief inspector?" she teased.

Anna knew Lori's work involved major crime and terrorist investigations and so was well aware that she often couldn't talk about her work.

"Thank you, Anna and it's all been a bit of a whirlwind, but yes, I can tell you, as it will no doubt be in tomorrow's press," she smiled. "I'm looking into what happened to Marcos Ramírez." Lori knew Anna had been on the island for over thirty years, since she'd moved there with Luis, her late husband and Sam, who was around five at the time, so she asked, "Did you know him, or the family?"

"Yes, I met him at a few business networking events, but I suppose I knew Eduardo, his father, a little better, as Luis and I used to sometimes go to charity functions with them. It's such a shame Lori, for the family to lose both of them in such a short space of time. Sounds like it was a dreadful accident? Do you know that Sam and Terri were on the rally too?"

Lori hadn't yet seen the list of the rally competitors and presumably neither had Nino, as he'd have made the connection straight away.

"No, I didn't, so that's really helpful and gives me another excuse, if I ever needed one, to stay on the island a little while longer," she smiled.

The two women had met less than a year ago, at the same time Lori had met Greg when she was looking into an organised crime group on the island, and they'd quickly grown very fond of each other.

Lori looked across the table at Anna. She could almost see the cogs going around in Anna's head.

"I gather that as you don't usually investigate traffic accidents, this perhaps wasn't the accident it's previously been reported as in the press?" smiled Anna.

Lori nodded, knowing that, with Anna's background in MI6, secrets were definitely something she could keep to herself.

"The prelim report suggests it wasn't a traffic accident."

It took only seconds for the next cog to click forward in Anna's head. She knew Ramírez Senior had died of a heart attack some six months or so ago, which given his workload and his penchant for fine food and wine hadn't come as a complete surprise. But if Lori was saying the son's death wasn't an accident?

"So," Anna said slowly, "does that mean you're now looking into Eduardo's…"

Anna let her words trail off.

"Let's just say I need to speak to the Ramírez family about an exhumation."

*****

8

Kat Reyes was sat in the Café Cappuccino close to the royal palace in Palma. Her laptop was open and she was looking at the news reports of the fatal road accident involving the eldest son of the Ramírez family.

She finished her trawl of the national and local news with the Majorca Daily Bulletin, the local on-line English daily paper. It seemed that no one was picking up on the possibility of this being anything other than another tragedy to beset the well-known Mallorquin family.

She closed the laptop and sat back. The more she delved into the workings of the Foundation, the more disturbing the whole thing became.

It had started with a chance remark from Arlo, one of the news agency editors she often freelanced for. Before taking a step back from front line journalism, he'd been a very well-regarded senior reporter for one of the big nationals. She knew he liked her work and he'd always encouraged her to look for investigative style stories, rather than simply reporting on events that had already happened.

She recalled the conversation that had led her to where she was today.

"Go deep and when you think you've gone as far as you can, then dig again and then again."

"Yes, but what if the same thing happens to me as happened to you Arlo?"

"Listen Kat, I had a good run, a very good run, but that was when I was single, with no ties. Then when I met Julia, everything changed for me. I had new priorities in my life and I found I wasn't maybe digging quite as deep as I used to." He paused. "You know the sort of people I went after and they wouldn't hesitate to kill off a witness. Therefore, they wouldn't think twice about knocking off a journalist, or their family, if they thought it would stop the journo writing an exposé on them."

"But you didn't stop completely, did you?"

The older man looked at her.

"I know, but maybe I should have, because it very nearly cost me my wife."

Kat noticed he didn't mention himself, as she found her gaze drawn to his right arm, or at least what was left of it.

"It nearly cost you your life too, amigo," she said quietly.

"Ah, this," he patted the elbow joint where his arm ended.

He couldn't help but grimace, his mind racing back to the memory. He'd been about to go out with his wife in their car and he'd forgotten his car keys. Julia had said she'd get them and she ran back inside the house. He'd walked down to the car and was standing by it when Julia came back out, locked the front door and then unknowingly, detonated a bomb that had been set under their car when she flicked the ignition key to open it.

That his wife had survived, was just through the sheer good fortune that he'd left the car keys in the house and that she had volunteered to get them. But according to the bomb investigators, he'd also done remarkably well to escape death, albeit he'd still suffered a significant and serious injury.

"The bomb investigators said I was lucky. Apparently, if I hadn't been waiting for Julia on the passenger side…"

"Like I said, you could have died, Arlo!"

"But I didn't and more importantly, Julia wasn't harmed."

Kat knew Julia wasn't physically harmed, but she had suffered nightmares as a result of the attempt on Arlo's life and the effect on Julia had been the primary reason for him stepping away from front-line reporting.

"You're not exactly selling it, Arlo."

He smiled at her. She was young, ambitious and brave. She was just like he was at her age. Wanting to find the truth in difficult stories, even if it meant putting herself in danger.

"Kat, you know I don't need to sell this to you. You've already bought into this. I just want you to go after something that others won't want to touch," he said, his trademark smile returning as he pushed a file across the table to her.

He explained he'd started putting the file together about three years ago, when something didn't feel quite right. At first he was just gathering snippets of information through the news channels and from his old informants, but over the past six months he'd heard more rumours that, on their own, you could argue meant nothing, but he had the skill and the knack to see connections when others didn't.

"You really think there's something in this, don't you?" she'd said, as she'd flicked through the open file again.

"I do. So will you take a look at it for me?"

She looked at him. His smile had gone, replaced instead by a deep intensity.

She put the file back down on the desk and closed it and stared at the words on the front cover.

'La Fundación de Palma.' The Palma Foundation.

*****

Greg Chambers had just chosen a light pasta-based lunch at Enoteca da Luca, one of his favourite Italian restaurants in London.

"What would you like to go with that, Greg?" asked Matt, the restaurant manager.

"Any recommendations, Matt?"

"I've got a bottle of Brunello di Montalcino? It's got the trademark black fruit and acidity of Brunello and the grape is 100% Sangiovese, the same as is used in Chianti Classico."

"Sounds perfect, but just a glass please, I've got some more work on this afternoon."

As he waited for his food Greg reflected on his morning visit to the London offices of Trent MacDonald, the global engineering company, who were still 3R's most important client.

He was sipping his wine and thinking through the issues that had been raised during the meeting when Matt came back with his food.

"Great choice of wine, Matt, it's excellent!"

"It's good isn't it, Greg? I'll try and keep a bottle back for you for next time you're in," said Matt with a wink. "Are you in London for long?"

"I'm popping across to Madrid to see Lori for a couple of days and then I'm off to Asia for a bit. But if you can hang on to a bottle, I'll be back in a couple of weeks' time."

"Say hello to her from me and you must bring her to see us next time you're both back in London."

Greg saw his phone screen flash and Lori's name appear.

"Talk of the good lady, she must have known we were talking about her," smiled Greg.

Matt smiled and mouthed *'Say hello,'* as he left Greg alone at the table.

"Hola, Inspectora Jefe!" He'd been delighted to hear she'd been promoted, as he knew how much of herself she invested in her job. "Oh, and Matt from Enoteca says hello."

"Say hello back to him," said Lori, remembering the very nice lunch she'd had there with Greg after he'd taken her to visit St. Paul's Cathedral.

He then listened, as she quickly moved into what he called her 'work mode.'

"You're in Mallorca? Look, I know you can't go into the details, but are you going to be there long, my love?" he asked.

She loved the Englishness in the tender way he always spoke to her.

"Not sure at the moment," she replied. "It depends if the victim's family are coming over here, or whether I need to get back to Madrid to see them, so I'm not sure where I'll be for the weekend."

"Don't worry, that's fine. Just let me know when you can and I'll come to you."

"I'd like that. So how was John?"

"He's good."

Greg had only managed a quick hello with Sir John MacDonald, the Chairman of Trent MacDonald. He'd been due to retire the previous year, but then his wife, Sheila, had been murdered in their Mallorcan home and since then Greg knew his oldest client, and now a firm friend, had thrown himself back into his work.

Although it had only been briefly, it had still been good to see him, but in any event, he was there to see

John's son Chris, one of the senior VP's who ran Trent MacDonald's Asia Pacific operation.

"By the way, John asked after you and wants to know when you're going to retire and come and join me at 3R?"

"Ha! You mean 'you' want to know when I'm going to retire, Greg Chambers!" she said. "Anyway, I don't know if you can afford me, can you?" she grinned, although she knew full well that Greg's company were doing very well. In fact, 3R was doing exceptionally well, partly because of the new staff Greg's daughter Terri had recruited, as well as now being able to call on both Sam and sometimes even asking Sam's mother, Anna Martínez, to help out on occasion.

"I'm sure we could find something half-interesting you could do," he teased, "and we might even be able to pay you a few euros too."

"Well, I'm not retiring any time soon, Señor Chambers, so stop asking me," she teased him back, although she knew that any salary he could offer her was likely to dwarf even her new chief inspector salary.

"Okay, I promise, I'll stop. Now, what about this weekend? When will you know where you're going to be?"

She was about to answer when she saw a number on her screen, recognising it as the one Rafa Ramírez had called from before.

"Actually, I might be able to tell you after I've taken a call that's just come in. Speak to you in a minute. She broke off from Greg and answered the new call.

"Señor Ramirez, what can I do for you?"

"Inspectora Jefe, I just wanted to let you know that my mother and I will be flying out later this afternoon. She wants to come and see Marcos and to see where he died. Now you mentioned you wanted to meet with us, so I thought you'd like to know. We'll be at our villa, I'll ping you the location."

"Muchas gracias, Señor. That's good of you to inform me and perhaps we can meet sometime during the morning?"

"That will be fine. Talk to you tomorrow, Señora."

*****

After she'd texted Greg that she'd still be in Mallorca over the coming weekend, she went to find Nino Castilla.

"This is going to hit the press very soon, Nino, so can you get the Comms team to work up some responses to the likely questions I'm going to get please?"

"I've already spoken to them and she's on it, Boss."

She smiled. She felt she was still thinking like an inspector, rather than a chief inspector, while Nino seemed to have already stepped up to the mark, even though they'd both only been promoted for a few days.

He realised what she must be thinking.

"I had a good boss, Lori. She trained me well," he winked at her.

She gave him a short nod of appreciation.

'I think I just need to believe in myself a bit more,' she thought, before she refocused.

"Now, the only good thing, if that's even the right way to say this, is that with the two Ramírez deaths, we've reduced the list of potential suspects," said Lori.

"What? You're not including Rafa then?" asked Nino.

"Good point, but there's nothing to suggest that he's had any involvement at all in the running of the Foundation. Yes, he's been to the quarterly Board meetings for the Ramírez Corporation, and if I'm being a bit cynical, that might just be to keep an eye on ensuring they're making enough money to continue to fund his lifestyle."

"Okay, so that leaves us with the other three founder members: Rodriguez, Lopez and Fernandez. Where do you want to start?" said Nino.

"Let's start with the former lawyer turned politician, José Rodriguez, but we shouldn't forget the rest of their families either Nino. We can't rule any of them out at this stage," said Lori.

She listened as he briefed her, with barely a reference to the file before him, on each of the remaining three founders of La Fundación de Palma. She was always amazed at his propensity to quickly assimilate information and just tell her what was relevant and important.

"His first wife died a couple of years ago, but he has a new one now, at least relatively new and she's much younger than him. There's one kid from the first marriage, Francisco, and he now heads up his father's law firm."

"Okay, what do we know about wife number two?"

Nino looked through the CNI files Mendez had given them on each of the Foundation families and pulled out a photograph.

"Maria Rodriguez. She's thirty-five, the same age as his son. She was one of his political analysts and known to be hugely ambitious. It seems she put her own political career on hold when she married him, which was a year after his first wife died."

"A bit soon?"

"There were rumours, but the first marriage was said to have been happy and it appears that Maria was just in the right place, at the right time, to pick up the pieces."

"And she put her career on hold?" Lori asked.

"Yes, although she supported him when he ran for President and it seems that she was doing a really good job of it too, judging by the polls, that is until he made a major faux pas on his environmental policy, after which even Maria couldn't save him and his campaign nose-dived and the latest guy got in with a landslide."

"What did he get so wrong?"

"He got caught in a scam, allegedly talking to a couple of oil company representatives. They were promising additional campaign funds, but only if he agreed to support their drilling options for further exploration in the Basque-Cantabrian basin."

"Who set him up?"

"It's interesting. The video of the scam was sent anonymously into one of the press agencies."

Lori frowned.

"Better get a copy of it and see if we can identify any of the players in it. You said his first wife died?" said Lori. "Do we know how?"

Nino flicked through the CNI files. It was clear that Mendez's people had done a very thorough job.

"Lung cancer. It says here she'd been a heavy smoker, so I'm guessing there's nothing suspicious there."

"Maybe, but mark it up for possible further investigation, as I don't think we can make any assumptions here, Nino. Anything on the son, Francisco?"

"He's bright, well-educated and seems to have taken his father's firm by the scruff of the neck and turned it into one of the very best places to go to if you need to build a damn good defence argument."

"Okay," she said slowly. "If I'm reading you right, you said they'll get you a strong defence, but it's not necessarily built around the truth?"

"That's pretty much what it says in the file."

"Okay, so what about Enrique Fernandez? Mendes told me he now owns a chain of hotels, Enfern Hotels, plus everything from sun loungers to sun umbrellas?"

"Yep, that pretty much sums him up. Two sons, Enrique Junior and Sebastián, otherwise known as Ricky and Seb. Both in the family business. Ricky runs the hotels and Seb the rest. They're European-wide and still expanding. Well regarded in the travel industry. Treat their customers and their staff well, but there are rumours that they're very hard on their suppliers."

"Do we know in what way?" said Lori.

"There's nothing specific, just that they demand a lot from their suppliers, and drive a very hard bargain."

"So maybe just astute business people, rather than anything untoward?"

"Maybe," said Nino. "There's certainly no intel to suggest anything else. It's just…"

"What?"

"Like Lopez Autoparts, they also seem to get the best sites when it comes to planning applications for their hotels."

"Okay, so maybe not just the astute business guys I suggested. Now what about Lopez? Isn't he thought to have been one of the main drivers behind the formation of the Foundation?" said Lori.

Nino nodded. "Before his illness, Manny was CEO and president of Lopez Autoparts, so he's come a long way from how he started. Originally he was a black marketeer in the Franco era, selling dodgy gear from the back of a mobile van, but he also got into some protection stuff too, although that all seems to have gone away by around the mid-noughties."

"He's done all right for himself then," said Lori. "So, what's up with him?"

"Near fatal heart attack about five years ago, since when he's had another near-miss two years ago."

"Seems to be a bit of a trend with him almost dying and then Ramírez not being quite so lucky," mused Lori. "Who took over from him?"

"If you mean the Lopez family business? It was his daughter, Hannah Luisa Lopez. He's been priming her to take over the family business since she was knee high apparently."

"She's got no other siblings?"

"No, and no mother either. She died giving birth to another baby a couple of years after Hannah. Neither survived."

"Lopez brought his daughter up on his own?"

"Pretty much so and she's the apple of his eye by all accounts and she dotes on him too."

"How did he manage to take a dodgy car parts operation and turn it into Lopez Autoparts?" asked Lori.

"Mendez thinks he's had a lot of help along the way."

"From the Foundation? That must have been a hell of a lot of help. And anyway, what sort of help are we talking about?"

"I think this is where we start to see what the Foundation was really up to. That, together with what he was doing with his protection stuff."

"What do we know about the protection element?" asked Lori.

"Seems he was raising a lot of cash through taxing local, mostly small independent shopkeepers, as well as putting a lot of his competitors, other car workshops and parts suppliers, out of business."

"Okay, but you say that dropped off a good while ago?"

"That's what it says in here," Nino indicated the Mendez file before him. "It seems to have all but gone away when Lopez Autoparts really started to take off around 2010.

"What about the Foundation, who was actually running that?" said Lori.

"It was Ramírez to start with, but they'd only been

going a year or so when Manny took over the day to day running of the Foundation."

"Was it amicable?" said Lori.

"On the face of it yes, so that no one lost face. But the rumour mill suggests that it was much more of an acrimonious coup by Manny, after which he and Eduardo rarely spoke, except to cross swords at the Foundation board meetings."

"What about Rodriguez and Fernandez? Whose side did they take?"

"Definitely looks like it was Manny's, although the intel doesn't say why. But it's clear that under his leadership it wasn't long before they all started to benefit from Manny's persuasive skills, as he helped each one of them, including Ramírez, to secure new business loans and fancy new premises."

"Persuasive skills?" Lori queried.

"Well, looking at this," he turned to a page in the file, "whilst the Foundation's influence, especially in the early days under Ramírez may have been limited, things quickly changed when Manny took over. Officially, the Foundation was helping its members by advising on the best way to apply for low cost banking terms and smoothing the process on planning applications."

"And how was Lopez making all this happen?" said Lori.

"The reality, according to Mendez, is that Manny quickly got in amongst some of the more, shall we call them amenable local bankers and politicians? Anyway, he started lining their pockets and the members benefitted from preferential banking rates and planning consents that were passed without challenge. But he seems to have been pretty smart in how he did all of this."

"How so?" said Lori.

"Because he also set about building the Foundation's reputation by supporting a wide range of local community initiatives. This obviously made the politicians look good too and very soon, everybody was starting to talk about the amazing generosity of La Fundación de Palma," said Nino.

"Clever."

"Yes, especially because Mendez thinks that most of the money they funded the charities with, came from either Lopez's protection money, or the bank loans they were getting at preferential rates."

"Very clever then," said Lori. "So, he was basically stealing the money off the local shop keepers or, bribing the bankers for preferential loan rates, and then giving the money to charities. Whichever way, it would certainly make the politicians look good to the local electors. No wonder then, that Manny and Co were getting their planning applications through without a question being asked, whilst others no doubt found themselves locked in dispute with their local councils, probably in some cases for years."

"Looks that way, Boss. There's also a couple of comments in the report that suggests the backhanders might have been relatively small to begin with, but then if you go down the road a few years, things changed and some of the particularly influential politicians were ending up with new houses. And it wasn't just on the island, as the Foundation soon gained traction on the mainland as well."

"Presumably as the original founder members' own businesses grew and they were growing their network?"

"Exactly, so the Foundation would come into its own when Lopez needed planning permission to build a new Autoparts superstore, or Fernandez a new hotel."

"Well, that's definitely a hike up the corruption

ladder, but a bit of corruption at a local level of government doesn't necessarily suggest a need to get the GEO involved Nino, so what was it that Mendez said about car fires that he thought we should take a closer look at?"

Nino looked through the file again.

"Yes, there's a comment here that suggests, no, it actually says it suspects the Foundation, or rather someone at the Foundation, got involved in settling a multi-million euro insurance claim."

"Why would they do that? And do we have any idea who it was?" queried Lori.

"The report doesn't specify why, but reading between the lines it looks like the Foundation acted as a go-between," said Nino.

"When was this?"

Nino checked the file again.

"Three years ago. The claim was against Lopez Autoparts Europe Limited for supplying counterfeit parts that were deemed unfit for purpose."

"What sort of parts?"

"This is where it gets very murky. The claim related to brake pads they were supplying to Lopez Autocentres, a subsidiary of Lopez Autoparts Europe."

"I'm thinking you're about to tell me the murky bit?"

"Lopez Autocentres service the vehicles for a hire car company part owned by the Ramírez family."

"Ah, so what was happening?" said Lori.

"Tests showed the materials used in brake pads were very poor quality, making them almost bound to fail under hard braking. But it didn't stop there, because they found the pads were highly likely to catch fire."

"That doesn't sound great," said Lori. "How did the claim come about?"

Nino looked up from the file.

"Ten people died."

"As a result of car fires?"

"Yes."

"That's awful," said Lori. Then a thought crossed her mind. "Were all the cars owned by the hire car company connected to the Ramírez family?"

"Yes, but the thing is, the incidents occurred across the whole of Europe. That's why no one originally picked it up."

"But they all point to the brake pads as the primary cause?"

"Yes, very much so," said Nino. "All the cars had recently been in for a service at one of the Lopez Autocentres. However, it seems that the new brake pads were fitted as a matter of course."

"So, they might not have even needed them?" exclaimed Lori.

"Looks that way."

"Shit!" said Lori. "But surely the people could still have got out of the car, couldn't they?"

"Fortunately a lot of people did, but where the people died it seems the automatic door release also failed. But this is where there's some uncertainty as to what caused the door release to fail, because there were a lot more reports of brake failure beyond the cases where the people died."

"How many are we talking about?"

"Close to a hundred, although not all of them burst into flames."

"But no one else died?" said Lori.

"No, but only by the good grace of God, although some were still seriously injured in the resulting accidents."

"Can they connect the brake pad fires to why the automatic door release sensor failed."

"That seems to be what the court case is set to determine and what Lopez Autoparts are pinning their defence on."

"What? That they aren't responsible, even though it was their defective parts that failed spectacularly!"

"Looks that way."

"Unbelievable. Those poor people, stuck in their cars as they burnt to death."

Nino nodded.

Lori thought for a moment. "Why were they changing the brake pads at the first service? Isn't that a bit soon? I mean, even for hire cars?"

"The Lopez lawyers tried to argue that it was good practice to change them early, they quoted 'safety reasons' would you believe? But industry experts hinted it was just part of a scam for Lopez Autoparts to fleece the hire company."

"Why would Lopez do that if his Foundation co-founder part owned the hire car company?" Lori said out aloud, but she answered her own question. "Because Manny didn't like Eduardo."

"'Didn't like' may be a little tame, Boss. Mendez thinks the two of them could barely stand to be in the same room together for any length of time."

"Okay, but how did the Lopez company get away with all this then?"

"They settled out of court, which wouldn't normally be an issue, but it was rumoured that it was at a much lower compensation figure than you'd expect in a case like this."

Lori frowned, "Are you saying the families were got at?"

"That's the most likely explanation. Things weren't helped by the fact that the ten deaths occurred in different countries. That meant ten different police forces and different insurance companies and no one pulled the whole thing together until it was too late, by which time Lopez Autoparts had got everything signed up through a clever bunch of lawyers, headed up by guess who? Francisco Rodriguez."

Lori swore.

"It gets worse. Now none of the families will speak to the police, let alone testify in a court of law. So we have no idea as to what really happened, except that they've all apparently willingly agreed to an out of court settlement and before you ask, I've got copies of all the case papers being sent to me from the various forces."

"We should still try to speak to them again."

"Could be difficult, Boss. They've all signed NDAs, non-disclosure agreements."

"I don't care. Start with the families based in Spain and then reach out to any contacts we've got in the other countries to try to get those families seen too."

Nino nodded.

"One more thing, Nino, who took over from Manny Lopez after his heart attack?"

"Eduardo Ramírez took back the Chairmanship, although Mendez reckons it was by then more in name only, as Hannah Lopez, Manny's daughter, was and still is the CEO."

"Of both Lopez Autoparts and the Foundation?"

"Correct," said Nino.

"What happened when Eduardo died?"

"Hannah was voted in by the Board as President and CEO, with just the one vote against her."

"Don't tell me, Marcos Ramírez?"

"Yes," said Nino.

"And now he's dead," said Lori quietly.

"Does that put Hannah Luisa Lopez in the frame for our most likely suspect?" asked Nino.

"Well, she's certainly very well-positioned, but

listen, how ill is her father? What if this is all just a front for Manny, as he was the one who seems to have originally started the corruption," she paused, "unless that is, they're all involved?" Lori grimaced. "I'm now beginning to understand why this has landed on us, Nino!"

*****

9

None of her police contacts had been able to give her any more information, other than what had been released in the short and uninformative press release the police comms officer had given out soon after the accident.

"They seem to be keeping things very much under wraps don't you think?" Kat Reyes said to Bella Santos, one of the local reporters she'd got to know from attending police media conferences on the island.

"It's probably just because of the Ramírez family. You know how much influence they have on the island. The local police chief is probably shit-scared of something getting out before the family know about it first. Anyway, it doesn't look like there's anything else going to come out on the accident. I mean, he wasn't a drinker or anything, so it's not going to be drink driving or anything like that, and there's no suggestion of any other cars being involved."

Kat could tell her friend was doing some fishing of her own.

"No, you're right," said Kat, who wasn't about to give anything away about what she suspected.

She changed the subject, but kept an eye on Bella's body language. It had been a risk asking the 'under wraps' question. However, Kat hadn't been on the island all that long and she needed to know if this was normal behaviour by the local police and as she'd seen Bella was a regular at the daily police media releases, she knew it was worth asking the question to see what reaction she might get.

But she was relieved when Bella moved on and started talking about the younger brother, Rafa, who she'd found out from a friend at the airport, had arrived in Palma by private plane.

"Do you think he's going to take over the family business? I mean, he's got a reputation as a bit of a playboy hasn't, he? And he doesn't seem much interested in business except to make sure it brings him in enough money to fund his lifestyle."

Kat smiled. It seemed that her new friend was more into celeb style stories, than necessarily hunting down one of the next Ortega and Gasset awards that were handed out for investigative journalism.

'But is that why I'm doing this?' Kat pondered, before she answered herself with a firm, "No."

"No what, Kat?"

Reyes hadn't realised she'd spoken out aloud. She grinned.

"Nothing, Bella, I was just agreeing with what you said about Rafa Ramírez," she said quickly.

"My source said he's brought his mother here. They've got a villa here on the island."

"I suppose she might want to see where the accident happened and presumably Marcos will be buried in the family vault alongside his father," said Kat.

"Yes, he will," said Bella, quietly. "But how did you know that Kat?"

She realised she'd said too much. Bella wasn't as daft as she sometimes tried to make out. She tried bluffing her way out of the question, but Bella was having none of it.

"What are you up to? You're sniffing around something aren't you? Go on, what gives, amiga?"

Kat did her best to back track.

"No, it's nothing, Bella. It was all over the papers, about Eduardo being buried here, so I'm just adding two and two together, that's all."

Her friend just looked at her, then started to shake her head.

"Nope, you know something."

Kat knew she had clearly been wrong, in fact very wrong indeed, to think Bella was just a celeb chasing reporter.

'How did I think she was just that?'

"Well? I'm waiting?" said Bella.

*****

Kat had to make a decision, and quickly. She didn't like it, but she'd screwed up and been found out by Bella. However, as soon as she started to tell her, Kat saw a different side to the young woman in front of her and quickly realised that some good might actually come out of a collaboration.

"Why haven't I seen any of this fire in your belly stuff from you before, Isabella Santos," grinned Kat.

"You mean you want me to lay all my cards out on the table for all to see?" her friend smiled.

"Point taken," said Kat.

The next hour saw multiple cups of coffee and ensaïmadas, the popular Mallorquin pastries, consumed as Kat slowly took her friend through the background story to her investigation of the Palma Foundation.

Finally, Kat sat back in her chair.

"Well, what do you think?"

Bella held up her hands.

"Jesus, Kat, first you're telling me Old Man Ramírez

was somehow bumped off, and now you're saying it wasn't an accident that killed Marcos and that it's all somehow tied in with corruption and protection rackets involving the Foundation?"

Kat nodded.

"Well, that's some story, Kat!"

"Don't you believe me then?"

"Of course, I believe you!" said Bella. "I'm just blown away by what this all means. I mean the Foundation! They're...."

"I know," said Kat. "They're like the biggest thing in charity on the island and they aren't far off being in the top five in the whole country," said Kat.

"What can I do?" said Bella.

"Now before I say anymore, are you sure you want to be involved? Because if I'm even half as right as I think I am about what the Foundation has been up to, for not just the past few years Bella, and I'm talking decades here, then they or at least someone in that organisation won't hesitate to kill if they think it's necessary."

She didn't want to unnecessarily scare Bella, but she needed her to know how high the stakes were.

Bella was quiet for a moment. "I do understand, Kat, but I'm really not the reporter that maybe you thought I was before we had this coffee."

"You're damn right there, girl," laughed Kat. "So, you're definitely in?"

"Like I said, what can I do?"

*****

Lori met up with Sam and Terri in one of the cafés on the seafront at Portixol, close to Terri's apartment.

They greeted each other with a hug and kisses on both cheeks.

"Hi guys, good to see you both again and thanks for meeting me."

"Good to see you too, Lori," said Terri. "But this all

sounds very official. Sam said you wanted to talk to us about the Classic Car Rally? Presumably this is to do with the Ramírez accident?"

"Yes."

"You don't think it's an accident, do you?" said Sam.

Terri looked at Sam and then Lori.

"He's very direct, isn't he?" laughed Terri. "But to be fair Lori, Sam said something wasn't right when it happened. See your old copper's nose isn't going off," Terri grinned.

"Copper's nose?" Lori looked at Sam, not quite understanding the English saying.

"You know, when you sniff something out from nothing?" said Sam.

Lori laughed, "Ah, yes. What was it that got you thinking like that then?"

"Hang on, can we backtrack just a moment, Lori?" said Sam. "Are you saying this wasn't an accident then?"

Lori nodded. "It's not in the public domain yet and I've not yet had a chance to meet the family in person to tell them, so please keep this under wraps, but yes, there's damage to the front and rear of the vehicle that's consistent with it having been hit deliberately, and more than once."

"You said something was wrong!" said Terri in a whispered voice.

"And I think your nose is probably right, Sam, because the damage suggests the car was literally rammed off the road. So, what was it, Sam? What was making this not seem right?"

"I don't know, Lori. It was after we'd had a bit of time to take it in. Terri and I were talking about Marcos's father and that he'd also recently died not too long after my father, Luis. It just struck me, you know? Probabilities and likelihood."

Lori smiled and nodded.

"I'm sorry you two, but you'll have to explain as I've never been in the police," said Terri.

"Sorry, Sis, but you've no doubt used these in planning scenarios when you were in the army. What's the probability of this happening? What's the likelihood?"

"Ah yes, gotcha. You're using the same thought processes to look at the probability and likelihood of both the father and son going within six months of each other?"

"Exactly. So, I'm not saying it's not possible, but both of them dying so suddenly and unexpectedly? Well, the likelihood is certainly questionable," said Sam. He paused and then looked at Lori again. "So, are you looking at his father's death as well then? That was a heart attack, wasn't it?"

"I'm going to have the body exhumed for a full post-mortem by a state authorised forensic pathologist."

"Does the family know yet?" asked Sam, who found himself drifting back into his old mindset. That of an SIO, a senior investigating officer.

"No, but we know Marcos's mother and brother are now both on the island, so I'll be seeing them after we've finished here."

Sam nodded, wondering how the family would take the news.

"I guess you're wondering if we saw anything suspicious during the rally, Lori."

"I am, but presumably you'd have told me already."

"Sadly, you're right, so I don't think we've got anything that's going to help you. We did see Marcos on his way up to the Sanctuary, but we were on the way down at the time and I don't recall seeing anything that stood out," said Sam. "But I'll have another think and if anything comes back to me, then of course, I'll let you know."

The conversation continued with Lori asking Sam how he knew Marcos and what, if anything, he knew about Ramírez's involvement in the Foundation. There wasn't a lot he could tell her. Although he'd known Marcos since he was a boy, it had only really been at something of a distance.

As they finished, Sam asked, "You probably won't want to say Lori, but do you have a possible motive for either of the two suspicious deaths?"

"You're right, Sam," she smiled, "I'd rather not say. Now, I'd better be going, but thanks guys. You might not think you've given me much, but it was still helpful. Let's catch up for dinner soon. Greg will be across later today or tomorrow, so I'll see you then."

Terri had been sitting, just listening to the two of them talking. One a serving detective and the other had been one in his former life. As they waved Lori off, Terri said, "Looks like a right can of worms."

"Lori's got her work cut out there, that's for sure. Glad we're not involved in this one, Sis," said Sam.

"Do you miss being in the police, Sam?"

He was a bit taken aback by her question, but he didn't need to think too hard about his answer.

"Yes and no. I certainly don't miss the politics at work. But the people, the interaction, the buzz and the investigation side of things? Yes, I do miss that. But hey, the work you've been getting me involved in with 3R is really starting to fill that gap, so don't go worrying about me, Terri." He went quiet for a moment before continuing, "The way I was at work, with the PTSD hanging over me? Something needed to change, and that either had to be me, or the environment, or perhaps both."

"You obviously changed your environment by coming back here, but what about you, how are you doing, mate?"

She asked, knowing exactly what impact PTSD could have on someone. She'd recently been through it not once, but twice. The first time when she was shot and almost killed by Marsden and then when she saw Simon die right in front of her, after he was shot by Diego Sanchez.

"It feels a bit like the horse and cart thing, Terri. You know what I mean? What comes first? Getting out of London definitely helped and although I know it's still there, it is getting easier for me to deal with...," he paused, "well, deal with myself I suppose. And hopefully, you've seen me a bit more chilled, Sis?"

She smiled, as like him, she'd seen Sam as a brother almost from the moment they'd found out Greg was also his biological father.

"I have, but I've got to be honest, Sam, you're making me think. Do I need to get away from here? From Portixol, or Mallorca, to clear away the memories?"

"Maybe it would help," said Sam. "But that said, and I'm thinking aloud here. All that being in London was doing to me, with the work I was engaged in, was stopping me finding the time to sort myself out. Whereas, you've done what I didn't. You've taken time away from work, from 3R, to get fit and I don't just mean physically. And you made time to work through some of the difficult stuff and maybe even to start to accept some of the things I haven't even got close to, at least not until recently. I know we can all hide things, and only you know how you're dealing with coming to terms with everything you've been through, Terri, but if it helps, I think you're doing pretty damn well."

She sat for a moment, taking in what he'd said, before she slowly nodded, "Thanks, Sam, that was helpful for me too and whilst I know I've still got a way to go, you're right, I do think I'm doing okay."

He saw the smile return to her face, the one he'd seen when he first met this radiant, confident and energetic young woman.

"Come on then, Sis, if Greg's flying in soon, we'd better get set to brief him on what's going on in the world of 3R International!"

*****

10

Lori slowed as she approached the gates of the Ramírez villa. It was an impressive brick-built arched entrance, with purple flowered bougainvillea growing all around it.

The electric gates opened and as they drove through, and then up the driveway, they started to see the extent of the beautiful gardens surrounding what was a large imposing country manor house.

"Where did they get their money originally?" asked Nino.

"I looked them up. The family were originally fishermen. They followed the tradition of selling what they caught to local people, but with the onset of early tourism catching on around the turn of the last century, they started buying in the catches of the other fishermen. This eventually led to the creation of Comida de Mercado. You'll know it better, Nino, as CDM, but it's still a private limited wholesale company, owned entirely by the Ramírez family."

He nodded. He'd definitely heard of CDM and knew they were one of the biggest, if not the biggest, wholesalers in Spain, buying and distributing every type of food all over the country.

"And it's not just food now is it, Lori? There's the

hire car company, but you remember that construction job, last year?"

Lori recalled an investigation from the previous year.

"Where the construction company wouldn't pay the going fee for 'protection' of their equipment?"

Nino nodded. "It was CDM who were supplying the cranes and construction equipment. It seems they have their fingers in many pies."

"Yes, they've come a hell of a long way and now they've definitely taken on the mantle of a much-respected blue-chip company in the Spanish economy," said Lori.

"Wow," said Nino suddenly.

The villa seemed to rise out of the ground before them. They'd approached it from the south, coming up from the coastline near Portals Nous, so they hadn't been able to see the whole villa until they got to the crest of the driveway.

"I was expecting something pretty big, but this is stunning!"

"That is impressive," said Lori.

She parked the car at the front of the villa and as they were getting out, she saw the front doors open and a man came out and started walking towards them.

Tall, in his mid-30's and yes, Lori thought, very handsome. He had to be the younger of the Ramírez brothers.

"Inspectora Jefe? I'm Rafa Ramírez."

Introductions over, Rafa spoke again, "My mother's waiting inside. I've told her that you now think Marcos's death may not have been an accident. It obviously came as a shock to her and she's still very upset, but she wants to know what you think really happened to Marcos."

Lori had been deliberating when to break the news

about wanting to exhume Eduardo's body and decided it was better to pre-warn Rafa about the question she'd need to direct to his mother.

His reaction, when she told him, was as expected, one of surprise and then anger.

"I don't believe it! You can't honestly be suggesting someone has not only killed my brother, but that they've also murdered my father as well!"

"I didn't say it was the same person, Señor Ramírez," said Lori.

"But the probability that it's a different person? I mean, how likely is that?" he scoffed.

She looked at him and Nino heard the change in her voice tone, when she went into her 'listen to me and listen good' mode as he called it.

"You're right of course, Señor. It is highly likely that it is either the same person, or organisation, who is responsible for Marcos's death. However, experience shows that it's essential to keep an open mind during an investigation, even when it seems perhaps obvious as to what has happened. To do otherwise means we risk missing other possibilities."

It was a firm and clear put down and Rafa realised he'd overstepped the mark.

"I am sorry, Inspectora Jefe, I meant no offence and at this time I have no doubts as to your professionalism."

He left the words hanging. He'd accepted her rebuke, but also let her know that he wasn't one to be shouted down if he discovered something was wrong.

"Good, I'm glad we're agreed on that," said Lori with a warm smile, her voice having returned to her usual intonation. "Now, I think perhaps I should speak to your mother."

"Yes of course, please come this way," said Rafa, with an equally engaging smile.

'*Smart cookie,*' he thought.

As he opened the doors to a room off the main hallway, Lori's first impression was of the amazing view, across the Bay of Palma, from the full-length windows.

She then saw a woman walk back in from the patio.

"Señora Ramírez? I'm Inspectora Jefe Lori Garcia and this is my colleague, Inspector Castilla. I'm so sorry for the loss of your son, Marcos."

"Good afternoon, Inspectora Jefe, Inspector and thank you. Thank you also, for coming here to see me. I understand from Rafa that you're with the GEO?" said Christina Ramírez.

Lori at once got a sense of the woman. A no-nonsense approach, even given her grief for her son.

"Si, Señora. Perhaps we should sit down, and I can tell you what we know so far?"

"Yes, yes of course, forgive my manners, I am a little distracted, particularly with what Rafa has told me of your suspicions."

Nino felt himself sink into the sumptuous leather sofa cushion as he sat down next to Lori.

"This is still not in the public domain," said Lori. "However, given the high profile of your family Señora Ramírez, it is unlikely that this will stay under the watching eyes of the press for too long. Which is why," Lori paused, "I wanted to ensure you were aware of what we have learned from the initial vehicle examination at the scene."

"I'm not sure I understand, Inspectora Jefe?"

"At first sight, it looked as though your son's car was damaged just by the fire, when the petrol tank exploded. However, our vehicle examiner is very thorough and he now believes that another vehicle hit the Mercedes and forced it off the road."

"You're saying this definitely wasn't an accident,

Inspectora Jefe?"

"No, Señora, it wasn't. The evidence is conclusive and indicates your son's car was struck on more than one occasion, at both the rear and the front, suggesting this was a deliberate act. Señora Ramírez, your son's death is being treated as a murder investigation."

Lori waited for the words to sink in and as they did, she saw a momentary flicker around the woman's eyes. She continued, but her voice was softer, gentler now.

"Thank you for informing us, Inspectora Jefe and I am grateful to your vehicle examiner's thoroughness. I'm sure you'll understand that Rafa and I will need time to try to come to terms with why this might have happened."

Christina Ramírez stood up.

"Of course, but if I may, I would like your understanding to ask you just a few questions?" said Lori.

Rafa looked at his mother. She wasn't one to readily back down, but like him, she had recognised this policewoman was not one to be underestimated.

"Please go ahead and ask your questions," said Ramírez, sitting back down.

"Thank you. Your son mentioned that Marcos had something he wanted to talk to him about, something about La Fundación? But he didn't say exactly what. Do you know what that might have been?"

"I'm sorry I don't, at least not specifically. I knew there were things Marcos was unhappy about with the Foundation. Do you know about the origins, Inspectora Jefe?"

"Yes, I do, but not necessarily about how the whole thing operates."

"Rafa can tell you about that later, can't you dear?"

"Yes, Mama, of course."

Nino was surprised and wondered if Lori was

too, that Rafa, the supposed playboy son of the family, might have a good working knowledge of the Foundation, although he noted Lori gave nothing away.

"That would be excellent, Señora and what about what Marcos wanted to speak to Rafa about? Do you know what he might have been concerned about?"

"I just know that since Eduardo died and Manny took back the reins, Marcos has," she stopped. "I mean Marcos had become increasingly unsettled with what he suspected had been going on behind the scenes."

"Do you know what exactly he suspected?"

Christina looked at her youngest son and then back to Lori and took a deep breath.

"Inspectora Jefe, you may already have gathered that the Foundation was set up to maximise opportunity and bring about certain benefits for its members. That meant that on occasions, this may have seen a favour returned with a favour."

"You're talking corruption then, Señora," said Lori quietly.

"No, I'm talking good business, at least that's how it was in the early days," Christina Ramírez said firmly. "As far as my husband was concerned, the Foundation was never intended to be anything more than a strong, and I mean a very strong, business network, where collaboration and cooperation would help our members' businesses thrive in the post-Franco era."

"By the way you talk, Señora, it sounds like things changed at some stage and in a way that your husband didn't necessarily agree with? Did he, or you, know about the protection racket?"

"No," she answered quickly. "I knew nothing about that."

"What about your husband?"

Lori saw the woman's eyes flicker in anger.

"He certainly didn't and neither did Marcos."

Although the way she spoke made Lori think that Christina didn't perhaps entirely believe what she was saying herself. "Look, my husband wasn't a saint when it came to business, Inspectora Jefe, but his father had very nearly lost CDM. They were in a time when running a business under Franco was difficult enough, without Eduardo having to deal with the fallout of his father's propensity for ill-conceived deals. The company very nearly went under, but despite everything, Eduardo rebuilt CDM to what it is today."

This time there was pride and a belief in the woman's face.

"But, Inspectora Jefe, you have to remember the times we were in. There was often still an expectation from some," she paused, "from some disreputable people who still expected bribes, even as Francoism was on its way out."

The look of distaste on Christina's face was plain to see.

"I admit, there were occasions, when he would literally be left with no choice but to agree to some additional payments, in order to allow him to complete a deal, or build a new premise, but if there was any of sort of protection racket going on then I think that could only have been down to Lopez."

Lori heard Christina almost spit the word 'Lopez' out.

"I see, but when you talk about 'additional payments,' Señora, then I assume you're talking about bribes."

Christina Ramírez started to speak, but Lori held up a hand, "I do understand, Señora Ramírez, at least to an extent, that it was a different time with different standards."

"Precisely," said Christina. "And Eduardo was always uncomfortable with the tactics Manny had brought in, using his backstreet dealing methods to either bribe, or intimidate people."

"Why didn't he stop him then?" said Nino.

"He tried, but Manny always had an answer."

Nino could again see the anger in her eyes.

"Manny never spoke about the protection racket as you call it, but he'd also swear blind that there hadn't been any sort of bribery or corruption, at least not real corruption," she paused, "and don't go trying to lecture me on what is 'real' corruption officer! We were bankrupt and we were trying to rebuild a business after a dictatorship and there were some things that had to be done. Eduardo didn't like it, but it was a necessity at the time."

Nino was nodding, "We've already said that we understand that things were different back then, Señora, but what about more recently? Was your husband still unhappy with what was happening?"

Christina Ramírez regained her composure and took a deep breath.

"Yes, and it has been worse in the last ten years or so, even with Lopez's daughter taking over. I thought she might at least be able to keep some element of control over her father when she took over as CEO."

"Manny's daughter, Señora? This would be Hannah?" said Lori, noting that the protection racket Lopez had been suspected of seemed to come to a halt when his daughter took over.

"Si, Hannah Luisa Lopez. Eduardo suspected things were happening, possibly because of some of the new members Manny had recruited to join the Foundation, a number of whom my husband felt came with a less than salubrious background."

"But you said he challenged Manny and presumably Hannah about this?" said Lori.

"And Marcos did as well," said Rafa. "None of what

they suspected ever went through the Foundation books. Marcos told me that Hannah had an answer for everything and that we were imagining things."

"Do you think she was protecting her father, Señora?"

"I don't know, I just don't know."

Nino changed the direction of the questioning.

"Where does the Foundation get its funding from?"

"It's a hundred percent funded by its members. Since the start, every member has paid a significant fee to be part of the Foundation," said Christina. "As you probably know, we started with just the four founder members, but part of the ethos was always to grow the membership, extend the network and therefore increase the circle of influence."

"It sounds as though you were part of all this in the early stages, Señora?" said Lori.

"Yes, to start with I had to be, and it wasn't necessarily because I wanted to. It was more a matter of anyone and everyone in the family helping to save what was left of CDM."

"Did the other three founder members know things were quite so bad with your business?" asked Lori.

"No, not at all. We were almost bankrupt because Eduardo's father had bled the family trust dry trying to prop up CDM. But to the outside world, including Manny, Juan and Enrique and not to mention the banks, the Ramírez family were almost like Mallorquin royalty, with land and money, and plenty of it. But it was all just a façade. Whilst we had a lot of land and property, there was little or no cash left. We were mortgaged to the hilt, borrowing from anyone who Eduardo could hoodwink into lending to us and of course in those days, the land and property wasn't worth anything like what it is now."

"Did the other three find out?"

"Yes, eventually. Eduardo managed to keep it away from them for about a year, but then it came out when we couldn't even pay the annual fee to the Foundation and then all hell broke loose. That was when Manny took over the helm of the Foundation and Eduardo felt he was from then on very much side-lined when it came to making any of the key decisions."

"That's really helpful, Señora, but tell me, with regard to your husband's suspicions, did Eduardo have any specific evidence?" asked Lori.

Christina went quiet. "If he did, then he took them to his grave, because Marcos searched high and low through his papers after he died."

Lori looked across at Rafa. He picked up on her look.

"Mama, the Inspectora Jefe also wants to ask some questions about Papa's death."

Lori saw her go visibly pale.

"Oh my god! I just knew, I just knew there was more to this, but when I said I couldn't believe it was a heart attack," she turned and looked accusingly at Rafa, "you and your brother told me to stop thinking there was anything more to it!"

"So, you suspected something might be wrong?" said Lori.

"I can't say I suspected, but I knew my husband, Señora and he was a lot fitter than people thought."

"But anybody can be subject to a heart attack, Señora," said Nino gently.

As she turned to face him, Nino felt the full force and intensity of a woman whose thoughts, at least most of her adult life, had never been questioned.

"Inspector, I think I just said that I knew my husband."

Lori saw where Nino was taking this, even if he was risking the wrath of the matriarch of one of Mallorca's most respected families.

"Yes, of course, so do you have any idea as to why he might have had a heart attack, Señora," asked Lori.

Despite the grief she was feeling for her son, Christina Ramírez also realised where the police officers had been gently guiding her with their questions.

"Rafa, what have they said to you?"

"Mama…."

"Señora Ramírez," interjected Lori. "I'm inclined to agree with you that your husband may not have been a likely candidate for a heart attack and for that reason, I would like, with your permission, to carry out a forensic post mortem."

"But he's already had one, hasn't he?" said Christina.

"Yes, but this would be undertaken by a state forensic pathologist, a specialist," said Lori.

"You want to exhume his body!"

"Yes, I do, and I'm sorry that I have to ask you for your agreement to do this, but I feel it's important."

"Do you need my agreement?"

"No," said Lori. "However, I don't do this without good reason and therefore I would much prefer to do this with your consent."

She saw Christina take a moment, digesting what had just been said.

"Gracias," said Christina Ramírez. "I appreciate you asking, and I will agree to your request, Inspectora Jefe. If there is the slightest possibility for you to discover that my husband didn't die through natural causes, then we would want to know. Wouldn't we Rafa?"

Her son nodded.

Christina said, "I have no idea as to who could have done anything to my husband, or indeed why, but we'll do everything we can to help you, but for the life of me, I don't know anyone who would want to kill either Eduardo, or Marcos."

"Your consent is really helpful, Señora," said Lori, knowing it would be a significant deciding factor when she approached the judge for the exhumation order.

But without any other likely reason for these two men to have been murdered, Lori needed to know much more about the Foundation, because it seemed to be the only connecting factor linking their deaths.

As she walked back to their car, Lori said quietly, "Nino, I think we're going to need some more help. Get Pérez to get the next ferry over here with half of his team."

Nino gave a quick nod of his head and pushed a speed dial number on his phone.

*****

11

Hannah Luisa Lopez stood in front of her father's bed, listening to his breathing. It was uneven again and the nurse was trying to help him adjust the oxygen mask on his face.

"Leave me alone, will you!" he yelled.

"Papa, try to calm down. Angelina's only trying to help."

"Calm down? How can I, when you won't tell me what the hell is going on, Hannah!"

"But, Papa, I don't think now is the time."

Manny Lopez looked at his daughter and sighed.

"Angelina, please leave us now. I need some time with my daughter."

The nurse looked at him and then across to Hannah, who nodded to her to do as her father said.

As the door closed behind the nurse, Hannah tried to re-adjust her father's oxygen mask, but he pushed her away and ripped it off.

Gasping for air, he took a moment to slow his breathing.

"Hannah, please don't tell me you, or rather Ortiz, were in anyway involved in Marcos's death."

He had always been able to see straight through her, so she knew there was no point in lying, or trying to hide anything from him. If she'd learned anything from her father, she knew there was nothing he didn't know about guile and deceit.

"He was getting too close, Papa. He kept asking questions and threatening to go to the press! I couldn't allow that to happen. But Ortiz did a good job, so there's nothing to worry about."

"Nothing to worry about!" She heard the anger boiling in his voice. "My darling girl, they wouldn't have found anything out! As far as most people are concerned, the Foundation is a generous charitable benefactor of worthy causes and that's all they ever needed to know."

"But it wasn't just Marcos, Papa. He was getting some of the members onside, especially some of the older ones. And whilst they might not have the balls to take you on, I know they see me as an easier touch."

He knew his daughter was nothing like an 'easier touch,' not by a long chalk. But she had a point, although he still felt it had been too much of a high-risk strategy to get rid of Marcos, especially so relatively soon after he'd told her to get rid of the boy's father, his oldest business collaborator, Eduardo Ramírez.

"I just wish you'd talked to me about it first."

"I'm sorry, Papa."

He heard the regret in her voice and his voice softened.

"Do the police suspect anything? I mean, are they linking his death with that of Eduardo?"

"Not as far as I'm aware at the moment and there's no reason they should. But don't worry, I've got our people in the local police keeping their ears to the ground. Problem is, the case is now being looked at by the GEO."

"Stop telling me not to worry, Hannah, because I bloody well am." He felt his anger rising again. "Now, why are the GEO poking their noses in?"

"I don't know, but I'm expecting a visit at some stage and Papa, you'd better be ready too," said his daughter.

"Oh, I'm sure I'll be far too ill to see anyone," he smirked. "But how are you going to play it?"

"Like you said, Papa, there is no paper evidence. I'm stonewalling the press for the time-being and there's no way the police will ever get a warrant to try and find the money trail. Even if they did, I can't see anyone they'd be employing on their pay scale getting anywhere near to our guy's payment maze."

"Well, I damn well hope you're right, but in any case, you just make sure you keep me informed of what's going on."

He looked at his daughter. She had always been the most important thing to him since his wife had died. He could see she was hurt. Hurt for him questioning her actions. He smiled. She was like him in so many ways, but she also had the impetuosity of her mother. A characteristic he hoped wouldn't come back to bite her.

*****

Kat Reyes looked across the table at her new collaborator.

"Things have gone far enough, Bella. What with Marcos's death and me being no nearer to finding the Foundation's corrupt money trail, I think we need to shake some trees and see what happens," said Kat.

"I can go with that, Kat, but what are you thinking? Will you try to see the Ramírez family? And what about the police?"

"I think we should go for both. And I'm going to see if I can take a crack at the CEO of the Foundation."

"Hannah Lopez?" said Bella.

Kat smiled. This girl was certainly quick on the uptake.

Bella spoke again, "Okay, I like that approach. Now,

should I try and front out the GEO officer? Lori Garcia."

Kat was taken aback.

"How do you know her name?"

Bella smiled, "Like I said, Kat, I wouldn't be much of a reporter if I'd laid all my cards out on the table the first time you'd asked me a question, would I?"

Kat grinned. "Fair point, but how do you know her name?"

"Garcia was here on the island last year. She was heading up the investigation into the murder of a British woman by an Armenian crime gang boss."

"You've actually met her then?"

"Yes, at one of the press conferences. She's good, and whilst she's tough to get anything from, she is fair when it comes to dealing with us lot."

"Even more reason that you should be the one talking to her then."

"Okay," said Bella. "I'll try and set something up for tomorrow."

*****

It had been a long day, but Lori was pleased when she saw the text from Greg.

'I'm at the airport.'

She hadn't expected to see him quite so soon, but she'd already finished what she had planned to do for the day, so seeing him would be good. She rang him.

"Hello, handsome. Do you want picking up?"

"Hola mi querida, hello my darling," said Greg. "No, it's fine, I'll get a cab. I'm sure you've got some work to tidy up. But what about some dinner? Have you got time?"

"Yes, I can't do anymore today, so a night off and a fresh start tomorrow would be really good."

"I'll go and drop my stuff off at Terri's and see you at, what? Shall we say eight, for a drink in Café de Lonja, the one just down from Abaco?"

"I think I know the one. It's got the beautiful traditional black and white floor tiles?"

"Yes, that's it. Let's meet there and then we can find somewhere to eat later. See you later. Love you."

"Love you too," said Lori.

As she put her phone back in her pocket, she saw Nino looking at her, with a smile across his face.

"What?"

"This is properly serious then, Boss?"

"Yes, I suppose it is, Nino," and she felt the smile appear on her face.

"It's about time, that's all I can say and I'm happy for you, Lori, really happy."

He rarely called her by her first name. She patted his hand. "Gracias, amigo."

She'd not exactly hidden her private life from her team since she'd joined them five years ago, but it was pretty much public knowledge that her husband Felipe, a serving police officer, had been murdered in front of her and her two young boys almost twenty years ago.

It had taken a while, almost ten years, before she'd eventually felt comfortable to go out on a date. But even then, she'd only managed a couple of what she called real relationships, when the boys were still in their teens, but nothing had lasted beyond just a few months.

She'd convinced herself that it was because of her job and the hours she worked. That was why she couldn't make things stick. But in reality she knew it was because she just hadn't found anyone who she felt as comfortable with as she had with Felipe.

'Until now,' she thought and the smile returned. 'Until now.'

*****

When she walked into La Lonja bar he was seated at a table with a bottle of red and two glasses.

"You look amazing!" he said, as he stood and kissed her tenderly on the lips.

She started to say it was nothing, but stopped herself. She'd gone back to the hotel to shower and change and yes, she'd made an effort and not just for him, but because she wanted to.

"Thank you, my darling," she said, standing back and looking him up and down. She grinned at him, "You look pretty good yourself, Señor Chambers."

He gave a small nod of the head.

"Well thank you. Now what shall we toast?" said Greg.

She thought for a moment.

"To us," she said, and she leaned forward and kissed him again.

"To us," he repeated.

"Now come on, tell me how your London trip went and more importantly, how long will you be on the island?" said Lori, as they both sat down.

"It went really well, but I have to admit, it's been a bit of a relief having Terri coming back to take over the day-to-day operations of the company. I mean, don't get me wrong, Sam has done a brilliant job, but he's got his own business here with Anna to run and the fact is, that if I want him doing anything with me and 3R, then I actually want him out in the field, managing some of the projects we've got coming in."

"Leaving you to do what you're best at."

"Exactly," said Greg.

"Which would be wining and dining the clients," she grinned.

He laughed back at her, although she knew that 3R International was very much built on the reputation Greg had established in the corporate security world over the past twenty-five years.

"Now what about you? Sounds like another high-profile case?"

"Yes, and it's a complex one."

"Corruption?" asked Greg, looking across the top of his wine glass.

"Why do you say that?" she said, trying not to give anything away, which was always difficult when she was dealing with a man who was a former spy.

"It's just a guess, honestly, Lori," he said. "But if you take the death of a high-profile individual like Marcos Ramírez, whose family are hugely wealthy, influential and I think I'm right when I say they're founder members of the Palma Foundation?"

She said nothing and he continued.

"Then add in what's in the international business news about some dubious business deals, then that often suggests corruption may be present in some shape or form."

"Greg!" Her voice raised slightly. "Please tell me you aren't looking into anything to do with this."

This had been how they'd first met, when she was investigating the death of Sheila MacDonald, the wife of Greg's oldest client, Sir John MacDonald.

"No, I'm not," he said quickly, "and I'm not prying, I promise. But I spoke to Terri when I dropped my stuff off and she told me Sam's old copper's nose had also been twitching, which is presumably why you're over here looking into all of this, and you've had a promotion to boot."

"To boot? What does that mean?" She tried to deflect what he'd been saying.

"I think you probably know exactly what I mean, so stop trying to ignore what I'm saying, Lori. I just want you to be careful that's all."

She took his hands and held them.

"Don't worry, my love, I know the stakes are high here, but it seems that I've now also got friends in high places too, but I am being, and will continue, to be careful."

"Well, that's good then, because I wouldn't want anything happening to you."

"Why would that be then, Señor Chambers? Don't tell me I've stolen your heart?"

"That and a whole lot more, Lori Garcia," he smiled back to her, because that's exactly how he felt.

She saw the intensity in him and realised this wasn't the time for a light hearted response.

"Okay, I promise, I'll be sure to be extra careful."

He relaxed and raised his glass.

"Here's to an unexpected, but hopefully a very pleasant few days together. Salud! Or is it ànims?"

She raised her glass to his, whilst a thought occurred to her that if Sam and Greg had pieced together the idea that the so-called accident was connected to corruption, then it wouldn't be long before the press would be wanting to hear from her.

She looked back at Greg, "Either, my love, but you're right ànims is the Mallorquin. Cheers."

*****

12

After breakfast in bed she left Greg in her hotel bedroom with a kiss and a promise to try to see him later that day.

As she walked into the office Sofi Delgado had arranged for her, she saw Nino was already at his desk.

Lori used the abbreviated greeting, "Buenas Nino!"

"Buenas dias, Boss. Good evening with Greg?"

"Si, Nino, it was lovely."

She checked in with Nino on his family, something he always felt she was so good at, always genuinely looking after her team. Taking a sip of the coffee she'd picked up on the way in, she sat down.

"Is there anything else from the vehicle examiner's report?"

"No, he says he can't accurately determine the exact number of hits the Mercedes took before it went off the road, but it was at least two, possibly three, front and back. He's assuming the Merc spun and then was rammed from the front to knock it over the edge."

"And the fire?"

"It's very rocky terrain. Therefore, it seems most likely the pipes have split as the car's bounced down the slope."

"Any update on the PM? The one for Marcos."

A post-mortem was automatically conducted on suspicious or unexplained sudden deaths of individuals.

"He died as a result of smoke inhalation, rather than the burns he received in the car fire. Something perhaps for his family, to know he didn't suffer too much. There was also a cut and some bruising to his forehead, but the pathologist was happy it was a result of his head hitting the steering wheel."

"No airbag?" asked Lori.

"No, apparently they weren't fitted till the early eighties."

"Okay, good. Anything new come in?"

"We've got some press interest. Isabella Santos, a local, has asked to meet you this morning if possible. I checked her out with the comms guy here. She's a local freelance reporter. Covers all the usual stuff. Crime, public interest and local celeb stories."

"Do we need to see her yet, or should we wait till the nationals get hold of this?" mused Lori.

"Well, this might help. One of the local Comms guys saw her talking with another journo, from Madrid."

Lori looked up. She could do with this not suddenly appearing in the nationals, at least without being carefully managed.

"Kat Reyes, she's also freelance. I recognised her name from a couple of things she's done. I spoke to our comms team back at HQ. Apparently, she worked for one of the big nationals before going out on her own recently. Seems to be gaining a reputation and is focusing on high profile stories, while still getting regular work off the nationals."

"Hmm, no point wondering how Santos knows I'm here. She'll have enough contacts to have found that out, but what's her connection to Reyes?"

"Will you see her?" asked Nino.

"Probably better that I do. At least, better than have her and Reyes go digging around before we're ready to let this stuff out into the public domain. Can you set it up for say ten o'clock please, Nino?"

"Yes, Boss."

*****

Lori got the message that the reporter had arrived. As she opened the access door to the public waiting area at the front of the police station, she saw an attractive young woman in her mid-20's, smartly dressed, with her sunglasses perched up on the top of her shiny black mass of hair.

"Señorita Santos?"

The young woman smiled and held out her hand.

"Inspectora Jefe Garcia, encantada. Thank you for seeing me and please call me Bella," said Santos, realising the police officer hadn't apparently remembered her.

Lori was always wary of first impressions, but there was something familiar about this young woman. Maybe on first sight she might look like she was more used to dealing with the local celeb stories Nino had mentioned, but if she knew Kat Reyes, she'd need to be careful. Lori took her through into an interview room, stopping at the coffee machine on the way.

Even before they'd sat down, Bella Santos had started asking a range of searching questions regarding the death of Marcos Ramírez leading Lori to immediately dismiss her initial view of the reporter.

"You've certainly done your homework, Bella, that's for sure," said Lori.

"Yes, but you haven't actually answered any of my questions Inspectora Jefe," the reporter said, with a hint of frustration.

"Well as I explained, I'm not yet in a position to make some of our findings public, Bella, but rest assured you'll be the first to know, I promise."

Bella threw in her final challenge.

"You don't think the death of Ramírez was an accident then?"

"I haven't said that, Bella, and I would not want you causing the family unnecessary suffering through pure speculation."

'*A firm rebuff.*' Bella thought.

"But....," she started to protest.

"I rarely make promises to reporters, Bella, so please take it in the spirit it is intended," said Lori, standing up.

Bella saw the look in the police officer's eyes and realised the interview was now at an end. To try to pursue it further risked losing any chance that Garcia might just keep her promise to keep her in the picture.

"Yes, yes, of course and thank you again for seeing me."

"My pleasure, Bella and I do now remember you from when I was here last year."

Bella couldn't stop a flush coming across her face, which Lori spotted and smiled at her. "One final thing, Bella, be sure to pass my best wishes onto Señorita Reyes as well."

Lori watched for her reaction.

"Señorita Reyes?"

"Come now, Bella, I think we both know you're working with Kat, but may I ask just one thing?"

"Si?"

"Please allow me to complete my investigation before you try to dig too deep. There are certain complexities to this matter that we're still working through."

Bella knew she was being warned off. But she wasn't about to just be told to go and sit down like a good little girl until teacher said she could move again.

She looked at Lori and held her gaze.

"Would these complexities be anything to do with Señor Eduardo Ramírez's death then, Inspectora Jefe?"

Lori was experienced enough with the media to know when not to blink at a direct question and also when not to give a straight answer. Instead, she bounced the question back at the reporter.

"What do you mean by that, Bella?"

Bella gave a slight smile, knowing she was dealing with a media savvy senior GEO officer who wasn't going to give anything away in a careless slip of the tongue.

"Oh, I think you know all too well what I mean, Inspectora Jefe. So, just to make myself clear, neither I, nor Kat, will be sitting back quietly whilst there's a story out there. But we will also do our very best to stay out of your way. So I do hope we can cooperate together?"

Lori heard the change of tone in the reporter's voice. She hadn't been threatening, or confrontational, but she'd certainly made her position very clear. It had definitely been a good decision to see Santos. Far better to keep this young woman onside, than see her running about like a loose cannon.

Lori stood up.

"Of course, Bella. I'm glad we understand each other. Thank you for coming to see me."

Bella nodded. The meeting was over.

*****

"She stone walled me!" exclaimed Bella when she met Kat in a café in a small square, close by to Avenguida de Jaume III. "And she knew we're working together."

"Hey, Bella, don't be so hard on yourself! Knowing we're working together isn't a problem and she's going to be media smart, so you did really well even getting to see her. And what you've done is get an 'in' with her."

"So, you didn't think she'd give anything up in the first place, did you?" said Bella quietly.

"Well let's put it this way. It would have been a first at this stage of a major crime investigation," said Kat.

"Why didn't you tell me that before I went in then," Bella asked.

"For one, you need to learn this stuff for next time and two, you might have approached your questioning in a different, more accepting way. Now she knows you're serious in chasing the truth on this thing. So, like I said, don't beat yourself up! You did a good job, in fact you did a really good job if you got a promise out of her."

"Okay, thanks," said Bella, starting to understand what the more experienced journalist had got her to do. "What about you Kat? How did you get on?"

Kat had tried to see both the Ramírez family and Hannah Lopez.

"I got nowhere with either of them, except a holding statement from their media people, which I guess was what I pretty much expected to be honest. But at least now they know we're interested in them and that they might do what we wanted."

"You mean, shake them up a bit?"

"Yes, but with that comes an element of risk, Bella."

Kat saw the half-hearted response from Bella's body language.

"I mean it, Bella! If these people, whoever it is, have killed not just Marcos, but his father, then we need to be really careful. Do you understand? This isn't a game!"

Bella saw the earnest look on Kat's face and nodded.

"I get it, Kat, I'll be careful."

"Not just careful, Bella. You be damn careful, you hear me?"

She'd not seen Kat like this before. Therefore, she

knew her friend was being deadly serious in what she was saying.

"I will, I promise."

As they left the café neither of the two women saw the man across the street. If they had, they might have thought he was just reading his paper whilst enjoying a coffee in one of the other cafés. But in any event, they wouldn't have seen the directional microphone the man had been pointing towards them. Secreted between the pages of his paper, it had recorded the women's entire conversation.

Jaime Ortiz carefully folded his paper, flicked a few buttons on his phone and sent a copy of the recording to his boss. Getting up from his table, he left some coins for the coffee and then phoned his boss as he headed back to his car.

"This had better be important," said Hannah Lopez gruffly.

He never liked it when she spoke to him like this.

"It is," he said curtly. "But no doubt you'll call me when you've listened to it and decided what you want me to do."

He rang off at the same time Lopez heard a ping, as the email arrived. There was a knock on her office door and her secretary started to open the door, to bring her a document to sign, but she stopped when she heard Lopez bark, "Not now," quietly closing the door as she backed away.

As Lopez sat listening to the recording Ortiz had sent, she saw her hand twitch. It was an involuntary movement, but it had been happening more often. Her doctor said it was related to high stress and had tried to prescribe some drugs, which she'd rejected out of hand. She'd been worried it was Parkinson's disease, so if it wasn't that, then she knew exactly when it was happening. It was when she didn't feel in control of a situation and she certainly didn't feel in control after hearing what these two women had been speaking about.

She called him back.

"Okay, you were right to call."

Her voice was softer this time. Ortiz knew she must have listened to the recording and realised she needed him, so he knew her acknowledgement was as close to an apology as he'd get from her.

"Looks like you have a problem," he said.

"No, we may have a problem," she said, emphasising the '*we.*'

"Okay, fair enough. What do you want me to do?"

"Warn the reporters off. Start with the younger one. But Jaime, just a warning, do you hear me?"

"Understood."

*****

13

He was born and spent his early years in a small country village in north west Spain. One of two children, Jaime Ortiz had a happy settled childhood, with loving parents and a sister who was two years older than him.

Nothing of which gave any sign as to the man he was to become. He was bright and above average intelligence and he'd subsequently read enough books, and done enough detailed research of his own, to understand how a child can grow into someone who is capable of calculated murder.

He knew exactly when and where it had all started. He was twelve and a change to his father's job had meant the family moving to a city. His parents had done their very best to help their two children settle in, but a difficult first day at his new school had ended up with Ortiz being pinned up against the wall by the school bully.

He'd had the odd, occasional bout of playground fighting with a couple of boys in his infant school, but the playground assistants had quickly intervened before things went too far and the boys were soon all the best of friends again.

But this was different. Two boys held him, one on

each arm, whilst the bully, a big, thick set boy named Hugo, punched him in the face. Ortiz heard the other two laughing as Hugo kept punching him and he soon felt the stickiness of blood dripping down from his nose. He'd sensed the tears forming in his eyes, but he held them back, determined not to give them the satisfaction of seeing him cry. This wasn't fighting, it was a beating and it seemed to go on for ever. He waited in vain for it to stop, for someone to help, just like the playground assistants had. But it was only when his sister, who had gone looking for him, came around the corner and saw what was happening and starting screaming at the boys, that the punching stopped.

His parents did all the right things that evening, talking to him and reassuring him, because he had been very quiet since he'd arrived home. Worried that they needed to try to help restore his confidence, his mother took him and his sister into school the following day and spoke to his teacher.

The staff were very sympathetic and understanding and Hugo, the bully, and the two other boys did get a telling off and were made to come and apologise to him. But he saw the smirk on Hugo's face and knew he didn't mean it. Which suited him fine, because he knew what was going to happen, although it was just a matter of time before it did. He'd pick his moment and then Hugo would pay for what he did to him.

He wasn't scared of him, but he couldn't take him and the two boys who were helping him, not altogether. So, he bided his time and kept clear of Hugo for the next few days. Although, when he did see Hugo, he kept his eyes down, as though he was scared of him.

A few of his classmates did ask if he was okay. They'd heard what had happened and told Jaime that Hugo always did it with new boys, and sometimes girls, who came into the school, so it was clear that he wasn't an isolated victim and that there had been many other victims of Hugo's beatings.

Jaime was going to make Hugo suffer, but not because he was some sort of knight in shining armour. No, he just wasn't going to get picked on. He got through to the second week, watching and learning about Hugo's movements. Nothing else happened to him either, but that was another part of learning more about Hugo. It seemed the bully wasn't completely stupid. He waited until the following week before attacking Jaime again, but this time Hugo didn't leave any sign of blood, as he punched him in the stomach, again and again, until Jaime threw up. Hugo had picked a place in the school to ambush Jaime where he knew there would be no one to stop him, not until Hugo himself was too exhausted to carry on hitting him.

"You tell anyone about this Ortiz and it's your sister who gets it next, okay?" Hugo panted at him.

Jaime was hurting, but he was more annoyed at himself for letting it happen to him again. This time he told no one and he made sure that night to hide the bruises on his body when he was getting ready for bed.

After his mother had said goodnight, he lay in his bed, a plan starting to come together as to how to separate Hugo from his two sidekicks. Next day he took his penknife into school and during one of the break sessions he sneaked back into the classroom and with the penknife, he scratched the names of the two boys into his teacher's new wooden desk, something she had told the children about with great delight.

When they went back into class after the break, Ortiz sat waiting expectantly for the teacher to discover the newly engraved initials in her desk.

He was a bit disappointed that she didn't see it straight away and as the lesson went on, he thought he might have to do something, just so she'd see it. The problem with that was that it might draw attention to him, which was clearly something he wanted to avoid.

He'd almost given up, as the teacher was bringing the lesson to a close. His plan was going to fail, even before it had got off the ground. But as the teacher moved some of her books across the desk, Jaime saw her suddenly sit bolt upright. She'd seen the carving of the two boys' names.

Although he'd not been at the school long, Jaime had thought of Señora Diaz, his teacher, as being quite a quiet sort of a person. So, he, together with the rest of the class, were amazed when she went bright red in the face and started barking at the two boys whose names were inscribed on her table.

"Get to the headteacher now and explain yourselves!"

"Explain what, Señora?" said one of them, clearly confused, if not a little petrified at the sudden explosion from his teacher.

"You know exactly what I mean. Now get to the headteacher's office now and tell her which one of you carved your names into my brand new desk! The rest of you can go and take a ten minute break whilst I sort this out."

'Ten minutes,' thought Jaime. *'More than enough time.'*

As they trooped out into the playground Jaime deliberately looked across at Hugo and waited, staring straight at him until the boy saw him.

"What are you looking at, Ortiz?"

Ortiz stood there, looking defiantly back at him.

"You're going to regret this, Ortiz. First, I'm going to beat you up again and then I'll get that cute sister of yours."

"Come on then," said Jaime and he walked towards Hugo, and not away, as the bully had been expecting.

At this point Hugo had his first sense that all was not as it should be. He looked around for his two sidekicks, but realised they weren't there.

"You've…"

"What? Set this up, Hugo?" said Jaime and in a voice that Hugo hadn't heard before and that was something that worried him.

Jaime moved closer towards him.

"Well, if you want some, then I'll happily give it to you," hissed Hugo, as he moved in on Ortiz.

Whilst Hugo was stocky, he wasn't as tall as Jaime, so as he tried to land his punches, they were wide or short as Jaime bounced one way or the other to dodge the blows.

Although Jaime wasn't a fighter, at least back then he wasn't, he knew what he was going to do, because he'd planned it all. He didn't think a straight punch would be enough against Hugo, so he'd decided he'd keep him moving, making the bully work a lot harder than he was used to, to tire him out. Even though Hugo landed the odd blow, Jaime was moving about so much that he hardly felt them, which seemed to infuriate the bully even more, making him even more reckless in his attacks.

He saw Hugo starting to tire and as the boy took a step back to catch his breath, Jaime made his move, running hard at him and knocking him to the floor. Then jumping down hard on Hugo's chest, squeezing the breath out of him, Jaime sat astride his chest, pinning his arms down with his knees.

"Get off me!" Hugo tried to yell, but he could hardly get his breath.

The other children were surrounding them now, but no one was there to help Hugo, instead they were urging Jaime on.

"Hit him, Ortiz!"

"Give him some of his own medicine!"

Jaime heard the shouts, but it wasn't going to affect his plan as he looked down at Hugo.

He saw a look of surprise on Hugo's face and realised it was because he was smiling, something he'd not done since the first day at the new school.

But to Hugo the smile actually sent a shiver through him.

He started blabbering, "Look I'm sorry, Ortiz, it was just a bit of fun amigo. I'm sorry, it won't happen again."

"Fun?" Jaime kept smiling. "Yes, just a bit of fun. Well so is this, Hugo."

He didn't know where it came from, but Jaime suddenly seemed to find strength in his arms that he didn't know he had. He'd rolled Hugo over, even before the boy knew what was happening and then he rammed the boy's right arm hard up his back.

Hugo screamed, tears rolling down his face. "Let go! You're hurting me. Let me go! Please!"

But Jaime pushed the boy's arm further up his back.

"No, I don't think so, Hugo," said Jaime. "Now let's just see how far your arm will go before it breaks shall we?"

The shouts from the other children had stopped as they weren't sure what was happening now, but to Jaime, he realised he was actually enjoying this, enjoying inflicting pain on this boy. He gave the Hugo's arm another sharp twist and heard the boy scream.

Then he recognised a gentle voice from behind him. "Let him go, Jaime."

It was his teacher. Señora Diaz had come to find the children to take them back into class.

"He needed to learn a lesson. He can't keep doing this to people," said Jaime calmly.

She heard the calm and control in his voice.

"Doing what, Jaime?" she said softly, worried at what she was hearing.

"The beatings, the threats. He said he was going to do things to my sister. I couldn't let that happen."

"No, of course you couldn't, Jaime, but I think he's had enough. So come on, let him go."

The teacher couldn't actually believe what she had seen. It was well known throughout the staff that Hugo was a bully and the staff did their best to watch him, but how on earth had young Jaime Ortiz got him on the floor, with his arm halfway up his back?

"Come now, Jaime. I think Hugo's got the message," she said, this time in a slightly firmer voice.

Jaime climbed off him and Hugo stood up, holding his arm, trying to wipe the tears from his face.

"Hugo?" said Jaime.

"What?" said Hugo.

"No more, okay?" Jaime's voice was quiet, but Hugo didn't miss the menace in the way he spoke. "Because next time you won't know I'm coming."

The teacher heard the threat and knew she needed to step in, but Hugo had and probably still was making some children's lives a misery, so she left the threat hanging just long enough for it to sink in.

"Right, that's enough of that, Jaime. Hugo, get to your class. Jaime, stay here with me please."

He'd listened to the teacher as she asked him if he was alright and that he should have told his teacher about what had been happening. Jaime nodded in agreement, but was more taken with the sight of Hugo slinking away, no longer a bully.

He'd stood up to Hugo and it had felt good. He'd beaten him and he knew if Hugo or anyone else ever gave him cause, then he could and would make him suffer and he'd enjoy it at the same time.

Of course, he knew Señora Diaz would speak to his

parents and for their part, they weren't sure whether to be proud that their son had stood up to the bully, or concerned that he'd suffered in silence. But most of all, they were just relieved that as time went on that Jaime seemed to settle down at school, doing well both academically and in sport, although he didn't make many, what he'd feel, were real friends.

As far as Jaime himself was concerned, he just made sure he was never going to be bullied again. He trained hard with the rugby squad, bulking up, as well as toughening up, as he grew in height. His coaches recognised that he was becoming a strong leader on the pitch too. He was always one of the first to be involved in any sort of rolling maul. One of the most devastating of attacking plays on the rugby field, it mirrored the Roman Legionnaires Phalanx technique, where the players copied the legionnaires of old, linking together into a single collective movement to move forward as one.

As he grew in physique and strength, there were only a few people who ever bothered him after that, whether he was at school, university, or when he later joined the army and those that did also soon wished they hadn't.

Whilst he'd hated being beaten up by Hugo all those years ago, he hadn't forgotten the experience either. He made sure he learned from it in the same way that he went on to learn how to fight, and to kill, in close combat training in the army.

Hugo's beatings had shown him how he could ignore pain. He knew it was still there, but he found he could box it up, to deal with it later and just focus on stopping where the pain was coming from, be it a physical challenge, or someone he was fighting.

But he'd perhaps been more surprised when he realised just how much he'd enjoyed inflicting the pain on the boy, when he'd twisted his arm up his back to breaking point. It was later, whilst reading a paper on violence as a response to crisis, that he wondered if he might have psychopathic tendencies. He'd had no previous inkling that he might, but after he'd beaten up one of his sister's boyfriends, who he'd found out was two-timing her, he realised that, just as with Hugo, he'd enjoyed imparting pain on the cheating boyfriend.

He'd never spoken to anyone about whether he might be a psychopath, not even his parents. Primarily, because he was worried about the label he was putting on himself. Psychopath in his mind meant killer, which he couldn't accept, certainly not while he was still at university. But later, in the army, he found that it became much more of a strength, particularly as he went through close combat training, where his direct and fearless approach enabled him to quickly close out the fight scenarios, earning him the nickname, el perro loco, 'Mad Dog.'

Although Jaime didn't appreciate the nickname, at least not to start with and he also resented the fact that his fellow officer cadets seemed to be intent on avoiding him being their training partner. That is, until his army combat instructor took him aside and explained that he'd rarely seen anyone, at least so early in their training, with the ability to close down a fight with such controlled violence, whilst also showing a complete disregard for any pain the opponent had managed to inflict on him.

"So, you see Ortiz? That's why we call you 'El perro loco!'"

The instructor saw the cadet smile back at him. It was a look he'd seen before, on those soldiers who could kill without compunction.

*****

He'd gone on to serve for almost seven years, ending

his time in a multi-country coalition force in Iraq. He'd never told anyone the real reason he left the army, but it wasn't because he'd completed his service contract. Instead, he had been given the heaviest of hints to look for a new career, after suspicion fell on him when two Iraqis were killed during a patrol he was leading.

His had been one of a number of patrols, deployed to find the people responsible for recently setting off a car bomb that had inflicted heavy casualties on his unit. His team found four men hiding in an unoccupied house. They detained and searched them and two of them turned out to be suspected of being involved in other attacks on the coalition forces. Ortiz released the two who weren't suspected and then his team turned the house upside down. However, they failed to find any evidence to link the men to the latest car bombing.

Ortiz told his team to go and wait outside for the transport to arrive to take the prisoners back to the base. His sergeant had been reluctant, unsure about leaving his officer alone with the two men, but Ortiz had insisted. He'd waited a few minutes until his men were out of sight, then to the horror of the remaining two prisoners, he raised his weapon, a semi-automatic rifle and shot and killed them.

He knew they might not be the car bombers, but even if they weren't, they were believed to have set off other bombs, so it was a message Ortiz was intent on sending to those responsible.

There was an investigation. But then, just as he was now, he had been very thorough. Careful not to make it look like the execution it was, he'd shot the men in different parts of the body. He'd then taken two handguns out from his rucksack, guns that he'd previously recovered from other Iraqi prisoners, and put one each in the hands of two of the dead men. He had to hope they were right-handed, but doubted that would be a level of detail the investigators would ever get into. Then after he took a final check around at the scene, he'd radioed in: "Shots fired, two suspects down."

Whilst there was no evidence that he'd done anything other than protect himself, the chief investigator knew something wasn't right and made that abundantly clear to Ortiz, suggesting he might want to terminate his service contract early, *'for everyone's sake.'*

Most of his unit thought he was a hero, but the sergeant who'd queried his order to leave him on his own knew better and said as such when they were alone.

"Job done, sir."

"Don't know where they got those guns from, but I got lucky."

"You certainly did, sir," said the Sergeant.

Ortiz had looked at him. He knew the soldier couldn't prove anything and besides it didn't look like he was going to anyway. However, he didn't like loose ends, so he did as the chief investigator had suggested and a week later, with the army's consent, he'd resigned his commission.

*****

14

Manny Lopez was worried. Worried about his daughter. She was too much like her mother. She'd also had the same streak of recklessness running through her. But until now, he'd always been able to tidy up any fallout, and when he couldn't, his fixer, Jamie Ortiz, had.

He'd sent for him, and the fixer was now standing at the side of the bed where Lopez lay.

"Thank you for coming amigo," whispered Lopez, pulling an oxygen mask to one side.

"Always a pleasure to see you, Boss," smiled Ortiz, although he was struggling to see him lying there, with the oxygen mask and a multitude of tubes connecting him to a set of monitors.

"I'm worried about Hannah, Jaime."

Jaime nodded. He'd worked for Manny Lopez for almost twenty years. During that time, he'd always felt he'd been treated well by the old man and in return he'd given him his total loyalty, a loyalty that included occasionally sorting out something his daughter may have caused.

Lopez noted his fixer's silence, knowing the man had never overstepped the mark by commenting on Hannah.

"The thing with Marcos? Presumably that was you?" he asked.

Jaime nodded again, although she'd expressly forbidden him to speak to her father, probably because she knew what he'd say.

"She told me not to tell you."

"I gathered that, and I don't blame you. You can't have two bosses, Jaime and I did say she was now in charge."

"I sense there's a 'but' coming, Boss," Ortiz said, with a grin.

Lopez laughed, although it started him coughing. When he'd stopped, he held out his hand to Ortiz.

"Jaime, I don't know how much longer I've got, but promise me one thing. Look after her. Whatever it takes, do you hear me?"

Ortiz knew the latest prognosis on his boss wasn't good. The doctors had said he'd got weeks, rather than months.

"I will, Boss, I will."

"No, Jaime, I want you to promise, alright?" Lopez grabbed Ortiz's hand and Jaime was surprised at the strength his boss still had. Then he saw the intensity in the old man's eyes.

"I promise, Manny. I'll look after her with my life."

Ortiz had never called him by his first name and Lopez could see the emotion in his fixer's eyes.

"Thank you."

Manny released his grip and took another deep breath. "Now, tell me, what's all this about a journalist getting involved?"

Ortiz smiled. Whilst the old man might have left the day to day running of the Lopez empire and the Foundation to his daughter, he clearly wasn't going to stay completely out of what was happening.

"Journalists, Boss. There's two of them. One from

the mainland and a local. Hannah wants me to go and scare them off, at least the local girl from Palma."

"Just scare her off?"

"Yes, Boss, she was very specific on that."

Manny thought for a moment.

"And what do you think, Jaime?"

Lopez had always sought his advice, almost since Manny had first met him when the young man walked through his office door at the back of one of his Lopez Autoparts workshops.

"Has she told you about the recording I got when the two journos met up. They seem to be making a few things add up, and we've got interest from the GEO."

"No, she didn't give me the details, but she did tell me about the GEO. I think that concerns me more than a couple of journalists, Jaime."

"Me too, Boss. I can give out the warning like Hannah wants, but if the GEO start getting close, I think we need to move fast and block them."

"You have an idea, Jaime?"

"I do, Boss, but perhaps it might be best if you run this past Hannah first?" Jaime spoke with sensitivity, because after all it was Manny who had built this whole business from just a bit of back-street marketing to what it was today.

"Good point, my boy. Go and deal with the reporter and expect a call from Hannah."

Ortiz left his boss with a wave of his hand and Manny started coughing again. He reached for his oxygen mask, but it fell on the floor. He lay still on his bed, trying to balance his breathing, cursing that he couldn't control what was happening to his body. As the coughing became worse, he gave in, pushing the help button for his nurse.

*****

Manny let the nurse re-fit his oxygen mask and his

breathing gradually settled. He told her off for fussing, as she adjusted his pillows. She frowned at him and then smiled as he then thanked her for all she did for him.

It was time for more of his medication. It didn't help much, but it did alleviate the pain to some extent and he lay back on his bed and thought about the time he'd first met his fixer, Jaime Ortiz.

It had been late one afternoon when he had a couple of his collectors, as he called them, in the back office of one of his Autoparts workshops in Palma. They'd brought him the 'taxes' they'd collected that day.

Even though Lopez Autoparts had really started to take off with new stores opening across the island, due in part to the help he was getting from his 'friendly' local planning councillors, Manny still needed cash and a lot of it.

That was why he was still running his protection rackets, a couple on the mainland and one in Mallorca. They were a fall back to the seventies, when he'd been building up his black-market business and it had been a useful side line, providing a steady source of funding, especially when things were tight when he'd helped start up the Foundation.

He remembered the moment he first saw Jaime Ortiz. He was checking the money the collectors had presented him and there was a noise outside the office door. He ignored it and continued his count. He knew they were probably skimming something off the top, but as long as it wasn't too much he didn't care. He was completing the entry in the journal he kept when he heard another noise. He assumed it was Carlos, one of his guys who was on the door, keeping anyone out whilst he went over the accounts with the two collectors, so he shouted, "Keep the bloody noise down, Carlos."

He went back to questioning the two collectors. It was always good to keep them on their toes and he knew they'd been having problems with one of their pickups who ran some sort of computer repair shop. They'd had to put the shop windows in a couple of times to convince him to pay up as he'd been bleating about not being able to pay.

He listened as the older of the collectors reassured him that it was all sorted now. It seemed that after a couple of warnings; the windows and giving him a broken nose, the store owner had seen sense and paid up, "Including a bonus premium too, Boss," the collector proudly said.

"Okay, good job then," said Manny, although he suspected not all of the bonus payment had been passed on to him.

He heard another noise. He was about to call out to Carlos again, but then it stopped as suddenly as it had started. He assumed his doorman had dealt with whatever it was.

Except that he hadn't, and the door opened and rather than Carlos standing there, it was someone saying he was a friend of the computer geek.

Manny thought back. *'Had it all just been a matter of fate?'*

The man was unarmed, but had demanded that he stop 'taxing' his friend, the same one who hadn't been paying until he got his nose broken.

"So you think you can just breeze in here and tell me how to do my business?" Manny had said.

"I'm glad you understand," said Ortiz. "Stop sending your thugs to tax my friend and we can all get on with our lives."

"And if I don't take your suggestion? What then?"

"Well, it might be something of an understatement, but I think you might regret it if we don't come to some sort of arrangement."

"But an arrangement, as you call it, generally means if I give you something then you'll do something in return. So, what exactly are you offering?"

"I'll walk out of here and you won't see me again," said Ortiz, with a smile that had the hairs on Lopez's back starting to twitch.

"I've had enough of your shit," said Manny and nodded to his men.

He smiled at the memory of the feeble attempts his two collectors had made when he'd told them to get rid of the intruder.

One had rushed forward, thinking brute strength would be enough to take Ortiz down, but he'd been met with an uppercut, delivered with such astonishing power that Manny winced as he heard the guy's jaw crack as his man collapsed to the floor.

Ortiz thought the second collector looked like he might be a little more savvy, but he smiled when he saw the man had momentarily panicked. Instead of going in quickly, to catch Ortiz off balance, he'd stopped. The hesitation gave Ortiz the time he needed to spring to his left and then kick out hard, with his right foot at the collector's left knee cap. The man had screamed as his leg buckled under him. If his kneecap wasn't broken, then enough damage had been done to ensure he wasn't getting up anytime soon.

Manny pulled out the drawer of his desk and took a handgun. Admittedly it was a bit of a relic from the past, but it had always been enough to scare someone off when he'd needed to.

"That's enough! I really think you'd better go now."

Manny pointed the handgun, but Ortiz stood his ground.

"I said, I think you'd better…."

Ortiz interrupted him.

"Listen, I gave you a simple request and in return I'd walk out the door, but now you're making it difficult. So just to make it clear, I'm not going anywhere until you tell me you'll stop 'taxing' my friend."

Lopez couldn't help feeling a little baffled at what was going on here.

"Look, I've no idea who you are, but I really don't understand why, when I'm holding the gun, that you think I'll do as you say."

Ortiz looked straight back at him.

"Because unless you agree, I'll have no option but to break your neck."

It was the look in his eyes and the tone in his voice that started raising doubt in Manny's mind. He was the one with the gun, but that clearly didn't seem to concern the man standing in front of him.

"Brave, or perhaps foolish words, Señor. Why shouldn't I just shoot you?"

Manny saw a flicker of another thin smile on the man's face.

"You could try, Señor, but have you ever actually fired that old thing? You see, you might think it's a Smith and Wesson, which is admittedly, one of the best handguns in the world. The problem for you is if it's a Spanish copy."

Ortiz saw it. Just a flicker in Lopez's eyes.

"And the other problem you might consider is that they weren't true copies. In effect they were poor fakes, made using substandard metals, suspect firing pins and the mechanisms were usually cast from hand drawn images someone had made from looking at an actual Smith and Wesson. So you see, they often fail to fire, and even when they do they're hopelessly inaccurate."

Ortiz saw more doubt appearing on the man's face. He continued, "As such I'd estimate you've got a less than a fifty-fifty chance of that thing actually firing and not blowing up in your face. Then even if it does fire, you've probably got about the same chance again of hitting me. Now given those odds, you might want to reconsider my suggestion to just stop taxing my friend, as believe me when I say I can one hundred percent guarantee that I will break your neck, even if by some miracle you do actually manage to hit me."

Manny saw the man's thin, menacing smile again. He looked at his two men on the floor. No use to man or beast. Then he looked down at the gun in his hand. He'd never fired it and given what this guy had just said, he certainly didn't fancy trying it now, not if he stood a chance of taking his own head off in the process.

"If it helps, Señor," said Ortiz, "if it's genuine, there will be a small, imprinted logo on the flat area between the hammer and the trigger," said Ortiz. "You could check that if you like and no, I won't use it as a chance to rush you, because like I said. I don't need to."

Manny couldn't resist. He glanced down at the gun. There was no logo, it was blank. He smiled and put the gun back inside the desk drawer.

"Perhaps you'd better sit down, Señor."

Ortiz nodded, pushing the one of the unconscious collectors out of the way as he sat down.

"How did you know, Señor?" About the gun?"

"I didn't, at least not for sure. But then again, there's literally millions of fakes out there and unless you're shooting something like that every day of the week, even if it is a real Smith and Wesson, then I'd have still fancied my chances of getting to you before you stopped me."

"Are you brave, or foolish then, Señor?"

"Neither, Señor. But I know about guns, and I know how to kill people. Two things that, given the level of ability I've seen in the people you seem to employ, you appear to know little."

"Ex-army?" asked Manny.

"Yes."

"Are you looking for a job, Señor?"

"I'm looking for you to stop taxing my friend, simple as that. You agree to stop that, and you'll never see me again."

"And if I don't?" said Manny.

"It's your choice, Señor."

"You're still threatening me? I thought we'd gone past you making idle threats towards me?"

"Oh, believe me, we're way beyond idle threats, Señor."

It was the way the man spoke that was making Lopez feel uncomfortable. The man wasn't saying anything like, *'I'll come and find you and kill you and cut your body into little pieces,'* but that's exactly how he was making Manny feel.

"Perhaps we should start again? My name's Manny Lopez and I'd like to offer you a job."

"Before we go on, Señor Lopez. Two things."

"Yes?"

"Stop sending your collectors to see my friend."

"Of course, of course, Señor, and the second thing?"

"I won't be one of your tax collectors, okay?" said Ortiz.

"Absolutely. I don't see you doing anything like that for me," he paused, "Señor?" Lopez looked at him expectantly.

"It's Ortiz, Jaime Ortiz."

"No, Jaime, you've no need to worry. I think that's way below the pay scale of what I have in mind for you."

*****

15

For almost twenty years Ortiz had worked for Lopez. Manny soon started to call him his 'fixer,' someone who would sort things out when everything else had failed. The nickname had stuck and he'd made sure Ortiz had been very well rewarded for everything he did for him and the Foundation.

Years before, Lopez had lost his wife when she'd been giving birth to their second child, who also died in the birth, leaving him alone to bring up their first daughter, Hannah.

He missed his wife, both as the woman he'd loved since he was sixteen, but also because she'd always been there to listen to his concerns and worries about his business. So as his reliance on his fixer's skills grew, so did his trust in the man who'd originally threatened to break his neck unless he stopped taxing his friend.

Lopez smiled as he thought about the relationship between the two men and how it had grown into a deep sense of loyalty, on both sides, knowing Ortiz would go to any lengths to protect his boss.

A protection that was sometimes required, because it seemed that the bigger both Lopez Autoparts and the Foundation became, then so the associated problems, in running the two organisations, seemed to escalate.

But with his fixer, Lopez knew Ortiz could settle most things through his own particular approach to persuasion. Although generally, a threat of violence, if a person didn't at first comply, was usually enough. And if that didn't work? Manny's smile was cold as he thought of the occasions when he'd made it clear to his fixer that a problem needed to disappear permanently.

Ortiz had never needed Lopez to ever give him a direct order as such, to go and kill someone. He'd soon learned to read between the lines and understand what was required, and from his perspective, he'd never had any remorse, or qualms about what he did to protect Manny, or the Foundation for that matter, for to him, Manny was the Foundation.

*****

Jaime Ortiz shook the hand of his boss before he left his bedside, not knowing if he'd see him alive again and left with the closest thing he'd ever had to a heavy heart. He'd never particularly rationalised why this man had become so important to him. He'd literally committed murder to protect the man, so to promise him he'd protect his daughter with his own life was the least he could do.

With that thought in his head, he set off to find Isabella Santos.

*****

Ortiz made a call to the mainland.

"Juan, I need to find a woman."

The man on the end of the phone laughed.

"Señor, I didn't think you usually struggled to find a woman?"

Ortiz ignored the man's attempt at humour.

"Just do your job. Her name's Isabella Santos. She's a local journo in Palma de Mallorca."

Juan Moreno realised this wasn't the time to mess with the 'fixer,' so he got on with his job, as an IT specialist for Ortiz.

"Okay, what do you need? The usual? Address, mobile, email?"

"That'll do as a start," said Ortiz.

A simple search gave up her social media accounts and from there the hacker easily got in behind the security walls, soon finding the woman's date of birth, email and mobile number, enough to then pose as her and access some other sites just by changing her passwords.

"She's not very clued up on keeping her identity protected, amigo."

"Makes your job easier then. What can you tell me about her?" said Ortiz.

"Okay, she's twenty five, single, but looks like she has an on-off relationship with a guy called Dieter, so presumably he's German."

"Address?"

"I'm getting to it, amigo!"

"Well hurry up then," said Ortiz.

"Apartment 4, 141 Calle de Mallorca, Palma."

"Thank you."

"No prob…." But the line had gone dead.

Ortiz flicked open an app on his phone and found the address.

He was less than fifteen minutes from Palma and he was soon parking in the city's underground car park. He locked the car and headed for the exit stairs. He took the steps two at a time and squinted as he came out into the bright sunshine. He set off towards the fountain in the middle of the roundabout and then walked down Passeig del Born. Halfway along he checked the app again. The woman's apartment wasn't far. It looked like it was in a side street off Las Ramblas, close to the Teatro Principal. Five minutes later and he was walking past it. He could see a security key code panel at the entrance and an old CCTV camera mounted on the wall above. The camera looked like it had been installed a good few years ago, probably when the apartment was built. Given the cobwebs around it and the very dirty looking screen, it looked like it hadn't been functioning for some time.

He double backed and checked the panel by the access door. It looked new and there were sixteen apartments listed. *'Bound to be someone along at some stage soon,'* he thought. He walked away and waited close by. Far enough so as not to be noticed, but near enough that he could make it to the door if someone came out, or went in.

After half an hour he was still waiting. He was about to call the hacker, to see if he could find the access code, when he saw a woman with a pushchair. She stopped by the apartment entrance.

He watched as she pushed the numbers. He couldn't tell the exact numbers, but he could see the position of the buttons. Second row left, third row right, second row middle and first row middle. 4-9-5-2. Then he quickly moved in as she struggled to open the door and manoeuvre the pushchair.

"Allow me, Señora," he said with a smile and held the door open for her. "I'm just on my way up to see a friend."

She smiled, but she was wary enough of people accessing the apartment to say, "I hope you don't think me rude, but what's the access code?"

"Not all, Señora, that's very sensible. I mean I could be anyone," he smiled. "I'd better whisper it, it's 4-9-5-2."

She grinned back at him. "I'm sorry to ask, but you just never know who you're letting into the apartment these days do you?"

He smiled back. *'No, you don't,'* he said to himself.

He helped her get to the lift and then took the stairs, as he didn't want the woman to see he was heading for the first floor. When he got there, he checked first that the woman with the pushchair wasn't getting out of the lift on that floor. It was clear. A quick look about for CCTV cameras confirmed there weren't any. The door to number four was on his right. The lock seemed to be a simple mortice and there was a spyglass in the centre. There was a box by the door to number three. It looked like a delivery of an on-line order. He picked it up and knocked on the door of number four.

He heard footsteps coming to the door. A young woman's voice. "Who is it?"

He recognised it from the audio recording he'd made at the café. It was Santos.

"Delivery for you. Sorry, but it needs a signature."

He imagined her looking through the spyglass and so he held up the package to the spyglass, making sure she couldn't see his face.

"I don't think I'm expecting anything, Señor."

Her voice was guarded.

"Ah, I should have said. Is that Señorita Santos? Isabella Santos? Your neighbour at number three has put you down to accept the package if they weren't in. I'm sorry if they didn't tell you."

Ortiz was careful to say 'they' as opposed to he, or she, when he referred to the neighbour.

Bella Santos was sure the woman at number three would have said something, but she knew she was always getting packages of some sort. She opened the door but left the safety latch on. She was being careful, just as Kat had told her to be.

"Can you push it through the gap, Señor?"

"No, sorry, it's too big."

"Just leave it by my door then and I'll pick it up in a moment," said Santos.

"I don't think so," said Ortiz and he smashed his shoulder into the door, catching her unawares and without time for her to try to slam the door shut. He knew he'd be unlikely to force the door open if it had still been closed. But once it was open he wouldn't have the mortice lock to deal with and the safety latch was probably only going to be fixed to the frame by a couple of screws.

"What the....," she shouted, as he burst through the door. She went to scream, but he grabbed her by the throat and the rest of what she was trying to say was lost as she started choking.

"Stop shouting. I said, stop shouting and I'll let go."

Bella was still trying to get her voice to say something, but he had such a tight grip on her throat that she couldn't get a sound out.

"I said, Bella, if you stop, I'll let go."

'How the hell does he know my name?'

"Who are you?" she tried to croak. Then she held up her hand, as in submission and she stopped trying to say anything.

"Now, you need to promise you won't yell if I let go, okay?"

She nodded, determined to start screaming the moment he released her, desperately hoping someone would hear her.

"Oh, and Bella," he said matter-of-factly. "If you try to scream, you'll be dead before you finish. Understand?"

He said it in such a way that made her shiver, and she knew the feeling flushing through her body was one of out and out fear. She looked at him. At his eyes and what she saw only convinced her even more that she should do as he said.

She nodded.

"I'm taking my hand away, okay?"

As Ortiz released his hand from her throat, he felt her body lose some of its rigidity as the fight slipped from her. She started panting, as the air rushed back through into her airwaves.

"Good, now we can have a little chat. Now I represent someone who would like you, and your friend Kat, to stop poking your noses into something that doesn't concern either of you."

"I don't know what you mean," said Bella, trying to massage her throat that felt like it had been crushed.

"Don't play games with me," said Ortiz and he touched the screen on his phone and she heard herself talking to Kat.

"You've recorded us!" she exclaimed. "You can't go around doing that!"

But she realised the futility of what she was saying. Why wouldn't he record the conversation? He'd just broken into her flat for god's sake and had tried to strangle her. *'No, he hadn't tried,'* she shuddered. *'If he'd wanted to actually do that, I'd be dead.'*

"What do you want?" she asked quietly.

"I've just told you," said Ortiz.

"But you can't just….," she tailed off.

"What come in here and threaten you?" She saw the look in his eyes again and another shiver went through her body.

"I just mean…, I mean you can't stop us!" she said, desperately thinking how to get out of this situation.

"Look, I can see what you're thinking, Bella. How is this happening to me? Yes?"

She nodded. The anxiety rising inside her with the realisation that she had no idea what he might do to her.

"Well, the sooner you accept it, then the sooner I'll be out of here. Just back off and go and tell your friend to do the same."

"But...," she started to say.

"But what? Listen, if you don't stop, then I'll start with you first and then I'll move on to your friend. You'll both be dead, but not before you've suffered a lot of pain and humiliation beforehand and we wouldn't want that now, would we? Not with a pretty little thing like you."

He ran his hand up across her cheek and felt her body initially stiffen, before it started to shake almost uncontrollably.

"Fear is a strange thing, Bella. Some people find it's thinking about what might happen is often worse than the actual thing. You know, when some people worry about having an injection? But when they have it, they find it's not actually as bad, so maybe you'd be the same?"

He saw the tears were now streaming down her cheeks and then saw a wet patch appearing around her crotch.

"Ah, Bella, a little mishap. Don't worry, it happens to a lot of people. It's when your body goes into fight or flight mode and you've got adrenalin pumping through it. It stimulates a link between the brain and the bladder, which often causes people to piss themselves."

"You bastard," she whispered.

But with that he suddenly flung his arm out violently at her, his hand catching the side of her head sending her to the floor.

"And you'd better remember that because if you don't heed this little message, then I promise I will be back for both you and your friend Kat." He let the words sink in. "Oh, and Bella," she looked at him. "Don't bother calling the police. I have my contacts in there and I will know if you talk to them."

With that he left her on the floor and walked out of the apartment.

'Message delivered.'

*****

16

It had been a while since they had all had a chance to get together, so Sam suggested the 3R team, together with Lori and Nino, all met up for a lunch at Contrabando, away from the city in nearby Llucmajor.

Miquel, Sam's friend and owner of the Contrabando Tapas Bar, was there to greet them after Sam had asked his friend if he could lay on a private lunch for them.

After a warm welcome from Miquel and his team, together with some of the usual teasing that Sam should settle down and marry Miriam, one of his Contrabando team who Miquel was always telling him was one of the most beautiful girls in Mallorca, they all sat down to a light lunch of Pa amb oli, a traditional Mallorquin lunch of brown bread with extra virgin oil, with the bread 'rubbed' with a local tomato and usually topped with Iberian ham and local cheese.

"Congratulations are in order to you too then, Nino, on your promotion to Inspector," said Sam.

"Gracias, amigo. It was a bit of a surprise, the way it happened, but the fact I get to stay in the same team is a double bonus."

"Tough boss though," said Sam with a grin.

"You're right there, Sam," winked Nino.

"What's that you're saying, Inspector?" laughed Lori.

"Just saying what a great boss I've got," grinned Nino.

"Ha! And there was I thinking I'd get someone decent to work with for once," she teased him back. "Now, seeing as we're all here, I don't want to spend all our time together talking about work, but I do have a couple of things I'd like to check with you guys." She looked at Sam and Terri.

"You're sure you're okay with us sitting in, Lori?" said Greg, tilting his head towards Anna.

"I think I can trust a couple of ex-spies like you two," grinned Lori.

*****

Lori asked Sam and Terri to talk her through the events of the day from their perspective.

"So, the thing is, we now know there was damage to both the rear and the nearside front wing of Ramírez's Mercedes."

"Front and back?" said Sam.

"Yes."

"That suggests the car spun and was then deliberately pushed off the road," said Sam.

Nino looked at his boss, Lori and then back to Sam.

"We think you're spot on, amigo."

"The garage who maintained the Merc says there was no damage at all to the car before it started the rally, but can you confirm for sure that there was nothing there as it went past you?"

"Absolutely, Lori," nodded Terri. "We'd stopped for a moment as we were on our way down from Santuari de Cura because Sam here, thought I was driving too fast, and we'd get time penalties for turning up at Bodegas Angel too early."

Sam raised his eyes at his half-sister.

"Well, you were, but I suppose that's not relevant here, except to say that we definitely saw him, Marcos that is, going up the puig, the hill, towards the time check in at the old monastery."

"Sam's right, we did. In fact, before he says anything, I have to admit I was a bit taken by Marcos, so I was probably concentrating a bit more than usual."

Greg looked across at Anna, who saw his look, acknowledging that it was good to see Terri being attracted to another man.

"So there was no damage?"

"No, definitely not on the front as I saw that close up," said Terri. "Then I watched the Merc in my rear view mirror as it went up the hill and it looked good to me."

"That's helpful, Terri, gracias. Did you see anything else, that now on reflection, seems a bit odd?" asked Nino.

"No, mate and there was no one immediately behind him, no one except the next participant who came later. They were in a beautiful little bright red Ferrari 246GT Dino, but it was about seven or eight minutes later, because the organisers had got us well spread out, to avoid us racing each other," said Terri, with a mischievous look sideways at Sam.

Nino looked at the papers he'd got from the rally organisers and nodded, "Yes, that's what it says here, the Ferrari checked in after Marcos and the guy actually saw him leave the monastery, but didn't see him after that. It was when the Ferrari turned up at Bodegas Angel, and had checked in, that the organisers realised Ramírez was missing."

"They thought he might have broken down. Not an unusual occurrence in classic car rallies, but when the Ferrari driver said he hadn't seen Marcos's Mercedes on the way down and nor had they had any phone call in from him, the organisers began to worry," said Lori.

"So, there was nothing else, Sam, that you can recall?" asked Nino.

"As we've been talking, I've been trawling through it again. You know? Going forwards and then backwards in my head and there is one thing, but it may be nothing."

"Go on," said Nino.

"I think there was a small hatchback, possibly a Fiesta, at the side of the road as we turned into Bodegas Angel."

"Colour? Occupants?" said Lori.

"Light coloured, possibly silver and I only saw someone in the driver's seat, but it's possible there could have been a passenger. No idea of an index plate I'm afraid, but it looked newish, so possibly a rental."

"Christ, mate, where did all that come from?" exclaimed Terri. "I don't remember seeing that at all."

"Once a copper, always…" said Greg, and the others joined in, "….a copper."

"We've not had any previous reports of that, Boss," said Nino, flicking through his papers. "I'm not sure I'll get very far going to the rental companies for a list of every silver or grey small hatchbacks that they had out on hire, so I'll start with just the Ford Fiestas."

"Agreed," said Lori.

"Boss?" He could see his boss was thinking.

"Just a thought, but I'll put a call into our two journalist friends. It could have been one of them keeping tabs on the rally,"

"Yes, good thinking."

"Sorry we can't help anymore," said Sam.

"No, don't worry, you've helped in clarifying the picture we had been developing."

"Which is?" said Sam.

"That whoever killed Marcos was waiting for him

somewhere between where you were parked up and where the Mercedes was forced off the road."

"So, this is now definitely a murder investigation then?" said Sam.

"Very much so," said Lori.

"And when we get the results of the forensic post-mortem, then we might have another one," said Nino.

*****

When Lori rang Bella Santos to see if she had been in the Fiesta Sam had seen she was surprised at the response she got. The young woman, who had been so upbeat and engaging, was distant and abrupt.

"I'm sorry, Inspectora Jefe, but I can't help you."

"I just wondered if it might have been you, or even Señorita Reyes, that's all. There's no problem, I was just asking to help piece something together.

"Like I said, it wasn't me. I don't know about Kat, so you'll have to ask her."

Again, the young woman's voice was short, curt even and nothing like how she had been when Lori had seen her just the other day. Something was wrong.

"Look, Bella, I said I'd help you if you'd help me, so if you know anything about this Fiesta then it…"

"I told you I don't know anything about a Fiesta. Now, I'm sorry but I've got to go."

The line went dead. Nino was looking across the desk at her with his eyebrows raised. He'd heard most of what was being said, including the tone of voice Bella had been using.

"Problem?"

"I think so."

Lori had seen enough examples of witness intimidation in her time to recognise it when she heard it.

"Can you try and find Bella Santos's address? And quickly Nino. Oh, and have we got a number for Kat

Reyes? She should know where Bella lives."

Nino had already got Reyes number, from a comms friend back in Madrid, so he passed it to Lori. Then he was back making another call to trace the home address. Journalists weren't in the habit of making their home addresses public, but he had enough contacts to ask in confidence.

Lori called Reyes and didn't have long to wait for her to pick up.

"Hello, who is this?"

"Señorita Reyes, my name's Lori Garcia, I'm a ….."

"I know, I know. Are you ringing about Bella? I've been trying to call her, but she's not picking up."

"I am. Do you know where she lives?"

"No! Call me bloody stupid, but we've really only just started to work on this job together and I never thought to ask her."

"Don't worry we're just checking with some contacts we have."

Just then Nino gave her a heads up.

"It's okay we've got it!"

Lori gave her the address.

"But Kat, can I call you Kat?"

"Si, si!"

"Do not, I repeat, do not go inside the building until we get there okay! I mean that. We'll be there in a few minutes."

"Okay, okay, please just hurry."

Nino was already at the door as Lori was taking her handgun from her drawer and slipping it into her shoulder holster.

"I've got Pérez and three more on their way as back up."

It wasn't far, but they needed to get there quickly. Nino wished he had a siren on the car they had, but they could hear a siren in the distance and hoped it was

Pérez and his team.

They arrived at the address and saw it was an apartment block. There was an unmarked Skoda, a GEO car, half parked on the pavement and an armed GEO officer was outside the door.

"Boss, the skipper plus one have gone in and are on their way up. It's on the first floor and Boss, we've got the back covered."

"Gracias."

Lori and Nino went through the door and took the stairs. As she got near to the first floor, Lori called out to avoid any chance of being mistaken for an offender, "Pérez?"

"Si, Boss, come on through. Premises secure and Señorita Santos is with us."

Lori breathed a sigh of relief as she moved forward with Nino. She saw the door was open and the safety latch was hanging off the door frame. Walking into the apartment she saw Pérez sitting with Santos. The young woman was shaking and sobbing, with tears streaming down her face.

"Boss," said Pérez standing up and tilting his head towards the damp patch on Bella's trousers.

Lori nodded to him and Lori took his place next to Santos.

"Bella? Shall we get these trousers off you and get you into something a little more comfortable?"

Bella said, "Please."

Lori steadied her as Santos got up from her chair and helped her up through into the bedroom.

"It's just wee," said Bella, as she saw Lori looking at the trousers, just to check if they might be needed for evidential purposes. "He didn't do…," she paused, "anything like that."

Lori knew what Bella was saying, that she hadn't been sexually assaulted.

"I couldn't help myself, but he was laughing at me, which just made it all the more worse."

"It's okay, Bella, it's nothing for you to worry about. And just so you know, Kat is on her way. She's been really worried about you."

"I know. She kept calling, but I couldn't answer her. I didn't know what to say."

Lori called out to Pérez, "Fernando, can you tell Alpha Four that Kat Reyes will be arriving any moment and can he bring her up."

"Si, Boss."

"Now then, Bella," said Lori gently. "I think you'd better tell me what's been going on."

She immediately sensed Santos tense up again.

"I can't, I can't. He said, he said….," Bella stammered.

"I know, I'm sure he said all sorts of things, but we're here now and we can protect you."

"But you can't, can you? Not forever I mean. He said he'd find me and Kat and he'd…"

She started shaking again. "I need to go to the toilet."

Lori watched as Santos rushed to the toilet. She'd said there'd been no sexual interference, so she didn't need to stop her from going to the toilet.

Lori went to find Nino, who was in the kitchen area.

"Is she okay?" said Nino.

"Yes, well, as good as expected."

"Whoever has done this, Boss, has done a damn good job of putting the frighteners on her," said Nino, with a grimace.

"I know and I'd really like to know exactly what happened to her. Poor girl looks like she was terrified and has wet herself.

Nino nodded and then they heard someone calling out.

"Bella! Bella!"

Alpha Four brought the journalist into the apartment just as Santos came out of the toilet. The two women held each other.

"I'm so sorry, Bella, I'm so sorry. I should never have brought you into this."

"Señorita Reyes? I'm Lori Garcia."

"Inspectora Jefe."

"Bella is a little reluctant to talk to us at the moment and I can understand why. Someone has clearly given her a very serious warning. So do you know who has done this?"

"I've got an idea....."

"No, Kat, you can't tell them!" shouted Bella. "He's been recording what we were saying and says he'll kill us both and do things, horrible, horrible things, before he does..." Bella broke down again into uncontrollable sobbing.

"You've got to do something, Inspectora Jefe, something to protect Bella."

"What about you, Señorita? I'm sure the message was equally meant for you too."

"I can look after myself," said Kat, although she wasn't as convinced of that as she tried to sound.

"Bella said something about the man having recorded a conversation you'd had recently?"

"I don't know anything about that, but we met a couple of hours ago in a café. Maybe she's talking about then?"

"I think it might be better if you tell me what you know," said Lori.

"No Kat!" screamed Bella.

"Oh my god! What did he do to you, Bella?" said Kat, who took her in her arms again.

"Nothing, nothing, but you mustn't say anything. Promise me you won't!" implored Bella.

"But Bella, if we don't stand up to these people, then

they will keep doing this to other people."

"But he said he'd kill us," sobbed Bella, her whole body shaking involuntarily.

Lori could see Santos was terrified and put her hand gently on her shoulder.

"Bella, it's okay, it's okay. Now I just need to ask you just one more question, is that alright?"

Bella nodded.

"Did the person harm you in anyway physically?" Lori asked gently.

Bella held her hand to her throat.

"He grabbed my throat and he…., he stroked my face with the back of his hand."

Lori and Nino both thought the same thing. "Touch DNA!" she mouthed to him, and he was already making a call to Detective Sofia Delgado.

"Sofi! Good, I need a DNA kit urgently. Can you bring it to Apartment 4, Calle de Mallorca, just off Las Ramblas?"

"Five minutes, Inspector!"

*****

17

"Bella, I'm sorry, but because you said he touched you, I do have another question. Have you washed your face at all since the man touched you, it was a man presumably?"

"That's two questions," said Bella, and Lori saw the beginnings of a grin on the young woman's face.

"Yes, you're right, I'm sorry, I slipped that one in by mistake." Lori smiled back at her.

"No, I haven't," said Bella. She'd heard the man with the Inspectora Jefe make a call. "Are you thinking about DNA?"

"I am and I know you don't want to tell me anything, but if you allow us to take a sample then I won't ask you any more questions."

Bella had stopped shaking and with armed police in her apartment and her friend's arms still wrapped tightly around her, she at least felt safe for the moment. She didn't want to ever feel as afraid as she had been again. Kat had said this wasn't a game and she needed to be careful and now she knew why.

"Okay."

Lori barely heard her as she'd spoken in such a low whisper, but she gently squeezed Bella's arm in acknowledgement.

Two minutes later, Sofi Delgado was at the door.

"Inspector?" She called to Nino. "Can I come in?" If they wanted a DNA kit, then she needed to treat the whole room as a crime scene until she was told different.

"Yes, yes, Sofi," he called out. "We're only focusing on Bella here. So, you can walk free within the rest of the apartment." As the detective came into the living room he said, "Have you heard of Touch DNA?"

"Si, Inspector. We covered it in the basic forensics training on my detective training course. 'Every contact leaves a trace.'"

"Exactly," Nino smiled as Sofi quoted Locard's Exchange principle from the 1930s.

"Bella?" said Nino. "This is Detective Sofi Delgado from the local police. She is on attachment to our team whilst we're over here."

"Hello, Bella," said Sofi, gently, but professionally. "I'm just going to take some swabs from where the man touched you on your face with some sterile swabs. Is that okay?"

Bella nodded.

"Where did the person touch you? Can you just point, rather than touch, where he touched you, please Bella."

Sofi remembered that Touch DNA, or sometimes known as Trace DNA, was still subject to a lot of debate. Research, especially about how long the DNA persisted on someone's skin in a skin-to-skin contact, was on-going, together with the best way to gather samples, whether it was using wet or dry swabs.

Lori watched the young detective, impressed by the way she went through the process of taking the DNA swabs from Bella. Lori was no expert, but she'd read a briefing paper recently where it discussed the best way to collect skin on skin DNA samples and the wet/dry method Sofi was using was currently considered to be the most effective.

Even if the DNA might not be sufficient to use in any subsequent court case, it might at least give them a positive ID on who had threatened Bella. It was a long shot, given that the skin contact to Bella's cheek had been so fleeting, and Lori knew that. But she hoped they might have a better chance where the man had gripped hold of Bella's throat, because that would have been a much tighter grip and could potentially have left sufficient cells on Bella's skin to secure a DNA reading.

"I've taken both wet and dry samples, Inspectora Jefe. We're well within the timeframes of what the research says, I think it's 96 hours that it will stay on skin, so I'll get these off to the lab."

"Well done, Sofi. Good job. Let's catch up later," said Lori.

"Thank you too, Bella," said Lori. "I know you aren't keen on telling me what's happened, but this has been helpful, very helpful. I know I said I wouldn't ask you any more questions, and I won't, except to say is there anything else you'd like to tell me?" Lori looked at Kat for support.

"I think it's for the best, Bella. We can't let these people get away with murder and then start threatening you too, can we?"

Lori waited. There was no point in rushing this. The girl had had quite a scare, but it looked as though she was about to start talking.

"But can you protect us? Both me and Kat, I mean?"

"Just look about you, Bella. These men here, they're all highly trained and armed and they will keep you safe, won't you Fernando?" She looked at Pérez.

"Yes of course, Boss," said Pérez with a warm smile. "Señorita Santos, you'll be safe with us. I promise you on my mother's life."

A half-smile formed on Bella's face and she mouthed 'gracias' to him.

"And Kat? She'll get protection too?"

Lori nodded, "Yes, of course, if that's what you want, Kat?" She looked at her.

"I was actually thinking that it might be helpful if I move in here for a while with you, Bella? We can keep each other company and it'll save you having to put two protection teams together, Inspectora Jefe?" This time it was Kat who looked to Lori for support.

"Absolutely, that's a great idea." Lori nodded in agreement, "Perfecto, then that's agreed. Now, Bella, perhaps you'll tell me what happened."

Bella had thought that there wouldn't be a lot she could actually tell the police, but she had a journalist's instinct for detail and by the end Nino had taken half a dozen pages of notes.

"Bella, that was amazing!" said Kat.

"Yes," said Lori, "and impressive too, Bella." She looked at the notes Nino had made. Quickly scanning down a couple of pages, she saw what Bella had been able to recall about the man's accent, his intonation, together with his smell when he'd been close to her. Whilst she couldn't identify the specific aftershave or cologne, she'd been able to describe it as a fresh scent, rather than anything woody.

"But does that sort of thing help?" asked Bella.

"It might and it might not, Bella, but it's far better to have too much detail than not enough, so this is great," said Nino.

"Kat, maybe you could now talk me through what you have been looking at in regard to the Foundation?" said Lori.

"Okay, but a lot of it is just supposition, with not a lot of proof to go with it."

"That's fine, just tell me what you've got and oh,

before we start, were you parked up in a silver or maybe grey coloured Ford Fiesta outside Bodegas Angel on the day Marcos Ramírez was killed?"

Kat looked at her, with a frown. She'd heard Garcia say 'Ramírez was killed.'

"Yes, but how did you…"

"One of the rally participants noticed your car and we just wanted to rule it out."

"Yes, that was me. I'd followed some of them from Castell de Bellver, where the rally started and was waiting for them to get to the first time trial at the Angel vineyard." She paused a moment, "So, Inspectora Jefe, you don't think this was an accident, do you?"

"No, I don't, Kat, it's a murder investigation. But listen, you need to keep this under wraps, okay? I'll tell you soon enough when you can go public with this, but not yet, because we're a long way from connecting anyone to this, right at this moment."

Nino had been taking a call. "Boss, something's just come in. A cyclist has phoned in a report of a burnt out van. It's in a quiet car park south of Puig de Randa."

"Can you get…" Lori was about to ask him to get it recovered for forensics.

"It's already happening."

She gave him a nod and quietly said, "Sorry" to him. He just grinned back at her, but she was annoyed with herself, because she kept forgetting he was now the Inspector and doing what she used to do. He was bloody good at his job too, so she needed to let go of the reins and give him the freedom to get on and do it.

"Can I leave you to tie up with Fernando on putting together a protection package, Nino?"

"Yes, Boss, of course, and I've also got a digital specialist coming down to work on an e-fit with Bella."

She nodded her approval and then smiled. He'd no doubt got Pérez working on the package already.

"Need anything from me? If not, I'll say my goodbyes to Bella and Kat and get out of your hair. I'm going to go and gate crash the Lopez offices again and I won't be leaving until either Hannah, or Manny Lopez has seen me."

"Okay, Boss, let's catch up later."

*****

18

Lori left Bella's apartment, having reassured the two women that they were in safe hands, then she set off for the Lopez Autoparts offices.

Situated in one of the smart, mostly IT dominated, business parks near to the university, Lori drove the short distance out of the city, turning off the Ma1110 at the Son Espanyol junction before parking at the front of an impressive set of offices bearing the Lopez Autoparts brand name.

The woman on the reception desk tried her best to stop her as Lori walked into the building, saying she would need an appointment, but she was in no mood to be fobbed off this time.

The benefit of what was an open plan set of offices was that once she was inside the building, Lori could easily access the senior executive suites without having to go through any sort of card entry system.

Ahead of her she saw a set of double doors. There was a plaque on them displaying 'Chief Executive' and Lori headed straight for it. A woman, presumably Hannah Lopez's PA, or secretary, jumped up from her desk and tried to intercept her.

"You can't go in there! She's in a meeting."

Lori kept walking, flipping open her warrant card, "I

think you'll find this gets me into any meeting."

"But you can't. She won't see you without…"

But Lori had got to the door and had already opened it. Inside there was a woman and a man sat at a low table.

"I'm sorry, Señorita Lopez, I couldn't stop her."

"Ah, Inspectora Jefe Garcia I presume? I didn't realise you had an appointment," said the woman.

"I think we both know I don't." Lori just stood there, waiting.

"Okay, Juanita, I can take it from here, thank you." Lopez waved a hand at her PA who nodded and left the room. "This is my legal advisor, Francisco Rodriguez."

"How convenient, Señorita, to have your lawyer here," smiled Lori.

"Are you saying I need a lawyer for whatever you want to talk to me about? It's clearly very important, as otherwise why would you have burst into my office uninvited?"

Lopez was smiling, but there was no humour in the way she spoke. *'Much more like the venom of a snake.'* thought Lori.

"I've just come from Bella Santos, a young journalist. She's had an unwanted visitor. Someone came to warn her off."

"That's awful, but who is this Bella Santos and why are you telling me?"

"She's been working with Kat Reyes."

"Again, I don't know who she is?" Lopez looked at Rodriguez.

"Officer, can I just ask you to get to the point. You've come in here making accusatory statements about something Señorita Lopez knows nothing about. Now, unless you have something constructive to ask, I'll have to insist you stop harassing my client."

Lori ignored the lawyer.

"Are you saying you don't know Kat Reyes?"

Rodriguez went to speak again, but Lopez raised her hand "It's okay Francisco, I have nothing to hide, although I am now late for an appointment. Now, Inspectora Jefe…, it's Garcia, isn't it? I don't know who this Kat Reyes is, but if she's another journalist, then I'm afraid I get a constant stream of calls from journalists, so I only know a handful of names, but they work for the major papers."

"Yes, she is a journalist and she's been investigating the car fires where your company was responsible for fitting sub-standard brakes that caused the death of at least ten people."

"Inspectora Jefe! I really must insist you retract that absurd statement before I have you in court for libel," said the lawyer.

"Ah, hit a chord, have I?" said Lori, "but with you, Señor, or with your client here? And what about the accusations that the Foundation has been involved in wholescale corruption? Do you have any comment on that and I mean either of you, seeing you as you were one, Señor Rodriguez, who seems to have managed to gag all of the families involved, unless it was the same person who visited Bella Santos! But don't worry, I've got people re-interviewing all of the families again."

"Oh, I don't think I've got anything to be worried about and besides, I think you've said enough, Inspectora Jefe," said Lopez, "and I certainly have nothing further to say to you on either of these two wild accusations, both of which I hasten to add, I know nothing about. So please leave now!"

"Don't worry, I got what I came for and just so you know, I'm not one who can be scared off an investigation," Lori stared at them both, but as she went to leave, she heard Lopez speak.

"Be careful, Inspectora Jefe," hissed Lopez.

Lori turned.

"Are you threatening me?" her voice hard and determined.

"Not at all," said Lopez, the thinly disguised smile had returned. "Just offering a friendly piece of advice. We wouldn't want anything to happen to you now, would we?"

Lori could hardly contain her anger at the gall of the woman. *'How dare she threaten her!'* But instead, she smiled. "Oh, don't worry, Señorita Lopez, it takes a lot more than a few threats to warn me off, I can assure you of that."

"Well let's hope it doesn't come to that then."

Again, the smile on Lopez's face didn't match the look on her face. "Juanita," she called. "Please show the Inspectora Jefe out of the building."

Lori didn't wait. Neither did she acknowledge the PA as she walked out of the building without looking back.

Lopez closed her office door.

"How much do you think she knows?" said Rodriguez.

"Clearly not enough to do anything official, but I don't like the fact she's getting those families re-interviewed. It took enough persuasion to keep them quiet last time."

Lopez was thinking.

"Hannah?" said the lawyer.

"Shut up, I'm thinking."

He waited. She was now very much the boss and not just of Lopez Autoparts, but of the Foundation after taking over following her father's heart attack.

"You aren't thinking of doing anything rash are you, Hannah?" he said quietly.

"Not at all, Francisco," she smiled. "But maybe the Inspectora Jefe needs something to divert her attention away from us."

There was a look in her eye. One that the lawyer had seen before and sometimes wished he hadn't, as he didn't like to feel compromised when he knew too much of what went on inside the Foundation.

"Hannah, I think it's time I went, because the less I know about what you're up to, the better."

"Yes, run along now Francisco and leave the dirty work to me." Lopez said it a way that left him in no doubt as to what she thought about him.

She picked up her phone after he'd left her office and pushed a quick dial button.

"Jaime? I have another matter for you to fix please."

*****

19

Ortiz listened, as Hannah Lopez told him about the visit she'd just had from the GEO officer.

"She's saying she's going to speak to the families again, Jaime. Are you sure they're all going to hold up?"

He thought for a moment. He'd used a combination of open threats and a lot of hush money. A thin smile appeared on his face, as he remembered the look of absolute fear in their eyes, when he told them what would happen if they reneged on their agreement.

The hush money had been carefully funnelled through so many different channels that it would be almost impossible to trace, especially because it had been paid in small, incremental payments, making it look more like a salary than any sort of pay-off.

"I can't see any of them changing their minds, but listen, I'll go and remind them, just to make sure."

"Jaime," she purred, "thank you, that would certainly reassure me."

"What about the GEO woman, Garcia? Why is she getting involved in the first place?" he asked.

"I don't know, but I need to find out. I think someone may have put them up to looking into the Foundation, but I don't know, at least, not yet. I think they're clutching at straws, but perhaps it's because of Marcos? Maybe it wasn't such a good idea to get rid of him?" mused Lopez.

"But you did say he was getting too close, asking too many questions."

"You're right, but the police may see it as too much of a coincidence. Shit!" she cursed. "None of this would have happened if Eduardo hadn't found that damn journal."

The journal was part of a physical handwritten ledger her father had religiously kept since he and the others had originally set up the Foundation. She'd known nothing about the ledger until Eduardo Ramírez had dropped it on to her desk after her father's heart attack.

He'd shouted at her, demanding to know what it was and she could still see the anger in his face.

"What the hell is this, Hannah? Did you know about this? What your father has been doing all these years, I mean?"

She'd had no idea what Ramírez was talking about. That is until she picked up the ledger and opened it. The first few sections were just entries relating to transactions over the early years, but then she found what Eduardo had been talking about.

She read down the entries and then flicked through more of the pages, not believing what she was seeing.

Ramírez had been quick to recognise that she'd never seen the ledger before.

"You haven't seen this either have you?" he exclaimed. "He could get us all put in prison if anyone ever saw this!"

It took a moment for her to regain any sense of calm. She was already reeling from finding her father on the floor in his office and then seeing the paramedics working on him, and now this!

"I'm sure my father has a perfect explanation for this, Eduardo."

"Yes, I'm sure he has! But whilst you might not recognise the names in here, young lady, because they were before your time, I do!" said Ramírez, picking up the ledger.

She glared at him. She hated the way Ramírez patronised her.

"It's got everything in here, including a list of hush money, Hannah!" He shouted as he flicked through the pages.

"Will you keep your voice down," she said, trying to calm him. "We don't need the whole building to hear your claims."

"Claims, claims! They're not just bloody claims, Hannah! This holds a record of every single bribe he's paid to people since we set up the Foundation! And let me tell you it includes that complete debacle surrounding the investigation into those poor bastards. The ones who died as a result of those faulty brake parts your company fitted!"

He took a moment, to regain his composure, then asked once again, but more quietly this time, "Hannah, did you know about this?"

"Do you mean the pay-offs, Eduardo, or the ledger?"

"Don't be facetious, young lady!" he shouted at her again and this time Hannah's PA opened the office door to see what was happening.

"Is everything alright, Señorita Lopez. It was just that I thought I heard…."

"It's okay, Juanita, please leave us. Señor Ramírez is just a little upset at my father's sudden illness."

"Yes, yes, quite. We're fine, Juanita, so please leave us," said Ramírez.

Hannah glared at him. Who the hell did he think he was? Dismissing her staff like that!

She turned to him again.

"Where did you find this anyway, Eduardo?" she asked calmly.

"I thought I'd help by tidying his desk up, you know, when you went in the ambulance with him. It was just lying there, on the desk. Anybody could have found it, Hannah!"

"Well, that's not quite true is it, Eduardo? I mean no one would be just wandering into my father's office, so it would only have been one of us, or possibly his PA and she's been with him over thirty years, so I can't imagine there's much she doesn't know about how my father worked."

"What? And you think that's okay? That his PA knows Manny's up to his neck in bribery and corruption? I don't believe I've just heard what you said, young lady!"

He was patronising her again and this time she couldn't contain herself.

"Will you just shut up, Eduardo," she snapped. "You need to stop pretending you're the innocent here. How the hell do you think your business, and those of your partners', succeeded when others failed. You stand there playing the high and mighty, but I reckon you knew what was going on, but chose to turn a blind eye. Now you've realised my father was perhaps always the smarter one of the lot of you and that he wasn't going to be the only one who went down if things ever came out. And don't forget, my father told me how you never let on that you were almost bankrupt when the four of you set up the Foundation and look where you are now!"

Ramírez shifted from foot to foot and started to say something, but she held up her hand.

"Without him, you'd be nothing and neither would your family. So don't come crying to me that you suddenly don't like the way he went about bringing you back the sort of wealth you once had!"

Ramírez started to look uncomfortable as the truth of what she said hit home, however, he tried again, "But Hannah! He was bribing people."

"And? Your point is?" she demanded. "Look, Eduardo, you may call it corruption, but perhaps you've forgotten?" She sneered at him. "In the business world it's called persuasive negotiation."

"You knew about it then?"

"Not the ledger," she conceded. "And yes, I'm inclined to agree with you. It isn't the best idea my father has ever had. But the money? Paid to help smooth the way for the deals that have helped turn Lopez Autoparts, Enrique's Enfern set up and your CDM outfit into collectively billion euro businesses? Then yes, I knew about that and whilst we're at it, we'd better not leave out how José's legal practice got to be where it is today now, should we?"

"So, the others knew about this?" Ramírez said slowly, knowing the answer even before he'd even asked the question.

"Of course, they did! But my father said he could never tell you, because he couldn't trust you to keep your mouth shut," she hissed at him. "So, you'd better make sure you keep it shut now!"

He was taken aback by the venom in her voice.

"Or what, Hannah? Remember, I'm not one of your minions who you can shout at. And I don't think you realise who you're talking to, young lady. I've got friends in some damn sight higher places than you will ever have! So don't think you can go threatening me!"

She could see he was shaking, but she couldn't risk what the stupid old man might go and do if she antagonised him anymore.

"Eduardo, let's just both calm down now, shall we?"

She smiled at him and went to sit down on the sofa in her office. "Come, sit down with me."

"I'm fine where I am, thank you," he glowered.

She felt the hairs on her neck start to rise again in anger, but she took a long breath in before speaking again.

"That's fine, wherever you're comfortable, Eduardo. Look, my father only did what he felt he needed to do to help not only the Foundation, but all of your businesses," she spoke in a more measured tone. "And Eduardo, I think even you have to admit, your business has done rather well over the years."

He was quiet for a moment. He looked down at the ledger in his hand. He knew how business worked, so he wasn't blind to the idea that corruption went on. But the ledger? It was a dangerous audit trail that could take them all down. *'Had he been just a touch too self-righteous when he'd complained about the corruption? Was he just more worried about being found out and that the ledger could...'* He rephrased his thinking. *'Not could, but would!'* The ledger would destroy everything the four of them had achieved through the Foundation.

She waited. She could see Ramírez was thinking. Maybe he was weighing up what to do, or perhaps realising that without her father, the Ramírez family would by now be well and truly bankrupt.

"Would you like me to dispose of the ledger, Eduardo?" she finally asked.

He didn't say anything for a moment, but then he smiled.

"No, I don't think so, Hannah. I think I'll hang on to this for now." He saw her blink. That had got her attention. "Yes, I think I should take back the reins at the Foundation, whilst your father is unwell."

He saw Hannah was about to say something, but this time it was he who held up his hand.

"And I assume I can count on your support, together with Enrique and José, Hannah? I mean, I don't suppose they know about the ledger either and we wouldn't want them to think Manny has been keeping some sort of evidence over the years that would incriminate everyone else, would we? I mean, whatever would they think of him?"

He smiled at her again and she knew he had backed her up against a wall.

"Of course, Eduardo. I think that's an excellent idea and I'm sure my father will be delighted to support you too."

He'd almost heard her teeth grinding as she'd agreed to what he'd said. "Good, that's settled then. I'll ring the others and let them know what's happened to Manny. Then I'll tell them about the arrangement we've decided upon. I think it's perhaps best that we say it was Manny who suggested it as he was on the way to hospital?"

She nodded, knowing she had nowhere else to go, but her nails were digging hard into her hands as she swore under her breath that he wouldn't get away with this, no matter how long it took.

*****

20

Lori Garcia was still fuming when she got back to her temporary office in the Policía Nacional HQ, situated just off Passeig de Mallorca.

Nino Castillo could see his boss was upset about something.

"You okay, Boss?"

"She threatened me, Nino! Out and out threatened me and she thinks she can get away with it. Well, I'm going to make damn sure she can't."

She took a few deep breaths and smiled as he put a coffee down on her desk.

"Gracias, amigo, I think I need that. Any luck with the CCTV outside Bella's apartment block?"

"We're still checking it, Boss. Sofi's on it. She's got a contact in the town centre CCTV unit and they've apparently got the guy on camera going into the apartment."

"Have we got a face?" Lori asked excitedly.

"Sadly not. He's kept his head away from the cameras, so he's no mug whoever he is. But that's what Sofi's got her contact working on. He went in behind a woman with a pushchair, so we've got another eyewitness. Pérez has got one of his team going door to door in the apartment block, so we should be able to locate the woman."

She smiled. He was such a professional, and at this rate he'd be chasing her down for the next promotion before too long.

"That's great, Nino, really great. Well done." She looked down at her SIO notebook, "Okay, so how are we doing with the families from the Lopez court case?"

She saw the look on his face.

"Not great then, I presume? God, they must have really scared the shit out of them."

"Looks that way. We've done a load of background work. You know bank details and credit cards on each of the families."

"Anything?"

"Nothing."

She saw the frustration in his face as he went on, "If they've been given any money then it's been bloody well hidden. I must admit, I expected to see a hundred grand, or at least something significant being dropped into their accounts, but there's nothing like that and there's been no new cars, or anything like that."

She thought for a moment.

"Get the economic unit to go back through it again, Nino. But this time, forget the big pay-outs they might have been looking for. This time ask them to drill down into any regular sort of payments. You know, something that looks like a salary for an additional job, or some sort of small annuity."

She saw he looked a little disappointed that he perhaps hadn't thought of that himself.

"Hey, amigo. It was something I learned the same way. I was looking into an organised crime set up and I went looking for the big fish, as in the big pay outs. But of course, there weren't any, because they were too clever for that. However, my boss got me to go through it all again, but this time to look at the minutiae."

"And the answer was there?" asked Nino.

"In a manner of speaking. It's where we found they'd made a mistake. They'd done a test payment and someone had been sloppy because they hadn't covered their tracks very well. It gave us a name and most importantly, it was the 'in' we needed. Once we'd got through that, we knew where to look when we started checking the other payments in that name."

"Okay understood, I'll get them on it straight away."

*****

Jaime Ortiz had already decided which families needed a face-to-face reminder and which ones would be sufficiently compliant with a phone call.

Only one caused him any sort of concern and it didn't particularly surprise him as to who it was. They'd been the most difficult the first time around. It had been the woman who was most vociferous. Her father had died in the car fire and she had showed a lot of grit then, and this time, she was being no different as she faced up to him. That is, until he broke her husband's arm.

"Señora, I admire your courage, but please do not confuse bravery with foolishness."

She went to speak, but he cut in quickly.

"Do not try my patience, Señora, or it won't just be your husband's arm I break next. You have had a very generous settlement from Lopez Autoparts, but with that comes a commitment to not disclose anything of our agreement and neither can you, or any of your family, support any police investigation."

She went to speak.

"Before you say anymore, please bear in mind what the consequences may be for you, your husband and your three beautiful children."

"Don't you dare touch my children!" she bristled.

"I hope I don't need to, Señora," he said quietly, "but

if I have to, then it will be your fault, so the choice is yours."

"You can't do this!" she shrieked.

"Oh, but you see I can, and I will," he said, and she squealed in pain as he grabbed her arm and twisted it hard.

The menace in his voice had been clear and he could see the fight in woman crumble as tears appeared in her eyes.

He looked across to the husband who was nursing his arm.

"Señor, I take it that I can rely on your family's agreement to honour the generous settlement from Lopez Autoparts, because I would not want to revisit your home any time soon."

Ortiz twisted the woman's arm again.

"Si, Señor, si! No more, please, Señor, I beg you!"

"I'm glad we have that settled then," said Ortiz, letting go of the woman before he casually walked out of the house without saying another word.

*****

"Boss, it's Sofi. She's got something!" shouted Nino.

"Put her on speaker phone, Nino."

"Sofi, what have you got?" said Lori.

"Inspectora Jefe, we've got an image. It's not perfect, but it's the best they can do. He came into view as he was walking past la Petita Llibreria, just past the theatre. Do you know it?"

"Yes, I do, Sofi," smiled Lori, because it, the Little Bookshop, was owned by Anna Martínez.

"We've got a side-on view of him and it compares really well against the e-fit the specialist did with what Bella was able to tell him."

Nino showed her the CCTV image and the e-fit likeness.

"That is good!"

She'd seen enough e-fits in the past which barely showed any likeness to the eventual offender. Can we get any sort of facial recognition from the CCTV image?"

"Hopefully, although it's not good enough for a specific hit, but Sofi's working through the possible matches. Problem is there's around a hundred."

Lori took in a deep breath, "I know that's a lot, but that's a whole lot better than I thought it might be, Nino. Listen, have you got the CCTV image and the artist's e-fit on your iPad?"

He nodded, "Si."

"Come on," she grinned. "Let's go and shove them under the nose of a certain Hannah Lopez and see what sort of reaction we get!"

*****

"You're sure, José?"

Hannah Lopez was on the phone to José Rodriguez who, after Hannah told him the GEO had been sniffing around, had been doing some digging of his own.

"It's not written down anywhere if that's what you mean Hannah? But of course, these things never are. But I have it on very good authority from someone in the president's office who saw something they weren't meant to see. I'm just adding two and two together."

"That it's this Cesar Mendez, from the CNI, who is pushing things?"

"He's certainly the one doing the pushing, but more importantly, it's coming direct from the President."

"Why now? What's changed to make him think he can do this now?" mused Hannah.

"Hmm, I don't know, but maybe he's had this planned for some time. Don't forget, Hannah, the President and I go back a long time and he clearly still sees me as some sort of threat." He laughed. "I suppose I should take that as a compliment."

"This isn't any time for laughing, José. I've already had the police banging on my door, not once, but twice!"

With that, Juanita, Hannah Lopez's PA was unsuccessfully trying again to stop Lori Garcia from walking straight into her boss's office.

"Señorita Lopez, I am so sorry. She wouldn't…."

"Don't worry, Juanita. You can leave us now. It seems the Inspectora Jefe thinks she can do as she likes."

She spoke into her phone again, "I'm sorry, José, I have unwanted visitors again. Do you think you could ask Francisco to start compiling a harassment case against the GEO and in particular Inspectora Garcia?"

"Just for the record," smiled Lori Garcia. "It's Inspectora Jefe. We wouldn't want Señor Rodriguez to get his facts wrong now, would we?"

Lopez put her phone down and as Juanita closed the door behind her, Lori turned to Hannah Lopez.

"And if that little display is supposed to warn me off, then you're badly mistaken."

"Little display, Inspectora Jefe?" Hannah exaggerated the 'Jefe.' "I've no idea what you mean."

"Stop playing games Lopez and just to confirm for your little harassment case, yes, I am coming for you and the rest of the board of the Foundation."

"And are you going to enlighten me as to why you have started this vendetta?"

"I'll tell you why. It's for the wholesale bribery and corruption your Foundation has been indulging in ever since it came into being, that's what."

Nino had been watching both women as they went at each other in a verbal barrage. Neither were giving an inch and it was hard to see how the stalemate might be broken.

"I have no idea what you are talking about. So, unless you have something else to ask which you can support with at least some sort of credible evidence, then I suggest you leave," demanded Lopez.

Lori had relaxed her pose and smiled at Lopez. "Yes, there is one more thing." Nino handed her the iPad and she touched the screen and the e-fit image appeared. "Do you recognise the person in this image, Señorita Lopez?"

She knew straight away who it was, but she wasn't going to tell them that and besides, even she knew that e-fits were notoriously difficult to secure a positive identification from.

"No, should I?" asked Lopez.

"What about this man?" Lori showed her the CCTV image.

Lopez made every attempt to hide any sort of reaction from her face. If the e-fit had been a half reasonable reflection of Jaime Ortíz's features, then the CCTV photo, even though it was side on, was an even better capture of him.

"What's up? Nothing to say?" asked Lori pointedly.

Lopez tried to regain her composure.

"I was just thinking it might be an ex-employee, but we have so many that I'm not sure I can remember his name. But why are you asking me? What has this man done?"

"He threatened a young journalist by the name of Bella Santos. Ever heard of her?"

Lopez tried again to not give anything away. She slowly shook her head, "No, I don't think so. But is she alright? This Bella Santos I mean?"

"Yes, she's the one who helped with the e-fit and now we have a corroborative image of the offender before he entered her apartment building."

"So, you don't know who he is then? That's such a shame," said Lopez, feigning disappointment.

Lori ignored her, "You just be sure to let us know if

you do remember his name," snapped Lori, just as there was a knock at the door.

"Señorita Lopez? I have your lawyer, Señor Francisco Rodriguez, on line one."

"Thank you, Juanita. Now if you have nothing else to ask me, then perhaps you'll leave and allow me to have a confidential discussion with my lawyer about this unnecessary harassment?"

"Absolutely, Señorita Lopez and be sure to ask him what the penalty is for not just bribery and corruption, but also for obstructing police in the execution of their duty," said Lori.

With that the two women smiled at each other, leaving both in no doubt as to what they thought of each other.

Lori was deep in thought as she and Nino walked out of the Lopez headquarters.

"She knew who it was straight away, Nino," she said under her breath.

"Didn't she just! Now we just need to find out who it is."

"And the sooner the better, Nino. I'm going to send those images across to my new friend at the CNI and get him to run them through their database."

Hannah Lopez watched the two GEO officers from her office window as they walked across the car park. Then picked up her phone.

"Yes, it's me. You've been careless and it's made things messy, very messy. Now I need you to do what's necessary to clear this up. Understand?"

Ortiz listened as Lopez told him about the images she'd been shown. He was shaken, because he prided himself on his professionalism and care in ensuring people didn't talk after he'd been to see them. Maybe that Santos woman had something more about her than he'd given her credit for?

"I could set something up, give her something else to think about," said Ortíz.

"My father said you had something in mind. Well, it had better be something good, but for God's sake don't kill her! That will only bring the rest of the GEO down on us." said Lopez.

'I'm not stupid,' he thought. But he didn't immediately say anything, because for once, he seemed to be the one who had left some unnecessary loose ends. He took a breath. "The usual thing. Drop some money into her account and tip off the anti-corruption cops. They love finding bad apples."

A thin cruel smile appeared on her face.

"Now that would be helpful, Jaime," said Lopez. "And it would certainly put her out of action."

"Wouldn't be surprised if she gets locked up."

Lopez's smile widened, "When can you make it happen?"

"Soon."

"I'll transfer the money to the usual account."

"And I'll let you know when it's done," said Ortíz.

She was still smiling as she touched the screen to finish the call.

*****

21

Ortíz knew exactly who to call as he'd used him before on jobs like this.

"How much?" the man asked.

"How much for the job?" said Ortíz.

"No, I meant how much do you want me to put in her account?" laughed the man.

Ortíz allowed himself a smile as well. He thought for a moment. When he'd done this sort of thing before, to get rid of someone who might have been obstructive towards a building application, he'd used somewhere between ten and twenty thousand euros for local officials and then upped the figure to around fifty thousand, if they were at a regional, or national level.

"I'll send you a hundred thousand plus your seven and a half percent on top. Take that off and drop the rest into an account in her name," said Ortíz.

"If it's a cop, especially a GEO, shouldn't I be getting a bit extra? You know, like ten percent?" said the man.

"You'll get nothing except a hole in the back of the head if you ask me anything like that again."

The man went quiet, knowing he'd not just overstepped the mark, but had gone way past where he should have with Ortíz.

"Sorry, I was just joking."

"I wasn't, so just shut up and listen."

He made notes as Ortíz spoke.

"Any preference where you want her account to be?" said the man.

"Nothing too clever, otherwise the anti-corruption guys won't be able to find it, even if you tell them where to look."

The man laughed again, feeling he was back on safer ground.

"Okay, shouldn't take long, an hour at the most."

"Good. Let me know when it's done and then send it in the usual way, anonymously and with no trail to Europol's European Financial and Economic Crime Centre."

"No problem."

*****

Two hours later the duty supervisor at Europol's EFEC Centre in the Hague, the capital of the Netherlands was looking through an electronic file one of her desk officers had sent her to review.

"And this came in on an anonymous email?" the supervisor asked.

"Yes, I tried doing some back checking on it, but it's properly hidden in a mass of weeds. Someone really didn't want us to know who they were."

"Is it genuine then?"

"Looks like it is. I've been to the bank and the account, and all the details check out."

As she flicked through the file on her screen the supervisor let out a low whistle.

"There's almost a hundred grand gone in here over the past four months!"

"Yes, all from accounts that have been hidden in a maze that I can't get into," said the desk officer.

The supervisor knew he was one of her best, so if

he said he couldn't find any trail, then she knew there weren't many who would.

"And the officer, she's GEO?"

"Yes, a Chief Inspector Lori Garcia. Just been promoted. Seems to have a really good track record. One point of interest though. Her husband was murdered by an OCG about twenty years ago."

"That's interesting. Why would she be taking bribes from, presumably an OCG, when they were the very people who killed her husband?" said the supervisor.

"Seems odd, but hey, people do strange things for all manner of reasons, don't they?"

"You're right," said the supervisor. "This looks genuine enough, I'll send it through to the Anti-Corruption Prosecutor in Madrid and leave it to them to decide how far they want to take it."

*****

Ortíz had already had a message from his man that the file had been sent to Europol, but then he got another.

'The file has been sent to the AC Prosecutor in Madrid.'

'How do you know?' he texted back.

'I buried a tracker in the file. It tells me who's seen it and where it is at any given time.'

'Couldn't someone find it?' Ortíz texted back.

'Nope.'

'I hope you're right.'

His man was going to type something back, but thought again. He'd crossed the line once today, so wasn't going to make the same mistake again, at least not in the same day.

*****

"Have you got some good news for me, Jaime?"

He heard the cheerfulness in her voice.

"You're sounding happy."

"I'm hoping you've got some good news for me."

"In that case, I do. A file has been sent from Europol to the Spanish Anti-Corruption Prosecutor."

"Good work, Jaime, good work."

"It shouldn't be long now," said Jaime.

"Do we have connections with someone who will be looking after the investigation?"

"We most certainly do," said Ortíz, looking at a name in the Anti-Corruption Prosecutor's unit. I've called them and they will make sure the file ends up on their desk."

"Jaime, perhaps we should do dinner soon?"

He smiled, but said nothing. She'd done this before. It was her way of rewarding him. Or was it? He knew she didn't have anyone permanent in her life, so an occasional nice dinner and a shag with the hired help was probably just as much fun for her as it was for him. Problem was, he knew she didn't think anything further of it once it was over. Whereas he'd found himself being more and more attracted to her, even though she mostly failed to show any feelings at all towards him.

"Or perhaps you don't want to?" she said, trying to be coy, but in his view failing miserably.

"That would be lovely, Hannah," he allowed himself to use her first name and smiled again when she didn't correct him.

"I'll get my PA to sort something out."

He almost laughed out loud at the thought of a 'shag with the hired help' being arranged by her PA.

*****

"Good day at the office?" Greg asked when he rang her.

She thought for a moment.

"Yes, I think so," smiled Lori. "Not a lot of progress, but we're making some headway.

It had been a long day, but she felt they were getting

somewhere, especially now they had a pretty good image of the man who had threatened Bella Santos, and she'd been able to get under the skin of Hannah Lopez.

"Good, so are we going to be able to do dinner?"

"I think that's a great idea. But can we just do a quiet one? Just the two of us?"

He could hear she was tired, even though she was obviously trying to be cheerful. He didn't know the detail around the case she was working on, but a suspicious death surrounding a high-profile member of Mallorquin society was never going to make things easy.

"Of course, my darling. Anywhere take your fancy?"

"No, you choose," said Lori. "I'll go to my hotel and change, and I should be with you for around eight."

"Perfecto! I'll have a glass of red waiting for you as you walk through the door."

*****

Nino said he had a little more work to finish off before he was going to look for somewhere to eat. Lori left him in the office and walked back to the hotel. It was a short walk from the police headquarters and whilst pleasant enough, the hotel could have been designed by a police finance manager for a one-night sleep over on a cost-conscious budget.

She showered, wrapped herself in a towel and went to the small wardrobe where she'd hung her clothes. As she opened it, she caught her reflection on the mirror on the inside of the door. She took a step back and let her towel slip away. She did the front and then the sideways look in the mirror, looking at her body and trying to resist the temptation to breathe in.

Like nearly all of her girlfriends, she wished bits of her body looked better than they did. But overall? Well, she was in her late forties now and she'd had to maintain a reasonable level of fitness because of work, particularly for the training she had to undertake as an authorised firearms officer, which was always tough and demanding. Lori took another look at herself and then allowed herself a small smile.

She knew she could sometimes still turn heads when she walked into a room, although it had taken a long time since she could think of herself as a woman, rather than the wife of her murdered police officer husband, Felipe. But eventually she had reached that place where she wanted to look and feel good when she went out.

Her overnight bag was primarily for work, but she always kept a couple of non-work looking clothes in there. She usually wore smart business suits whilst on duty, so it was her way of helping to wind down after work, even when she was staying away from home.

It was a warm spring evening in Palma, so she chose a loose strappy cream patterned dress and a pair of blue high heeled shoes before she set off from her hotel. As she walked, she could feel the tiredness from a tough day start to lift as she looked forward to spending the evening with Greg.

She crossed the road into the main high street, Avenida de Jaume 111, but as she walked towards Passeig del Born, Lori had the sensation that she was being followed, or at least watched. She couldn't put her finger on how she knew. It was probably years of surveillance experience and training, or just pure instinct, but she just knew.

She stopped a couple of times. The old anti-surveillance trick of pretending to look into a shop window, whilst actually looking at the reflection. Who would be following her? Could it be the man who threatened Bella Santos? That seemed unlikely and why do it in the middle of the shopping area known as Palma's Golden Mile? She continued, but now with an air of caution, occasionally turning or glancing over her shoulder.

With the feeling not disappearing, she took out her phone as she turned left into a side street, Carrer de Sant Jaume 3, and rang Nino.

"Silly question, but have you got anyone watching my back?"

He didn't get what she was talking about immediately.

"Sorry, Boss? Watching your back? Oh, you mean tailing you. No, why?" he said, suddenly becoming concerned.

"It's nothing. I'm probably just imagining things. Anyway, I'm almost here now at Greg's hotel, so I'll….."

She went silent. Then Nino heard her cry out.

"What are you doing!"

"Boss, Boss, are you okay?"

Lori's phone had gone dead.

*****

22

Nino Castillo rang Greg immediately.

"Nino, good to hear from you."

"Is Lori with you?"

Greg could hear the urgency in Nino's voice. He looked at his watch. It was 8.05pm. "She should be here any moment. She said she'd be here at eight."

"Greg, Greg, listen! I was talking to her and then her phone went dead. I think something's happened."

Greg was struggling to take in what he'd just heard.

"What? What do you mean, something's happened. We're in the middle of bloody Palma, nothing could have happened to her, Nino. Maybe her phone's just died?"

"I don't think so," said Nino slowly. He'd seen she'd had her phone plugged in to a charger when they'd been in her office debriefing the day. "Listen, she told me you're staying at the Born?"

"Yes."

"I've got the team on their way now to do a loose search and I've got Sofi Delgado checking with the local police if there's been any sort of incident."

"Incident? What do you mean incident, Nino?"

He could hear the anxiety in Greg's voice.

"I'm covering all bases, Greg, that's all. One minute

I was talking to her and then her phone went dead and…"

"And what?" demanded Greg.

"It just doesn't feel right."

Greg had got his composure back and had parked the fact that this was Lori they were talking about.

"I understand. What can I do, Nino?"

"There's not a lot you can do, Greg. I know there's probably not a lot of point of me telling you not to go out looking for her, because I suspect that's exactly what you'll do anyway."

"Correct," interjected Greg.

"But just keep in touch, okay?"

"Of course, Nino and I know you'll do the same. One question before you go? I assume you've tried ringing her back?"

"Yes, sorry, I should have said. It just goes to ansaphone."

"Sorry, another question, Nino. Do we know what she was wearing?"

"Not sure. She left the office in a blue suit. A jacket and skirt, but she was going back to the hotel, so presumably she was going to change before seeing you."

"Okay, thanks," said Greg.

He took a moment to stop and think. Nino's guys would be outside the hotel, so there was little point in just rushing outside looking for her.

He rang Sam, who listened as he told him what had happened.

"What?"

"She's just disappeared. One minute she's talking with Nino and then her phone went dead, mid-sentence."

"And she was on her way to you?"

"Yes. She'd told Nino she was going to her hotel to

shower and change and then she was going to walk down to me at the Born."

Sam started to suggest that perhaps Lori's phone battery had died.

"No, Nino had seen her charging it up before she left the office. Remember Detective Delgado?"

"Yes."

"She's checking for any local incidents."

"What can I do?"

"It feels a bit 'needle in a haystack' time, Sam. Nino's team are out searching the immediate area, so we'll only be falling over each other if we go out looking for her too."

"Agreed." He knew this wasn't like a usual missing person case, where the police would have other, in some cases, just as pressing priorities to deal with. All of the GEO would have been despatched by Nino to be out looking for their boss, so they'd be best to leave them to get on with their job.

"Greg, you might get a knock at the door too. They will go through all the basics and that will include checking in with you, so don't be put off if they start asking you questions okay. You're not a suspect, but they need to look at this from every angle."

"Yes, yes, of course, but thanks for the reminder."

"No problem, now have you told the others yet?" He meant Anna and Terri.

"No, I thought I'd start with you and come up with a plan."

"Okay, so here's an idea. I'll ring Terri, you ring my mum and let's meet in your hotel." He looked at his watch. "As quick as we can all get there, but by nine at the latest. Then we should run through who we need to be talking to, but in the meantime, I'll check-in with Sofi, I mean Detective Delgado."

Greg didn't need Sam to spell out what he was

thinking. They needed more information on what Lori had been doing before they could do anything more. Yes, he knew Nino would leave no stone unturned, but that didn't mean he was going to sit about and wait to see what happened to the woman he loved.

Yes, he loved her, something he hadn't really felt about a woman for some considerable time.

Sam seemed to sense what he was thinking.

"Greg, we'll find her, I promise."

"I know, I know we will." He just wondered if he'd find her alive.

*****

"Sofi?"

"Sam, I guess you're ringing about Lori?"

"Yes. Have you got anything?"

She wouldn't usually be keeping friends of a missing person updated on a moment-by-moment basis, but this was different. One, Sam Martínez was ex-job, a former Met DCI and two, she really liked Lori Garcia and, she smiled to herself, she knew she liked Sam too.

"Nothing, at least nothing yet. We've had no reports of any street robberies, or assaults. I've got the city CCTV manager going back to their office to coordinate the review of the footage from the area from HQ to Lori's hotel and then down Avenida Juame 111 towards the Hotel Born."

"That's great, Sofi."

He knew she was good, as she'd shown what she could do when she'd been involved in the investigation into Lily Green's kidnap the previous year.

"What are you guys going to do?" asked Sofi, who had met the rest of the 3R team during the kidnap investigation.

"We're all meeting up at Greg's hotel at nine, plus I'm thinking someone, either Nino's GEO, or someone locally will want to come and see Greg?"

"That would be me then," she said. "I've just had a call from DI Castillo and he's cross referenced all of this with my Inspector and he's asked if he can use me as a liaison officer."

"Thanks Sofi, that's great. I'll see you soon."

Terri and Anna had been just as shocked as Sam to hear that Lori had seemingly disappeared. But by the time they were all at Greg's hotel, Anna had already started putting things into action.

"Okay, we can't work out of Greg's bedroom as it's too cramped for all of us, so I've sorted out a meeting room downstairs with the duty manager. He's laying on coffee and tea and we just need to ask for anything we might need."

"Impressive as always, my dear. But how did you get all that done so quickly?" said Greg.

"The owners are old friends. It just took a quick call," said Anna.

Sam smiled at his mother's almost infinite ability to quickly manage the logistics for any given situation.

"Sofi Delgado is meeting us here too," said Sam.

He saw his mother and Terri both give him one of their 'looks.' They knew he liked the detective, but from their perspective, he'd so far spectacularly failed to follow up on what had seemed like a promising start to a relationship with her.

"Stop it you two, will you!"

Terri was about to say something when there was a knock at the door. "Saved by the bell, well, a knock," she said, opening the door.

"Sofi," said Terri, giving her hug. "Good to see you again, although the circumstances could be a lot better."

"Hi Terri, hello everyone. Señor Chambers, we've got every available resource out there working hard to find out what's happened to Lori."

"Sofi, please, Greg is fine and thank you."

"Gracias. Now this might sound strange, but do you mind showing me your bathroom?"

Greg understood what she was asking, so he nodded across to Sam.

"Of course, Sofi. I understand what you need to do. Please feel free to check the whole room."

Anna and Terri both realised what was playing out and stood up to let Sofi get on and do what she needed to do to eliminate the room as a possible crime scene.

Sofi knew that to most people it might seem a little over the top to be searching a hotel room for a body, but she was an experienced enough detective now to know that the basics still needed to be covered, even when they seemed to be unnecessary.

"Thanks for that," she said, having quickly and efficiently checked the bathroom and then under the bed and inside the wardrobes in the main room. "I appreciate your understanding."

"No problem, Sofi. Sam said you'd need to do it, so I'm fine with you doing your job."

"Okay, now I'm just waiting on a video to come through from the CCTV room."

"Have they said what's on it?" asked Sam.

"They can see two people, probably men, judging by their build and posture. They're walking a woman out of Carrer de Sant Jaume 3."

"Right outside the hotel then," said Sam.

"Yes, and then they take her to a van, well it looks like a people carrier. It was parked in the main street."

"Kidnapped?" said Greg.

"There doesn't look to be any sort of struggle," said Sofi.

"Maybe they had a weapon?" said Anna.

"It should be with us any moment, so we can have a

look," said Sofi.

Her phone rang.

"Si, Boss, I'm with Señor Chambers at the moment and I've done the room search." Greg saw her give a reassuring smile, before he saw her expression change. "Si, Detective Delgado speaking."

The others watched her as she listened to whoever had joined the phone call. Sofi seemed to become even more self-conscious the more the call went on, eventually turning away from them and walking towards the corner of the room.

"Something's wrong," Anna whispered to Sam.

*****

23

Lori Garcia had just been about to go through the doors into the Hotel Born, when she'd felt someone tap her on the shoulder.

She had tensed and then turned suddenly, getting into a fighting arc position, ready to respond if necessary. Then she recognised the man before her. He was smiling at her, but it looked like a forced smile. He was one of the detectives from the local office. She'd been introduced to him during the time she'd been over on the island.

It was enough to distract her and so she missed what happened next. A second man quietly slipped through the hotel doors and came up behind her and grabbed her phone out of her hand.

"What are you doing!" she yelled, before he switched the phone off.

"Inspectora Jefe Lori Garcia, you're under arrest on suspicion of corruption in public office contrary to Section 422 of the Criminal Code."

It took a moment for her to register what the second man had just said to her.

"Is this a joke? And who are you anyway?"

"Comisario Gutierrez, Head of Balearics CID."

At least that made sense, she thought. It was usually

always an officer of the same, or a more senior rank, who would be involved in the planned arrest of a police officer. She looked at him, still clinging in vain hope that this was some sort of elaborate joke at her expense. But there was no smile and no engagement.

"Comisario, there must be a mistake. What am I supposed to have done?"

"I'm not sure feigning ignorance makes for a great defence, Garcia," said Gutierrez. "I'm only doing this because the Anti-Corruption Unit couldn't get across from Madrid in time. But here's some free advice. They've got you bang to rights. I've seen the arrest file."

"Bang to rights on what though?"

By now the first officer was leading her back down the alley to where an unmarked van had arrived up and parked across the entrance to the side street.

At least they hadn't put her in handcuffs, but that was the least of her worries for the moment. She still didn't know what she was supposed to have done. Section 422? That was bribery! Who was she supposed to have bribed, or taken money from?

"Head down and in you go, Garcia. You've this officer to thank for you not being cuffed, well that and we're trying to avoid any further reputational damage you've done to the service," he almost spat the words out.

Even though she knew she hadn't done anything, in some way she could understand his disgust. She was no different to every other hard-working officer in the service who despised those officers who accepted bribes. She'd even been involved in a number of high-profile investigations where officers had been corrupted by major crime gangs. They'd been paid to either look the other way, or sometimes it was to help with the processing of drug shipments going through one of the south coast ports.

"But you still haven't told me what I'm supposed to have done?"

"Look, I appreciate you haven't kicked off, or put up any sort of a fuss, Garcia, but you'd be better off thinking about your defence than whinging that you haven't done anything."

Lori was trying to think straight. This man, the Comisario, was clearly convinced that she was bent, and he'd made it clear that he wasn't going to listen to anything more she said. She sat back in the seat in the rear of the van, wedged between the two men who had arrested her.

The Comisario barked an order at the driver to take them, through the back entrance. Lori knew that meant only one thing. She was being taken to the cell block at headquarters, which was both good and bad. It was good in that the custody officer on the main desk would have to tell her exactly what it was she was being detained for.

But it was bad, because she'd end up in a cell where she'd have little or no chance of sorting this out. Whatever 'this' actually was.

*****

As Sofi came off the call Sam had been the first to speak.

"Problem?"

"I've been called back to the station and told I'm not to speak to you, or Greg, or any of you for that matter."

"Why the hell not?" demanded Greg.

Sofi stiffened, clearly taken aback by his reaction, but Anna quickly stepped in. It was obvious that Sofi had been put in a difficult position.

"Can you tell us who you just spoke to, Sofi?"

"I'm sorry," she said quietly. "I can't tell you anything more."

"Just a name, Sofi," said Anna gently.

She stood there. She knew she shouldn't, but something was happening and it didn't feel right.

"It was my boss, my DI."

Anna pressed her again.

"And then someone else joined the call?"

Sofi hesitated, unsure what to do. She liked these people, especially Sam Martínez. But the man on the phone had been very clear, telling her not to discuss the arrest of Inspectora Jefe Garcia on corruption charges with anyone, including the GEO.

She almost whispered her answer, as though that meant she wasn't actually telling them anything.

"It was the station commander."

They all knew straight away that it was very much out of the ordinary, for a station commander to be ringing a junior detective.

Greg was first to break the silence.

"Is she dead, Sofi?"

"No!" Sofi exclaimed.

"Well, that's one good bit of news," said Greg.

Sam spoke next.

"Has she been arrested, Sofi?"

Greg looked at Sam first and then at Sofi, who didn't answer.

So, then they knew. Lori had been arrested and must be on her way to a police station.

"I'm sorry to put you in a difficult position, Sofi," said Greg.

She knew a 'but' was coming, to ask her what Lori had been arrested for. She thought for a moment, then made her decision and told them.

Greg took a deep breath.

"I know you can't be seen to be getting involved, but corruption, Sofi? I know you don't know Lori very well, but I think you know her well enough, don't you? I mean, can you really see her being in any way involved in anything like this?"

He was right, she didn't know Lori Garcia particularly well, but from what she'd seen of her, she'd put money on the fact that she wasn't corrupt.

Greg could see whose side the young detective was leaning towards.

"Sofi, I know I'm prejudiced, but this has all the hallmarks of a set-up. Is there anything else you can tell us at the moment that might help, as we're going to need to know as much as we can if we're to be able to help Lori." He smiled at her, "Look, I know you shouldn't be divulging anything to us. However, I think you probably know all of us well enough by now," he looked around the room, "to know that we can probably get most of what we need to know anyway, but I think that the time taken for us to find it would be better used trying to establish why this has happened."

Sofi nodded. She didn't know how much help it would give him and besides, it certainly wasn't a state secret, but the Station Commander had told her who the order had come from not to talk to Greg and his team. Knowing the resourcefulness these 3R guys had shown since she'd first met them, she was fairly certain it wouldn't take them too long to find out his name.

"The arresting officer, the one who gave the order for me not to talk to you? His name is Juan Gutierrez. He's the Head of CID for the Balearics."

"Thanks, Sofi, that's a big help," said Greg.

"Shit," said Sam under his breath.

Greg looked at him. "What?"

"If the Head of the islands' CID is dealing with this personally, it suggests that this isn't someone local trying to make something out of nothing, so he must think there is something substantial against Lori."

*****

"Nino, it's Greg."

"Greg, I haven't got anything for you yet, I'm….."

"Nino, let me speak. I've got something, but you aren't going to like it. Lori's been arrested."

"What?"

"Something to do with corruption and the guy who arrested her is the Head of Balearics CID, Juan Gutierrez. Ever heard of him?"

Detective Inspector Nino Castillo was rarely, if ever, lost for words, but hearing his boss had been arrested had rocked him.

"Er no, never heard of him, but I'll get him checked out. Do we know where she's been taken?"

"No, I was hoping you could find out," said Greg.

"Of course, sorry, Greg. It'll probably be here, at HQ. I'll check it out and call you back."

As he put his phone down, he looked up to see the station commander standing at the door to his office.

"Sir, I was about to come to find you."

"Concerning Lori Garcia?"

"Si, so you already know? Thank God! Boss, someone must have their wires badly crossed. I mean, this has to be a mistake?"

The look he got back from the station commander took the wind out of his sails.

"It's Nino, isn't it?"

Castillo nodded.

"It can be bloody hard to accept sometimes, Nino, when someone we've worked so closely with is finally caught out."

Nino flinched at the way the other man had said 'finally.'

"But…"

"There's no buts, Nino," the Commander said. "And if you need any more convincing, which I can see you do, then given the sensitivity of the arrest of a senior GEO officer, especially as she's currently investigating two high profile deaths, I can tell you that the Head of CID has allowed me access to the evidence file. And I'm sorry, Nino, but it's very clear. She's been on the take for at least the past six months."

Nino stood there, trying to take in what he'd just been told.

"But Sir, there's got to be some sort of explanation?"

"Look, there isn't, okay? She's downstairs being processed and the only thing you need to understand, Inspector," said the senior officer, his voice taking on a much firmer tone, "is that you are expressly forbidden from trying to see, or contact her, in any way." He paused. "And nor are you, or any of your team, allowed to discuss this matter with anyone. Do I make myself clear?"

"Crystal clear, Sir," said Nino, through gritted teeth.

With that the station commander turned and left. Nino took out his personal phone. No point using his work phone, just in case someone in anti-corruption might be tracking his calls.

Greg saw the call coming in from a 'No ID' number. He was about to ignore it, but changed his mind at the last minute.

"Yes?"

"Greg? It's Nino. Lori's in trouble, big trouble."

"Go on." Greg flicked his mobile onto speakerphone and put it down on the table.

"She's being booked in here, downstairs I mean in custody. I've been read the riot act by the station boss and I'm not to try to see her, or to speak to anyone about what's going on."

Greg then twigged why Nino was using a different phone.

"I appreciate you calling then, Nino, but don't go getting yourself...."

"Greg don't waste your time worrying about me. I'm

a big boy, but they, and I mean the anti-corruption guys may be watching me, so I'll be picking up a few throw-away phones just in case. But for the time being, I've just texted you this number."

Greg heard a ping as the text arrived.

"What will happen now, Nino?"

"Okay, so she'll be interviewed. If you haven't had a call from her and I certainly haven't, then I think we can assume they've withheld her right to a phone call."

"They'd need a judge's authority to do that, so someone's really done their homework," said Sam.

"Yes." Nino then went quiet. "Sorry, there's someone just wandered into the main office and I don't recognise him. I'll call you back."

Castillo rang off and Greg stood up, his hands in the air.

"Guys, I'm sorry, I'm reeling a bit at the moment, so can someone suggest what the hell we're going to do?"

It was Anna who took control.

"Sam, you will probably have a better idea of what the process may be, even given the fact we're dealing with Spanish law."

Sam nodded.

"Nino's right, Lori will be interviewed at some stage and even though they've refused her a phone call, I doubt they have any legal grounds to deny her access to legal advice. Problem is, if she doesn't have a named solicitor then she will get a local brief."

Terri looked at him.

"Sorry, by brief, I mean solicitor."

"And what does that mean? Aren't they any good?" asked Terri.

"Just depends on who you get," said Sam. "Most are absolutely fine, but they're often just frazzled because they're running around chasing the next job. Despite the public perception that every lawyer, and barrister, earns a fortune, the reality is that many of them, especially the newcomers, just about scrape a living whilst trying to get a foot on the ladder."

Anna said, "Greg? Has Lori ever mentioned having a family solicitor?"

"No, can't say it's ever come up. Maybe Nino could suggest someone? He must have run into enough good ones in his time, mustn't he Sam?"

"Yes, although how quickly they could get anyone out here might be an issue, and they may just try to refer her case on to a local company here and we'd be back to square one."

"What about Sofi? She might know someone here who she trusts?" said Terri.

"I like that idea better, Terri," said Sam. "I know she's been told not to speak to us, so I'll see if I can get hold of her through Nino."

"Yes, good thinking," said Greg, "I've got Nino's private number. I'll zap it through to you."

Terri looked at her father and couldn't hold back a smile.

"What?" said Greg.

"Zap? Really Dad? You've got to get a grip of this techno-speak."

It was what they all needed, and it broke the tension in the room, allowing them a moment to laugh.

"Okay, now I think one of the first things we need to do is to somehow get to see Lori and make sure she's alright," said Anna.

"What are you thinking?" said Greg, as he could see she was working on an idea.

"We know she's in police headquarters and until we can get some help from Nino, or Sofi, we need to look at other options."

The rest of them looked at her, waiting for her to continue.

"I've just done a very quick search on criminal lawyers in Madrid."

"Are you going to try and get hold of one of them?" Sam asked his mother.

Greg smiled. He'd already guessed what Anna had in mind.

"No Sam, she's going to get in to visit Lori posing as a solicitor. Right?" said Greg.

"Well, I'm going to try," said Anna. "I'll start with a phone call into the police station and then see if I can make arrangements to see Lori." She looked at Terri. "I'm going to need a couple of business cards."

"No problem. I'll get it sorted. I know a printing place not far from my apartment. They turn out good quality stuff. I can get something done for first thing tomorrow morning. But won't Lori need a lawyer, or is it a solicitor, tonight? I'm thinking if they try and interview her tonight?"

"It's either or, really Sis. Although lawyer is more of an Americanism. Both are an acceptable umbrella term of all roles in most legal systems," said Sam, "and in Spain, a lawyer is an abogado. But regarding your thinking about whether she might be interviewed tonight? I think it's doubtful, because the police will want to properly prepare for the interview. Plus, they may even want to wait until an anti-corruption prosecutor, who I think are based in Madrid, to come across from Madrid to oversee the investigation. Therefore, it's more likely to be sometime tomorrow."

"What name do you want on your business cards Anna?"

Anna showed Terri the search details on her phone screen.

"This one please. I'll be Señora Anna Dominguez, Especialista en Derecho Penal, Criminal Law Specialist."

"What if they check?" asked Greg.

"Sam?" said Anna. "What's your experience suggest?"

"Can't say I saw custody sergeants doing that back in the UK and if they do look them up, then they'll find… who's the company you're supposed to be with?"

"She's with Jimenez and Co.," said Terri. "And although they've got some of their senior partners listed, there's no other details on the lawyers who work there."

Greg smiled. He knew Anna would have already checked that to give herself a back story, something that would at least hold up to some low-level scrutiny.

"But we are still going to get her some proper legal representation? Yes?" said Terri.

"Yes, of course," laughed Anna. "I'm not that good, Terri. Right, since it may take a while to get through the system, I'll make a start and put the call into the police station now and see if we can find Lori and get to talk to her."

"Okay, whilst you're doing that, I'll ring Nino and see if he can get Sofi to come up with a name of someone locally to represent Lori tomorrow," said Sam.

*****

The custody officer hadn't immediately recognised Juan Gutierrez, the Head of CID for the Balearics, when he saw him getting out of unmarked van in the waiting area for the custody cell block. But he did when he saw the Comisario approach the back door to custody and look up at the CCTV camera screen and motion to be let in.

The custody officer, a sergeant, saw Gutierrez was with another man, a local detective, together with a woman. She was dressed in a cream summer dress and high heels, so it took a moment before he recognised the senior GEO officer who had spent time working out of HQ during the past year.

The sergeant called out under his breath, "We've got visitors everyone. Best behaviour please for a couple of bosses."

He saw some of his team grinning back at him. A visit from a senior officer to the cell block wasn't that uncommon. But then again, nobody wanted them coming down and finding something not being done right. The team quickly went through a quick review of the live custody records for all the detained prisoners, to check they were all up to date.

"We're all good, Sarge," whispered one of the corporals after a final glance at the timings on the custody record checks on the computer terminal in front of them.

"Gracias, amigo," said the Sergeant, as he buzzed the button to allow the senior officers through the back door into the custody block.

"Comisario, what a pleasure to see you, Sir. What brings you down here this evening?"

"Sergeant, this is Lori Garcia. A serving officer with the GEO." There was an intended pause before he added, "At least for the time-being."

By the way the Comisario sneered, no one listening was left in any doubt as to his contempt for the woman standing next to him.

"Sir?" said the Custody Sergeant. "Is Señora Garcia under...."

"Under arrest? Yes, Section 422 of the Spanish Criminal Code."

The Sergeant entered the details on the computer terminal and then looked first at the Comisario and then at the woman before him.

"Bribery and corruption?" he said, with a look that was somewhere between disbelief, mixed with disgust, at what he'd just seen and heard.

"Yes, Sergeant. I've got bank statements in the accused's name showing payments of amounts totalling nearly one hundred thousand euros made to her in the last six months."

There was a low chatter of noise from the custody staff.

Gutierrez passed a bundle of papers across the table. The sergeant looked at them and his manner changed as he took in the evidence he'd been presented with.

"Can you explain these payments, Inspect..," he started to say her rank, but changed mid-sentence. "I mean, Garcia?"

The sergeant waved the papers in front of her. Lori saw her name and home address on the statements and she didn't have to look too closely to see some of the data figures on them.

Lori was struggling to keep her composure. She had been thinking that whatever was going on was something she'd be able to clear up once she was back at the station. But that all changed when she'd caught sight of the bank statements. Gutierrez saw her reaction and smiled. Just as he'd thought, *'Bang to rights.'*

"I've never seen these documents before and I have never accepted, received, or solicited, any sort of bribe," she said with as much confidence as she could muster, whilst all the time she could feel her stomach churning inside.

She saw the officers were smirking at her. They'd heard it all before. Defendants proclaiming their innocence, even with the most damning of evidence. And Lori had to admit, she'd done it herself too when arresting people who she believed, with one hundred percent confidence, were guilty.

"I'd like a phone call and legal representation please," she said, as calmly as she could.

"Sergeant, I have no objection to her receiving legal advice. God knows she'll need it, but given the seriousness of the offence I have already received authorisation from a judge to deny any request for a phone call at this stage. This will be reviewed after we have had an opportunity to search her home address and her offices both here and in Madrid."

"Understood, Sir, and presumably no visitors?"

"Correct."

"I assume you understand what has just been said?" the Sergeant said to Lori. "No other phone calls except for legal representation and you will not be allowed visitors for up to a period of five days as laid out in the care of prisoner regulations. This may change before the five days has elapsed, should the Comisario decide the authorisation is no longer required, but I expect you know all this already?"

She nodded. It was often the case, in a serious matter, to deny an arrested person access to visitors. "Who was the judge?" she asked, but then immediately wished she hadn't. There was nothing to be gained by antagonising the situation. If the Comisario said he'd got a judge to agree to it, then he must have.

"Forget it, I believe you." said Lori.

"Thank you, that's very gracious of you," said the Sergeant sarcastically. "Now do you have your own legal representative, or would you like me to arrange for the court to appoint you one?"

She didn't have her own solicitor, so Lori tried to think of someone she knew, someone she could really trust. But she was struggling to think straight. Then the sergeant's desk phone rang.

A custody assistant picked it up, listened and then handed the phone to the sergeant.

"It's her brief, Sarge."

"Thought you said you didn't have legal

representation?" said the Sergeant, who missed the look of confusion on Lori's face. "Take her to the side interview room and I'll put the call through in a minute, but Dani? Search her first. A thorough search too mind you," he called after the assistant.

Lori grimaced as Dani, the custody assistant, took her by the arm and steered her towards a nearby room. Yes, she'd been searched plenty of times before during practice training sessions, but this was for real.

The sergeant picked up the phone. "Yes, Sergeant Nunez speaking," he said officiously.

He listened to the woman on the other end of the phone.

"I think you have my client in custody, Sergeant? Lori Garcia of the GEO?"

It was a typical lawyer voice, thought the Sergeant. Where they try and show they're well above your status. He huffed, "Yes and she has just asked for you to be contacted. Can you give me your name and your firm, Señora?"

"Of course, Sergeant, I'm Señora Anna Dominguez and I represent Jimenez and Co., of Madrid."

The sergeant had never heard of them, but quickly looked them up on his terminal. "Phone number?"

She could hear he wasn't happy, probably because he thought she was some hotshot lawyer from the mainland trying to be smart with the island police. Using a Madrid law firm may not have been the best option, but he'd probably know all the local ones in Palma, so it had been the best bet. Anna used her most charming and hopefully engaging voice and gave him the main switchboard number from the Jimenez website.

The sergeant checked it matched against the one he could see for the firm on the list of accredited lawyers on his terminal screen.

"Thank you," he said. "I'll just put you through."

"Before you do, Sergeant, can you please tell me what my client has been arrested for?"

"I'm sorry, I thought you'd know seeing as you seemed to know she was in custody, Señora," he said with a smirk. "Anyway, it was for bribery and corruption, Section 422 of the Criminal Code."

*****

24

Anna waited whilst the phone call was put through.

"Hello?"

A man's voice.

"Please wait, whilst my colleague finishes searching your client, Señora."

Anna could just about hear two women's voices in the background. One was presumably one of the custody staff and the other was Lori, who was answering the other woman's questions.

"Have you got any weapons on you?"

"No."

"Any drugs?"

"Really?"

Lori had been unable to hold back. But regretted it as soon as she said it. She saw the woman's expression harden and couldn't blame her. The woman was only doing her job and she was only asking standard questions.

"Yes, really! Look I can make this as difficult, or as easy, as you want, it's up to…"

Lori butted in, "I'm sorry, Señora. I shouldn't have said that. I know you need to ask these questions. I apologise and no, I haven't got any drugs on me."

She saw the other woman's features relax, just a little, although she still conducted a very thorough search, patting Lori down and then using a search wand across her chest and groin.

Lori breathed out. The woman could have been a lot more vindictive if she wanted, citing a reluctance from Lori to answer questions and she was pretty sure her sergeant would have granted a strip search just for the hell of it.

"Gracias, Señora," said Lori quietly. Both women knew why Lori was thanking her.

"Seems you're in enough shit, Señora, without me adding to your woes." The women turned to the other custody assistant and said, "She's clear."

"Gracias, Dani. Here, Garcia, take the phone. It's your brief. We'll be outside."

Lori waited until the custody staff were outside the interview room and the door had closed.

"Hello?" she said.

Anna recognised Lori's voice.

"Try not to react, Lori. It's me, Anna. Is anyone still with you in the room?"

Lori couldn't believe she was hearing her voice. "How did you...? Stupid question." Lori knew something of Anna's background in the British security services, so getting a phone call into a police station, to speak to her whilst posing as a solicitor, wasn't going to be too much of an issue for her friend. "Sorry, I'm a bit...well, shaken if I'm honest. But no, there's no one in here now. They're outside the room."

"Good, now we just wanted to check on you, to see how you are. We know you've been arrested and we will get you proper legal representation before they interview you, which given the time, is probably going to be tomorrow, okay?"

"Yes."

Lori went quiet for a moment. "Is Greg there?"

"Of course, I'll put him on. And just so you know, you're on speakerphone."

Greg was trying to stay in control, so he could make sense of the mess Lori was in and somehow sort it out. But just at that moment, there didn't seem to be anything he could do about it any time soon.

"Greg, I didn't, I mean I haven't…"

"I know, I know, my darling and we all know that, and you don't need to say anything more."

He heard her take a deep breath, as though she'd been more worried that he might somehow believe she'd taken a bribe, than how she was going to deal with the allegation.

"Are you okay?" he asked gently.

"I am," she said. He heard her take another deep breath. "I'm a big girl and I can handle this."

"I know you can. But we don't know how long they might try to detain you, so just take each hour, and each day, one at a time," he said. He thought back to the time he'd been captured during the Bosnian War and held captive for months whilst people bartered for his release. Whilst this was a different situation and that they couldn't keep Lori for months without some sort of court appearance, he knew that whatever the length of time you had to deal with, it was always much easier to do so, if you had 'hope' to hang on to. As he spoke, he tried to reassure her.

"We'll sort this out, Lori, I promise. Whoever has set you up has no idea who they have just taken on, so please, try not to worry."

He knew that was far easier to say, than for her to believe. Someone had clearly done a very good job on setting her up, as even he knew that senior police officers didn't get arrested on just a whim and so there must be some convincing evidence trail to back up the corruption allegation.

"I'll be okay, Greg. But I'd be lying if I said I wasn't worried. They've got bank statements showing over a hundred thousand euros going into an account in my name!"

She heard a low whistle from Greg.

"Someone has done a proper job on me, Greg, so make sure you tread carefully too."

"Don't worry, we will. Now, can you give me any pointers at all as to where to start?"

"Yes, get hold of Cesar Mendez from the CNI. This has to be tied up with the Palma Foundation. But Greg, I think I've massively underestimated these people. I thought it was maybe just Manny Lopez and his daughter, but if they can get this sort of thing off the ground in double quick time? Then their influence must be a lot more widespread than I'd initially thought."

Greg looked around the room. Anna had been taking notes and she nodded back towards him.

"Yes, we've got all that and we'll make a start straight away."

"Greg, I said be careful, and I mean that for everyone. Please guys, do not do anything to put yourselves at risk. These people have shown what they are prepared to do."

"Don't worry, we'll be careful," said Greg, but there was an edge to his voice.

Lori managed a half-smile. She knew Greg well enough by now to know that he, and the rest of the 3R team, would do whatever it took to prove her innocence and bring those responsible to justice, but perhaps not the sort of justice she, as a police officer, had sworn an oath to follow.

There was a bang on the interview door.

"I think they want me to cut the call. Does Nino

know?"

"Yes, but he's been warned off from seeing you, or even speaking to us, but of course he's ignoring that."

"What about my boys? They're going to be searching my house, Greg. You need to...."

He heard the anxiety rising in her voice.

"I'll ring the boys and explain everything."

"Thank you. I love you," she said.

"I love you too. Now, try if you can, to get some rest and Anna will appear in the morning as Anna Dominguez."

The door opened and this time it was the sergeant standing there. Lori ended the call with, "Gracias, Señora Dominguez, I'll see you tomorrow."

"She's not coming tonight then?" said the Sergeant.

"No, I told her to come tomorrow as I don't imagine the Comisario will be interviewing me tonight."

He looked at her. She was clearly worried, but she still had some fight in her.

"Cell 4," he said to his assistant, Dani, before he grinned at Lori, but it wasn't a pleasant look. "Best you get your head down and get some rest then, Garcia," he almost spat her name out as he threw a blanket at her.

Lori was going to say something, but there seemed little point. He wasn't the one she needed to convince she'd been set-up. That would need to be the special prosecutor, the person responsible for taking the case through what would be a three-stage trial process.

She said, "Thank you," although she wondered why she was even bothering with the pleasantries, especially with the sergeant who seemed determined to make things as hard as he could for her.

Lori watched as the custody assistant opened the door to Cell 4 and then stood back and waved her in, adding, "Shoes."

Lori slipped off the blue heels she'd put on to go to

see Greg and felt the cold of the floor. She left her shoes outside the cell and walked through the door.

Less than an hour ago she'd been looking forward to seeing the man she'd fallen in love with. Now she was standing in a police cell. She'd obviously been in cells before, but never before as a detained person. As the door slammed shut the reality hit her. Feeling the tears welling up inside her, she suddenly felt very alone and very cold as the walls started closing in on her.

She bent down and picked up the blanket and went and sat on the bench at the end of the cell. It was a standard cell of around five square metres, with a solid wood-topped bench running the length of one of the walls. Behind the door, out of immediate view from the spyhole in the cell door, was a metal toilet bowl in a small alcove.

She shivered. Whilst it had still been a warm evening in the city, she now felt cold in the cell, especially in the thin dress she was wearing. She pulled the blanket around her. It smelled of industrial disinfectant rather than the usual washing detergent. But it was still early in the evening, so Lori realised it was probably getting its first use of the day, so it should be clean.

She kept looking straight ahead, knowing they'd probably be all stood around the custody desk watching her on the CCTV monitor to see how she reacted. She didn't need to look to see where the camera was. It would be in one of the corners of the cell, high above the door.

She lay down on the foam mattress on the bench and turned her head away to face the wall, not wanting them to see the tears she could feel on her cheeks. She shut her eyes, knowing she needed to sleep because tomorrow was going to be tough, but she could only hope that she could bring some sense to what was already starting to feel like a nightmare.

*****

25

Walking towards his office, Pablo Hernandez, a state anti-corruption special prosecutor, was enjoying the morning sunshine that was filtering through the trees that lined the city streets of Madrid.

He felt his mobile phone buzz, it was a text. *'Call you in a couple of minutes?'* He smiled. It was from Francisco 'Frankie' Rodriguez, who he'd known since they were boys. They'd met at junior school and they'd stayed friends ever since.

He texted back. *'Perfecto!'*

Like Frankie, Pablo had studied law and whilst his friend had the benefit of joining his father's corporate law practice, Pablo had wanted to do things his own way and he'd started out with a much smaller firm. He'd done well and was already making something of a reputation for himself, when he'd received the invitation directly from Frankie's father himself, Juan Rodriguez, to become a member of the Palma Foundation.

To start with, Pablo hadn't been sure whether to accept or not. Nearly all of what he had heard about the Foundation was positive and Frankie was obviously all for it, but even then, almost ten years ago, there was the occasional rumour of something that perhaps didn't sit quite right with the image of the Foundation as being an integral and charitable member of the business community.

That all changed when he had his membership 'interview' with Frankie's father. Juan told him that even though he hadn't been a member of the Foundation, he'd been keeping a watchful eye on the young lawyer's development. The older lawyer explained that it had been easy enough to create the opportunities for the young man to shine in a number of high-profile cases, opportunities Pablo had thought he had won on merit, but which instead, had been manufactured by Rodriguez, on behalf of the Foundation, to ensure Pablo's name was regularly discussed in the highest circles of the justice system.

Pablo wasn't sure if he should be pleased that he'd had such hidden support, or to be disappointed that he hadn't achieved all he had through his own efforts.

"But how do you make things like that happen?" he asked.

"Let's just say I have a number of ways that help to make the wheels of justice turn smoothly," said Juan. "Now, Pablo, can I assume you will be joining us in the Foundation? I mean after all, I'm sure it won't harm your continuing journey to the very top of our beloved profession."

Pablo heard the emphasis Rodriguez put on the word 'top' and as they shook hands, it was all he could do to stop himself fawning all over the older man. Both men understood the extent of the younger man's ambition, but Juan Rodriguez also knew he now had someone who he was going to ensure got to the very top of the criminal law system. Someone who would be of significant benefit to the Foundation for many years to come.

Following that fateful meeting, almost a decade before, Pablo had found himself on something of a whirlwind route to the top. Through invitations to Foundation networking events and introductions to people who mattered in the judiciary, all arranged by Juan Rodriguez, Pablo moved swiftly through the ranks of public prosecutors to his current position, as a special prosecutor with the state anti-corruption unit.

His phone rang.

"Frankie! ¿Qué tal? How are you doing?" he said warmly.

"Muy bien amigo, but hey, Pablo, I hear you've picked up a big case yesterday?"

Pablo had long ago realised the extent of the influence of the Foundation. Therefore, he didn't bother asking his friend how he knew any of this before it had become public knowledge.

"Yes, mate, a bent cop, but I think you know that already."

"Word gets around quickly and nobody wants someone like that high up in the GEO."

"No, we don't." Pablo paused, "But what's your interest in her, Frankie?"

"Nothing really. Just interested, as she's been trying to make something out of nothing from poor old Marcos's death."

As soon as he heard Frankie say, *'Nothing really,'* Pablo knew there was much more to this than Frankie was saying, but he decided to play along to see where this was going.

"Yes, I was gutted to hear about Marcos, Frankie and so soon after his old man had a heart attack! How is his mum and Rafa taking it?"

"They're doing okay in the circumstances, amigo, but it's obviously been a tremendous shock."

Pablo already knew this wasn't a chance call from

his friend. Why had the policewoman, whose arrest he'd been told about last night, been looking into Marcos's death? According to the press, it had been an unfortunate and tragic accident.

"I gather she must have been digging around in something you'd rather she didn't then, amigo?" probed Pablo.

"She was just causing unnecessary distress for Señora Ramírez and of course Rafa, that's all it is Pablo," said Frankie dismissively.

Pablo instantly knew that there must be much more to this that he didn't know. But maybe it was better that he didn't know? The Foundation had been good to him, very good and he'd realised a long time ago how things worked with them, so he wasn't about to start prying into something he didn't need to.

"Well, your troublesome Inspectora Jefe Garcia is now under arrest and in a cell in Palma police HQ."

"What happens next?" asked Frankie.

"Well, I'm heading over there myself shortly, to oversee things when it goes to court."

"Has she been charged already then?" asked Frankie.

"No, but from what I've seen the interview is more of a formality, unless she can magically come up with some plausible explanation about a hundred grand turning up in her bank account."

Francisco Rodriguez whistled.

"That's a proper bung, amigo! When are you likely to get her before a court?"

"We've got to go through the usual process. She'll be interviewed later this morning. Then the case papers will officially be presented to me by the police and the local investigating magistrate. He's a good guy and is already keeping me well briefed. From what he's said, it seems she's been picking up bribes for the last six months or so. I'm anticipating she'll be charged by midafternoon and if I can arrange it, I'll get a special court to sit later today."

"Impressive, Pablo and let me know if you need any help arranging the court. My father has a lot of old friends on the island and I'm sure they could help move things along if you need them to."

'I bet he has,' thought Pablo. "Yes, will do, Frankie. That could be useful as I'd like to be back in Madrid tonight, if possible, as I've got a lunch meeting tomorrow that I'd like to keep."

"Who is that with? Or is that so secret that you couldn't possibly say?" laughed Frankie.

Pablo smiled. He guessed his friend already knew who he was seeing. It was one of the Supreme Court judges he'd met at a recent Foundation meeting.

"It's Judge Torres."

It was Frankie Rodriguez's turn to smile.

"Well, I hope everything goes well in Palma then, so you can get back to see the judge. Give him my regards too when you see him."

"I will," said Pablo, once again realising the extent of the Foundation's influence where his friend, who was the same age as he was, had a network of contacts that included Supreme Court judges.

"Timing couldn't be better for you really, Pablo, given this bent cop has been caught and you're handling what's obviously going to be another nice high-profile case for you!"

"Yes, very good timing," said Pablo.

"It won't do you any harm, that's for sure, Pablo. Good stroke of luck that you were the duty prosecutor when the job came in."

Pablo Hernandez nodded. He was about to say that it was a bloody good coincidence, because a really high-profile case like this would of course only help with his ambition to become one of the youngest judges on the circuit, but he knew, *'Nothing of this has been any sort of coincidence at all.'*

"Pablo?" Frankie said again, sensing something in his friend's silence.

"Sorry, amigo." Pablo stalled for time and said he'd had another call coming in. "Yes, very fortunate, Frankie," he said, slowly. "Looks like I was in the right position at the right time."

"Definitely and it's cases like this, Pablo, that will have the king-makers looking at you again."

Pablo Hernandez smiled. *'The King-makers.'* Frankie was talking about the people like Judge Torres who would oversee the next round of senior judicial appointments. *'So that was the message, loud and clear. Get the bent cop locked up and the Foundation will see you get to be a judge.'*

"I can't be thinking about things that are out of my control amigo. I'll just be glad if I can help to get a bent cop off the streets," said Pablo, just a little bit too glibly.

'Out of your control amigo? Maybe, but not mine,' thought Frankie, almost smirking at his friend's efforts to hide his blind ambition, before replying, "Absolutely, Pablo."

*****

Lori had been awake for some time before Pablo Hernandez's call with Frankie Rodriguez.

She'd awoken to the sound of the hatch in the cell door being slid down and then banged shut, as the outgoing custody staff made their final checks before the new team came on duty at 7am.

It took her a moment to remember where she was. She shivered. It hadn't been the nightmare that she desperately hoped it had been. This was real, very real, but at least Greg knew where she was and she knew he'd be doing everything he could to help. But would it be enough?

She remembered the last words the sergeant had said before the cell door slammed shut. *'Get your head down.'* But even if she had been able to sleep, it seemed they hadn't made it easy, as they'd left the cell light on all night.

On purpose? Probably, but rather than taking her further into a spiral of despair that she had been in danger of going down, Lori had felt something stirring inside her. Was it hope, or maybe the first glimmer of a determination to fight this? Whatever it was, it had helped her to get some much-needed sleep and when she'd woken up, she still had the same feeling. She was going to fight this, with everything she had.

"If they think I'm not going to fight this," she whispered to herself, "then they've got another think coming!"

*****

26

Sam texted Detective Sofia Delgado. It was early, but he asked if he could meet her at 8.00am at Cappuccino in Plaça Rei Joan Carles, at the top of Passeig del Born.

He was waiting outside the café when he saw her walking down the main high street, coming from the direction of the police headquarters. Dressed in a smart business suit; a blue jacket and matching trousers, she had her dark chestnut brown hair tied up in a loose ponytail.

They shook hands, which felt awkward to Sam, but he didn't know what else to do, whilst Sofi felt a slight flush in her cheeks.

"Let's go inside," he said, as he held the door for her.

"Gracias, Sam."

The table just inside the door was free, so they sat down and ordered coffee and pastries.

"Thanks for coming, Sofi, I really appreciate it. Sorry to dive straight in, but have you got any news?"

"It's okay, I want to help if I can, but I've got nothing, Sam. The bosses are keeping a really tight lid on this."

"Can you get to see her?"

"No, not a hope. We can't even get into the cell block to deal with the overnight prisoners at the moment, although I got a quick two minutes with one of the custody staff from my old shift. He thinks they're going to keep her isolated on one of the wings. They don't want anyone knowing what's going on, so they'll shift all the other prisoners into different wings and keep Lori in a sterile corridor."

"Jesus, she's not a bloody terrorist!" said Sam.

"I know," said Sofi gently, "but she's a senior ranked GEO officer and this will bring a lot, and I mean a lot, of press attention Sam."

"Of course, yes, you're right. I'm starting to read things into this which aren't there."

He thought for a moment. "What's the guy who arrested her like?"

"Gutierrez? Tough, but he is fair."

"That's a good thing?"

"The best we could hope for, but I should have said, he really doesn't like corrupt police officers, particularly senior officers."

"But Lori's not...."

Sam stopped himself. It didn't matter what he said to Sofi, if the evidence was so overwhelming that it gave Gutierrez no reason to doubt what he had before him, then Lori was in real trouble.

"Sam?" said Sofi.

"I just can't believe someone has managed to create such a shed load of what's obviously falsified evidence that's left this guy, Gutierrez thinking he's got Lori bang to rights."

She looked at him. "Bang to rights?"

"Sorry. You know? When the evidence is overwhelming?"

"Ah, yes, I understand. But we can't give up hope. It has to be a set-up, so we need to dig deep and find out how they've done it."

Sam smiled, as she'd said 'we.'

"Look, Sofi, it's great that you're willing to help, but I don't want you getting in any trouble."

"Don't worry, I'll be careful and besides, it's not just me remember? We've got Castillo and Pérez and their guys too. They're all one hundred percent loyal to her, you know?"

Sam thought for a moment. "We know from what Nino has said that they might be watching him, but having Pérez and his guys on hand might be really helpful, especially if we start to get anywhere with this. But are you sure they're up for it?"

"Oh, yes, I've had texts and calls from both of them on their personal phones. They're just waiting for the nod, at least until someone tries to shift them off the island, although Nino says he's sticking with the Ramírez investigation and he'll dig his heels in if anyone tries to tell him otherwise."

"That's fantastic and talking of Nino, did he speak to you about a brief for Lori? Sorry I mean an abogado, a lawyer."

"It's okay, I've seen enough English TV shows to know what you mean by brief, Sam," she smiled.

They sat back in their chairs as the waiter, smartly dressed in their Cappuccino uniform of pressed white shirt and black trousers, arrived with their order.

Sam looked at Sofi and she smiled. It was a smile that made him smile too.

"Thanks again, Sofi," said Sam, once the waiter had gone.

She was a bit confused.

"For what?"

"Just, just for being here and helping. It means a lot to…" He stopped for a moment. "It'll mean a lot to Lori."

She reached out a hand to him, "And what about you, Sam?"

For a moment she was worried that she had misread

him, but he gently took her hand, "Yes, you mean a lot to me as well."

He looked at her and seeing the response in her eyes, he leaned forward and as she met him halfway, they kissed.

"That didn't take us too long then," grinned Sofi. "I've wanted to do that almost from the moment I first saw you!"

"What? Even when I was an assault suspect?" he joked.

"You were never a suspect you idiot!" she laughed. "I just needed a way to try to keep close to you."

It was his turn to laugh then.

"Okay, well now we've got that sorted, shall we try and see what we can do about Lori?" said Sofi. "So, you asked if DI Castillo had spoken to me about a lawyer? And yes, he did, and I have got someone in mind. She's an old girlfriend. We were at school and then Uni together. We both studied law and whilst I joined the police, she joined one of the better-known legal practices in Palma. But last year, she branched out on her own."

"Have you spoken to her?"

"Yes, I rang and left a message last night and she's messaged me this morning to call her at 8.15am."

Sam looked at his watch. "It's almost that time now."

"You're right. I'll ring her now. I know she'll be up for it, Sam. Shall I tell her to meet you at Greg's hotel?"

"Yes, that will be perfect."

Delgado flicked through her contacts and made the call. Sam's Spanish and Mallorquin was good, really good in fact as he'd lived on the island since he was a little boy, but even he was struggling a little to keep up as the two women spoke so fast.

"Did you get all of that?" Sofi grinned as she put her phone down.

"I got something about her meeting me at the Born Hotel in about quarter of an hour. As for the rest of it...."

"Okay, I know, we talk fast." Another broad smile flashed across her lips.

"Fast is an understatement," laughed Sam. "But yes, that's brilliant. And Sofi, you think she's, well you know, good?"

"Oh, yes, she's definitely good, Sam, I can guarantee that. Even with their so-called water-tight case, Maggie will have them scrambling around chasing shadows."

"Maggie?"

"Margarita Cruz, but she went out with a Scotsman for a while and he called her Maggie and it somehow stuck," Sofi laughed.

Sam checked the bill and left some euros on the table before leaving the café. Outside, they hugged and kissed with a tenderness that comes with new love, before going their separate ways; Sofi towards police HQ and Sam crossed the road junction and made his way to the Born Hotel.

He went through the lobby and straight up to the meeting room Anna had arranged the night before. There was just Greg in the room.

"Morning, Greg," he said.

"Morning, Sam. There's coffee and some breakfast things over there, but please tell me you've got some good news."

Sam poured a coffee and outlined the conversation he'd just had with Sofi.

"Sofi's friend, Sam? She's good? I mean good enough to take on this sort of conspiracy?"

"Sofi reckons she's really good, Greg. So, I think we need to go with that, but she'll be here any moment."

With that there was a gentle tap at the door. Sam opened it and in swept a young woman.

"Buenas dias, gentlemen. I think you're expecting me? I'm Margarita Cruz, but please call me Maggie."

It was quite an entrance and Greg thought that if she had even half as much guile, then she'd be doing a pretty good job, when it came to defending Lori.

After the introductions were over, Greg found he was even more impressed when Maggie got straight down to the business in hand. "Okay, we're starting off on I think you call it a 'sticky wicket'?"

The two men smiled back at her.

"You're definitely right on that one, Maggie," said Sam.

"But, Señores, we all need to remember that their case is just a pack of cards. If we can find something, anything, that will make one of their cards start to wobble, even just a little bit, then I can do some serious damage to their case."

Sam liked what he was hearing and he'd seen enough defence solicitors and barristers in his time to recognise a good one when he saw one.

Greg clocked the look on Sam's face and visibly took a deep breath in. *'Hope'* was what they all needed and this young lawyer had just given them a massive injection of it!

*****

27

The three of them talked some more about what the process would look like for the day, before Anna and then Terri joined them just before nine o'clock.

So, you are the other former 'spook' Sofi told me about then Anna?" grinned Maggie.

"That was all a long time ago my dear, but yes, I worked for the British Secret Intelligence Service, or MI6, as they're better known."

"And Greg says you'd like to come into the station with me, under the pretext of being my associate?"

Anna nodded, "Yes, that's the plan, just to give Lori some extra support, but if you think it's not a good idea, then we'll be…"

"No, I think it's a very sound idea. She won't know me and so won't necessarily trust me to begin with and we don't have time for me to build up the kind of trust I need her to have from the very start. So yes, you can be this 'Señora Anna Dominguez' of Jimenez & Co. They're a top outfit, so I'll have to be at my best to be working with those guys," laughed Maggie.

The way she talked left everyone in the room feeling the tension they were feeling starting to ease. Yes, this was going to be a hard battle to overcome, but they could all see this young woman had a lot about her.

Maggie could see the confidence rising in the four people before her and whilst she wanted them to feel there was still a fight to be had, she also needed them to understand the likely stages of how things would play out.

"When Lori is interviewed, we'll get a chance to see more of the evidence, but given what you've told me already, we need to be prepared for the fact that the Anti-Corruption Special Prosecutor will have enough to proceed with a charge."

"Okay," said Greg, slowly. "So that's when you talked about a court hearing?"

"Yes, and that is likely to be tomorrow, but you guys need to be prepared for the fact that Lori is likely to be remanded in custody."

Maggie saw the concern on their faces. Sam especially knew that prison, even when on remand, was not a great place to be if you were a police officer. Lori would literally be a sitting target for anyone wanting to take out their own frustration on their own circumstances, or just for the sheer hell of it.

Sam stepped in, "But you will ask for bail, Maggie? I mean we have access to significant funds that we could offer as a surety."

"I don't think all the money in the world will help in Lori's case, Sam," said Maggie. "Not that I'm completely writing bail off as a possible option. I just think it's highly unlikely to be granted."

She could see this had hit home, particularly with Greg. Sam seemed more accepting, but then again, she knew he was an ex-detective from the police in London.

"Look, I'm just painting worst case scenarios here, so there's no surprises for you, or Lori, for that matter. Now, Anna, if you're ready, I think we should go down and present ourselves as Lori's legal team. What do you say?"

Anna liked her, especially her business-like approach to things. She smiled. The young lawyer reminded her of her younger self, back when she was training undercover officers like Greg. She looked across at him and could see the worry on his face, but knew that he needed to focus on what he and Sam could be doing.

"Yes, let's go Maggie and don't worry, Greg, or rather try not to worry. I'll give you an update as soon as I can. In the meantime, I have a thought. Terri? I think it might be best if we keep you out of things for the time-being."

"Okay," said Terri. "I'll head back to my place. I'm going to get Tommy over here too and maybe a couple of the other guys. Just in case."

"Good idea," said Greg. He knew Anna must have something in mind for Terri, but gathered, from her silence, that now wasn't perhaps the time to explore what she was thinking.

"Sam? Any thoughts?"

"I think we should do our own digging on the Palma Foundation. Let's start by going to see the Ramírez family. I can say we're coming to offer our condolences."

"Yes, and give them mine too," said Anna, as she was taking something out of her shoulder bag.

"Maggie, give me two minutes, whilst I just use the bathroom."

"Yes, of course," said Maggie.

And it was only two minutes later when Maggie looked up to see a woman with dark black hair in a 'bob' style, wearing a smart black business suit coming out of the bathroom. Even Terri had to double check, but Maggie had to take a really close look to see it was Anna.

"Impressive," said Maggie. "Señora Dominguez I

presume?"

"Encantada," smiled Anna, in a very passable Madrid accent. "Shall we go?"

*****

Lori had taken the breakfast she had been offered. A pre-prepared packed breakfast in a disposable carton with a plastic spoon.

She had to smile when she saw the label on the side of the carton. It was produced by CDM, the catering and distribution company owned by the Ramírez family and the food wasn't actually too bad, especially seeing as it would have been microwaved by one of the custody staff. She finished the last spoonful and bent down to put the carton on the floor.

As she sat back up, she noticed the label on the mattress she was sat on. It had 'Enfern' printed on it, the company owned by Enrique Fernandez, another of the four founding partners of the Foundation. She shook her head. It was presumably just another example of the extent of the Foundation's influence, and ability to achieve multi-cooperative contracts for the benefit of its founder members.

She was brought back to the present when she heard one of the custody staff shouting, "You finished?" whilst not bothering to open the cell hatch.

She called out, "Si." Then added "Gracias." Better to keep the custody staff onside, rather than give them any excuse to make things difficult for her.

"Hold your carton up for me."

Lori picked it up and held it by the hatch and passed it through. She heard the custody assistant, a woman and one of the new morning team say, "Gracias."

"May I have a phone call now please, Señora?"

"You're still not allowed any calls, or any visitors."

The woman's voice was firm, but not vindictive.

Lori knew there was no point in arguing with her, as

she would not have the authority to overturn what was clearly a decision Gutierrez had made.

"Okay, no problem, gracias."

"I think your brief is here though. I'll be back for you shortly," said the woman.

"Thanks again," said Lori. A little bit of humility and humble pie had given her something back from the custody assistant. It wasn't much, but it was something.

Two minutes later the cell door opened and the custody assistant called her out.

"You can put your shoes on if you like."

Lori looked down at the high heels she'd been wearing when she was arrested. They were perfect for a night out, but not so great for keeping her feet warm in a cold cell block, but they were still better than nothing on the cold floor.

The custody assistant had already sized her up and recognised Lori wasn't going to be a problem, at least not whilst the interview process was going on. Walking alongside her, rather than holding back, the custody assistant guided her towards the interview rooms.

Lori knew where she was going, because it had only been a few months since she was using these rooms to conduct her own interviews. The memory brought with it a sense of disorientation and she stumbled.

"Are you okay?" said the custody assistant, steadying Lori's arm.

"Yes, yes, sorry, must be the heels," she lied.

"Look, if it makes you feel any better, there's a lot of us in the nick who don't believe you're bent, okay?"

Lori squeezed the woman's hand.

"Gracias, Señora."

"But we still have to do our job," the woman added.

"I understand. And I won't be a problem, because

you and I both know that isn't going to help. But thank you. Knowing what you said does help and I am going to fight this, so please, please, tell me anything you might hear that could possibly help."

"Okay," whispered the woman. "So, I don't know if this helps or not, but one of the anti-corruption special prosecutors is flying over today."

"Do you know their name?"

"I think it's Hernandez, but that's all I know."

The custody assistant opened the interview room door. "Señoras, here's your client."

Maggie Cruz also knew the benefits of treating the custody staff with respect. "Buenas dias, Señora y muchas gracias."

"De nada, you're welcome, Señorita Cruz," the custody assistant smiled.

As Lori walked into the room, she saw two women. The younger one, who had thanked the custody assistant and an older woman. It took her a moment to recognise it was Anna, dressed in a smart business suit and with a black coloured 'bob' hairstyle.

Anna smiled at Lori and saw her return a forced, half-smile. She had been worried about what sort of state Lori might be in, but she was looking better than perhaps she'd expected. Not great, but she looked like she was holding up, but Anna was also too experienced to give anything away, except for a warm and encouraging greeting.

Maggie spoke first.

"Inspectora Jefe Garcia, I am Maggie Cruz, a lawyer and I will be representing you. Please just give me a moment."

Lori watched as Maggie took out a small black object, the size of a computer desktop mouse. She saw her flip some sort of switch and put it down by her notepad.

"It's a blocker. I think we both know that the police aren't supposed to listen in, or record confidential discussions between defendants and their lawyers, but I'd rather be safe than sorry."

Lori smiled.

"So, we can talk openly now?"

"Yes, but just watch yourself. The cameras are probably still on, okay?"

"Yes, understood."

"Good, so I know you obviously know Anna, but just for the moment you need to remember she's your brief, Anna Dominguez from Madrid, working for Jimenez & Co." Cruz smiled.

Lori nodded and forced another smile.

Anna said, "I've brought you in a change of clothes. They're Terri's, but we think she's not far off your size and we can get more of your things from your hotel later."

"Thank you, Anna."

"Now two things. First of all, Greg sends his love, as do Sam and Terri and secondly, how are you doing?"

Lori let out a deep breath. She knew the cameras were still likely to be on, but it didn't stop her wanting to hug and cling on to her friend.

"Thank you. Give them all my love too and thank them all for what you're doing. I'm okay, but it's early days, although I'll feel better wearing those," said Lori, pointing to the smart black business suit Anna had partially taken out of a bag.

"When we go, Lori, I'll get you to authorise the removal of your hotel key from your belongings, so the custody staff can release it to us," said Maggie.

Lori nodded again.

"Now, I know you don't know me," continued Maggie, "but I've been briefed by your friends as to what's happened. At least with as much as they know.

And by friends, I include Sofi Delgado. She's the one who's brought me in to help."

Lori looked back at Cruz.

"We grew up and went to school together, all the way through to Uni. We go back a long way."

"Lori," said Anna, "we're really happy we've got Maggie on board."

Lori took another deep breath. It was a clear message that they'd checked this young woman out and that she could trust her.

"I think they're planning to interview me today."

"Yes, that's what they've told us too and it looks like it's going to be the Comisario and a detective sergeant," said Maggie. She'd spoken with the custody sergeant, who she knew from previous visits, and she'd managed to worm out of him that it would be Gutierrez and a DS who would be interviewing Lori.

Lori smiled. It was usually customary for a police officer being interviewed under caution to be interviewed by someone of a higher rank. However, Lori knew from her own experience of investigating professional conduct cases that it was also the norm for the senior officer to have an experienced interviewer alongside them, regardless of their rank.

"Do you know they've got a special prosecutor flying in this morning?" said Lori.

Maggie shook her head, "No, that's news to me."

"One of the custody team let me know. He, or she, is called Hernandez."

"Hmm," said Maggie. "Pablo Hernandez. He's a high-flyer, destined to be a judge before too long. He's got some serious backers."

"Don't tell me," said Lori. "Juan Rodriguez?"

"Yes, how did you…?"

"Rodriguez is one of the four main partners in the Palma Foundation."

"And you're convinced that this is what this is all about, Lori? That you've been digging too deep and someone in the Foundation wants you out of the way?" said Anna.

"It certainly looks that way."

"Do you think Gutierrez is caught up in this?" asked Maggie.

"I've no reason to think he is. But hey, given the fact that the Ramírez family's company, CDM, supply the food in here and one of the other partners, Enrique Fernandez? Well, his company Enfern supply the mattresses in the cells, I don't think we can discount anyone until we know for sure they aren't connected."

Maggie swore in Spanish, something both Anna and Lori understood.

"Sorry," said Maggie.

"No, don't worry, that was my thought exactly," said Anna.

Maggie laughed. "Now Lori, when you were being booked in, did you see anything of the evidence the Comisario presented to the custody sergeant.

"He showed it to me very briefly. He wasn't hiding it, I think because he thinks I haven't got a leg to stand on. But the bank the statements are supposedly from, BCB? Banco de Costa Blanca, well it's not one I've ever had an account with."

"And the statements were showing €100,000 in there? Did you see if it was just one deposit?" said Maggie.

"No, it looked like maybe four of five deposits over five or six months."

"That would usually be how it's done, Maggie," said Anna.

"You've done this sort of thing?" Maggie asked.

"A long time ago now, but yes, we'd have bank accounts either already set up and we'd just get the names changed, or it was sometimes possible to hack into the bank and create the accounts and a back story of transactions. If we couldn't do something like that then it was easy enough, for a quick low-level job, to just get a set of papers printed up to look like there was an account."

"What would you think they've done here?"

"With what they'd need to prove here? It's going to be more than just a set of fake statements," said Anna. "So, I think there will be a bank account, or even a number of them, in Lori's name. Probably created by a hacker, or a friendly in the bank."

"What do you mean by a 'friendly'?" asked Maggie. "Someone who's on the take?"

"Yes, either susceptible to bribery, or they might be someone who they have a hold over. Well, that's how we used to do it anyway."

"My, you did operate in a shady world, Anna. But what about hacking into a bank. I know it's possible, but they're supposed to be super-secure, aren't they?"

"Maggie," said Lori. "Anna did and in fact still does work in, as you say, a very shady world and she has access to people with skills to get into even the most secure of sites if they need to."

Maggie nodded, "So what you're saying is, that if you can do it, then with their resources, so could someone at the Foundation?"

"It's obviously not something every hacker can do, but a good one? Yes, they'll definitely be able to do it. But on the positive side, any sort of hack, or incursion, into a secure site will generally leave a trace. It's down to the skill of the hacker as to whether or not their trace can in effect be re-traced," said Anna. "That's what we'll try and action now we know which bank this money is supposed to be in. If we get someone with a high skill level and maybe a good bit of luck, we might be able to discover the origin of this money," said Anna.

"How long does all this take?" said Maggie.

"Difficult to give timelines, as it really depends on the security systems of both the bank and the hacker. But if we haven't got an answer within 48-72 hours, then it will become ever more difficult."

"And you've got someone who could do this re-trace?"

"No one specifically, but I know some people who do," said Anna. "I'll make some calls when we leave here."

The conversation continued, with Anna listening, as Maggie asked Lori about her career and then how she had become involved in the Foundation investigation, including how she had been contacted by Cesar Mendez.

Content that she had enough of the background detail, Maggie then turned her focus to working through the interview strategy with Lori. They agreed on the tactic of a pre-prepared statement, after which Lori would go 'no comment' to any further questions in the interview, to try to draw out from the police exactly what they had in terms of evidence of her alleged corruption.

The last half an hour was spent drafting and editing the prepared statement before they sat back, satisfied with what they'd achieved.

"You ready?" asked Maggie.

"Yes, and thank you again, Maggie," said Lori. "I really appreciate your help. I'd better get changed, as hopefully it won't be too long before they want to get started."

She stood up and walked across to the door, opened it and called out to the custody staff, to ask if she could be allowed to change her clothes. Anna and Maggie waited in the interview room whilst one of the custody assistants took Lori to a side room.

"How do you think she's holding up?" said Maggie.

"She's okay," said Anna. "In fact, I'd say she's better than okay. She probably had a bit of a wobble last night, but it looks like she's woken up this morning ready for a fight."

"How do you know that?"

"I've been there, Maggie, so it helps to have a sense of what she's going through."

Maggie raised her eyebrows. Sofi had said she was some woman, but Maggie now wondered if even Sofi knew half of what Anna appeared to have been in her past.

"What's your take on the special prosecutor coming over here, Maggie?"

"Not good, if I'm honest. I didn't bother to say anything to Lori, as she will know this anyway, but I'd guess they're going to go for a court hearing late this afternoon. So, we were right when we thought they wouldn't really be playing ball with bail."

As Anna nodded, she saw Lori reappear at the door.

"That looks better."

"Yes, and it feels much better too," said Lori. "Oh, and I've signed something that releases my hotel room key to you, Anna. You can pick it up at the custody desk."

"Great."

"One last thing and I almost forgot. Anna, can you, or can you get Greg or Sam, to track down Cesar Mendez?"

"The intelligence guy from CNI?" said Maggie.

"Yes, if anyone can help get this sorted out, then Mendez can," said Lori.

"Yes, of course, Lori, I'd already got that in mind. I'm going to leave you now with Maggie, as the interview process is a lot more her area of expertise, than mine.

I'm going to use some old channels I've got to try to get into Spanish Intelligence, as I wouldn't be surprised if our Señor Mendez might be a bit reluctant to respond to just a cold call from Greg, or Sam. And Lori?"

Lori looked at her.

"Stay strong. We're going to be working on this until we get it sorted, okay?" She held her friend's hands in hers.

"Thank you, Anna, and you too Maggie. And don't worry, I know this is going to be more of a war than just the one battle, but I'm ready for that, honestly."

Anna smiled back, but she'd already detected the slight waver in Lori's voice that gave away the concern she was trying to hide.

*****

28

Terri had gone straight back to her apartment and started making phone calls and booking flights.

Tommy Williams, an ex-para and Greg's longest serving member of his 3R team was already checking his bag as he finished his call with Terri. All of the team had 'ready to go' bags and after a quick glance he zipped it up and went to his small wall safe and took out his passport and a quantity of euros from the assorted currency he had in there.

Next, he texted James Porter and Penny Hastings. Terri had said she'd ring them direct, but he just wanted confirmation they'd both had the call to get to Mallorca ASAP.

Tommy's phone rang. It was James. Like Simon Barnes, he was a former SAS officer and had been recruited to the 3R team on Simon's recommendation. Simon had been James's mentor in the Regiment and his murder had hit him hard. But Tommy also knew, after many hours of talking to him, that operationally James was fit and ready.

"You set, Tommy?"

"I'm all good," replied Tommy in his warm Bajan accent. "I'll see you at Gatwick and do you know if

Penny's coming too?"

"Yes, mate, Terri mentioned it. Are we going to have to hit the ground running?"

"No, we're just going as backup for the moment whilst the others figure out what the hell's going on."

"Okay, that's great, Tommy. Flight's in a couple of hours, so I'm heading off now. See you there."

It was like talking to Simon. It must be an SAS thing, Tommy thought. They get straight down to business and want to know what's happening and what their role is. Tommy swore to himself. If he ever got hold of that shit Diego Sanchez, he'd make sure he paid for what he'd done. He felt his knuckles closing up as he remembered his friend, Simon, but he snapped back out of it when he felt his phone buzz again. He looked at the screen. It was Penny. He rang her.

"Penny, you all okay?"

"Tommy, lovely to hear you, and yes, I am."

He had a real soft spot for her, although despite his apparent gregarious and outgoing nature, he was often quite shy when he was in the company of a woman. And it was like that with Penny, as he'd never been able to string more than a few words to say to her outside of a professional setting.

But it didn't stop him loving everything about her, from the sound of her polished English accent to the fact that, in his words, 'she was one tough cookie.'

A former MI6 undercover agent, she had been deep undercover, posing as the P.A. to a Russian billionaire in a long term MI6 sleeper operation, but even Tommy didn't know she'd been doing it for almost ten years. It had only been when Martin Carruthers at MI6, sanctioned Greg's 3R team's investigation to target Oleg Makarovich, Penny's boss, that her role as an MI6 officer became increasingly more likely to be exposed.

With the successful conclusion to the Makarovich

operation, Penny was clearly not going to be able to safely resume her role as an undercover officer anywhere within the intelligence service. Therefore, with Carruthers's blessing, she quietly retired and joined the 3R team.

"Looks like we're going on a trip then," said Tommy. "You all packed?"

"As always," she laughed. "See you at the airport."

He smiled, then it was back to business. It sounded like Lori was in some serious trouble and he and the rest of them needed to get out there as soon as they could.

*****

Sam phoned the main switchboard of CDM, the Ramírez family business, and speaking in the Catalan dialect of Mallorca, he asked to speak to the youngest son, Rafa. He didn't know Rafa and so wasn't even sure if he'd take his call, so he was a little surprised when he heard a voice on the other end of the phone.

"It's Sam, isn't it? Sam Martínez. My brother spoke about you. He was delighted you agreed to take the spare car on the rally. It really helped out a lot."

"I was only too pleased to help, but can I first say that my mother, Anna, and I both send our sincere condolences to you and your mother, Rafa. It must have been such a shock after losing your father too?"

"Thank you Sam and I know you understand, as it's not that long since you lost your own father, is it? My mother was telling me about it. And now you're back on the island, so I take it that you aren't in the police anymore, back in the UK?"

"That's nice of your mother to remember my father too. And you're right, I'm back home, although strictly speaking it's still what they call a career break, where I could go back after five years if I chose to."

"But in the meantime, you're helping your mother?

My mother says that might be something of a full-time thing, given you own a significant property portfolio?"

Sam didn't know if Rafa was just making small talk, or if he was genuinely interested, but this sounded nothing like the playboy image Rafa Ramírez seemed to have in the Spanish press.

"To be honest, Rafa, I had no idea. I thought they owned the little bookshop my mother runs, plus a couple of villas across the island. I confess I was a bit stunned when I found out the exact extent of what the family own, but listen, I'm taking up your time. As well as offering our condolences, I wanted to ask you for your help and possibly your mother's, if she's up for it, as we have a very close friend who is in trouble."

"What sort of help, Sam? And is this anything to do with the GEO officer? I think her name is Garcia?"

"Yes, it is, Lori Garcia. I don't know what you've heard, but we think she's been framed?"

"We've only heard what's been in the news. It said it was a GEO officer who had been arrested and since we can't now get through to her on the number she gave us, we've put two and two together."

"And you've heard nothing from anyone in the Foundation?"

Sam heard the change in Rafa's voice.

"No one there is likely to tell us anything, Sam, so if that's who you're looking to help, then yes, I'll do whatever I can and I'm sure my mother will be the same."

Sam gathered there was no love lost between the Ramírez family and the rest of the Foundation founding partners.

"Can we meet?"

"Yes, of course. Come this afternoon if you like? Probably best if you come to the villa. My mother isn't really feeling up to going out much at the moment."

"I understand and thank you, I'll be across to see you around two thirty, if that's okay?"

"Perfecto."

*****

Anna made her way from the police headquarters back to Greg's hotel, The Born and went straight to the meeting room.

"She's doing as well as can be expected, Greg."

"Okay, what aren't you telling me, Anna?"

She had to smile. Back in the day, when she was the experienced MI6 training officer and he was the rookie field agent and she'd trained him in undercover techniques, he'd always had a natural instinct when it came to people and especially when it came to whether they were telling the truth, or even the partial truth.

"Can't hide anything from you, can I?"

"Nope, but then again, you see straight through me too. So come on, give. How's she really doing?"

"Like I said, as well as can be expected, but she's definitely shaken up Greg, even though she's putting a brave face on this. I think it's because she knows someone has done a very good job on her and she can't see a way out of it, at least not at the moment."

"What about physically?"

Like Anna, Greg had been exposed to significant periods of confinement, usually in very demanding situations when he'd been an MI6 field agent. He therefore knew the potential impact on someone like Lori, who wasn't used to and certainly wasn't trained in coping strategies to deal with even a short period of captivity.

"She's fine physically, Greg. She's fit and strong and as long as she eats and exercises, then she'll have no problems from that side of things. It's really her mental state I think we need to be mindful of."

"You're right. This could end up being a long-drawn

out affair."

She could see the concern growing in his face.

"The good news is that Maggie is as good as we hoped she'd be. I'm certainly no expert on court room skills, but she went through everything with Lori and she's already prepared a written statement for the interview, as she sees no point in trying to refute every question Gutierrez throws at her."

"That makes sense. Anything else?"

"Lori gave me a possible lifeline. I just need to see if I can get hold of it."

Greg nodded, looking for more detail.

"Cesar Mendez. He's the one who tasked her with this job. He's CNI, but apparently this was authorised by the President himself."

Greg eyes flashed. "Then surely there's real hope we can get this sorted quickly then Anna, especially if it's come from the President himself and Mendez is the gateway to him?"

"That's what I'm hoping."

"And the CNI? They're the national intelligence people, aren't they?" said Greg.

"Yes, so Mendez really does look to be the key that could literally unlock Lori's cell door!"

*****

Anna knew she might get the run around if she tried to just ring Mendez, or even the CNI direct, so she first of all made a call to Martin Carruthers. For want of a better word, he was her boss at MI6 and he worked out of the Vauxhall offices in London.

"Anna, lovely to hear from you, although I wondered if you might be giving me a call."

"Why would that be then, Martin?"

"Perhaps because your friend Lori Garcia has been arrested on suspicion of corruption?"

MI6 had specific 'desk' experts to monitor

information and news from across the world and then decide on what needed to be classified as intelligence, in other words, information that required further action. Nevertheless, Anna was still a little surprised that Martin knew about Lori.

"So you're keeping tabs on 3R then, Martin, or is it just Greg?"

"Well, it's both actually. I promise you, it's nothing sinister Anna, but since the incident with Makarovich I've had Greg flagged."

Martin had seen an opportunity for a return on his decision to provide some assistance to Anna and Greg's 3R team, when she had reunited with Greg and they'd found themselves tackling an Armenian major crime gang.

Anna's return to the Service, on an occasional and ad-hoc basis as determined by Carruthers, had worked very well since then. However, a subsequent 3R investigation into the kidnap of Anna's friend's daughter had pulled the Russian billionaire, Oleg Makarovich, into the spotlight. As someone who was very definitely a person of interest to MI6, Makarovich's involvement moved to ensure 3R and especially Greg's activities were from then on flagged.

"Okay," said Anna slowly, knowing Greg would not be pleased to know he was on an MI6 flag list. It didn't matter that he had nothing to hide, but it could affect the level of confidentiality he could offer his 3R clients. But she decided to move on. Nothing she could say, at least at the moment, was likely to make Martin remove the flag and besides, she had other, more important things on her mind at the moment.

"Well, yes, you're right, Martin. It is about Lori."

"Presumably it's a very good setup?"

She hadn't expected him to think any differently, but it was reassuring for him to voice his disbelief that

Lori could be guilty of corruption."

"It looks very good indeed, Martin."

"Interesting that someone should go to the extent of targeting a senior GEO officer. It suggests they have someone, or something to protect," mused Martin. "However, I'm not sure how I can help on what is an internal police corruption inquiry, not to mention it's in a foreign country, Anna, but I imagine you have something in mind?" He smiled at her.

"I think you know this is something that goes far beyond just an internal police inquiry. Ever heard of Cesar Mendez? He's apparently reasonably high up in the CNI?"

"Doesn't ring any bells, but I can get him checked out with the Spanish desk."

"That would be excellent, Martin. If I say that he's supposed to be one of the good guys, then hopefully that's what you will get back from the Spanish Desk."

"What's his part in all this then?"

She knew he couldn't resist digging to find out more, but she needed his help and she wasn't giving anything critical away by telling him.

"He was the one who tasked Lori with the job she's investigating. It seems it came from the President himself."

"Interesting and then there was the death of the Ramírez boy," said Carruthers.

"Yes," said Anna.

"And so soon after his father, Eduardo."

Martin Carruthers left his words hanging.

She knew he was waiting for her reaction. *'But did he know about all of this before Lori's arrest?'* Nothing much surprised Anna anymore when it came to the MI6 man.

"So, what's your interest in this then, Martin?"

"Oh, curiosity, nothing more."

Anna smiled. She knew Carruthers had more than

enough on his plate to be just looking at something out of curiosity.

"You aren't going to tell me then?"

"Well, I suppose it's nothing I can't share with you, Anna, but it's not for general discussion at this stage."

"Understood."

"Presumably your Señora Garcia was being asked to look into the Palma Foundation?"

Anna shook her head in disbelief. Yes, Martin Carruthers was a senior MI6 officer, but why on earth would he have the Foundation on his watch list?

"I gather by your lack of an immediate response that for once, I seem to have surprised you, Anna?"

She could imagine the satisfaction he was getting from catching her momentarily lost for words.

"Well, yes, you certainly have. So go on tell me, why are you looking at the Foundation?"

"We monitor anything that might unsettle the political landscape in countries with whom we have close diplomatic links and Spain is obviously included in that list, particularly because of the continued rumblings about Gibraltar. You'll no doubt know about the four founding partners?"

"Yes," said Anna.

"And that one of them, the lawyer Rodriguez, ran for President in the last election?"

"Yes," said Anna.

"And he could have got in, if it hadn't been for the gaffe he made at one of the campaign events."

"Do you think it's Rodriguez, or the Foundation, who are really growing their influence?"

"It's both and even the current President seems to have one hand tied behind his back when it comes to tackling them. To the general observer, the Foundation is nothing but a source of good, bringing wealth to the economy and much needed funds to charities across the whole of the country."

"That's why he's had to resort to some clandestine activity involving the CNI?"

"Exactly," said Carruthers.

"But you're not looking to interfere in anyway?"

"Oh, goodness me, no. This is strictly something the Spanish will have to sort out for themselves. But we'll obviously need to keep an eye on any potential impact on UK interests, whether that's Gibraltar, or trading conditions with Spain.

"Did you know about Mendez before I mentioned him then?" asked Anna, slowly.

"No, I didn't. So, all the more reason for me to help you."

"Thanks, Martin. If you can get me an in with him, then this could really blow this whole thing wide open and help get Lori released."

"Let's hope so. I'll get back to you as soon as I can."

*****

29

As Maggie Cruz was going over the final preparations with Lori Garcia for her interview under caution with Comisario Gutierrez, Sam and Greg had driven to the Ramírez villa.

Sam pushed the button on the intercom at the electric gates.

"Sam Martínez and Greg Chambers to see Señora Ramírez."

A moment later the gates swung smoothly open and they drove in and Sam saw an athletic looking young man come through the front door and walk down the steps towards them.

"Sam, Greg? Rafa Ramírez. Welcome."

He spoke in perfect English and thanked them for coming.

"I wish we were meeting under better circumstances," said Sam. Once again, he was somewhat taken aback by the man before him. Rafa was engaging and business like and so different to the playboy image usually portrayed in the headlines of the celebrity magazines.

The two men followed Ramírez into the villa and he took them to a large reception room with an amazing view of the bay of Palma.

"My mother will join us in just a moment, Señores."

Sam nodded. "Thank you again for seeing us at such short notice."

"That's no problem. Ah, here you are, Mama. Señores, my mother, Señora Christina Ramírez."

Greg stepped forward.

"Señora Ramírez, encantada. It's a pleasure to meet you and please accept both my and Sam's sincere condolences for losing Marcos at far too young an age."

"Gracias Señor," said Christina and she nodded appreciatively to them. "So, my son tells me that the police woman who's been arrested is a friend of yours?"

"Yes, Señora, a very dear friend of mine," said Greg.

Before he could say anything else, Christina spoke again.

"Presumably you believe she is innocent of the allegations against her?"

"Yes."

"But you would think that wouldn't you?" she said, and he felt her eyes boring into him.

Greg held back a smile, because it was a statement seeking clarification, more than an accusatorial question. She was sharp and quick witted, that was for sure.

"You're right, I would. But you've met her, Señora, what do you think?"

This time Christina smiled. "Well of course, it's clearly a set-up Señor. But you must go carefully. Do not underestimate these people, because I think that's exactly what Marcos did. Now I've warned Rafa that he must not make the same mistake, Señor Chambers. I could not stand to lose another son to these people."

"Who do you mean by 'these people,' Señora?" asked Sam.

"I hope you are looking for clarification here, Señor

Martínez, because I certainly do not take you for a stupid man."

"You're right, Señora Ramírez, that was a clumsy question, I'm sorry."

"Don't worry young man, I was just teasing you."

They saw her visibly relax and gathered they must have passed some sort of test, although what sort they had no idea.

"Señores, as I told your Señora Garcia, my husband was no angel when it came to business, but he wasn't a crook and he didn't go around hurting people. It all started out with good intent, with the Foundation, I mean. We were at the point of having to file for bankruptcy with CDM, a business his family had founded well over a hundred years before, but through the connections and network he now had through the Foundation, Eduardo was able to rejuvenate CDM's fortunes."

She checked they knew about CDM, the family's catering and wholesale business. Seeing Greg and Sam nodding, she continued, "But Manny Lopez was a different being altogether. I'm talking about the way he did business. And his daughter? Well she's inherited all of his traits and then some. I think she's the one behind this, killing my Eduardo and now Marcos."

"Mama, we don't have any evidence to that effect, so we must be careful before we go around throwing allegations we can't substantiate," said her son, Rafa.

"It's okay, Rafa," said Sam. "We won't be going and repeating anything we hear from you and your mother. We just want to hear what the two of you really think has been happening with the Palma Foundation."

Christine Ramírez took a deep breath.

"My husband had no history of heart disease and for his age, he was reasonably fit. Therefore, although the post-mortem determined the cause of death as being a sudden heart attack, I do not believe it, and nor I have to say does our doctor who has tended my family for the past thirty years."

Sam looked at Rafa. "My mother is right, Sam. Papa having a heart attack? I know these things can happen, but it just doesn't stack up and then to lose Marcos less than six months later to an apparent car accident? Well, it's just too much of a coincidence."

"That's what we're beginning to think too, Rafa," said Sam, "and I think Lori was of the same view. So much so, that we think they've gone for her, although this time, they've held back from resorting to physically harming her."

"Because killing a police officer, a senior GEO one at that, would bring far too much unwanted attention down on them?" asked Rafa.

"You've got it in one," said Sam.

"So, you will dig deeper into this? And not just to clear Inspectora Jefe Garcia's name?" asked Rafa.

"Yes, that's the plan," said Greg.

"Thank you, Señores," said Christina. "These people cannot be allowed to get away with this, but as I said before, you must tread carefully. Hannah Lopez, Manny's daughter, uses a man called Jaime Ortiz to do her dirty work. Before he died, my husband told me about him and how he suspected him of having interfered with the witnesses and the jury in the Lopez Autoparts corporate manslaughter case."

"I didn't know about this, Señores," said Rafa. "Mama, did he give you anything concrete to support his thinking?"

"No, that's just it. Your father said he had something, some sort of book that Manny had kept for years and recorded all his shady deals in. But then a day or so later, he told me the book had been stolen from his office, so then he had nothing."

"Do you know what sort of book your husband was talking about?" said Sam.

"No, I'm sorry, but he was surprised Manny had it. He said he couldn't believe Manny had it for so long, ever since the Foundation had started."

"Did he go to the police about any of this? asked Greg.

"Well, he thought about it, but I think you need to understand, Señor, that the Foundation network stretches far and wide."

"Are you suggesting corruption?"

"Perhaps, but not necessarily as in the usual sense, where money changes hands, Señor. But if he had gone to the police, then all I'm saying is that there was a very good chance that it would have got back to Manny, or Hannah."

"Okay, that's useful to know, although not necessarily helpful," said Sam.

"No, not with what you're trying to do with your friend, Señora Garcia. Anyway, my husband went and challenged Hannah, demanding to know why she had taken the book."

"Did he know she had taken it?"

"Not for sure, but he was certain that it must have been her, or Ortiz."

"What did she say?" said Sam.

"She admitted it. Said she'd taken it back because it was her father's personal property."

"She's got some front!" said Greg.

"Front, Señor?" said Christina.

"Sorry, Señora. I mean she is very full of herself, very confident."

"Ah yes, she is certainly all of that. She told him the book was nothing more than an internal record her father had kept for his own purposes."

"What did your husband do then, did he say?"

"Nothing immediately, but he was furious and said he needed to sit down and talk it all through with Marcos."

"And did he?" asked Sam.

"No, he never got the chance," she said quietly.

Greg saw her stiffen slightly.

"How soon after did he suffer the heart attack, Señora?" Greg asked gently.

"It was the same week he had the argument about the book with Hannah. Within thirty-six hours, he was dead."

*****

Hannah Lopez realised she was drumming her fingernails on her desk. It was something she did when she was stressed and the phone call she'd just finished, had certainly increased her stress levels.

Garcia had been brought in to investigate the Foundation by this Cesar Mendez of the CNI.

She sent a text to Jaime Ortiz.

'Need to speak urgently.'

Within two minutes he'd called her on one of the new burner phones he'd given her. Mobile phones that she could use without fear of the calls being traced and which she could easily dispose of in the chemical bin he'd given her.

He listened as she told him what she wanted him to do.

"Can you do it?"

"Of course, I can do it, but there's a risk it will bring a lot of police sniffing around and not just the police. The intelligence services won't take kindly to losing one of their guys."

"Can't you make it look like ETA?"

Ortiz knew there was little point trying to pin anything on ETA, the Basque separatist terror group, because they'd effectively dissolved back in 2018.

"Making it look like ETA won't stand up to any sort of scrutiny, but," he paused, "I could put something together that could suggest it was someone like ISIS."

"That sounds good," she said.

He heard the change in her voice, as she relaxed, but wondered if she'd really understood the potential backlash of what she was asking him to do.

"Hannah, I don't often question your decisions, but are you sure you want to take this one on? I mean, you held back with Garcia to just get her out of the way, but if we get rid of Mendez? That could bring a whole lot of trouble your way."

She heard him use the words 'we' and then 'your way' and wondered where he would be if they reached a day of judgement. Could she rely on him in the same way her father clearly did?

He could sense she was thinking about something. Maybe he'd said something unwittingly that had unsettled her, which certainly hadn't been his intention.

"Hannah, I don't know if you're worrying about anything else? But if it helps, let me just say that I swore an oath to protect your father and all of his family many years ago and so I will never do anything to bring harm to you, or your father."

She smiled. *'What was she thinking?'* Ortiz was of course, totally loyal, and she needed to banish any other thoughts she might otherwise have.

"Thank you, Jaime," she said warmly. "I don't doubt your loyalty for one minute. But I need to put this thing with Garcia and Mendez to bed. You seem to have effectively sorted the Garcia woman, at least for now, but I think we also have to get rid of any opportunity of a 'get out of Jail' card that Mendez could offer."

"If you're sure?"

She didn't mind him questioning her once, but once

was enough.

"Jaime, just get it done!"

He knew when to stop.

"Okay, you're the boss."

'I am,' she thought, but she didn't bother acknowledging him. "When can you get it done?"

"Tonight, or first thing tomorrow. It'll no doubt be on the news."

*****

"You ready?" Maggie Cruz said to Lori, as they sat waiting in the interview room.

"Yes, I just want to get this part over and done with," said Lori.

They both looked up as the door opened and Comisario Gutierrez walked in accompanied by a younger woman in her mid-thirties.

"This is Detective Sergeant Vega. She will be supporting me during the interview process." He didn't wait for either woman to say anything before adding, "Señora Cruz, I'd heard you were representing Señora Garcia. I would have thought that this is a case you wouldn't have wanted to be involved in?"

"Why ever not, Comisario?" said Cruz, expressing genuine surprise.

"Oh, it's just that you seem to specialise in cases where there is an apparent miscarriage of justice. Where you stand a fair chance of getting your client found not guilty."

Gutierrez was baiting them and Maggie sensed Lori was about to react. She gently laid a hand on Lori's arm as she answered, "And that's exactly what I propose to prove here, Comisario, so should we cut the crap and get on with this? My client has a prepared statement which I will read to you. After that we will not be answering any further questions."

Lori resisted the smile she felt coming as Maggie hit

back at Gutierrez's intimidation tactics, but she knew this was only some gentle sparring before they got into the serious elements of the interview.

The interview was digitally recorded and Maggie read out the prepared statement. It contained Lori's sworn declaration that she was innocent of any corruption and reaffirmed her claim that she had been tasked by a senior member of the intelligence service, the CNI. Despite Maggie's advice, there was no mention of the involvement of the President. They had discussed this at length, with Maggie trying to persuade Lori to include it from the start. However, Lori was insistent they should hold back on it until absolutely necessary, especially given the fact that Mendez had already effectively told her that the President would not come forward to sanction this as an official operation.

"So, for the purposes of the recording, you are not going to answer any further questions?" asked DS Vega.

"That's correct," said Lori.

"You understand that the Comisario and I can still ask further questions, whether or not you choose to answer them, and failing to answer our questions could be taken as an inference of guilt at a subsequent court hearing?"

"My client understands that," said Maggie Cruz.

There followed thirty minutes of pre-prepared questions with the inevitable no comment response from Lori. The police officers outlined their case in detail, producing the appropriate bank statements as evidential exhibits. Although she wasn't answering any questions Lori still looked at the copies of the statements whilst taking care to not touch any of the originals, to avoid inadvertently adding her fingerprints to the documents.

Lori was getting a nagging pain in her stomach. She

knew it was a sense of panic and it was getting worse. She was innocent, but the two officers before her had what they firmly believed to be cast iron evidence of high value corruption. To make things worse, from what Lori had seen, she couldn't blame them either, as the evidence did appear to be clear cut.

She whispered in Maggie's ear, who looked at her and then nodded.

"My client wants to say one final thing to you, Comisario."

"Okay, I'm listening."

"Comisario Gutierrez, you seem to be a fair man and so all I ask is that whatever you see before you, which I accept appears to show evidence of my alleged corruption, just please consider the possibility, however far-fetched it may seem, that this is an elaborate set-up to discredit me and my investigation into the Palma Foundation."

Lori saw Gutierrez was listening intently to her and when she'd finished, he nodded in an acknowledgement to what she had said.

"For the benefit of the digital recording of this interview, I have heard what you have said and as with everything I do, I will of course keep an open mind. However, in fairness to both you and your legal representative, I should advise you that on the basis of the evidence I currently have before me, I will be recommending that you are charged with bribery and corruption under Section 422 of the Spanish Criminal Code."

Neither Lori or Maggie were surprised by what he said, but it didn't stop Lori getting another bout of stomach cramps and she had to fight hard from wincing with the pain.

"Will you be looking for the court to sit in the morning Comisario?" asked Maggie.

Gutierrez looked at his watch.

"Oh, I don't think we need to wait till then. I'm sure the anti-corruption special prosecutor will be able to get something set up for late this afternoon."

With that, he spoke briefly to the policewoman, asking her to turn off the recording and deal with the administration paperwork around the digital recording, before he left the room.

"Lori, give me two minutes to make some calls and then I'll be back for a debrief. Officer, is that okay? Can Lori stay in here with you?"

"Yes, that's fine," said Vega.

Left alone with the police officer, Lori didn't much feel like talking, so just sat there, with a hand across her stomach trying to control the cramps.

After she'd finished the process of detailing the interview documentation, Vega sat flicking through her iPhone, then put it down and looked across at Lori.

"I've heard about you and on the face of it, I wouldn't have said you were bent."

"Thank you," said Lori.

"Nothing to thank me for and if you don't know, Gutierrez might come across as a bit bullish, but he is fair."

Lori gave a slight nod. Perhaps he would dig deeper into all of this? But then the officer dashed even those thoughts of hope.

"But with the evidence he's got, it's hard to get away from the fact that you look as guilty as hell," said Vega.

Lori looked at the ceiling. Vega was right. Everything pointed towards her guilt. She really needed Anna to get through to Mendez, as he seemed to be the only person who could end this nightmare.

*****

30

The three of them, Greg, Anna and Sam had regrouped back at Greg's hotel in the meeting room which they'd now booked for the whole of the next week.

Terri had dialled into the room's speakerphone and was listening with the others, as Anna took them through what had happened with her visit to see Lori.

"How was she when you left? Is she okay?" asked Greg.

"She is for the moment. But I am worried, because she looks like she's right on the edge."

Sam spoke first.

"I think we need to plan for what happens next."

"Do you think there is any chance of getting her out on bail, Sam?" said Greg.

"I'd say, no. Not that we give up and I'm sure Maggie will do her best and will say we can put up all sorts of sureties, but in these circumstances? I think a remand in custody is the much more likely outcome."

"Okay, not what I wanted to hear, but that all makes sense," said Greg. "Anna? Are they still not allowing her any visitors?"

"No, they can do that for five days according to

Maggie," said Anna.

"So at least it's good we've still got you to get in to see her as her legal representative if we need to." He emphasised the 'legal representative.'

"Yes," said Anna. "I think we can still make that work, at least whilst Maggie is happy to go along with it. I'm a bit concerned that there's a risk to her professionally if the police found out what we were doing, but she seems okay with it."

"It's actually really good of her to be doing that. I think Sofi found us a good'un when she suggested Maggie," said Sam.

The rest of them nodded in agreement.

Terri then spoke up, "What happened with the Ramírez family, guys?"

Sam filled Anna and Terri in on the conversation they'd had with Christina and Rafa.

"Do you think this book they mention is that significant then?" asked Terri.

"It's possible. But quite why Manny Lopez would keep a written record of the Foundation dealings I don't know. Why would he?"

"Old school?" said Anna. "He just prefers a written record?"

"Maybe," said Greg.

"Could it be that he didn't want some particular transactions stored on any sort of electronic database?" said Anna.

"You mean like the dodgy sort of dealings the Foundation are rumoured to be involved in?" said Sam.

"Well, it would give some logic as to why he's kept a separate ledger for all these years," said Anna.

"So, if we could find Manny's book then it might give us some sort of bargaining power?" said Terri.

"Yes, quite possibly," said Greg. "But other than it's a book of some sort, we have no idea what it looks like.

Manny Lopez and Eduardo Ramírez seem to be the only people who have seen it, although of course it looks like this Hannah Lopez may now be in possession of it."

"And that possibly means that her guy Ortiz may have had a hand in removing it from Ramírez's office," said Sam.

Greg breathed in deeply.

"Guys, whilst I don't feel we're necessarily getting any nearer to getting Lori out of custody any time soon, we at least seem to be making some kind of sense of what this is all about."

"I agree," said Sam, "and the more we understand what we're up against, then the better the chance of us helping her."

"Next steps?" asked Greg.

"Chasing down Mendez and getting the update from Maggie," said Anna.

"Getting Tommy, James and Penny in position," said Terri.

"I'll speak to Rafa again. Maybe his father's secretary might have caught sight of the Lopez ledger?"

"Good and I'll check in with Nino to see how he's doing, oh and I'll also call Lori's boys to update them. Her oldest boy wanted to come across with his brother, but I've suggested he doesn't for the time-being. I just feel that if they're targeting Lori in this way then we also don't want to bring her boys into the field of play. What do you think? Am I right to be thinking like that?"

"I think you're bang on," said Terri. "But do we need to be keeping a watch on them too? Without scaring the crap out of them, or their families?"

"I agree too," said Sam, "and with Terri's thinking about keeping a watch on them."

"I'll get Sharon to get over to the mainland with her team. We'll keep it low profile for the time-being, but do you think we should at least tell the boys to be on the lookout?"

Greg thought for a moment.

"You're right, Terri. I'll tell them, but not that we're baby-sitting them. They're big lads now, well into their twenties, but I know from what Lori's told me that the memory of seeing their father gunned down in front of them has never left them."

"I guess it won't come as any sort of surprise to them that whoever has framed their mother, might be watching them?" said Terri.

"Exactly," said Greg. "I'll just tell them to ring me if they see anything out of the ordinary."

"Guys?" Terri called out. "Have you got anything else for me at the moment. I confess to feeling a bit like a spare part," said Terri.

"Nothing yet," said Greg, "but it'll be good to have the others out here."

"I've got Penny coming along to sort out logistics and admin to free you up, Anna. I've got a room booked for her where you're staying, Dad and I'll get Tommy to stay with me and I was hoping you'd have room for James, Sam?"

"Of course, no problem."

"That's all good then," said Greg. "I feel like we've got enough resources to deal with what we at least think we're looking at. We just need to get something concrete for us to make some sort of inroad into this, especially to getting Lori released. Anna, when do you expect some news back from Martin about this Mendez fella?"

"I've had nothing yet, but I'm hoping I'll get something by the end of today."

Greg tried not to show his disappointment, but he knew that Mendez seemed to be their biggest hope in making any progress quickly.

"Hmm, well I hope he comes up trumps when we do finally get hold of him. Can you check in with Maggie, Anna and see what happened during the interview and come back with an update in…," he looked at his watch, "let's say two hours? Is that good for everyone?"

"Good for me," called out Terri and the rest of them nodded.

*****

"Señora Martínez? I think you have been expecting my call. My name is Cesar Mendez, but shall we get through the formalities? Please call me Cesar."

"Thank you for calling me, Cesar and I'm sorry to have had to contact you via," Anna paused, "via my friend in London."

"That is absolutely no problem and may I say your Spanish is excellent, but I gather from your 'friend' that you've lived in Spain, or should I say Mallorca, for some time now?"

"Thank you, that's kind of you to say, Cesar. Now, have you been told of the reason for the call?"

Mendez smiled. She was straight down to business, just as Carruthers had suggested she might be.

"Yes, I know why you were calling, Anna. Lori's been arrested on some trumped up charge of bribery."

"I need to know, Cesar, can you help to get her released?"

"I can and I will, although the people who have done this and I think we both know who that is, well they've done a very good job with the evidence trail."

"You've already looked into this then?"

"Yes, as soon as I heard she'd been arrested, I started doing some digging."

Anna was a little puzzled.

"Cesar, I feel like I'm stating the obvious, but can't you just get the President to declare she's been operating under his direct order?"

"Well, I could, but I have to give credit to them." Mendez clearly wasn't comfortable with mentioning The Foundation on the call. Whilst his phone was no doubt encrypted, Anna's certainly wasn't and he wasn't taking any chances that someone may be listening in to their call. "They're attacking Lori from a completely different angle from her investigation."

"Of course, so even if you come out and say she was operating under your, or rather a Presidential order, the bribery charges remain a separate issue. Yes, I see. So, what can you do?" said Anna.

"It seems reasonable to assume that they'll go for a remand in custody. Therefore, I'm going to try some backdoor negotiations to get her out as soon as I can."

"Maggie Cruz, our lawyer, told us a remand in custody was likely," said Anna.

"And she's right. Hernandez, he's the anti-corruption state prosecutor?"

"Yes, I've heard his name."

"He's already set up a special court for late this afternoon."

"How can he do that so quickly?" asked Anna.

"Because he can, Anna. He wields a considerable amount of power and when he says 'jump,' then people jump. He's also called in people who he knows he only needs to point in the right direction, to get the result he wants."

"What? Corrupt judges?"

"Not necessarily corrupt. But if you have a state prosecutor saying he's got a corrupt senior police officer who has good reason to fail to surrender to court bail, or may even interfere with witnesses...."

"Then it paints a picture that most judges wouldn't think twice about when deciding whether, or not, to remand them in custody," said Anna.

"Yes. But that doesn't mean we can't build a case to

get her released at the next court hearing."

"When will that be?" asked Anna.

"It's usually a week after the first hearing."

Anna was thinking quickly and starting to feel more than a little concerned at what Lori was going to have to go through. "So, Lori will be in custody for at least seven days?" she said.

"Look, Anna, I won't bullshit you. I don't even know if I'll be able to get her out in seven."

He didn't know if he was expecting some sort of outcry back from Anna, but Mendez was surprised at how the woman, who he'd heard from Carruthers still had a working connection to the British Intelligence Services, reacted in such an unemotional and calculated way.

"Right, in that case, we need to start thinking about alternative help for her then," said Anna.

"I'm not sure what you mean," he said slowly.

"If we can't get Lori out, then I think we need to consider the possibility that whoever is doing this may not stop at merely incarcerating her. Prisons are dangerous places at the best of times, therefore, I'm starting to worry that Lori might become a target in there."

"Just because she's a police officer?"

"Well that and because whoever wants her out of the way in prison may see it as an opportunity to silence her for good."

"You're right. I hadn't thought about that. Yes, they might go after her in there. I could see about getting her put into solitary confinement?"

"That would help. But in my experience, some prison staff can be susceptible to corruption or, often as not, it's coercion. Now whether she's in solitary or not, a prison officer could still allow or enable a situation to occur that could leave Lori in danger."

Mendez didn't know enough about the way prison culture worked to be able to make an informed comment, whereas it appeared that Anna Martínez clearly did. He wondered where she'd gained this experience, because she certainly talked with authority and knowledge of what happened inside a prison, but he knew better than to ask.

"I've seen her career record, Anna, but you know her personally. Do you think she'll be able to handle herself in there?"

"One on one? Yes, definitely. She's fit and tough, but that's not the way these things work, Cesar. Now I've got the start of an idea, but it's complicated and I need to be face to face with you to talk it through, as it's not something I want to go through over the phone."

Mendez realised that whatever she was thinking about required complete secrecy, with not even the slightest chance of their conversation being eavesdropped.

"Okay, well I've got a few things to finish off here and then I'll be on the first plane out of Madrid tomorrow morning."

"Thank you, Cesar, we all appreciate your support and I look forward to seeing you tomorrow. Message me when you're at Madrid airport and I'll be ready to meet you when you land over here."

*****

31

The next meeting they'd planned went ahead on time, two hours later in the hotel meeting room, with Terri again listening in on speaker phone.

"Two things from me. I spoke with Maggie and it's as we thought," said Anna. "The special prosecutor, Hernandez, has set up a court for this later this afternoon. Maggie and I are going to go there shortly, but Greg, I wondered if you would like to come along too?"

"Yes, I'd like that."

"Sam, I'm thinking it might be perhaps better if you didn't come? I know it's highly unlikely because I'll have the wig on, but I wouldn't want anyone, who was watching out for who comes, seeing you and then putting two and two together and realising we're related and I'm not in fact a solicitor," said Anna.

"I agree. No point chancing it," said Sam.

"And bail?" asked Greg. "Do we still think we've got no chance?"

Anna shook her head.

"Okay, my second thing. I talked to Mendez. I think we can almost guarantee that the bail decision has already been made Greg. In fact, he's not even sure he'll be able to get things turned around at the next hearing, which before you ask, will be in a week's time."

"But I thought this Mendez guy was our big bright hope of getting her out of custody?" said Greg. Anna could see his frustration starting to surface, so she spoke calmly when she replied.

"I thought so too, but he's already been looking into the case and even he had to admit they've done a bloody good job at setting Lori up. Yes, he can come in and say she was acting on his and even the President's authority, as regards the investigation into the Foundation, but whatever he says effectively has no bearing on the allegation that she has received a significant amount of money into a bank account in her name," said Anna.

The room went silent as they all absorbed what Anna had just said.

"Not good, not good," said Greg quietly, almost to himself. But then he straightened his back, as though he'd re-engaged with himself as he went back into professional mode. "Right, that's disappointing to say the least. Immediate thoughts people?"

"Can I suggest we don't go jumping too far ahead until we know exactly what we're dealing with?" said Anna. "I've got an idea as a backup, but I need to talk it through with Mendez in person to see if it's even got a chance, so I'm not going to even bother telling you all about it at the moment, as it could be a complete non-starter."

Greg felt his right hand shake. Involuntary reaction to stress was what his doctor called it. He was used to being able to come up with solutions to even the most complex of problems, but even he was struggling to see what he could do to help Lori. He wanted to know more about what Anna had in mind, but he knew better than to ask her about something that she still had in the very early planning stages in her head.

Anna saw his reaction and put her hand on his, to cover up the slight tremble she'd seen.

"As soon as I've got something more concrete to say, I'll bring it to the table."

Greg nodded and mouthed thankyou to her, although it was more for what she'd done, rather than what she'd said.

"Okay, I think Anna's right. We need to do a bit of sit and wait, as frustrating as that is. Let's reconvene tomorrow morning at 8.00am."

As the meeting broke up Anna whispered to Greg, "Is that causing you a problem?"

He looked down at his hand.

"Not really. It's more of a distraction than anything, but I don't like the fact that it might make it appear that I'm not in control. You know? To the team and especially to clients."

"Well, I don't think you've got any worries with the team thinking anything like that, but maybe don't try and hide it. Better they know, so they don't go worrying about it, hey?"

"Sound advice as always, Anna. Thank you."

*****

Pablo Hernandez's flight had landed on time and he had been in Police Headquarters within half an hour of landing.

"Comisario, it looks like you've done a good job landing this one?"

"Gracias, Señor. To be fair it was pretty straight forward given the evidence that we've had sent through, although that said, I'd still like to get some corroboration."

Hernandez had been looking through his case papers and looked up at the officer.

"But this looks like the evidence you have is

overwhelming?"

"Well yes, it is, it's just that…"

Hernandez wasn't liking what he was hearing. Since the road to becoming a judge had started to open up after he joined the Foundation, he had tried to ensure that any case he dealt with was as watertight as it could be.

"Just what, Comisario? She's guilty as hell, isn't she?"

"Well, it looks that way. I would just like some confirmation from the bank, because we have no other corroborating evidence to the bank statements."

Hernandez made a point of not showing any sign of the slight concern he was starting to feel.

"Ah, I see, and I completely agree then. Better to be prepared in case she tries to come up with some cock and bull story at the hearing."

Hernandez saw the look of relief on the Comisario's face, who had obviously felt a little uncomfortable raising the issue with him. It was a useful reminder that even this senior detective was still many levels below the status and influence that he wielded as a state prosecutor.

"Agreed, so, let's get her before the court, shall we? I've arranged something for late this afternoon. That won't be a problem getting a basic set of court papers from your people, will it, Juan?"

The prosecutor saw the policeman's reaction to hearing his first name being used.

"No, that won't be a problem at all, Señor Hernandez. What are your thoughts on bail?"

"A hundred thousand euro isn't an enormous amount of money in the great scale of things is it, Juan, when it comes to bribery, but…." Hernandez paused for a moment, drawing the police officer in closer to him, as though in confidence. "I know what I think, but I'm interested in what you think, Juan. I mean, should we be setting an example of Garcia? To send a message to all the good and honest officers out there, that we won't stand around and let a bent cop mess things up for all the good work they do with the public?"

Gutierrez was a fair man, just as Detective Sergeant Vega had said he was to Lori Garcia. However, whilst that fairness applied to suspects under investigation, he applied in equal measure to the police officers within his command, who were diligent, hard-working and honest professionals.

Hernandez had guessed as much and so wasn't surprised when Gutierrez came back with the response he had hoped for.

"You're right, it's not a huge amount of money, but we need to ensure all our staff know that when we find a bad apple, then we will root them out. I strongly suggest, if I may say so, Señor, that you go for a remand in custody. It will send out a really positive message and negate any risk of her failing to turn up for the court."

Hernandez looked at the officer, as though deep in thought. "You're right. That's very sound thinking, Juan and I'm very happy to go with your idea. I'm actually having lunch with Judge Torres tomorrow. I'll make a point of mentioning you as I hear they're looking at the candidates for the next round of police chief promotions." He winked at Gutierrez, "You can never get your name mentioned too often by those in high places, eh, Juan?"

Hernandez saw the police officer's chest puff up at the recognition he was apparently getting. He then felt his phone vibrate and he checked the screen. 'Frankie.'

"I'm sorry, Juan, I need to take this. State business," he grinned. "Now, I'll leave you to it and I'll see you in court around five."

He'd left the room before Gutierrez had managed to say anything.

"Frankie, two calls in a day? What's up, amigo?"

"Just checking in, that's all, Pablo. I've just had my father on the phone," lied Frankie Rodriguez. "He's wondering where you might be in terms of bail, or are you going for a remand?"

"Nice of him to be interested, but why do you think he's asking about this particular case, as he doesn't usually get you to ring me about my cases?"

Pablo knew he was playing with fire, at least with a little bit of fire, but he wanted to see just what his friend might say.

"I think he's just interested," said Frankie, and Pablo heard just a slight edge to his friend's voice.

A smile crossed Pablo's face. Deep down he'd always suspected the reach of the Foundation went a long way further than he'd ever thought possible. But now he knew. Getting a high ranking GEO officer arrested on corruption charges? Someone in the Foundation had made this all happen. Whether it was Frankie, or Hannah, or maybe even Frankie's old man, Juan Rodriguez, someone in the Palma Foundation had decreed this should happen.

"Frankie?"

"Yes, Pablo?" said Frankie, but he'd heard the change in tone in his friend's voice. He knew Pablo wasn't stupid and so he'd guessed that Pablo had realised what was playing out here. "Oh, Pablo, before we go on. I had an interesting chat the other day with my dad. I probably shouldn't tell you this, because it was something he told me in confidence, but I know you won't go shouting this about."

"Won't go shouting what about?"

"Well," Frankie said, almost conspiratorially, "my dad was at a meeting discussing the possible candidates for the next round of judicial appointments."

"And?"

"Your name came up, mate! Congratulations!"

"What? I mean, it's only at the candidate stage yet, isn't it?"

"Oh, I think we both know that if my father's involved and your name is being talked about, then that means you're very much a shoe-in. That is if all goes well and you don't make any cock-ups in the next few months," said Frankie.

'So that was it,' Pablo thought. *'Get this GEO officer sent down, don't ask too many questions and we'll make you a judge.'*

It was Frankie who smiled this time when his friend didn't hesitate.

"Frankie, that's amazing and please thank your father for all his support and please reassure him that I won't let him down."

Frankie understood his friend's response. It was loud and clear and the extent of his ambition above all else was beyond doubt.

"That's very good to know, Pablo. And the question of bail for the bent cop?"

Now it was Pablo's turn to act out the pretence of confidentiality.

"Now I know you realise I can't talk in detail, but in a case of this seriousness, with the amount of corruption involved? I wanted her remanded from the start. Get the bad apples out of the basket, you know, that sort of thing. But I've also been through due process and asked the OIC, the officer in the case and he's definitely up for her being remanded. Seeing as he's the Head of CID for the Balearics, then I feel it's only right that I should heed his advice, so we'll be pushing for her to be remanded in custody."

Hernandez almost heard his friend take a deep breath. *'Was that relief, or satisfaction at what he'd just said,'* wondered Hernandez.

"That's very helpful," said Frankie. "I'm sure Señora Ramírez will be relieved to know that as well, Pablo. I understand that she was becoming quite distressed about some of the things Garcia had been insinuating."

The State Prosecutor didn't particularly care what any of the Ramírez family thought, just as long as he was at the top of the queue when they announced the next list of high court judges, but nevertheless he played along.

"Well, that's good to hear," said Pablo, with as much feeling as he could muster.

Frankie hadn't missed the lack of empathy in his friend's voice as he logged out of the call and then immediately rang Hannah Lopez.

*****

32

Lori Garcia had attended many court hearings and given evidence on numerous occasions as well, however, this was different. It was the first time she had ever stood in the defendant box.

She had sat in the back of a marked police car in handcuffs, wedged between by two officers as she was driven a short distance, less than two kilometres, from police headquarters to Avendida d'Alemanya, to the courthouse, the Juzgado Primera Instancia #12.

The Primera Instancia court is where criminal cases are first heard by a judge to establish if there is sufficient evidence for the matter to proceed. Lori stood as she confirmed her details to the clerk of the court. She then waited until she was told she could sit down, something she was grateful to hear, as she had started to feel her legs twitch with anxiety.

She looked across at her legal team, Maggie Cruz, her actual lawyer and Anna Martínez, her friend who was purporting to be another lawyer, Anna Dominguez. Immediately behind them was Greg Chambers, the man she loved and who she prayed would make this whole nightmare disappear. He saw her looking at him and he smiled at her. She forced herself to smile back, although she could see right through his smile. It was the same look of helplessness on his face that she could feel taking over her entire body.

Behind Greg, Lori saw another face. It was a woman, although it took her a moment to place her. It was Kat Reyes, the journalist, sitting there on her own. Lori wondered where the younger woman was? The other journalist. She mentally flicked through her head, trying to recall the other journalist's name. Bella? Yes, that was it, Bella Santos. *'At least I'm not completing losing my mind,'* she thought.

Greg saw Lori looking past him, but stopped short of immediately turning around to see who was behind him. Judging by the look on Lori's face it wasn't anyone she was concerned about. He let a few minutes drift by before he casually half-turned and caught sight of a woman in a red coat sitting three rows behind him.

He sat quietly and listened as best as he could to what was going on as obviously the whole hearing was being heard in Spanish. Occasionally Anna would turn her head slightly and tell him what was going on, but within five minutes the judge had banged his gavel and Lori had been told to stand up.

The judge said something in Spanish that Greg couldn't follow and then he said, "El acusado es puesto en prisión preventive."

Greg didn't understand exactly what had been said, but when he heard 'acusado' and 'prisión,' he knew the judge must have said there was enough evidence to proceed and that Lori had presumably been remanded into custody.

Maggie stood up once more and asked if she could speak for a moment with her client and the judge had agreed.

Maggie and Anna stepped forward and huddled around Lori who had sat back down in the defendant's box, more because she couldn't trust herself to stay upright as she tried to take in all of what was happening.

"We're not giving up, Lori," said Maggie quietly.

"No, we're not," said Anna, "but please look after yourself in prison whilst we continue to try to work things through."

Lori was nodding, but Anna was worried she wasn't taking any of this in.

"My boys, Anna, my boys," she said, with tears filling her eyes.

"Try not to worry, Lori. They're okay and they send their love. We've got some of Greg's team out there with them, so they're fine and he's in regular contact with them. Maggie thinks that now that you've been charged and remanded, the ban on visitors and phone calls to you might get lifted. So, hopefully you'll be able to speak to them and see them if you want."

Lori couldn't bear the thought of her boys seeing her inside a prison.

"Just phone calls, Anna, please. At least whilst we try to sort this out. I don't want them seeing me in prison, okay?"

Anna could hear the tension in her friend's voice.

"Yes, understood, Lori."

Then she heard a noise behind her. It was a court officer. He was saying something in Spanish to Greg who had tried to walk across the court floor towards Lori.

"Señor Chambers," said Anna, maintaining her cover, "he says you can't come any closer. You must stay that side of the court."

"Just two minutes. Please!" said Greg to the officer.

Anna also tried to persuade the officer, talking to him in Mallorquin, but he just looked at her and then at Greg and then said firmly, "¡Sin excepciones!"

Greg didn't need Anna to interpret 'No exceptions,'

realising there was no point taking things any further, so he backed away.

Pablo Hernandez was looking on and wondered for a moment who the man was who had been sitting behind Garcia's legal team. He then checked his watch. His flight back to Madrid was in less than an hour and he'd need to be quick if he was going to catch his flight, so he shook hands with the Comisario and made his way out of the building to a waiting car.

Greg started to walk towards the back of the court and saw the woman in the red coat was standing by the main doors. *'Was she waiting for him?'*

He glanced back at Lori, not knowing when he'd be able to see her again. He smiled at her as she caught sight of him. Then he thought he saw something in her eyes. A look. Then she inclined her head, just slightly, but enough for him to notice and to realise she must be trying to get him to go after the woman in the red coat.

He gave the briefest of nods back, lifting his right hand to his lips and then motioning as if to send her a kiss. But when he looked back towards the woman in the red coat, she had gone.

He walked quickly out of the court buildings and stopped. The late afternoon light was failing and it took him a moment to adjust, but then he heard a woman's voice call out in accented English from behind him.

"Are you a friend, or foe?"

He turned and saw her. She was leaning on the wall, just to the right of the court entrance.

"Depends on who you are?" replied Greg. "But the fact you've waited and that Lori seemed to suggest I follow you, then yes, I guess I'm a friend. Greg Chambers," he said. "And you are?"

"Kat Reyes."

"And how do you fit into all of this then, Kat Reyes?"

"You don't know?" exclaimed Kat.

"I wouldn't be asking if I did. This has all been moving along very quickly. So, there's things the police know, and by the police I mean Lori and DI Nino Castilla, and there's things that I'm only just starting to find out."

"So, who are you, Greg Chambers?"

"A good friend of Lori's and someone who wants to help get her out of this mess. So, if you know anything that might help Kat, then I'd be very happy to hear what you've got to say."

Kat slowly nodded.

"You definitely sound like a friend to me. Perhaps if we go somewhere quiet, then maybe I can fill in some blanks for you?"

"That sounds good to me."

There were plenty of coffee shops to choose from, as they walked from Avendida d'Alemanya back towards the centre of the city and Kat eventually pointed to one as they came to it.

"This one should do and we can make sure we aren't overheard."

He looked at her questioningly.

"It's a bit of a long story."

"I've got the time if you have, Kat and better I understand everything than miss something that might turn out to be important."

Kat nervously looked around the café once again.

"You said something about being overheard before. What was that all about?"

Kat told him about the man who had attacked Bella and that he had played a recording of a conversation she and Bella had had not all that long before, when they'd been sitting outside a coffee shop.

"Directional mics," said Greg, more to himself than to Kat.

"What?"

"I'm sorry. He must have used a directional microphone. Easy to use and you can hide them under a newspaper or magazine. You just point them at the people whose conversations you want to hear and it records direct to your smart phone."

"But isn't that illegal?"

As soon as Kat spoke, she realised she was stating the obvious. Anyone who then went and threatened the person they'd been recording was hardly going to worry about the legalities, or otherwise, of listening in to private conversations.

"How do you know about this sort of stuff? Are you an ex-cop or something?" she asked.

"Probably best described as a something," he smiled at her.

"Intelligence services then?"

He nodded.

"But you're not officially investigating the Foundation or Marcos Rodriguez's death?"

"Well, I wasn't and just to clarify, I now run a private security consultancy called 3R, so I'm not here in any sort of official capacity. That said, after the meeting I had today with the Rodriguez family, then I can tell you that they have now asked me to try to establish the true cause of Marcos's death."

"And the old man's death? Eduardo. Do they still think that was just a heart attack?"

"You're right. They're not convinced, but I've probably got zero chance of getting anywhere near the truth of that without someone telling me point blank they gave him something to induce the heart attack."

"What about a post mortem?"

"I'm not well up enough on how you'd go about that, but I'll check it out with Nino."

"DI Castillo?"

"Yes," said Greg.

"He seems like a good guy," asked Kat.

"Yes, definitely a friend. And if you come across her, there's a detective in the local force called Sofi Delgado. You can trust her too."

"Okay, thanks, that's useful to know. What do we do now?"

"We?" said Greg.

"Yes, we! I don't know what I can do to help, but you can use me if you need to for any sort of research."

Greg thought for a moment.

"Have you heard anything about Manny Lopez having some sort of book, a ledger of all the more dubious transactions the Foundation have been involved in over the years?"

Kat shook her head. "No, but I can do some digging around." She saw the look on his face. "And yes, after what happened to Bella and now Lori Garcia, don't worry, I'll be extra careful."

*****

33

The late afternoon sun was coming in through the car windows making Lori squint.

The evening commuter traffic on the city ring road was doing its usual job of slowing everyone's journey home, but for Lori, it was just delaying her arrival at the Centro Penitaciaro de Mallorca.

The police car she was in had been laid on especially by the Comisario, together with a police driver accompanied by a court officer she'd not seen before. They seemed determined to get her into the prison system as soon as possible after the court hearing.

The car slowed and Lori flinched as she saw the entrance to the prison. The court officer sitting next to Lori felt her tense up.

"Getting worried, are we?" she almost spat the words out at Lori. "Well, you've probably got good cause to be scared. Someone's going to make mincemeat out of you, girl!"

The court officer laughed, but Lori dug deep to not show just how vulnerable and yes, how scared she was feeling. She thought about coming back with some sort of tough response, but thought she'd be wasting her time and effort on a woman who probably wasn't going to worry about what she said anyway.

"What's up?" snarled the woman. "Cat got your tongue?"

Lori shifted her back against the back of the car seat. If anything, the woman's taunting helped her hit the reset button inside her head. *'It is what it is,'* she thought. *'You just need to get on and deal with it.'*

Even the court officer suspected something had just happened. She didn't know what, but the woman seated next to her seemed to have changed and now had a very different look about her to the one she'd had when she first got in the car.

"Look, you aren't going to play up, are you? Because if you do, I'll have a reception committee waiting for you and that's really not going to help you, is it?"

Lori knew she'd turned the tables on this woman and just for a moment she thought she'd enjoy taunting her and seeing how she reacted.

"I promise I'll do you a lot of damage before we ever get to your reception committee, Señora, so how about you just be a good girl and shut up and sit there quietly."

This time it was Lori who felt the court officer flinch. It wasn't much, but it was enough to know she'd made her point.

Lori had spoken quietly, so much so that the driver, the same male police officer who had been particularly hard on her in custody, called out, "What's that? What's she saying?"

Lori looked at the court officer next to her and winked, but the look in her eye was enough to make the officer's voice tremble slightly as she replied, "Er, nothing. It was nothing. She was just asking me something about the prison."

"You'll find out soon enough because we're here now, darling," the driver called out. "Welcome to your new home from home."

"Gracias, Señor. Thank you and I'll be sure to remember you."

The driver looked in his rear mirror and saw the look on Lori's face.

"What do you mean by that? You're the one who should be worrying here. My mate reckons you'll get five years."

"Maybe you had better just hope I do!"

"Just get out, get her out of the damn car before I do something I'll regret."

Lori didn't know how it was helping, but standing up to them had given her a burst of energy that she knew she would probably need to hang on to whilst she was inside the prison.

She pulled away from the court officer and walked head held high towards the prison doors. Her two escorts had to hurry to catch up with her before one of the side doors swung open electronically.

A female prison officer was waiting there.

"Someone's in a hurry," she laughed. "Come in, Inspectora Jefe! We've been expecting you, as have a few of our other guests."

*****

The prison was a relatively modern looking facility that took both male and female prisoners on remand and sentence from the courts.

There were a total of fourteen modules, thirteen for men and one for housing women prisoners, with 142 cells in each module and 450 prison staff looking after nearly 1000 male and about 100 female prisoners.

As Lori walked through the door, a guard immediately shouted at her to stop and hold her hands out. The handcuffs were removed from her and handed back to the court officer who, having handed over some paperwork to the duty officer behind a reception desk, left with the police officer through the same door they'd come in.

Lori listened to the duty officer as he went through what was obviously a pre-prepared list of questions for every new inmate. She already knew most of what was being said because when she had been formally remanded, Maggie Cruz had given Lori a rundown on what to expect.

When Lori had heard there were fewer women than cells her hopes had risen that she'd be in a cell on her own. That is, until Maggie told her that the prison had mothballed some of the cells to reduce cleaning costs, but also because a prison review had found that most of the inmates preferred to be housed in pairs, rather than be alone.

"Given a choice, I'd prefer to be on my own," Lori had said to Maggie.

But then she was brought back to the present moment, when she was asked if she wanted to stay in her own clothes, or wear prison clothing. Lori knew she'd be asked this question. It was standard procedure in all Spanish prisons for prisoners to be given the option on what they wore, at least to a certain extent, as clearly, she wouldn't be allowed to keep her high heeled shoes because they would make too good a weapon in the wrong person's hands.

But having changed for her court appearance, Lori was wearing Terri's clothing. They were nice clothes. She looked at them again. *'No,'* she thought, *'they were really nice clothes.'* She knew they'd be too much of a temptation for someone to get their hands on, especially when she'd have to leave them unattended when she was in the shower.

But as well as that, she had a big enough target on her head, without making herself stick out anymore, by wearing an upmarket two-piece business suit.

The duty officer made some notes on the desk top

terminal before him and said something to one of the female prison officers. Lori didn't quite hear what he said, but it was presumably something about her getting an inmates uniform for her. He then said, "You'll get treated fairly whilst you're in here, Garcia, but don't go looking for any favours and don't go starting any trouble. Understand?"

Lori nodded at him.

"I know you're a police officer and I won't presume your guilt by suggesting you aren't one any longer, Señora. However, whilst you may think you know what goes on inside a prison, let me tell you that you may know some, but you definitely do not know everything." He paused as he took a breath in. "So be prepared to learn fast. Play ball with the prison officers and you'll get no trouble from them. Now I probably don't need to say this, but I'm going to anyway. Do not go antagonising any of the other inmates and do not react to any of the baiting you can expect to get. I say this for two very good reasons. One is because it could seriously impact your health and well-being and secondly, because what we do not want is for you to turn up dead on our watch and have the prison authorities all over us like a bad rash. Do you understand?"

"I do understand, Señor and thank you for your warnings," said Lori.

Whilst he clearly had his job to do, she could see he had no malice or ill-feeling towards her in anything of what he had said.

Within five minutes Lori found herself being taken to a waiting room where there were two other female prisoners who were seated on chairs watched over by two new female guards. One of the prisoners was tall, dark and olive skinned. *'A local,'* thought Lori. Whilst the other was younger, darker skinned and had tears in her eyes.

"Finally," said the first woman in Mallorquin. "We've been waiting for you for like, forever. So, you're the bent cop?"

Lori ignored her.

"Do you know what happens now?" said the second woman in English. She was younger than the first woman and in her early twenties. Lori could see she was shaking. Her accent was African and Lori guessed she might be Nigerian, but purely on the basis that English is the national language there and she knew there were a fair number of Nigerian immigrants on the island.

Lori looked across at the first woman, the local. She wasn't into pre-judging people, but the woman looked like she knew her way around the place.

"Are you going to tell us then? What happens now?" asked Lori.

"We've struck out today, but not in a good way."

"What do you mean?" said Lori.

"The screws in here are mostly okay."

"I'm sorry, but I don't understand you," wailed the younger woman.

"Best you learn a bit of Catalan, or Spanish then," said the woman, but still in Mallorquin.

"Give her some slack, will you? Maybe remember what it was like your first time?" said Lori.

"Whatever," said the local.

"First time inside?" said Lori in English to the younger woman.

"Yes, and I haven't done anything!"

"That's what we all say love," said local, but this time in English.

Lori glared at her, then looked back at the younger woman.

"What are you in here for?"

"A man asked me to carry his bag for him through the airport because his back was hurting. Then the police came and this dog starting barking at me. They said it was drugs! But I was just helping him! I'd never met him before."

It was clear that the older Spanish woman understood a lot more English than she had previously let on, as she said, "Are you stupid or what?" She threw up her hands in disbelief. "Jesus, that's the oldest trick in the book and you fell for it? Well, you bloody deserve to be in here."

Lori felt the anger rising inside her, but remembered what the duty officer had said about not reacting.

"Look, you and I know that, but maybe she didn't. Give her a break, will you?" said Lori. "Surely that doesn't take much does it?"

The local looked at Lori and then down at the younger woman. Lori thought she saw something in the Spanish woman's face, maybe something that took her back to her first time in prison.

"Okay, I'll take it slowly and my English isn't great," she started. "The screws..."

Once more she saw a look of confusion on the young woman's face.

"My, you have had a sheltered life, haven't you? Screws? That's what we call the guards. Anyway, like I said. Most are okay. Like the guy on the desk. He's firm and you can't mess with him, but he's fair."

Lori knew enough about how tough prison life could be just from talking with offenders over the years, but she still listened to what the local was telling the younger woman.

"Some of the screws like to have some fun and it's obviously all at our expense, darling. And, if the duty officer isn't looking, they might even sneak in a couple of the guys to come and watch the show."

"Guys?" Lori said.

"The male guards. There's a connecting door and they sometimes let some of them through to see the fun."

"What do you mean by fun?" asked Lori slowly.

The local woman laughed.

"Like now. We're supposed to shower, but I've seen who the screws are and I reckon we're going to get hosed. It's happened to me a few times now, but hey, don't worry, it'll all be over before you know it. Just ignore the men. They've never taken things any further, at least not yet." She regretted what she'd said as she saw the look on the young woman's face. "Forget that, forget it. What I mean is, you just need to let this happen. Let them have their bit of *'sádico'*...?"

She looked to Lori for help.

"Sadistic?" said Lori.

"Yes, let them get off on their sadistic fun, but make sure you stand strong, hold your head high and don't give them the satisfaction of seeing you cry. You can do that later okay, when you're in the cell and no one can see you?"

Lori looked at the local woman and mouthed, *'Gracias.'*

"That's good advice," said Lori and looked at the local, inviting a response.

"Elena," said the first woman, with a nod to Lori.

"I'm Bimpe," said the younger woman. "You say it like Bim and then pay," she explained in a way she'd had to do a thousand times and more before.

"Do as Elena says, Bimpe and you'll get through this," said Lori. "It's not going to be fun for any of us, me included."

"Especially you, Inspectora Jefe Lori Garcia, GEO," said Elena. "You're all over the news, babe, but not in a good way."

"You're a police officer? What are you doing in here?" said Bimpe.

"She's a bent copper," said Elena.

Bimpe looked at Lori in disbelief. "I don't believe that."

"I'm glad you don't," smiled Lori. "But for the time being I've got the same problem as you in proving I'm innocent. What about you, Elena? Are you wrongly charged?"

"Me? No! Guilty as hell, I'm afraid." The three women broke into laughter and only stopped when one of the guards yelled at them.

"Shut up and get your clothes off, Señoras! It's wash time. Come and show us what you've got!"

*****

34

Lori heard the smirk in the guard's voice.
Then she heard Elena whisper, "I'll go first, okay? Just follow my lead."

Lori and Bimpe nodded.

"And remember, hold your head up high and stare them straight in the face!"

The guards watched them as they took their clothes off, seeming to take delight in the embarrassment as they got down to their bra and pants, waving at them to take those off as well.

Lori had carefully folded Terri's clothes and put them on a chair. She then had to dig her nails hard into the palms of her hands, as one of the guards moved alongside her and intentionally tossed the clothes on the floor, before standing back and waiting to see if Lori reacted.

"I see you're a quick learner, Inspectora Jefe," scoffed the guard. "Now ladies, what follows is a time saving project. So just remember this is purely to help in the efficient and effective running of the prison," laughed one the guards.

"So, in other words, don't go complaining to anyone about it, or otherwise, all three of you will find yourselves down here every time I'm on duty," yelled another one. "Now get in there!"

'Head up high,' Lori said to herself as she followed Elena and then Bimpe into the shower room.

There were four more guards already waiting for them as they walked in; two women, who started shouting obscenities at them, whilst two men were just stood, arms crossed, leering at them. Too many for Lori to try to do anything about, especially as she had no way of knowing if either of the other two prisoners would help if she tried to stand up to what was going on.

"Come on, ladies, don't be shy," said one of the male guards; a man in his fifties, with dark black hair and a beard who was wearing a crumpled uniform.

Bimpe began to cry again and Lori held out her hand to her. She felt the younger woman's fingers curl into a ball inside her palm, as she looked for any crumb of comfort.

"We'll start with your backs, shall we? So, turn around ladies and face the other way and get those arms up high now."

It wasn't a request, but an order. Lori didn't know why, although maybe it was because she had at least been able to partially cover the front of her body with her hands, but now she felt even more exposed with her backside to these people.

The three women stood there naked, arms aloft and feeling very vulnerable. Lori heard the noise of the hose opening up, a split second before the jet of ice-cold water hit the middle of her back. The guard was playing the water jet back and forth across the three of them and Lori had to fight to keep her balance against the force of the water. She heard more laughter from behind, as the guards seemed to take delight in watching as the water bounced off the women's buttocks. Lori could feel Bimpe was tensing up and her arms were starting to sag, so she grabbed her hand and held it tight and whispered to her to straighten up and keep looking ahead.

"Turn around now, ladies," yelled one of the women guards. "Time to show off those beautiful bodies of yours!"

Lori heard the laughter from behind her once again. Then another shout, this time from one of the men, "Come on, turn around!"

Lori really couldn't believe this was happening to her. Less than 48 hours before she had been leading a murder investigation into one of the most well-known and influential families on the island and now she was now providing so-called fun to a bunch of gawping prison guards.

Elena seemed to sense what was happening with Lori.

"Don't go doing anything stupid, Garcia. You'll end up getting hurt. The sooner they get a face full of what they want to see, then the sooner the hose goes off, okay? Now, on my count, we all turn around, arms out wide and we look right through them. You too, Bimpe. Ready?"

She heard Lori and Bimpe say, "Yes," but clearly with enormous trepidation of what was to follow.

Elena didn't hesitate, "3-2-1, go!"

The three of them turned as one and stood there, as though they were midway through a star jump. Arms out to the side and legs slightly apart, but with their heads held high and even Bimpe's eyes were bright and fierce.

Lori initially looked straight ahead as Elena had said, but then she let her focus pull back to the six guards she saw before her. There were four women and two men. The men and even some of the women were letching at them, eyeing her and the two other naked women up and down.

Suddenly it was over, as Lori heard one of the female guards shout something. The water jet had been turned off and was being quickly packed away and the two male guards had slipped back through to the men's side of the prison.

A moment later a man in a white coat appeared at the entrance to the showers. He looked at the three women standing there naked and turned to the guards.

"What the hell's going on here? They should have finished their shower ten minutes ago? And why are they all still naked for God's sake? Get them some towels, I haven't got all day to do this."

One of the guards nodded and quickly passed a towel to each of the women who took it and covered themselves up. Lori guessed he must be the prison doctor. She wondered whether he knew if there was anything untoward going on. But if he did, then he didn't let on as he went back into the side room where Lori had originally met Elena and Bimpe.

Elena had been right. The hosing hadn't actually lasted that long, but the jeering and heckling from the guards had made Lori shake with anger at the humiliation they'd been subjected too.

Lori took a deep breath and looked at each of the female guards again. She'd already made a point of looking at the men, but she wanted to be certain she'd remember these women's faces too, promising herself she'd make sure they paid for this, that is, if she ever managed to get out of this hell.

*****

The three women stood there, with their towels wrapped around their bodies waiting for what was going to happen next.

"Okay, time to see the Doc and then a final search," sneered a guard. "You first."

She pointed to Bimpe who then went with two of the guards into the side room to see the doctor, leaving Lori and Elena waiting in the changing rooms. They sat in silence, both dealing with the ordeal they'd just been through. One of the guards came back and took Elena, leaving Lori to await her turn. She wondered about saying something to the doctor. But what was the point? It was only going to antagonise the guards, which was definitely something she didn't wanted to do.

Whether by intent or design she didn't know, but Lori was last to be seen by the doctor. Pushed, or rather shoved, into the side room, she stood as the man she'd seen in the white coat introduced himself.

Dr Aguero, like the duty officer, went through a list of pre-prepared questions, although this time it seemed to be in a more half-hearted manner, making Lori wonder just how interested the doctor was in her medical and mental state.

Lori watched as he made some notes on the papers before him before adding his signature.

"Okay, she's fit to detain."

"Thanks Doc. This way, Garcia."

Lori went with the guard into another room next door, where there was another guard waiting.

"Okay then, one last thing," said the guard.

Lori thought she detected something in the woman's voice.

'What now?'

"Take your towel off whilst we search you."

Lori couldn't stop herself.

"Search me. What for? I'm naked, for Christ's sake!"

"Standard procedure. We don't know what you might have secreted on your person."

'Secreted on your person,' thought Lori. *'Typical bloody legal speak.'*

"Drop the towel and turn around," said the guard again.

Lori tried to reset herself and just get it over with. She turned around and let the towel slip to the floor, but she could feel her body tensing up.

"Now bend over and spread your legs."

Garcia grimaced. She'd known something like this was coming, but it didn't make it any easier, but she did as she was told.

"Wider, Señora."

"You've got to be kidding me?" said Lori.

Surely they weren't going to do an intimate search, an internal examination? Lori knew that legally, she'd have to sign to agree to that or if not, they'd have to be doing it with a doctor, or some other sort of health care professional being present.

"Are you laughing?" one guard said to the other.

"No, I'm not. You see, Garcia, no-one's laughing here. So, just do as your damn well told and spread your legs!"

Lori heard the note of enjoyment in the guard's voice and decided she'd had enough. She stood up, but still had her back to them.

"Look, do you intend to do an intimate search? Because if so, I want to know on what grounds. And in any case, I'll tell you now, I'm not agreeing to it. So, if you want to do it, you're going to have get that quack back in here and the duty officer and then you can explain to me the grounds of why you think you can do it."

Whether or not they needed her to show any sort of resistance was something Lori had time to think about later, but it soon became clear they had decided she was going to get taught a lesson.

The guards exchanged a look, knowing what was going to happen next.

With Lori still facing away from them, they each grabbed one of her arms and pushed her hard to the floor and held her there.

She was pinned down and after struggling for a moment, she stopped trying to push back, knowing it wasn't going to do any good in the long run.

"Does this look like I'm kidding, Inspectora Jefe Garcia?" The words were spat out by the guard. "Just remember you're nothing in here. You understand? Nothing! Whenever you see me on duty, you need to just wait until I tell you to jump. Do you get that, Garcia?"

Lori had no idea why this woman was intent on exacting out some kind of violent one-upmanship on her in the way she was, but for now, she knew this wasn't something that was up for debate, at least not with both her arms pinned behind her back.

"I said, did you get that, Garcia?"

The easiest thing to do was just say 'yes' and move on. Lori relaxed for a moment, having decided she was just going to give in and let whatever happen, happen. Then she didn't really know what happened next, but something came over her. Maybe it was a thought that something like this was going to happen sooner or later, so she made her choice there and then.

"Oh, I got it alright. But just as long as you understand that you just need to make sure that you always have one of your buddies around you too," whispered Lori.

"You what?" said the guard, almost disbelieving what she had heard.

"Which bit didn't you understand?" said Lori, before she braced herself.

Although she was expecting it, it still took her breath away. The guard who had been talking to Lori, punched her hard in the lower back, sending a sharp, stabbing pain through to her kidneys. Then another punch came, quickly followed by another. The other guard joined in, with three vicious punches, before they hauled Lori up by her arms and threw her against the wall.

"Assistance required! Assistance required!" the first guard shouted. "Prisoner's kicking off."

Lori was trying to deal with the pain she could feel around her kidneys, but she somehow managed to turn and take a step forward towards the two guards, but she stopped when she saw two more come into the room, batons drawn.

"On the floor, now!" shouted one of the guards with a baton.

Lori stood still for a moment, but there was no attempt to move in and strike her. *'Different team?'* she wondered. Then she heard the woman shout at her again.

"Down, now, Garcia!"

Lori didn't wait. She knew it was likely to be a tactical message between the guards. They were going to move in on her if she didn't immediately comply and she could end up getting seriously hurt. She dropped to the floor with her legs and arms held apart.

"What happened?" said the baton guard.

"She just kicked off for no reason," said the first guard.

Lori knew then that the baton guard was from a different team. The guard was trying to take in the situation, wondering why Garcia was still naked, especially after the doctor's examination appeared to have finished some time ago according to the prisoner's detention log they'd been reviewing.

Something was wrong here, but she knew better than to question a colleague in front of an inmate.

"Garcia, pick your towel up and get covered up and

go through there," the baton guard pointed to the next room.

Lori did as she was instructed and was escorted through by the other baton guard, where they re-joined Elena and Bimpe.

"Trouble?" asked Elena.

"It was nothing," said Lori, feeling her back where her kidneys had taken a bit of a battering. "Lucky for me, I think a new shift is just starting."

"Yes, I saw that. Most of those guys are okay. Like that desk officer, firm, but fair."

The other baton guard joined them.

"Right, you're officially clean. Collect your uniforms and get to your cells. You've missed dinner, but breakfast is at 7.30am. Oh, and we don't do room service," but this time it was said with humour, rather than any malice. "But here, we've got you some sandwiches to be going on with."

The guard handed out the sandwiches and Lori let Elena sort out who had what, as it looked like she was the one who needed some food inside her more than the other two did.

"See, I told you it wouldn't be too bad and we'd get through it didn't I?" said Elena, although she could see Bimpe was holding her hands together, trying to stop them shaking.

"Moreno! What the hell are you doing back in here?" said one of the new guards cheerfully.

Elena looked at the guard and grinned.

"Wrong place, wrong time, Señora," replied Elena Moreno. "Hey, Señora, who am I with this time? Please don't put me with the bent copper!" she joked.

"Oh, alright then, darling," laughed the guard. "I've got your usual room for you and you can take your new friend here. But no hanky panky, do you hear?"

"Thanks so much," grinned Elena. "C'mon Bimpe.

You're with me, girl."

"I'll look after her," Elena whispered to Lori, "but you watch yourself, okay? There's a team in here who think they run the whole show. They might just want to take a pop at you."

"Thanks Elena, and for taking Bimpe. One thing before you go? Can you tell me anymore about this team and who I might need to watch out for?"

"The main woman in here is Valeria Morales. She's part of a crime gang on the mainland."

Lori knew the name and the gang she ran with who worked out of Benidorm. But she hadn't personally had any dealings with the woman before.

"Okay, thanks."

"And Lori? Basically, just don't trust anyone, including me, alright?"

Lori saw the serious look on Elena's face.

"Even you?" said Lori, feeling a little knot in her stomach.

Elena shook her head.

"Especially not me," she gave a laugh, but it was one filled with sadness, rather than humour. "Look, if they find out I've told you even this, you'll find me in the toilet block with my throat slit. So, I'm sorry, but if I have to give you up, then I will."

Lori understood. It would be dog eat dog in here, or *'Should that be, bitch eat bitch?'* she thought.

*****

35

Jaime Ortiz had made a better job of things like this in the past, but he'd had to act quickly, that meant missing out some of the meticulous planning he had always prided himself on.

However, he was now happy with where he'd got to and with what he had set in place. It had been simple enough for his scammer contact to track down Cesar Mendez. Despite the fact Mendez was a senior intelligence officer in the CNI, the country's national intelligence central agency, the scammer hadn't taken long to locate sufficient details on the dark web to find and identify his place of work.

Ortiz had waited outside a block of non-descript offices and then followed Mendez as he drove home in a dark blue SEAT Arona, a small SUV, that Ortiz had the scammer check the plates on. It was registered to a company, so Ortiz guessed it was probably an agency vehicle provided for Mendez to use in the course of his work.

As Mendez turned into his road and then parked on his driveway, Ortiz slipped the white VW van, stolen a short distance away from Madrid airport, into a parking space on the opposite side of the road.

He wasn't interested in disguising the identity of

the van as he'd make sure it was clean of all his prints before he left it. But as an added precaution, Ortiz had worn a cap and sunglasses, just in case there were any CCTV cameras either near to where he'd stolen the van, or as was more likely, here in the street where Mendez lived in a smart district on the outskirts of Madrid.

He had parked where he had a view of the house and the driveway. There was another car on the driveway; some sort of an estate car, which Ortiz guessed was probably the family car. He had a set of binoculars, but used them sparingly to avoid attracting too much attention, but it meant he could get a better look inside the house. There were two large windows on the ground floor and two smaller ones on the first, which he guessed may be bedrooms. He'd already seen Mendez greet and kiss his wife after he'd gone through the front door and moments later he'd seen two girls come and hug him. They must be the children who the scammer had said were seven and nine.

Ordinarily Ortiz would have sat and watched the house for at least two to three days before making his move. However, Lopez had been quite insistent that Mendez should not get to Mallorca on tomorrow's flight.

'What the lady wants, the lady gets,' Ortiz thought to himself.

He'd had to make a number of assumptions in order to get the job done quickly. With it being a government supplied car, it was unlikely that the woman would have clearance to drive the SEAT. Therefore, whilst there was still an element of risk in what he proposed to do, he'd calculated that the worst outcome might be some collateral fallout, but only if Mendez chose to take his wife and kids to school the following morning in the SEAT.

Ortiz took another look through the binoculars.

Mendez was carrying a bottle of wine to a table where his wife was seated. He sat down as well, presumably to have their evening meal. Ortiz then raised the binoculars a little higher to check the upstairs windows. The curtains on the bedroom windows were now drawn, suggesting both children were now in bed.

He looked at his watch. It was 9.00pm and the light from the sun had all but gone, just leaving the last remnants of its shadows as dusk, the darkest stage of twilight, approached. There would be no need to wait for the full darkness of nightfall, since he was well-practised, when it came to fitting devices to cars, in making the unusual look ordinary.

He unzipped the holdall on the seat next to him. He pulled out a small rectangular device that he'd collected from a Lopez Autoparts site situated on the outskirts of the city where, as in several other sites across Spain and Europe, Ortiz maintained a small covert weapons cache secreted in purpose built safes in the management offices to which only he, Manny and his daughter, Hannah Lopez had access.

Ortiz stopped for a moment to admire the quality of the device. He bought them direct from someone he'd known in the forces who had subsequently worked with ETA, the Euskadi Ta Askatasuna separatist group, until around 2011 when ETA had effectively ceased any further armed activity, leaving the bomb maker looking for a new client.

Ortiz didn't have cause to use such things often, but each time he'd used one of the bomb maker's IEDs, an improvised explosive device, it had delivered a one hundred percent success rate.

It was the size that always surprised Ortiz. It was like the mobile phone makers making their products smaller and yet more powerful and more effective, he thought. The bomb maker seemed able to constantly refine his production process and make his killing devices smaller and smaller, whilst still delivering a devastating blast effect.

Ortiz held it carefully in his hands, even though the bomb maker constantly reassured him that it was never live until the action code was inputted. He knew the bomb maker used a number of different triggers, but this one would activate when the sensor picked up any significant tilt or movement from the car.

The device was no more than six inches long, four inches wide and two inches deep, yet it had more than enough capability to destroy the car he was about to fit it on and because the blast was designed in such a way as to go up, rather than spread sideways, anyone outside a radius of about twenty yards was unlikely to suffer any sort of serious harm. However, this meant anyone inside or close to the car would be killed, or seriously maimed.

Ortiz adjusted his cap, pulling it down over his eyes, but with the light failing, he took off his sunglasses, knowing he was more likely to draw attention to himself at that time of the evening. Instead, he pulled his shirt collar up around his neck to help partially cover his face, before he got out of the van and walked across the road towards the Mendez driveway.

A quick glance around and without hesitating, he dropped to the floor alongside the SEAT, leaving a set of keys he had with him tucked under the front tyre. He had only needed the excuse once, when someone had come out of their front door and demanded to know what he was doing under their car. He'd told the guy he was looking for his keys and the guy actually helped look for them, all whilst Ortiz had still been able to fit what was an electronic tracker on that occasion.

There was no movement from inside the Mendez house and no one else came out to challenge him and nor did anyone pass him in the street. Ortiz rolled onto his side and within seconds he'd fitted the device to the underside of the car; under the driver's seat. A flick of the activation switch and then he was up on his feet and on his way back to the van, without a thought in his head that, because of his actions, at least one person would be dead within the next twelve hours.

Twenty-five minutes later and he was covering his face with his hand as he went through the airport long term car park entrance to avoid the facial recognition cameras. He found a space and although he'd worn latex gloves for all of the time he'd been in the van, he still went through his usual practice of thoroughly wiping down the inside, before he left it knowing it could be weeks before it was found and identified as a stolen vehicle.

Lopez had wanted him back on the island as soon as possible so he had booked on the 10.40pm Iberia Express flight to Palma. He'd used two different names when he booked two single flights, one to Madrid and then a return to Palma. It didn't guarantee anonymity, but any chance of identifying him would need more than a cursory name check of the flight manifests.

He waited until he was onboard the Airbus A320 before he called her.

"It's done?" said Lopez, her voice brusque and business-like.

"Yes, on my way back now."

"Thank you. Why don't you come here after you land?"

Her voice had changed. He could sense the excitement in her. He knew it was the thought of the impending violence and carnage that seemed to stimulate her more than anything he might be able to give to her as a lover. *'But why not?'* he smiled.

"That would be nice. I should be with you in just

over an hour."

*****

Lori stepped through the doorway into the main prison area thinking she knew what to expect. But the level of hostility she heard in the baying and howling that greeted her from the other prisoners, still took her by surprise. She'd experienced it before when she'd visited prisons to see someone, but then of course she'd always known she'd be leaving the prison within an hour or so. This felt very different, and she could feel the hairs on the back of her neck rising up as she tried to control the knot that was forming in her stomach.

She knew she couldn't afford to show any sort of weakness, let alone fear. Sticking her chest out, she walked on, with her head held up high and making sure she stared straight back at anyone she caught in her eye line.

A few looked away as soon as Lori stared them out, but there were more than enough who weren't intimidated. She heard several of the guards make a token effort to stop the prisoners making such a racket, but it was clearly some sort of rite of passage that Lori was expected to go through and besides, she knew there was likely to be worse to come.

It was still a relief to get through it and even more so when the guard stopped by an open cell and Lori found she was at least going to be on her own.

"In you go, Garcia. There's a bell on the inside, but only push it if you really need something okay?"

Lori nodded. "Gracias."

The guard looked at her, unused to being thanked for anything by the inmates.

"De nada. You're welcome."

The guard was about to go, but turned back, "Watch yourself, Garcia. There are people in here who will want to hurt you for no other reason than to get you as a notch on their hit list."

"I know, but thank you again. Please can you shut the door?"

It was early, too early really for lock down, but the guard thought she'd give the woman a break. She nodded and then manually shut and locked the cell door as she left.

The rest of the other prisoners on the women's module were either in their cell, or they were gathered in small groups still out in the main corridor. Seeing the guard had locked Garcia in for the night wasn't lost on one particular group of women. There were four of them, including Valeria Morales, a tall, dark haired woman in her mid-thirties and they were soon crowded around Garcia's cell door.

"Don't think you're going to be able to hide away from me in there, Garcia," said Morales. "You have a good night's sleep, because you're going to need it tomorrow when we see you in the exercise yard."

Lori heard the women move away and did her best to control her breathing. She wasn't scared of a one on one fight, even one against two didn't overly concern her. It would just depend on the other women and how well they could scrap, because this wasn't a place where any sort of rules might apply. What with her police unarmed training and having grown up as the only girl in a family with four brothers, she'd had to learn how to look after herself in vigorous and often over-enthusiastic play fights, so she knew she could handle herself pretty well.

But against three, or possibly four? They were much more likely to be the sort of odds she'd face and therefore, it would be an entirely different type of fight, where she'd need to be in a totally defensive mode just in order to survive.

She lay down on the lower of the bunk beds and

looked up at the wooden slats of the bed above her. She could feel the bruising around her kidneys, where the guards' punches had rained in on her. Tomorrow was likely to be even more difficult. She knew that, so she needed to try to get as much rest as she could. But judging by the shouting and screaming coming from some of the other prisoners in the module, getting any sort of decent sleep wasn't going to be easy.

*****

36

She had only managed to sleep in fits and starts and was awake much earlier than she'd hoped. It had been the cries and howls coming from some of the prisoners that had awoken her, presumably as the medication they'd been given to keep them calm had worn off during the night.

The cell doors had opened electronically a short time later and Lori had sat up on her bed knowing she needed to be ready for anything.

But she had kept herself reasonably fit with trips to the gym and regular runs and even though she was not far off fifty, the self-defence trainers at the GEO Academy gave her no quarter when it came to going through the training routines, so she felt as ready as she'd ever be.

She changed out of the pyjamas she'd been given the night before and into a t-shirt and leggings. There wasn't actually much difference between the two sets of clothing, but she felt fresher in the day clothes she'd put on. They weren't new, but why would they be? However, they did smell clean, albeit with more than a hint of a strong biological washing liquid that she wouldn't let anywhere near her own clothes back home.

'Back home,' she thought. '*Whenever would that happen?*' But she was quickly bounced out of that train of thought by a guard banging on her cell door.

"Get yourself down to breakfast for seven sharp, Garcia."

"Si, Señora. Gracias."

The guard did the same double take as the previous one, not knowing if the police officer was being sarcastic or not, but decided she wasn't.

"De nada. And watch yourself out there."

Lori didn't know if she should be grateful for all these warnings or not, although on reflection, she knew it was much better to be forewarned.

She got on the floor and started doing press-ups. The she rolled over onto her back, being careful to face the cell door, so she wasn't caught out and then started doing sit-ups, forcing herself beyond what she'd normally expect to do in a gym session.

She then looked down at her hands. They'd taken her rings off when she'd been processed at the police station, but that's not what she was thinking about. She was feeling them, flexing them, putting her hands into a fist. There was a good chance she was going to have to fight someone before the day was out, so she needed her hands to be able to manage in a bare fist fight.

She stood up and pulled the mattress off the bed and rolled it up and stood it up lengthwise, jammed on the underside of the top bunk bed frame. It gave her a makeshift punch bag which she could punch into, using the wall as a back stop. Even rolled up it wasn't very thick, so she tested it with a few well-placed practice punches, to make sure she wasn't going to smash her fist into the wall.

With a bit of adjustment and by adding in her pillow as some extra protection, she'd given herself something half-decent to work on to help strengthen and toughen up hands, as well as get her arms and shoulders working.

The fact that no one had stopped by her cell had been good, but as she finished off the last couple of attacks on the punch bag before she put it back in place on the bed, she began to wonder if she was going to be faced with some sort of welcome party, either before, or after breakfast.

She didn't have long to wait to find out. As Lori stepped out of her cell and started walking towards where the guard had said the food hall was, she heard the baying start up again. The module was long and rectangular, with cells along both sides of the walls, with space between the walkways where you could look down onto the ground level below.

Lori walked along an empty walkway, while on the other side of the module she could see the other walkway was busy and the inmates were having to squeeze by each other. She caught sight of Bimpe and Elena. Elena quickly looked around and then glared at Lori, mouthing something at her.

She couldn't tell what it was Elena was trying to say, but it didn't take much working out that she was warning her that something was about to happen.

Lori's senses were on high alert. Her body was tingling with anticipation. She knew she wasn't afraid, although she could feel the tension in her muscles which was doing her best to ease by rolling her shoulders and flexing her fingers.

Then she heard a voice.

"Garcia!"

Two women stepped out of one of the cells that was just ahead of her. She hadn't seen them before. Lori did a quick one hundred and twenty degree glance to her left, to check no one was behind her. It was clear, but as her eyes returned to what was ahead, she caught sight of Valeria Morales on the opposite walkway just looking at her. A cruel smile across her lips.

"Where are you going?" one of the women said. Heavily muscled with tattoos all over both arms, she was short and stocky, whilst the other one was taller, but of a heavier build, probably more used to bullying and intimidating people through her size than necessarily having to actually fight anyone.

"Breakfast, what does it look like?" Lori answered back.

"I don't think you really want to go for breakfast, do you?" the stocky one said.

Lori knew this was a test, to see how she reacted. She decided she wasn't going to mess about with what were obviously just a couple of Morales's foot soldiers, but she wasn't going to do it so everyone, especially Morales, could see.

She didn't change her pace, or say anything, but Lori just turned right into the empty cell where the two women had come from. The stocky woman looked across at Morales for guidance and her boss quickly flicked her thumb in a way to tell the woman to get in the cell and sort Garcia out.

The two women followed her in and then took a step back as Garcia was waiting for them. Whether they'd expected her to be worried, or even scared, Lori didn't know. But she could see they were very much taken off-guard and if they'd have known some of the subtleties of the art of fighting, they might have recognised Lori was now standing in such a way as to protect her fighting arc.

The two women were muttering threats and obscenities at her, but Lori was focused on their body language. There seemed to be no cohesion as to how they were intending to attack, if indeed that was what they were going to do. That was good for her, but bad for them. The two women were standing one slightly behind the other. In some ways that might have been a good tactic, but Lori didn't think they'd planned it that way, to give one another some cover, therefore she was going to make sure it quickly became a weakness, rather than a strength.

Lori took a step back on her right foot, rocking on it as she did. The lead woman, the stocky tattooed one, made the mistake of following her move, as did the woman behind her. Their forward motion meant they were then too slow to react when Lori suddenly sprung forward and threw an arcing right hook at the woman. The punch caught the woman square on the nose and Lori felt the nose flesh squash and the nasal bones fracture, leaving blood pouring down the woman's face, whilst the force of the punch sent her flying backwards into the taller woman behind who lost her balance and fell to the floor.

Lori was on the taller one in a moment, knowing she had to seize her chance. She punched her hard in the face as she desperately tried to get Lori off her. She was clearly strong and wasn't giving up easily, but Lori hit her again as hard as she could with a straight right punch to the head, followed by another right and then a left jab to the face.

"Stay down, Señora, if you know what's good for you."

But the stocky woman, the first one, wasn't going to give up either. Wiping the blood from her mouth, with her nose looking a very different shape after Lori's punch had rearranged it, she managed to get to her feet.

"Who do you think you….."

She tried to finish, but Lori wasn't about to wait to hear what she was going to say. Lori arched her back and launched a flying kick at the woman's head. She was only wearing soft plimsoles, but Lori's feet were tough from years of road running and this was an unarmed combat technique she'd perfected over time.

The kick caught the woman just under the jaw, so with the upward force the kick literally took her off the floor and launched back against the cell wall, where she fell to the floor.

Lori was breathing heavily and her knuckles were bleeding, but she'd got through it, just. But it had confirmed in her own mind that dealing with any more than two was going to be very difficult, especially if they had a better idea of fighting than these two.

Lori looked down at the women. The were both out cold. She checked they were breathing and their airways were clear, then shook her head, wondering how and why her automatic care button had somehow kicked in when these women had clearly meant to do her some serious harm.

She rinsed her hands in the sink, before walking back out of the cell and onto the walkway, where a crowd was waiting expectantly on the other side. She saw the look of surprise on Morales's face and Lori even managed to smile at her before she carried on heading towards the food hall.

She could hear a few murmurs from the rest of the crowd and even a few handclaps of applause, as clearly not everyone in there was a Morales supporter, although then again, she thought, *'No one's likely to come to the aid of a GEO cop anytime soon.'*

*****

Greg had arranged for everyone to attend, or dial into, a 9.00am meeting at his hotel. Penny Hastings had arrived early to help set things up and as Greg helped himself to a coffee, he looked on as Penny dialled Terri's mobile to link her in by conference call from her apartment in Portixol.

"Morning, daughter," said Greg cheerfully, as he heard Terri's voice over the Telcom phone. "Have you got Tommy and James with you?"

"Just Tommy. James is already out and about, but Sam knows more about that," said Terri.

Greg heard Tommy call out, "Morning, Boss."

He smiled. He'd never asked to be called 'Boss' by any of them, but Tommy had called him that from Day One when he'd become the first and now the longest serving employee of his fledgling new 3R company, Risk Reduction and Resolution. Now, over twenty years later, the company had been rebranded 3R International, after Terri had proposed a change to more accurately reflect the extent of their global work portfolio.

"Morning, Tommy. Thanks for getting across here so quickly. Are you all sorted and settled in?"

"Yes, Boss," said Tommy. "We're both up to speed on what's happened and we're all good to go when you need us."

"That's great." He turned to the rest of the team in the meeting room.

"Now where are we with Mendez, Anna?"

"I'm going straight to the airport after this. He texted me first thing. I've got his flight number and he should be landing in about forty five minutes."

"Good. Maggie, can you remind us again about the next court hearing?"

"It won't be for a week, Greg. But I've got some good news. They've definitely lifted visiting restrictions and Lori will be able to make and receive phone calls from this morning."

"That's great. I'll tell her boys and let's get a visit organised to get into see her. I know she doesn't want her boys going in, but I'd like to see her."

"Me too," said Anna.

"I can set that up," said Maggie.

"Sam?" said Greg.

"I've got some feelers out on finding out more about this Jaime Ortiz, together with anything we can track down about the more dubious dealings of the Palma Foundation."

"And anything about this book? The ledger?"

"Top of my priority list, Greg."

"Good. Oh, I've also asked Kat Reyes to do some digging around the ledger too, so I hope that's okay?"

"Yes, of course. Although I think anything we find is probably going to be word of mouth stuff, rather than anything concrete."

"That's all it needs to be. After all, we're not likely to be taking any of this to a Court. It's a means to an end," said Greg. "So, what's James up to?"

"I've sent him out on plot to sit up on Hannah Lopez. It's a long shot, but I want to know who she's meeting and where she goes."

"Anything so far?"

"Maybe. A car turned up at her place late last night and I mean late. It was sometime after midnight. James got the plate and we're trying a number of sources to get it checked."

Maggie listened in, wondering who these sources might be that Sam was talking about, as she knew that checking car registration details wasn't something that could be done quickly by anyone outside of the usual law enforcement agencies, at least not legally.

"I'm assuming that because you've not mentioned it, he couldn't tell if it was a man or a woman?"

"You're right. He's in the back of a van and he only got a side view. So, what with that and the poor light, he could only just make out that it was just one person in the car."

"Maybe he'll have better luck in the daylight if they come out today," said Greg.

"Guys!" Terri suddenly called out, an urgency in her voice. "Have you got a TV there?"

"Yes," said Penny, picking up the remote to a 42" flatscreen.

"You'd better turn it on and quick! I've just seen something on the Spanish news that does not look good."

*****

37

Penny flicked the remote until she found the La 1 channel, Spain's principal public-service television network.

Although the broadcast was in Spanish, the pictures showed a car, at least the remains of a car, that looked to have been literally blown apart outside a house in a tree lined avenue.

Greg saw the word 'Madrid' on the teletext going across the bottom of the TV and looked towards the others for help.

"What's it saying?"

Anna was taking it in, as was Sam and Maggie Cruz.

Anna spoke first, "It's a suspected terrorist bomb attack in a quiet Madrid suburb this morning. It was an attack on a car just after eight o'clock. The police believe there to have been one fatality, the driver, who they think was going to work. He's got into the car and then the bomb's exploded as he's turned off his driveway and into the road."

"Tilt switch," muttered Greg, and Sam nodded, knowing that the movement of the car dropping down off the driveway onto the main road would be sufficient movement to activate the tilt switch to detonate the device.

"He's yet to be named; however, police sources suggest he may have been targeted because he is a member of Spain's...," she paused, a look of concern appearing on her face, before she continued, "...of Spain's national intelligence service."

"Shit!" said Greg.

The room had gone very quiet.

"I know we're all adding two and two together and making four here," said Penny. "But it might not be Mendez."

"True," said Greg. "So we need to find out. And quickly!"

"I'll ring Martin and see what he knows," said Anna.

"If it is Mendez, then this really ramps things up," said Sam. "If they're prepared to take out a national security officer then we really need to be on our guard."

"And how the hell did they know he was involved and that he was getting on a flight to come here?" demanded Greg.

Anna had been about to push the dial button to Martin Carruthers in London, when she put the phone down.

"Other than the people around this table, only three other people knew Cesar Mendez was Lori's contact at the CNI. That was obviously Lori herself, Mendez and the only other person was Nino Castillo."

"Hang on, Anna, what are you saying?" said Greg.

Anna knew who had given up Mendez's name.

"Maggie," she said quietly. "What have they got over you?"

Maggie Cruz's face had gone pale and her whole body seemed to have shrunk.

"I don't know what you mean."

"We know these people can manipulate in a way that makes it very hard to refuse something, even if it results in the death of someone."

"I didn't know they were going to kill him," Cruz blurted out. "They just wanted to know what Lori had said to me."

No one spoke. They didn't need to. Mendez had been the big hope to help turn everything around and get Lori out of prison and put an end to the ridiculous sham of the bribery charges.

Cruz slumped into a chair. "I'm so sorry, so sorry. They've never asked for anything before, but they said if I didn't tell them, then they'd…"

"They'd what?" asked Anna, gently.

"They'd release a video and put it all over the social media," sobbed Cruz. "It would ruin me."

"I'm guessing they've compromised you at some stage?" asked Sam. "Yes?"

Cruz nodded, tears streaming down her face. "I met him through a dating agency. He said he was a foreign currency finance trader and I just fell for him. He seemed perfect, but then all of a sudden, after we'd been going out for about a month, something horrible happened and then I never saw him again."

"I don't need the lurid details, but presumably they've filmed you in bed with him?" said Sam.

"Not just him….." said Cruz quietly. "I don't even remember any of it. We'd been out together one evening and everything had seemed fine. Then all I remember is that I woke up in a hotel room the following morning with a blinding headache and with no recollection of what had happened. I tried calling him, but his phone was dead and after that I never saw him again. At least not until the video appeared on my email. Then I had a call from a woman who told me not to worry and she said they were sorry this had ever happened. It had all been some sort of terrible mistake and that she'd try to help me from then on if she could."

"What was this woman's name?" asked Anna,

although she had a good idea what Maggie was going to say.

"It was Hannah, Hannah Lopez."

Greg couldn't help himself as he slammed his fist down onto the table, making Maggie jump.

"And did she help you?" asked Anna, calmly and gently, trying to settle the lawyer.

Maggie was wiping the mascara that was now running down her face. "Yes, she was great and has really helped boost my career, giving me advice and new client contacts to get me set up on my own. I'd even managed to block out the video and those horrible, horrible images out of my mind and they've never asked me for anything before."

She went quiet. "Not until now. Oh my god, I'm so sorry, but I could never let that video get out. Never!" She started trembling, and then shaking, before she rushed towards a side door, to the toilet, barely getting inside the door before they heard her vomiting.

"I'll go and sort her out," said Penny.

"Sounds like a classic set-up," said Sam. "Some sort of date rape drug, probably GHB or Rohypnol. Compromise her, then help her, that is, until they want something."

"It shows the extent the Foundation is prepared to go to secure influence across a whole range of people," said Anna. "And that doesn't happen without some sort of deep planning to get someone, either one of their own supporters, or someone like Maggie over whom they have some sort of hold, into a position of power so that they might be able to help the Foundation at some future stage. It's impressive, I have to give them that."

"I can't help feeling just a bit sorry for her," said Terri.

"I know what you're saying," said Greg. He knew from what had previously happened to his daughter, that she understood more than most the effects of a date rape drug on the body, "but it doesn't escape the fact that what she did has led to a man's death, someone whose help we could really have done with."

Penny popped her head out of the toilet door.

"She's asking what you're going to do with her. She says she'll do anything. Give herself up to the police, or anything else you want her to do."

"We really need to turn her in," said Sam.

Greg held up his hand.

"Let's just pause and consider this for a moment, shall we?"

"What are you thinking?" said Anna.

"Well, first things first. Hannah Lopez has clearly acted on the information Maggie has given her. That suggests they are either very confident that she won't say anything, or….," he paused. "Ask her where she stayed last night, Penny."

The toilet door closed and they heard voices before Penny opened the door again, this time with a dishevelled looking Cruz.

"I went to my parents' house. Why?"

"Greg, do you think they're going to go after her?" said Sam.

"Loose ends," said Anna, quietly.

"What do you mean, loose ends?" said Cruz.

"Sam, can you get Nino to covertly check Maggie's address, especially her car?"

"Oh my god, oh my god!" cried Cruz. "You think they're going to kill me?"

Sam didn't see there was a lot of point in trying to play this down. The Foundation had already used and abused Cruz and now she was of no more benefit to them, there was every chance they'd get rid of her.

"Maggie, we can't discount it, so we'll put an alarm in your apartment and give you a panic button that will get you help very quickly, okay?"

She nodded, although clearly didn't look completely reassured.

Sam continued, "Now, do you have any photographs of this man?"

"No, he always said he wanted to take the photos and if he did a selfie of us, it never came out properly. I used to tease him about being such a crap photographer...," said Cruz, suddenly realising what she had just said and more importantly, what it meant. "He was doing all that on purpose, wasn't he?"

"Yes," said Sam. "Okay, I think we're beginning to get the picture now, Maggie. We need you to sit down with Penny and talk her through everything you did with this man, do you understand?"

"Everything?"

"Yes, I mean everything, from your first date, to when you first went to bed with him and everything thereafter. Penny, you got that?"

Penny nodded. "Come on, Maggie, let's get you a coffee and freshened up. Greg, can we use your bedroom, perhaps it's best if we have some privacy?"

"Of course, of course," said Greg, knowing Penny was also making sure Maggie wouldn't overhear anything else the team might be talking about.

*****

"Where does this leave us now?" said Greg.

"I've just phoned the prison to ask how you go about arranging visits and phone calls, and for a visit, you just turn up and book in, simple as that," said Terri.

"You're Spanish is coming on then, Sis," teased Sam.

"Well, I have to admit," Terri laughed, "it took a while. But, hey, I got there and that's why I was watching the news on La 1, to improve my lingo."

"What about a telephone call?" asked Anna. "Especially from a lawyer."

"Sorry, I didn't ask about legal calls, but phone calls can be booked through the main switchboard."

"Let's get a call in then," said Greg. "She's not going to be happy, but we need Lori to know we see this as a setback rather than a disaster."

"I'm on it," said Terri.

"Good job you were watching the news, Terri," said Anna, coming back into the room after making her call to Martin Carruthers. "Because sadly, Martin has just confirmed the man in the car was Cesar Mendez."

Anna looked for any sign of the hand tremble from Greg that she'd seen the previous day, but this time there was none.

"Okay, but we presumed the worse anyway," said Greg. "So, there's nothing to really change our mindset here. We've got a bunch of actions we've got to do and I hope Terri can get an early call into Lori for us, as I'd really like to know how she's doing."

Terri shouted out, "Call booked for 11.00am this morning."

"That's quick. I was expecting it to be later, but it'll be great to talk to her. Now, Anna, what was it you were going to speak to Mendez about? And you said you had an idea of some sort of plan?" said Greg.

"It was a possible proposal for us to consider and then action if and only if, it was absolutely necessary," said Anna.

"Go on," said Greg.

"Now this is still very much my early thoughts, so please hear me out before you say anything, especially as I haven't even mentioned it to you, Terri."

"Whatever it is, I'm up for it if it'll help Lori, Anna."

Greg smiled as he heard his daughter blindly volunteering without knowing anything about what Anna was about to say.

"I didn't think for a moment you wouldn't want to

help Terri, but what I have in mind will not be easy," said Anna.

"What are you thinking, Mum?" said Sam, who rarely called his mother, mum, when they were in a work setting.

"I think under ordinary circumstances, Lori could take at least a week on remand in a prison, without it being too much of an issue."

She raised her hand when she saw Greg was about to say something.

"Hear me out, Greg. She's fit, healthy and tough, even if someone in there might have a go at her just for being a police officer."

"I sense there's a 'but' coming," said Sam.

"I'm worried that with the trouble the Foundation has gone to get Lori locked up, to kill Mendez and then to possibly try to get rid of Maggie Cruz, then they may think nothing of going after Lori whilst she's in prison." Anna continued, counting the three issues off on her fingers.

This time she did see a slight tremor from Greg's hand.

Sam spoke first, "The Centro Penitenciaro isn't a high risk prison, but you've got a point. For the right incentive, which inside is usually drugs, someone could take a pop at her."

"What if she's in solitary?" piped up Terri.

Anna looked at Sam, who took his cue.

"She wouldn't be in there for twenty-four hours a day, Terri and that means someone could still get at her when she was taken out for exercise, or when she's in the shower block."

"Wouldn't she be accompanied by prison officers all the time though?" said Terri, but she didn't wait for an answer. "You're insinuating that one or more of the prison officers could be on the take?"

"Either on the take, or just even subject to coercion of some sort themselves. You know? They'll be told to turn a blind eye to this, or that, or otherwise one of their family will get hurt. It's that sort of thing," said Sam.

"Understood," said Terri. "Sorry, Anna, I'm interrupting, carry on."

"That's okay, Terri, because you, more than any of us, need to understand all of this, because what I'm proposing is that we get you in there to give her some back up."

Anna sat back and waited for them to take in what she'd said. And she didn't have to wait long, as Terri didn't hesitate.

"Sounds good to me, but I guess I would need some sort of background story, or whatever you guys call it?"

"Thank you, Terri, I knew you'd go for it, and yes, we'd sort you out a back story," said Anna. "Greg, Sam, what do you think?"

Greg wasn't sure what to say for a moment. He'd been that person who'd been sent into prisons to get information or protect someone. But he'd been trained for that sort of thing and understood the considerable risk and danger. His daughter was tough, and an ex-soldier, so he knew she could handle herself. But this was undercover work and deep undercover at that.

"I'm struggling a bit on this one, trying to separate this all out. Maybe I'm too emotionally connected because of Lori and Terri? Let me think about it, but, Sam, what do you think?"

"Guys, you know I've managed U/C jobs before and putting someone inside a prison isn't anything new to me, so it's certainly feasible. But, and it comes with one hell of a 'but,' because Terri, as far I know, you haven't done any sort of U/C work of any kind. Is that right?"

Greg shook his head. He was sure his daughter

hadn't done anything either.

"You're right, mate, I haven't," said Terri.

"But that's not a complete deal breaker, because, and maybe more importantly," said Sam, "to even get this started you'd usually have a big chunk of inside help for things like background documentation and computer records. So I don't mean to sound defeatist, but in practical terms," and he held up his hands, "without Mendez and unless you've got a trick up your sleeve, how are you going to get this idea off the ground?"

Anna smiled. Her son thought he knew something about her past in the intelligence service and even what she'd told him had at times been uncomfortable to explain. However, there was a lot more in her previous life within MI6 that she couldn't tell him about, because it was either still classified or, was something she'd rather he didn't know, for fear of possibly damaging the view he had of her.

"You're absolutely right, Sam, it is going to be a bit harder without Mendez, but I've already spoken to a couple of other contacts to sound out one or two possibilities."

"So maybe not one, but two tricks up your sleeve then, Anna?" grinned Greg.

Sam just looked at his mother and shook his head, suddenly realising he might not know as much about her, as he had thought.

*****

38

The guard stood in the cell doorway and banged on the door. It was the same one who'd told her about breakfast.

"Do you happen to know anything about two inmates being badly beaten up this morning, Garcia?"

"No, Señora. Why would I?" said Lori.

"Because we have someone saying they saw you going into a cell followed by two of Morales's enforcement girls. They were just a bit surprised to see you walking out, seemingly unharmed, rather than the other two."

"Sorry, I don't think I can help you."

"Be careful, Garcia. We don't mind if you knock off a few of Morales's thugs, in fact you can be our guest, but be warned, she won't take it lying down, okay?"

"Again, thank you for the advice."

"You're welcome, and Garcia?" Lori looked at her. "Maybe wash your hands, you've got blood coming through on your knuckles again," said the guard, with a grin.

Garcia looked at and flexed her hands.

"Gracias, and Señora? I wouldn't say they were that badly beaten up," said Lori, with a smile.

"Maybe not, but just enough to send a message, eh?"

said the guard, with a wink. "Anyway, I've got a phone call for you at 11.00am. I think it's your brief. Stick close to me and I might just be able to get you down there and back in one piece."

"Gracias," smiled Lori, as she followed her out of the cell.

This time she noticed the baying was considerably less. Whether it was the presence of the guard, or the mob were regrouping after the events at breakfast, Lori didn't know. But it was a relatively quiet and peaceful descent down the stairs to the relaxation area and the telephone rooms.

"There's no specific time limit, just don't take the piss, okay?"

Lori nodded to the guard and waited till the door had closed before she spoke into the phone.

"Hello?"

She was expecting it to be Maggie Cruz.

"Lori, it's me."

"Greg! Oh, my darling! It's so good to hear you. Are my boys okay?"

He smiled. They were always the first thing she thought and cared about, and it seemed to settle her when he said he'd been in regular contact with them.

"They send their love and will come and see you, but only if you want them to."

"Tell them I love them with all my heart, but I don't want them coming here," she paused. *What if I don't get out?'*

"I will, my love and they'll understand." Greg took a deep breath. "There's something else I need to tell you, but it's not good news I'm afraid."

She heard the edge in his voice and knew something was wrong.

"Whatever it is, just tell me. After the past couple of days, I don't think there's anything else that could be so bad."

Greg wasn't so sure that what he had to tell her wasn't actually right up there with all the other crap she'd had to contend with.

"There was a car bomb this morning. In Madrid."

She knew right away what that meant.

"They got Mendez! And it was definitely them, The Foundation? Jesus! How on earth did they know about him?"

"It was Maggie Cruz, so yes, we're pretty sure it was them."

He didn't have to explain about Maggie, as Lori had already guessed.

"They had something over her then?"

"Yes," said Greg. "She was compromised a few years ago. Usual thing, a porn video. But since then, they've kept out of her way. In fact, they've gone the other way, sucking her in even more by giving her career a major helping hand. You know the sort of thing, pushing new clients her way, networking and promoting her name."

"Once they get their claws in to someone they really go for them. Poor Sofi, she'll be devastated when she finds out," said Lori.

"Good point. I hadn't thought about her. Not her fault, but I'll get Sam to drop it to her gently. In the meantime, Penny is debriefing Cruz to see what, if anything, we can get from her."

"Are you going to turn her over to the police?"

"No, at least not yet. I think we're better off keeping things under wraps, plus we think they'll try and take her out as well."

"I suppose I should tell you. I had my own visit this morning and before breakfast too."

Greg thought he almost heard her chuckle.

"Are you okay?"

"I'm fine, bruised knuckles, but they're not. Anyway,

the guards were worse last night."

"What?"

"Yes, seems there's one of the teams who have a bit of a reputation to dish out some punishment beatings when they fancy it. They'd be one reason I really want to get out of here. To sort them out. But the rest of the screws all seem pretty fair."

"Screws, eh? Sounds like you're settling in already. Don't get too comfortable in there now, will you?"

"There is absolutely no chance of that my darling and besides I have another reason to get out. I'm missing you so much."

"I know, me too, very much so."

They both went quiet for a moment. He could hear her breathing down the phone. She was taking deep breaths and holding them for a while before exhaling. He knew she was trying to keep herself calm, but suddenly her breathing quickened as she lost control.

"But Greg, without Mendez, how am I ever going to get out of this?"

He could hear it in her voice. The first real signs of panic. She might be putting a very brave face on things up until now, but it was clear that this latest piece of news had really got to her.

She needed some sort of uplift and quickly, but he didn't want to tell her anything about what Anna was planning, just in case they couldn't pull it off.

"Look, we're working on a number of things at the moment. We're trying to get into what the Foundation is all about to find a weakness we can attack and there's a couple of things I can't go into on the phone, but I'm really hopeful we'll start to make some progress soon Lori, so please try to stay focused on what you're facing in there."

She felt herself becoming calmer as she made the conscious effort to slow her breathing. She took in a deep breath, feeling as though it went down past her lungs and into her belly, then she held it there for the same amount of time, about five seconds, before slowly letting it out. She was well practised in this and not just from yoga, but from her firearms training. It was amazing how quickly her body reacted to what she was doing and with it came a calmness, allowing her to refocus.

She knew Greg would be trying everything he could do to help her, so she just needed to get on with what she had any sort of control over and that was dealing with what was going on inside the prison.

"I know you're doing everything you can my love. Please don't worry, no sorry, that's a stupid thing to say. What I mean is, I can cope in here, that's what you don't need to worry about. Okay?"

"I know you can, but please take care."

"I will, I promise."

"There's something else, Lori. From what we can tell, it seems that whenever the Foundation have loose ends, they look to tidy them up, and permanently."

Greg let the words sink in.

"So that's why you think they were looking to find Cruz?"

"Yes," said Greg.

"You think they may try to do more than just get someone to give me a beating, don't you?"

"I think it's possible, yes."

"But why go to the trouble of having me arrested on some made up charges? Why not just get me taken out on the street, like Mendez?"

"To be honest, Lori," said Greg, "I don't know. Possibly because the murder of a police officer would bring too much interest down on them?"

"Whereas a bent cop, killed in prison by another inmate ….." Lori's words trailed off.

"….just looks like a vengeance attack," said Greg.

"Okay, in that case, can you get Nino to look into a Valeria Morales for me?"

Greg heard a definite change in her voice. It was brighter, more energised. Lori felt it as well. Rather than the threat of someone trying to kill her further dampening her spirits, it seemed to have boosted the adrenalin in her body. She was now back into fight or flight mode, and there was no question as which one it was!

"I know the name, but I've never dealt with her. I know she's part of a crime gang on the mainland, but it would be good to know the likely extent of her influence."

"I'll get on to Nino straight away," said Greg.

Lori saw the guard at the window, motioning to her to end the call.

"I need to go, they're calling time's up."

"Okay," he said. "My turn to sound stupid now. Please take care in there."

"I will. Love you, my darling."

"Love you too," said Greg.

*****

Hannah could tell by the look on his face that her father had seen, or at least heard the news by the time she went to see him. Manny Lopez waited until the private nurse had left his room before he spoke and when he did, there was no disguising the anger in his voice.

"Hannah, I'm not even going to ask if you sanctioned this, because it has all the hallmarks of Jaime Ortiz's work all over it!"

She stood there, unsure if her father actually wanted her to reply to the statement he'd made or not.

Lopez knew his daughter was no fool, but he worried about her reckless streak, something she'd inherited from her mother.

"My question is, why, Hannah? Why did you see this as necessary? You must have known the consequences of taking down a national intelligence officer?"

"It was something that had to be done, Papa. Mendez was about to leave for Mallorca, and I didn't know how much he knew about us."

Her father gazed out of his bedroom window, taking a moment to think about what to say to her. She needed to learn from what he saw as errors of judgement, because he knew he wouldn't be around for too much longer to tidy up after her.

It wasn't that he was necessarily averse to the tactics she'd used. Far from it in fact. Manny Lopez had been running the Foundation almost singlehandedly from its inception and there had been occasions when the end had, at least in his view, justified the means, even when that meant certain people had to disappear, forever. However, he did sometimes wonder whether he might have kept the Foundation free from corruption if his wife had still been around. But she wasn't and he still felt the heartache as though it was yesterday. Losing her, as she'd tried in vain to give birth to their second child, who also hadn't survived, had left him without the balance she had given him in his life. Since then, he'd had no one and not even his three founding partners were prepared to stand up and tell him when he was doing something wrong, something his wife would not have approved of.

He looked back at his daughter.

"Did you at least consider getting Ortiz to grab him and interrogate him? I know the end result may have had to have been the same, but you might now know more about what he, or the CNI knew."

She hated it when her father was able to pick her up on something. The problem was, as in this case, he was rarely wrong. She hadn't thought about it, primarily because of the time pressures to get Ortiz across to the mainland to set up the hit.

He saw the look on her face and knew he'd made his point and there was no need to go on. What was done, was done. Now he just needed to know that she was fully focused on what she intended to do next.

"Okay, I gather that's a 'no' then. Okay, then what now? Any more loose ends?"

"Maggie Cruz," said Hannah.

Her father lifted an eyebrow.

"The brief," said Hannah, "the one who told us Garcia was working with Mendez on this."

"Isn't she watertight? You've got that video with her and Ortiz, haven't you?"

"Yes, Papa, but…"

"But you think she's going to roll over?"

"She might, especially now she knows she's an accessory to Mendez's murder."

"You have a point, but you're in danger of turning this into a blood bath, Hannah and that will have the cops poring all over us."

"But we still have contacts in the police, don't we?"

"Yes, but I'm not even sure they've got enough clout to keep the dogs off us if there's too many bodies."

She didn't often ask him for direct advice these days, but now seemed as good a time as any.

"Papa? What should I do?"

"With the lawyer, Cruz?"

"Yes, Papa?"

"Leave her alone, at least for now. She's got little she can give away."

"Okay, Papa. Anything else?"

"I'm going to call in a favour from someone. It should help get rid of another issue, but without any comeback on us."

"Garcia?"
He smiled. His daughter knew him too well.
*****

39

Anna knew that without being able to get Mendez's help, then what she had in mind was going to be even more difficult to pull off.

She had already made some headway with the people she had already spoken with, even before Mendez was killed, but she needed to talk to the same people again, to see if there was another way, now she had lost the option of using Mendez.

"Anna, I don't speak to you for something like thirty years and now two calls within twenty-four hours?" laughed Lucas Iglesias, before the tone in his voice changed. "But I guess you're calling because of the CNI guy, Cesar Mendez?

"Yes, I am, Lucas."

She wasn't sure whether or not she was surprised that Iglesias knew Mendez's name. She'd met him almost forty years ago. They'd been working together on a joint British and Spanish Security Services operation and kept in contact after that. Then later, after she was 'retired' from MI6 having fallen pregnant with Sam, and she'd transferred to the Foreign and Commonwealth Office, the FCO, in Madrid, they'd had the occasional lunch. However, they'd lost touch after she met Luis and later moved to Mallorca.

"It was too much of a coincidence after our conversation yesterday, so I made a call to an old friend to see what I could find out."

"And?"

"Well, if nothing else, amiga, you need to tread very carefully. It seems there are enough supporters of the Palma Foundation to make things very difficult for you, as I think you probably already know, by the way they have your Señora Garcia incarcerated."

"Okay, that's the bad news, but have you got anything more positive, Lucas?"

"Yes, yes, of course, Anna. I just don't want you thinking this will be anything like easy."

"Oh, don't worry, Lucas, I'm under no illusions at all about that."

"Good, but it's not impossible either, my dear."

She smiled. He was old school. Always a gentleman and although there had been an attraction between them many years before, when they'd been working together undercover, they'd both known the last thing they'd needed had been any sort of a relationship between them, other than a professional one.

"So?"

"Like you, I still have some friends within the Service," Iglesias paused.

Another smile crossed her lips. *'How on earth did he know she was back working with Martin Carruthers at MI6?'* But she decided to let that go and just listen to what he was saying.

"Okay, you spoke to me yesterday about getting a back story dropped into the judicial system. Well, my contact says it is achievable. It just won't stand up to too much scrutiny. But I don't think you need perfection, do you?"

"No, not at all. I don't see this lasting more than a few days, because if we haven't sorted things out by then, well, let's just say that if we're not in trouble now, then we really will be if we don't get an early resolution."

"I understand. Now, my contact is a very old friend." Anna noted that he hadn't specified his friend by using he or she. "So, they are doing this as a favour, Anna, but it's a very big favour and…"

"They want something in return?" said Anna. She knew only too well that this was how things often happened in the security services world. "But you need to know, Lucas, that I'm only on the periphery these days. I'm in more of a consultancy position."

"That may be so, Anna, but you still have friends in very high places, yes?"

"Some, yes," she agreed.

"My friend would like an off the record conversation with your friend, Señor Carruthers."

Anna thought for a moment. She didn't like asking for help from Martin and not just for fear of compromising him, but every time she went to him for help, it gave him another ace card to hold over her. But she needed Lucas and his friend to get the operation off the ground. She could use an outside source, but breaking through the security firewall of the Spanish Judicial system would take time and that was something she, and certainly Lori, didn't have.

"I'm sure that's something I could ask Martin. Presumably your friend wants this to happen soon?"

"Yes, my friend has an issue they need some help with, but they can't be seen to be intervening."

"That's all you can tell me?"

"I'm afraid so, yes," said Lucas.

"Leave it with me."

"Thank you my dear. In the meantime, my friend will arrange the creation of the back story for you, so please send me the outline details of your person, together with a photograph as soon as possible."

"I will. And Lucas? Thank you again. Your help means a lot."

"What are old friends for, Anna, if you cannot call on them for help when you're in need."

*****

When Manny Lopez called in a favour, Diego Sanchez didn't hesitate to respond to the man who had been helping to keep him safe and out of the hands of the police.

Diego's father, Alberto, had first met Manny Lopez years before when Diego and his brother were both still in nappies. His father later told them the story about how Manny had tried to open one of his first Lopez Autoparts stores on the mainland. His store manager had reported receiving a visit from a security advisor suggesting that for a monthly fee, he could guarantee Lopez Autoparts would be protected from a spate of criminal damage attacks on new businesses within the region.

Alberto Sanchez had laughed when he'd told his sons that the man, who was to become a close friend, had understood exactly what was happening and that Manny had made sure he was at his new store when the Sanchez 'security advisor' had next visited.

Diego knew that this was all back in the day when his father was only just getting established, setting up protection and vice rackets, as well as developing the drugs side of the business.

Alberto had said he hadn't known at the time, but Manny had enough experience, of running his own protection racket back in Mallorca, to know exactly how to play the situation. But when Manny had demanded to meet the man's boss to discuss the possibility of a multi-site payment option as he planned to open many new stores along the Spanish coastline, Alberto had met with Manny and had found something of a kindred soul.

What started as a business deal, with Manny being more than willing to pay for Sanchez to keep anyone else away from his Autoparts stores, later became a firm friendship between the two men that had now lasted for well over thirty-five years.

That was until Alberto and his wife, Adelina had been arrested and their eldest son, Alejandro, had been shot dead by the GEO during a raid on their villa in Mallorca.

Diego had somehow managed to escape and had since been on the run, but with nearly all of the Sanchez assets seized or frozen, he'd soon found himself struggling for money, and he'd gone to Manny for help.

Lopez had immediately arranged a series of hideaways and untraceable bank accounts to help his old friend's youngest son stay out of the hands of the police, as well as personally funding the legal costs for Alberto and Adelina.

For over six months now, with Manny's continued help, Diego had not just been able to stay undetected, but he'd also managed to resurrect what was left of his father's organised crime gang.

"Uncle Manny, that's no problem at all. The woman who runs the place, Valeria Morales, is someone I've done business with before. I know for sure that she has no love for the GEO, so I think she'll be more than happy to help," Diego hesitated, "although she may want a return of some sort."

"But of course, my boy. That's the way these things work, isn't it? A favour for a favour."

*****

Anna had arranged for them to meet at one of the properties she owned as part of the Martínez family property portfolio. The secluded villa had an electronic gated entrance and was about ten miles south of the city and even though she thought it unlikely, Anna had still reminded them all to take extra care to ensure none of them were followed.

As they sat around the kitchen table, Terri listened intently as Anna and Penny talked her through some of the basics of U/C work. Whilst Penny had much more up to date experience, having been deep under cover for nigh on ten years as personal secretary to the Russian oligarch, Oleg Makarovich, Anna had also been a very successful U/C agent, as well as having been a trainer in her days with MI6.

"How did you keep it up, Penny? The pretence I mean?"

"Well, I suppose the thing to say in my case, Terri, is that I was much more of a sleeper than Anna probably ever was."

"So, by sleeper, you mean you were actually just being you for most of the time?" Terri asked.

"Yes, very much so, or at least as much as I needed to be to ensure I came across as authentic."

"So, what was the difference with how you operated, Anna?"

"Penny's right, Terri. If you can bring some of your own personality to whatever role you're doing, then it can really help. It's a bit like acting, but adding in something of yourself can make it just that little bit easier, just as long as you aren't impersonating someone."

"So you could do that when you were playing Frankie Walker's mother-in-law?"

Anna nodded. "Yes, at least in as much as I could be the protective mother," she grinned. "But it was much more of an impersonating role than yours will need to be, as we can create your character to be whoever we want you to be."

Terri knew Anna had got into her role as Mrs Saoirse Murphy by imitating her Irish accent and then matching her look, as far as she could, to the woman's hair and dress style.

"So, I'll be playing a made-up part, yes?"

Anna nodded, "But even though it's a made-up part, you'll potentially be doing it for long periods of time, so we need you to be able to turn off and separate yourself from the part you're playing," said Anna.

"And that's important? The turning off bit?" said Terri.

"Keeps you sane," said Penny, "but it also keeps you focused and helps you to regroup, often with just the shortest of breaks."

"But how do you do that then when you're with people all the time?" asked Terri. "Because I think that's the thing I'm most worried about. Slipping out of character, whatever that might look like in itself."

"Yes, and that will be harder for you in a prison, especially if you're sharing a cell," said Anna. "But it's not impossible. When I was in the Sanchez villa with Maggie Walker and her kids, there were times when I would pretend I needed the bathroom. I'd go and sit on the toilet, with the seat down, and just take a moment to just be me. Then I'd pick myself up again and go out the door, back in character as Saoirse Murphy."

"Okay, I understand, and I reckon I could do that. Toilet breaks sound good and presumably I could do this at night too? After lock down? As long as I'm not sleeping with some badass."

Anna grinned, "Yes, that might complicate things, but we're going to try to get you hooked up either in a cell on your own, or in with Lori."

"I'm not even going to ask how you might make that happen, but it all sounds good to me. I'm not great on accents like you Anna, so who am I going to be?"

"I've been thinking about that. But we can't leave you as you are, just in case someone in the Foundation takes a closer look at Lori and finds a link between her and Greg that could lead to discovering he's got an Australian daughter."

"Agreed," said Penny. "So, I get you aren't great, or at least you don't think you're great with accents, Terri, but let's run through a few that you might be able to get by with. And remember, we're in Spain, so it would be like me trying to discern a distinguishable difference between say, a Queensland and a South Australian accent. Which in reality, as you probably know, there isn't a lot, except maybe in certain words, where a vowel might be shortened, as in South Australia, whereas it's extended in Queensland."

"Mate, I'm not so sure I do know, Penny, so how the hell do you?" laughed Terri.

"It was before I did the Makarovich job, I was doing something in Australia."

"Ah, you were doing 'something,'" grinned Terri. "You ladies are something else!" And she laughed again. "Okay, I think I've got this. As long as we keep away from anything Spanish, then any of the locals aren't likely to pick up on whatever accent I'm trying to use anyway."

"Got it in one," said Penny.

They then spent the next half hour going through a multitude of accents that Terri then tried to imitate. Some of her attempts had all three women in fits of laughter, which helped relieve the tension, but it was as Greg arrived at the villa that they finally decided on one where Terri felt confident. It was Greek and she found she could draw on the sounds she'd heard as she was growing up, when she'd gone to school with two sisters whose family had originally moved to Australia from

Greece after the Second World War.

"Not bad, not bad at all," said Greg, when he heard his daughter talking. "But are you sure you've got enough Greek in you if you need it?"

"To answer your question, yes I do, although there'll be a lot of swear words in there!" she laughed.

"That'll be no bad thing," said Anna, joining in the laughter.

"Okay, so what about a name? And what about her hair colour? Are you thinking, wig?" said Greg.

"Too risky," said Anna. "Terri, I love your beautiful hair, but I'm afraid it's going to have come off."

She didn't bat an eye.

"No worries. It grows like a wildfire!"

"Good, so with your lovely Mediterranean tan you've picked up, let's go for brown hair. It's the more traditional colour of the Greeks, rather than the super-blonde colour that people usually think of," said Anna.

"Learn something every day," said Greg, with a grin. "I'll leave you to come up with a look and some outfits and let's catch up later."

*****

40

Lori heard one of the guards shout something, then saw some of the other inmates start to move along the corridor past her cell and realised it was a call for her side of the module to go out into the exercise area.

She joined the others and walked out into the concrete exercise yard that sat between two of the modular buildings. It was surrounded by high walls with flat razor wire that sat above the walls like a flexible tube. It looked like one of those children's play tubes they could crawl through, but this would cut anyone to ribbons who tried to get through it.

The scene was the same as she'd seen many times before on prison visits. But now of course, it was different. Not that she had any thoughts of trying to break out, as that would only seal her guilt. Just looking around and knowing she wasn't in control of her own movements, and that she couldn't just get up and leave, suddenly made her feel very alone.

Things got worse when Lori saw one of the guards. She was one of the team who had been on duty the night before and who had hosed her down. Her heart sunk. There was no way she could rely on her, or any of the others, to intervene in the yard, where out in the open, she was much more vulnerable and susceptible to an attack.

Then she saw two familiar faces. Bimpe was smiling at her, clearly trying to put on a brave face, but the look on Elena's face was enough to make Lori's senses go straight on high alert. Lori quickly looked around for some sort of cover, an empty wall or somewhere that surely the guards, even those up in the watchtower who were looking directly down into the exercise yard, couldn't ignore if she was attacked.

She started walking slowly around the outside wall of the yard, keeping her distance as best she could from anyone who came near her. Then she came to a more crowded section ahead of her. She tried to move to the side, but she got boxed in and one or two of the women deliberately walked into her, muttering sarcastic apologies. Then one of the women who'd attacked her at breakfast, the stocky, tattooed one, now with a nose bandage, came and stood right in front of her, blocking her path.

Lori looked at the woman. There was a look in her eye verging on hatred. *'What the hell had she ever done to this woman to warrant such a look?'* Whatever it was, now was not the time to try to rationalise with her.

"Where's your friend? Still in the hospital wing?" said Lori.

"You were lucky this morning, Garcia. But I think your luck might just have run out."

Lori had decided she wasn't going to duck any sort of confrontation.

"I don't think luck had anything to do with it. And, if you don't get out of my eyesight in the next five seconds, you'll be joining her."

The woman stood her ground, but as Lori started counting, "Two, three…," she saw a look of uncertainty appear on the woman's face, before she heard another voice. It came from someone who was approaching her from behind.

"Rosa, leave the Inspectora Jefe alone please. I wish to have a little chat with her."

Rosa looked past Lori and nodded her head towards whoever had been speaking, then glowered at Lori before she walked away.

Lori turned to see who had spoken. It was Valeria Morales. She half expected her to have some sort of bodyguard with her, but she didn't. She was alone.

The two women stood and stared at each other. Lori was trying not to let on how uncomfortable and exposed she was feeling. This was very definitely Morales's patch and she was very much the top dog in here. Therefore, if anything was going to happen to Lori, then there was every likelihood that it would have to be sanctioned by Morales.

"I suppose you know who I am, Inspectora Jefe?"

"A crook who's banged up in prison?" said Lori.

Morales smirked at her.

"Then hey, I'm just like you! Although the difference is, Garcia, I run this place. So you'd better believe me when I tell you, you're going to suffer every day. Every day that is, until I decide otherwise, but then of course you'll be dead."

She tried not to show it, but what unsettled Lori most was that Morales spoke not with venom, but with certainty. Knowing she couldn't afford to show any sign of weakness, Lori laughed and said, "What like this morning? That didn't seem to go to well for your two girls now, did it?"

"Ah, that little welcome from Rosa? Well that wasn't actually anything to do with me. That was just Rosa having her own little bit of fun. I think it's because she has a thing about cops."

"Oh, well that's okay then," said Lori, with a mock

laugh. "But she's clearly not very good at it, is she?" She decided to go on the offensive. "But what about you, Morales? Are you going to take me on, one on one? Or are you too much of a chicken-shit?"

Lori wasn't sure what reaction she might get from baiting the other woman, but she saw nothing but a steely look in the other woman's face.

"You'll wish it was just me by the time some of my girls have finished with you, Garcia. And by the way, this all comes with love from someone I believe you know?"

Lori looked at her, unsure what she meant.

Morales saw the hint of confusion in the policewoman's face and grinned.

"Diego Sanchez says to say, hello."

Lori felt a knot twist in her stomach. She wasn't scared of the woman in front of her, but if this was being generated by Diego Sanchez? That changed things because he clearly had a major grudge against her and if he'd called in a favour from Morales? Then that meant she really needed to take heed of Morales's threats towards her, as she wasn't likely to give up easily.

"Shame he's not here, but he's running scared, isn't he? Won't be long before we pick him up," said Lori.

As soon as she said, 'we,' Lori knew she'd made a mistake. There was no 'we' anymore, certainly not at the moment. She was in prison with little hope of her getting out any time soon.

Whether or not Morales saw something in Lori's face, or heard it in her voice, she knew she'd seen a chink in Garcia's armour.

"Ha! Brave words, Garcia, but that's all they are. There is no 'we' for you anymore and you'd do well to remember that. Hey, if you come and beg, then I may just let you off and get it all over with quickly. Now go and enjoy the rest of your exercise today and take care not to trip over anything."

With that Morales walked away, over to where she was then joined by a group of three other women, all showing evidence of a lot of workouts in the gym. Her bodyguards.

Lori decided it would be best to keep moving and to stay in the eye line of the guards in the vain hope they wouldn't want anything too serious to happen on their watch. She started walking again, increasing her pace, partly to actually get some proper exercise in, but to also try to stop herself being cornered. She glanced across again at Elena and Bimpe. They looked worried, which was pretty much how Lori felt too, but she didn't want to show it. Then she spotted someone coming towards her.

She'd not seen this woman before. She was tall and athletic, with cropped black hair. The woman broke into a jog, that quickly became a run. She was heading straight at Lori, whose fighting senses took over and she automatically started to move into a protective stance, side on with her legs slightly apart.

Too late, Lori realised it was a diversion. She didn't even see the second attacker coming from behind. Smaller, but just as athletic and well built, the woman was approaching fast, swerving to get to Lori through the groups of women who had started closing around Lori, providing cover from the guards and the CCTV.

But the second woman didn't stop. Instead, she kept running past Lori, but as she did Lori felt something sting her left arm. She instinctively wrapped her hand around her arm, whilst trying to refocus on the taller woman who had been running towards her. But the woman had suddenly stopped and was smiling at her.

The stinging in her arm continued, but Lori still had eyes on the woman who was still standing still just ahead of her. Then she saw the woman was nodding her head, motioning with her eyes down towards Lori's arm.

Lori looked down, lifting her hand away and saw a purple patch spreading across the sleeve of the light blue top she was wearing. She pulled back the sleeve and saw the cut on her arm. It was deep. She'd been slashed. Lori started walking towards one of the guards, then caught sight of Morales who just stared at her.

"Guard, Señora, por favor!"

"What do you want, Garcia?" snarled the guard.

Lori held up her arm, with the wet sticky blood glistening in the afternoon sunshine.

"Bloody hell, Garcia! We told you to be careful." She turned to the guard next to her. "Get her to the hospital ward now and pick up a new top for her on the way."

The other guard nodded.

"And Garcia?" The first guard lowered her voice. "This was an accident, right? I don't want any reports going in on this if you know what's best for you."

Lori didn't say anything. There seemed little point in arguing and whilst it might have been caught on CCTV, the whole thing looked to have been well orchestrated. She knew she needed to be better at spotting what was happening. There had suddenly been a whole bunch of people around her when the attacker struck. It was clever because they'd used speed to make it difficult, if not impossible, to identify the attacker even by slowing the CCTV images.

Although Lori hadn't seen who had attacked her, it was clear, judging by the whistles and howls, that whilst the other inmates knew exactly who was responsible, they were never going to say anything.

As she left the exercise yard holding her arm up, to stem the bleeding, Lori couldn't help thinking her nightmare had just got worse.

*****

41

Greg had convened another meeting the following morning to allow everyone to catch up on progress. This time Penny was at Terri's apartment, where she was helping her get into her role.

Greg heard the video call coming in and clicked accept on the monitor and then he had to look twice at the young woman before him to recognise it was his daughter.

"Impressive. I like the whole look. But tell me, how are you feeling about it all?"

"I'm good," said Terri, but in heavily Greek accented English. "I'm staying in role pretty much all the time to get used to me hearing myself.

"I have to say it sounds very good from here, Terri," said Sam. "Your inflection, the way you're speaking just a little slower than usual, together with the Greek accent is really disguising your voice."

"I agree," said Anna. "That's a real skill, Terri. Your father here was pretty rubbish at that sort of thing if I recall," she teased.

"Harsh, but true," said Greg, with a grin. "Anyway, keep working on it because I think Anna has some news for us?" he looked across the table at her.

"Yes, and things are moving very quickly. I sent

all the details through to my old contact last night. He's clearly still got some very strong ties in Spanish Intelligence, and he sent me an encrypted file first thing this morning. It's got your back story and copies of the arrest and recall to prison papers. We should be able to get you delivered there by 3.00pm this afternoon."

Even through the video screen Anna didn't miss the sudden look of doubt on Terri's face.

"You've no need to worry, Terri. Both Penny and I think you're ready for this and the sooner you get in there, the sooner you can absorb yourself into the part of Rhea Raptis."

Anna saw Greg making notes.

"That's, Rhea Raf-tis," repeated Anna. "It's spelt with a 'p,' but is pronounced as an 'f.' We thought it would give Terri something to use as a distraction during any questioning."

"Clever," said Greg. "And Terri, I know I don't need to say this, my girl, but thank you for what you're going to do."

"Don't go all soppy on me, Papa. I might just slip out of my accent," she said with a grin.

She was still his little girl and she hadn't called him 'Papa' in a long, long time. He tried to smile at the beautiful young woman on the video screen, but had to clench his fists to avoid showing her how worried he was.

"Okay, so what next?" said Greg, regaining his composure.

"I've got something," said Tommy. "We've got some pictures of the guy who stayed overnight with Hannah Lopez. Penny has loaded them up on the laptop and shared them, so you should all be able to see them?"

"Yes, got them," said Sam. "I've sent them through to Nino on his private number. He's having to go around the houses to get them checked, just in case he's still got his bosses looking at him."

"Could that be Ortiz?" said Anna.

"What? Getting some fringe benefits off the boss?" said Greg.

"Wouldn't be the first time that's happened," said Sam. "I'll see if I can get my mate Jimmy in the Met to run it through their systems too."

"Great," said Tommy.

"Any more from Maggie Cruz?" said Greg.

"I've debriefed her and got the whole sordid story of how she was taken in," said Penny. "And thinking about it, I'll get her to take a look at Tommy's picture too."

"Great. I've had a couple of catch up calls with Kat and Bella, the two journos," said Greg. "Kat wants to go to print about the Foundation. Print an exposé on the Lopez Autoparts car deaths story, with the backdrop of both the Ramírez deaths. I wasn't sure at first, but she thinks it might bring things out in the open. What do people think?" said Greg.

"Well it's not as though they don't know they're being looked at, does it?" said Sam. "And on the plus side, it might, as Kat says, put a fire under them and force something out. Presumably it might depend on how averse her editor is with regard to possible litigation. But that's something she'll know."

"I'd say go for it," said Anna. "Don't think we've got anything to lose, and we can at least protect both Kat and Bella."

"That's agreed then," said Greg.

"One last thing from me," said Terri.

Greg smiled as he couldn't recognise his daughter's voice at all.

"Who is going to take me to prison?"

"We're hoping we can get Nino or Sophie to help there," said Sam. "It's a big ask, but I know they both think a lot about Lori, so they might be willing to put themselves out on a limb."

"It is a big ask," said Anna, "but I agree with you."

"I've got a meeting with Sofi this morning. I'll report back after that, together with any news on the pictures from Jimmy."

*****

Sofi Delgado had told her detective sergeant that she was just popping into town to collect a statement. Sam had asked to meet her at 10.00pm and he was there waiting for her outside the Cappuccino Grand Café in Carrer de Sant Miquel.

"How's Lori?" was the first thing she asked after they'd sat down inside.

"Doing okay, but she's had some trouble already and not just from the inmates."

"We've heard rumours that some of the guards are a little punchy, but we can never get anyone to come forward. I'm not sure I can do anything to help? Maybe solitary?"

"Possibly, Sofi, but that's for later, if we need it. However, there is something I'd like to ask you. But I have to say, it's a big ask, Sofi, so you need to tell me if you don't think you or Nino can do it."

She listened as Sam explained.

"And you've got someone in Spanish Intelligence to put this whole back story together?" she asked incredulously.

Sam smiled at her. "Yes, I thought I knew a lot about policing and investigation, but even I'm learning that it's much more about who you know, rather than what you know, when you're dealing with the Intelligence Services, regardless of the country."

"And the story will hold up? And the paperwork?"

Sam took out a file from a rucksack.

"You tell me, Sofi. I've not seen one of these

documents, at least not here in Spain or Mallorca before, but presumably you've had prisoners you've taken direct to prison before?"

"Si, although they're not that common, but that should help."

She then pored over the file, taking several minutes to flick through the papers, backwards and forwards.

"Okay, this is a fixed term recall to prison arrest warrant that stipulates the person is taken directly to prison and held there for a period of 28 days. I've handled a couple of these before, when I was in uniform."

"Yes," said Sam. "We thought it better to avoid any court appearance and make it a direct to prison and do not pass go."

"Like Monopoly," smiled Sofi.

"Yes."

"Are these forgeries Sam? Because they look like they're original."

"That's because they are," said Sam.

Sofi swore. "I'm sorry, but how the hell has someone created all of this?"

"Look, I don't know if I'm honest, but they have and for the time-being at least, Rhea Raptis actually exists in the criminal justice system."

"What? Terri's actually in the system for real?"

"Well for the next 28 days she is, but hopefully she'll be out a lot sooner than that and Terri's character, Raptis, will be released and then the record will miraculously disappear off the system."

Sam saw she was deep in thought.

"Look, Sofi, if this isn't feasible, or you think Nino would rather not do it, then I'll totally understand. The last thing I want is to put you, or him, in a position that will get you in trouble."

"It's okay, Sam, I'm just thinking that's all." She

looked at the documents again. "Clever, very clever."

Sam smiled, "You'll do it then?"

"Listen, if someone can get away with putting an innocent senior police officer behind bars and get away with it and I stand still and do nothing, then there's not much point me being a police officer. Of course, I'll do it!"

*****

Maggie Cruz had told her office that she was taking some unexpected leave because of a family issue. The people in the 3R team had told her to be careful when she went out and only to do so for supplies and they had fitted a camera activated alarm. But she still jumped when the doorbell went and grabbed the panic button they'd also given her, even though Penny Hastings had sent her a text to say she was on her way.

Penny looked at the young woman before her. She was a long way from the confident lawyer she had first met only a few days before.

"I just want you to take a look at a photograph for me, Maggie and tell me if you recognise the person. Is that alright with you?"

"Will I have to go to court?"

Penny shook her head.

"That's for a later discussion. For now, I'm more interested in whether you can ID him for us and not necessarily if you know his real name."

Penny held out the photograph and at once saw Cruz shrink back.

"Yes, that's him. He was the one who…"

"Okay, that's good. What name did he go by?"

*****

"I've got a name!" said Penny.

Sam punched the air. It was the first good bit of news into the investigation.

"Jaime Ortiz."

"Do we know if it's real or an alias, Penny?"

"Possibly real, because she saw him pay for a meal a couple of times and that was the name on the credit card. I suppose it could be an alias, but it may just be his real name."

"I'll give Nino and Jimmy the name and see if they can match it to the photo."

"Please tell me it's some good news," said Greg, who'd seen Sam's celebration.

Sam smiled and told him about Cruz identifying the photograph. "I'm going to ring the guys now and see if that helps them."

Jimmy had been running the photo through his systems and even when he added Ortiz's name he still came up with a blank. But Sam had better luck with Nino Castillo.

"I was about to call you, Sam. I've got something and he's a very nasty piece of work."

"Would his name be Jaime Ortiz?" asked Sam.

"Yes, how did you find out?"

"It's just come in from a witness, or I should say a reluctant witness. Although I have to say I'm a bit surprised that he used his real name with her."

"Probably because there's very little against his name, Sam. In fact, it's pretty much all intel, with no convictions or even an arrest."

"What's the intel saying then?"

"He's believed to be an enforcer for one Manny Lopez."

"Our Manny Lopez, of Lopez Autoparts?"

"And the Foundation," said Nino.

Nino took Sam through a summary of the intel on Ortiz. Most of it was uncorroborated information that hadn't been able to be actioned any further, but it all led to strongly suspect Ortiz of leaning on local and regional council officials, particularly in regard to planning applications submitted by anyone connected to the Foundation.

"Anything else?" said Sam.

"There's the key witnesses in the brake pad deaths litigation case against Lopez Autoparts," said Nino. "When we started looking at the Foundation, we decided to re-interview all of them. There were a few who seemed to have been happy to take the money in return for keeping quiet, but most of them, Sam? They weren't just scared, amigo, they were absolutely terrified. I've no idea what Ortiz did to them, but judging by the state Bella Santos was in when he threatened her, well, I can only imagine what he said he'd do if these people talked to the police."

Sam was trying to pull his thoughts together. Ortiz was a clear link to the way Lopez Autoparts and presumably the Foundation had been running their operations. But that still didn't give him anything to help get Lori out of prison.

"I can see what you're thinking. That this doesn't help Lori," said Nino. "But what if we can get Gutierrez to just see the possibility that he's been duped? That this is all a set up."

"Do you think he'd listen?"

"He didn't seem up to listening before, but he's fair, if nothing else. But I probably need some more to put to him."

"Rafa Ramírez said that his father thought there was a ledger of some sort, hand written by Manny himself. Eduardo, Rafa's father had it, but Manny's daughter, Hannah, grabbed it back off him. Does that make sense, as that's a lot of names I've just thrown at you?"

"Yes, got it. You reckon it's with Hannah Lopez," said Nino.

"Yes, but with my old SIO head on, Nino, I can't see

you getting a judge to give you a warrant based on what you could tell them at the moment."

"Sadly, I think you're right there, Sam." He thought for a moment. "What if we pick Ortiz up?"

Sam thought for a moment. It might shake things up, get Lopez to wobble. "I just don't see him giving anything up without us having some leverage. It all feels like a stack of cards, you know? Like a pyramid and if we can just pull the right card out, we could bring the whole thing crashing down."

"What about this reluctant witness, as you call them? I won't bother asking who, but why are they reluctant? I'm assuming fear of reprisals? But can't we promise them protection, Sam? You know, the full witness protection programme, the works?"

Sam knew it wasn't just fear of reprisals. Maggie Cruz was also very aware that she might face charges for giving up Cesar Mendez's name that resulted in his death. Plus of course, she potentially faced sanctions, and even an end to her career, because of breaching client confidentiality.

"It's a bit more complicated than that, Nino. We need something, but you've given me an idea!"

*****

42

Sam had briefed her on what he wanted her to do and Penny Hastings was now sat with Maggie Cruz in her small, but very smart apartment that looked out across the Bay of Palma. She looked up from the mug of coffee Cruz had made for her.

"I wouldn't be asking you to even consider this if it wasn't really important, Maggie."

Cruz was trying unsuccessfully to hold back her tears. "But Penny, I don't know if I can do it."

Penny knew she couldn't give any guarantees as to what would happen about her having given up Mendez's name to Hannah Lopez, so she went straight to what Sam had described as Plan B.

"I really do understand, but I want you to know that you are not alone in this. You've got all of us at 3R who will be looking after you and I've got a couple of other people I'd like you to meet."

"But I don't want anyone else involved," moaned Cruz.

There was a knock at the door and Penny saw the anxiety heighten in Cruz.

"It's okay, it's just the people I want you to meet."

Penny didn't wait, but went and opened the door.

"Thanks for coming, Bella," she smiled. "I'm Penny

Hastings. Nino, good to see you again."

Nino smiled at Penny and then gently ushered Bella Santos, who was showing a similar level of concern as Cruz, into the apartment.

"Maggie," said Penny, gently, "this is Bella Santos and DI Nino Castillo. Nino's from the GEO, he works with Lori Garcia."

Cruz nodded, wiping the tears from her face.

"Bella is a journalist." Penny immediately saw Cruz stiffen. "She has been investigating the deaths of Eduardo and Marcos Ramírez and looking into the way the Foundation operates."

"I can't help you with anything," blurted Cruz.

"Perhaps hold that thought until you've heard what Bella has to say, Maggie. I'll get some more coffee."

Penny stood up and left Nino and Bella talking to Cruz whilst she went and phoned Sam.

"How's it going?"

"As expected, she was very shaken when I first talked about it, but the tears have gone now and she's listening to them."

"If you can make this happen, Penny, then…"

"I know, Sam, I know. Leave it with me."

Penny turned back and saw the three of them, but now it was a two, or rather a three-way conversation, because Cruz was engaging now. However, she wasn't going to get too excited until she heard Cruz agree to the plan.

*****

Detective Sofi Delgado had taken Pedro Romero, a young officer who was on a temporary attachment to CID, out on a general enquiry with her. That was the story Sofi gave him anyway.

"I've just got to get a statement signed from a witness in the old part of the city."

She eased past a few tourists, who were presumably

walking to the Banys Àrabs, the ancient Arab Baths, and looked for somewhere to park. The old streets were narrow and it was tight, manoeuvring the unmarked police car, as she headed for the location Sam had given her. There was little or no parking available, so she soon gave up looking for an actual space and tucked the car in as close to the wall as she could. She knew she wouldn't be there long as Terri would be close by, waiting to be 'spotted.'

"This should do. I'll just be a minute, Pedro, you stay here and watch the car in case you need to move it," said Sofi.

She got out with her briefcase, containing the unsigned statement she was supposedly going to get signed, and then went through the sham of going into a nearby apartment block. Once inside she phoned Terri.

"Are you ready?"

"Yes, ready as I'll ever be."

The voice threw Sofi, as it didn't sound anything like the woman she'd met when she'd been out a couple of times with Sam Martínez.

"Terri?"

Terri realised Sofi wasn't sure it was her, so she answered in her usual Australian accent. "Yes, it's me, mate."

"Wow, you had me fooled! Okay, so just to confirm, you've got brown hair, blue jeans and an orange top? Si?"

"Yes, yes." But now Terri had reverted to her heavily Greek accented English.

"Two minutes," said Sofi. Then she waited until she saw her leaving another apartment block on the opposite side of the street, before she stepped back out into the street. Terri was about twenty yards ahead of her, heading towards a café. Sofi quickened her pace and as she reached the police car, she opened the back door and threw her case down on the seat and quickly opened it up and took out some papers.

"It's her!"

"What? Who?" said Romero.

"Look at this!" Sofi thrust the papers with Terri's photograph on the front into his hand. "It's her! Rhea Raptis. Wanted on a return to prison warrant. She's just up there, blue jeans, orange top, early thirties, brown hair." Sofi grinned at him. "Want a good arrest to go on your attachment record?"

"Yes, please."

He was out of the car in a second, with Sofi following close behind. She was concerned that with his inexperience he might rush in, but she needn't have worried. He waited until he was close enough to Terri. Then with a final check that Sofi was in position to cover any possible attempt to escape, he calmly moved alongside Terri and firmly took hold of her arm.

"Hey, what are you doing?" said Terri, acting surprised.

"Señorita Rhea Raptis? I'm Temporary Detective Romero. I have a warrant to return you direct to prison. Are you going to come with us quietly?" He tightened his grip around her arm.

"It's pronounced 'Raf-tis,' Temporary Detective Romeo," said Terri, deliberately mis-pronouncing the officer's name. "And take your hand off me before I break your arm."

Sofi took her cue and moved in alongside Terri's right arm, grabbing it and quickly pulling it back towards her, twisting it as she did, forcing Terri to bend forward and let out a yell.

"What the hell are you doing? I'm not resisting okay, I'm not resisting."

"Didn't look like that to me, 'Raf-tis,' so just behave and everything will be okay," said Sofi, emphasising the woman's name.

Terri grunted, but allowed them to put the handcuffs on her.

"Good job," said Sofi, winking to the young officer.

'*Good job all round,*' thought Terri.

*****

Sam started to walk away. He'd been watching Terri's 'arrest' and had immediately called Greg. "Sofi's got her. She even got the young lad on attachment to do the arrest. Nice touch, as nothing will come back on him, but it also means Sofi's name won't show up as arresting officer."

"So, she'll take Terri straight to prison?"

"Yep, no need to go through police custody. They should be there in ten, fifteen minutes depending on traffic."

"Stage One done then, Sam. Any news from Penny?"

"Cruz is listening and Penny's confident she'll get her to cooperate. Hang on, she's calling. I might have more news for you by the time I get back to the hotel. See you in about ten minutes."

*****

"You want me to wear a wire!"

Cruz had seemed to be coming around to the idea of helping to get to Ortiz, even if it meant confronting him face to face. But as soon as Nino mentioned the recording device, she'd reeled back in her seat.

Penny stepped in to calm her, or at least to try to.

"Maggie, it's the only way we can secure the evidence we need. There would be little point in you doing it otherwise. I've told you already that this isn't necessarily going to be used in a court of law." Penny's voice was soft and calming and she saw Cruz starting to breathe a little easier. "We want to use what he says to go against Hannah Lopez and her father Manny. They are the ones who put Ortiz up to do what he did to you, so they're the people you might really want to punish."

"But it might still go to Court?"

"I can't give you any promises on that, Maggie," said Nino, "because it wouldn't be my final decision. But now you've listened to Bella about what happened to her, as well as the families in the brake deaths' court case, I really get the sense that you want to help. Am I right?"

Cruz nodded and tears again streamed down her face.

"No one should go through what that man did to me, no one! And he shouldn't get away with it, but if he is just the weapon of the Lopezes? Then, yes, I'll help you and…," she took a deep breath, "…I'll wear a wire if that's what it's going to take, but I just don't know if I'll be able to do it, to be in the same room with him on my own."

Penny could see Cruz had started to physically shake. Slowly at first, but then her whole body was twitching, as though she was having some sort of epileptic seizure. *'If Cruz was reacting like this when just thinking about Ortiz, then how would she be when she confronted him face to face?'*

Bella had seen Cruz was shaking and she changed seats to sit next to her. As she spoke, she took hold of the other woman's hands, "I don't think you need to play act when you're with him Maggie. In fact, it might be better if you don't try and hide anything. Maybe it'll be a little easier for you if you let your real emotions come out, just as they are now."

Cruz was trying to assimilate what the journalist was saying, whilst Penny Hastings had already realised where Bella was taking the conversation.

"If you're super-cool with him, then he's bound to suspect something. But if you just let yourself and your body react naturally when you see him, then it's going to come across as a lot more convincing, yes?"

Cruz had been taking in what the journalist was saying and the body shakes were slowly subsiding.

"What would you need me to say to him?" Cruz said.

Penny brought her hands together in satisfaction.

"Nino, over to you on this one. I'll ring Sam."

*****

It was more like fifteen minutes before Sam joined Greg and Anna back in Greg's hotel meeting room. There was fresh coffee on the table and five minutes later they'd brought each other up to date with how things were progressing.

"Penny's done really well to get her onside, hasn't she?" said Anna. "I mean, Cruz was a bit of a wreck last time we saw her in here."

"Yes, she's done a cracking piece of work there. And Anna? That was such a smart move getting her to join 3R," said Greg.

"It all worked out very well, didn't it? She could hardly have stayed on with Martin's lot after finishing the Makarovich operation as it would be just too risky for her to do any more undercover operations with them and she's certainly not one to sit quietly behind a desk," Anna replied.

"Well, their loss is very much our gain," said Greg. "And with Cruz now willing to front out Ortiz, I think that has to be our main focus."

Sam and Anna both nodded.

"Definitely, then we can hopefully use what he says against Hannah and Manny Lopez," said Sam.

Anna smiled. Her son and his biological father made a pretty good team.

*****

43

Terri stuck to the 'script' as she went through the prison reception process. She mostly cooperated with the guards, but swore at them in Greek when, whilst being searched, one of the women guards seem to take delight in running her hands over her breasts.

"Just behave Raptis! And you'll make things a lot easier on yourself if you just speak in English or Spanish when you're in here," said the Duty Officer.

"It's pronounced 'Raf-tis'," said Terri, with a huff. "And I'll behave if you tell her to stop fondling my tits!" snapped Terri, pointing at the female guard who'd searched her.

"Get used to it, Raptis," said the guard, exaggerating her name as 'Ruff-tits.' "Pretty girl like you will have lots of admirers in here."

The duty officer looked to bring things back in hand.

"Okay, that's enough. Look Raptis, you've only got to do 28 days and then you're out of here. Why you couldn't have just stuck to your Probation Order, only you know!"

Terri played along, keeping her head down, as though she knew he was talking sense.

"So, you understand? Don't get into trouble and

you're out of here in 28 days and if you play ball, we won't bother to transport you back to the mainland."

"Gracias, Señor, I appreciate that," said Terri.

"Okay, go with this officer and once the Doc has seen you, you'll be taken to your cell. Do you want to wear your own clothes or prison uniform?"

"Uniform please, Señor."

She was then taken through to the same rooms Lori had been in. But this time Terri was alone with just two female guards. She was also allowed to shower properly, with even a modicum of privacy, before being seen by the doctor, who quickly signed her off as being fit to detain.

"Okay, we've got a nice roommate for you, Raptis," said the guard, leaving Terri wondering if the Spanish Intel officer, who'd set up her back story, had somehow miraculously got into the prison cell management system to pair her up with Lori.

But when the guard stopped at a cell and opened the door, it wasn't Lori who she saw, but a woman with a recently broken nose who was sitting on the top bunk bed.

'Ah well, they got me this far,' she said to herself.

The woman glared at Terri as she entered the cell, then muttered something that Terri took to be anything but a traditional warm Mallorquin welcome.

"Encantada de conocerte también. Nice to meet you, too!" And she glared back at the woman.

Terri didn't know if it was because she stood up to the woman or not, but the look on the woman's face softened, just a little.

"Sorry, it's been a bad day. You sound like Spanish isn't your first language? What are you? Italian? Greek?"

"Greek, and isn't every day in here a bad day," said Terri, with a grin.

"Rosa," said the woman. "Welcome to Mallorca! My English isn't great, but it might be better than your Spanish," she laughed.

"Gracias. Rhea, encantada."

"What are you here for?" said Rosa.

"I messed up. Missed some probation meetings and they've hauled me back in here, but it's only for 28 days. How about you?"

"Three more years."

"Bummer," said Terri. "Who's the Queen around here, you?"

Rosa laughed, "Me? No! But me and her, we're tight."

"You do a bit of enforcement then?" Terri asked slowly. She knew she needed to be careful, so as not to arouse suspicion.

"You know how these things work. She needs something done and I'll make sure it happens. You look like you can handle yourself, so if you're interested, then maybe I could get you onside with her?"

"Appreciate the offer, but no thanks. I'm looking to stay clear of any trouble as I want to be out of here as soon as I can. So, do me a favour, Rosa, and keep me posted on anything that's going to kick off? I want to make sure I'm well away from it when it does."

"I can, but it'll cost you."

"Depends on what currency you're talking about, Rosa," smiled Terri.

"You're good looking, Rhea, but you're not my type," grinned Rosa. "Let's stick to xigarros."

Terri looked at her, not understanding.

Rosa pronounced it more slowly. "Shig-ar-ros, it's Mallorquin slang for cigarettes."

"Okay, deal. Give me a day to get some delivered, but in the meantime, who or what do I need to watch out for?"

"Okay, so Valeria Morales runs things in here. She's

from the mainland. She was running a crime gang on the Costas. She took it over after her husband was murdered by a rival gang."

"What she doing in here then?"

"She went after the guy who killed her man. Killed him herself apparently, but not until she'd done a lot of very nasty things to him. She's on remand, but they keep putting the case back. She kicked off where they had her before and beat up a guard, so they moved her here. Just to piss her off really," laughed Rosa. "So one bit of advice you can have for free. Don't go annoying her. She's very well connected and I mean over here on the island too, so she's got a lot of influence, including with some of the screws."

"Okay, gracias, I appreciate the heads-up. Any inter-gang stuff going on?" Sam and also Sofi Delgado had briefed her well on prison culture and who might be rubbing up against who in the prison.

"No, Morales has got everything sewn up. Anyone steps out of line and they get a visit from me, or one of my girls." Rosa looked at Terri. "You look like you've done a bit of time then, Rhea? What are you in for and I don't mean the 28 day recall?"

"Bit of drugs, bit of enforcement stuff. You know? That sort of thing."

That seemed to fit with Rosa's impression of Rhea Raptis, as she looked at Terri's muscular and athletic figure and nodded.

"I'll introduce you to Morales at some stage. Now, in terms of staying out of the way of things. You must have been living in a cave if you haven't seen or heard about the arrest and remand of the senior GEO cop?"

"Ha! Yes, I saw something about that. Is she here?" laughed Terri.

"She is and I've already had a pop at her!"

"Looks like you didn't come off so well though?"

laughed Terri.

The friendly tone in Rosa's voice disappeared.

"Careful, Rhea. Let's not let our new friendship go all sour now."

"Hey, I was joking, Rosa. No offence, honestly."

Rosa was still glaring at her, but then her face softened.

"She caught me by surprise that's all. But to be fair, she was better than I thought she'd be, I'll give her that. But she won't be so lucky next time."

"I'm sure she'll get what she deserves. Just remember to make sure I know when it is, so I can be well away from the action."

"Don't worry, I will. Stay in the cell this evening, as she's going to get another little visit just before lock down, and then another, first thing tomorrow morning. But they're just the warm up. The real thing will happen either later tomorrow, or the following day. It depends on when Morales decides to do it, as she's going to do it herself, just to remind everyone she's in charge."

"The real thing? Is she going to take her out then? Permanently?" asked Terri.

"Yes, seems so."

"Sounds like it'll be fun, for you guys anyway," added Terri, trying to make herself sound as though she didn't care at all what happened to Lori.

"Well, like I said, we're just the warm-up act. It's Morales who is going to get the final bit of fun."

Terri thought about asking if Rosa knew anymore about Morales's plans, but that might risk making her suspicious and besides, she could sense she was struggling to keep the Greek accented English going, so she'd do better to rest her voice.

Whilst she'd originally been disappointed not to end up in the same cell as Lori, Terri was now realising that being with Rosa might just play out to their advantage.

*****

James and Tommy had been tracking Ortiz since they'd seen him leave Hannah Lopez's villa. They'd already reported into Sam that they'd been able to identify what appeared to be Ortiz's base on the island, a small apartment block in a smart area just off the Passeig Marítim, the dual carriageway that runs parallel to the city's seafront.

"What's the latest, Tommy?" asked Sam, when they met at a café on the promenade opposite the marina.

"James is sat up on Ortiz at his flat. He's been there since we took him back there after he'd been out for lunch."

Tommy used the terminology often spoken by surveillance teams, to 'take someone back.' was to follow them from one location to a known location, which in this case was Ortiz's apartment.

"We've also tied him to two vehicles he seems to be using. One's a blue Seat Cupra SUV and the other's a dark grey Mercedes S class, which he seems to mostly use if he's ferrying the Lopez woman around."

"Good work, mate, especially as there's just the two of you."

"We've had a little bit of help," grinned Tommy. "All on the QT, mind you."

Sam looked at him.

"Nino rang me. It seems that Fernando and a couple of his guys asked to take a couple of days annual leave whilst they're on the island. Just whilst they wait to see what's happening with Lori."

"A couple of days off, eh?" grinned Sam.

"Talk of the devil," laughed Tommy, as Sergeant Fernando Pérez, dressed in casual shorts and t-shirt, crossed the road and came and sat down next to them.

"Fernando," said Sam. "Good to see you, amigo. Enjoying your time off?"

"Very much so, Sam. We've been getting a bit of sightseeing in." He winked. "But it's good to see you too, amigo and I just want to say how much me and the team appreciate what you're doing for the boss."

"Mate, she's almost family with how things are with her and Greg, so it should be me thanking you guys for sticking your necks out and helping Tommy and James."

"So, what's next, Sam?" asked Pérez.

"I'm about to put an idea to Nino if you want to come along? We've got a plan for our Señor Ortiz, but it's going to need your team to protect a vulnerable witness."

"Looks like we'd better cancel our leave then," grinned Pérez.

*****

44

It was fifteen minutes before the lock down and some of the inmates were starting to move back to their cells. Terri was in the central walkway on the ground floor and to anyone looking at her, she had her head buried in a magazine.

Her heart was telling her to go and find Lori, to let her know she now had some back up. However, she also knew she needed to bide her time and that she'd be better off watching and listening, ready to help when the time came.

But she had at least seen Lori. It was only a glimpse as she saw Lori on the side of the walkway, walking towards the stairs, and she didn't think Lori had seen her. That probably wasn't a bad thing, Terri thought, because as much as she was worrying about her, Terri wasn't sure how Lori might react if, by some chance, she did see through Terri's disguise, of the different hair style and colour, and realise it was her.

Terri could see Lori had her head held high and her shoulders pushed back, a classic piece of tactical body language. It might be a bit of play-acting, thought Terri, but Lori was putting on a good show and most of the other inmates were keeping out of her way.

But watching Lori, Terri was distracted, so missed

Rosa coming up behind her, until she heard her whisper in her ear.

"Maybe now's a good time for you to go back to your cell, Rhea."

Terri gave her a nod to thank her for the tip-off and slowly moved away. She wasn't certain if she was doing the right thing, leaving Lori to fend for herself, but Rosa had said it was just a 'warm up,' so she had to hope Lori could fend for herself.

But as she reached her cell, Terri stopped before she went in. Maybe it was a sixth sense, or intuition, or whatever people chose to call a gut feeling, but something made Terri change her mind and she turned and headed back towards where she could see Rosa.

She knew Lori could handle herself well enough, so if it was only going to be a couple of them trying to have a go at her, then she might just leave Lori to deal with it herself.

But whether it had been her intuition, or a gut feeling from her years as a combat soldier, Terri knew she'd been right to take notice when she saw Rosa had three other women in tow as she headed towards Lori's cell.

The three women walked in a 'V' formation, clearing the walkway ahead of them as Rosa followed behind them. Then Terri saw two more women creating a space behind Rosa by blocking anyone from passing them.

Terri walked towards the two blockers and saw the two women push back their shoulders and fold their arms. Then one of them spoke.

"You can't go up there. Come back in about ten minutes."

"It's okay, ladies, I'm sharing a cell with Rosa and she said I could come and watch. You know? To see Rosa get her own back and rough the cop up a bit."

Terri grinned at them.

The two women looked at each other. Rosa had said no one was to get past, but this woman seemed to know what was going on and they knew Rosa had a new cell mate who was Greek and this woman seemed to have some sort of accent that sounded Greek to them.

Terri saw the uncertainty in their eyes.

"Honestly, girls, I'm just here for a quick look, nothing else. Go and ask her if you want."

"Oh, go on then, but just a look alright, don't get involved."

"Promise and cross my heart," said Terri, crossing her chest with her hand. *'God forgive me, for telling lies to these poor unfortunate souls,'* she smiled to herself.

She quickly caught up with Rosa and the three women with her.

"I thought you wanted to stay away from any shit that was going on, Rhea?" said Rosa.

"Call me fickle," laughed Terri. "But I couldn't resist seeing the look on the cop's face when she sees what's happening. Is that okay?"

"Yes, of course, but better you stay back and just watch. These girls have first call on knocking her about."

"That's fine by me, but hey, Rosa? What about the guards?"

"It's okay. Like I said, Morales has a lot of influence, including with those guys over there." Rosa flicked her head towards two of the guards who, despite being at their posts, were conspicuous in the way they were looking in the opposite direction.

After one last check, Rosa banged on Lori's open cell door.

"Knock, knock, Inspectora Jefe! I heard you had a little accident and thought we'd come and see how your arm is."

Terri wondered what the issue was with Lori's arm and tried to see past the four women, but her view was blocked as they crowded through the door into Lori's cell.

"Ah, you again."

Terri recognised Lori's voice, but it sounded harder than she was used to hearing it, so, she clearly wasn't backing down. Standing by the cell door Terri tried again to somehow attract Lori's attention, but still couldn't catch her eye.

"Brought some reinforcements, have you? Ha! So, you don't fancy going one on one with me then?" laughed Lori.

Terri smiled. She could see what Lori was trying to do. She stood little chance if all four of them went at her, as sooner or later, one of them would get in a lucky punch, or a kick that would take her to the floor and once they were on top of her, Lori would be in real trouble.

But Terri knew that if Lori could force the issue, to embarrass Rosa into having to take her on, just the two of them, then things could be a lot different. Yes, Lori might still come off worse and take a beating, but better it was from one woman, than four.

"Go on, Rosa."

Lori heard another voice. Someone at the back of the cell who had shouted.

Terri called out again, "Go on, you take the bitch!"

Lori heard the shout. It was in broken Spanish from someone with some sort of Mediterranean accent, but there was something familiar about it. She tried to look over the other women, to see who had shouted, but could only see a mop of short brown hair on a woman's head behind Rosa.

One of the three sidekicks then shouted, "Yes, Rosa, beat the shit out of her and then we'll finish her off."

Rosa turned on the sidekick and snarled.

"Shut up and remember what I told you! We're just to soften her up, nothing more."

"Let's see how you get on with that then," said Lori, raising her arms, fists clenched in readiness.

As she did, Terri caught sight of a bandage on Lori's left arm and realised that must have been what Rosa was talking about when she mentioned the 'accident.' Watching anxiously as the four women moved as one towards Lori, Terri suddenly realised the women were about to create a problem of their own and her anxiety turned to hope.

She'd done a lot of house entry searches whilst on active service in Iraq and they rarely went in en masse. It was usually in ones, or twos, and they'd go in quickly and file off and hold a position, be it straight on, left or right, depending on where they determined the most danger was.

The cell was small, so there wasn't much room to move about in, therefore, Terri knew the women would have been better off trying to back Lori into a corner by attacking her on two fronts. But they didn't, and nor did they just rush her to try to overwhelm her with their sheer numbers.

Terri hoped Lori would be thinking the same. She knew a little about Lori's work and thought she would have done enough house and building entries, both real and in training, to understand both dynamic and deliberate entry tactics, because what Terri was seeing played out before her was neither.

Lori had realised what was happening and was standing her ground in the middle of the cell. With only limited room ahead of them, the women were forced to squeeze through the doorway in twos. She watched them closely, seeing what they might do. To be fair, they were making a reasonable effort at a deliberate entry, slow, but sure, as the front two waited a moment for the two women at the back to get through the door and then close up behind them.

Lori expected the attack to happen at any moment, probably a rush, in which case she would be in trouble. Her eyes were darting back and forth, looking for the most immediate danger. First at Rosa and then at the other woman next to her, a short, stocky woman of about thirty with a blonde, Mohican style haircut. Just by the way Rosa was standing, Lori decided she looked the more dangerous. She was also the leader and in this scenario was the most likely to be the one who made the first strike, so Lori focused on her, waiting for an opening.

It came when the two women at the back bunched up too closely behind Rosa and the Mohican. Too late Rosa saw what had happened as the four women suddenly lost all manoeuvrability. She started shouting frantically at the two behind her, to get back and out of her way, but she was too late.

With Rosa momentarily distracted, Lori seized her chance. Springing forward, she let fly with a massive right hook that stopped Rosa in her tracks, caught as much by surprise at the length of Lori's reach, as the force of the punch.

Even Terri winced, as she heard the resulting noise of a sickening crunch and a crack, as Lori's fist connected with Rosa's face, breaking her left cheek bone, as well as loosening several teeth and leaving a stream of blood gushing from her mouth.

Rosa screamed, or tried to, as she reeled back clutching her face and fell over the woman behind her, before she scrambled back out of the cell clutching the left side of her face, whilst uttering a muffled cry of, "Get her!"

Terri saw her opportunity to help Lori, by slowing

the woman down who was directly in front of her. She clipped the back of the woman's heels, sending her sprawling into the blonde Mohican in front of her and knocking her off balance, all of which gave Lori valuable seconds to reposition herself.

Lori then looked up and saw the fifth woman at the back, the one with the short brown hair. *'Who are you?'* she thought. But then the woman winked at her and flashed a smile, a smile Lori recognised at once.

'It can't be.' Lori thought she must be hallucinating!

Lori very nearly said something, but then saw Terri give a slight shake of the head that brought her back to reality.

"Come to watch, have you?" said Lori.

"Thought I'd see how the great GEO officer is getting on," said Terri, keeping to her Greek accented English.

But then the Mohican was back up on her feet and moving in on Lori. She was big and strong, but had little or no technique, presumably being more used to just using her size as an intimidation factor to overcome people. Lori feigned one way and then the other and as the Mohican lunged at her, easily fending her off with a hard, two handed, open palmed strike to the woman's chest, which sent the woman crashing backwards.

"Are you Italian?" Lori called to Terri.

"Do I sound Italian?" smirked Terri. "I'm Greek, alright? Anyway, my new friends here seem to want to try to leave a few bruises on you, so I'm going to leave you to it. Although I won't be far away if you decide you need to make a run for it." She winked at her again. "But I promise to be back in the morning."

Lori looked at Terri. There was a reason she wasn't intervening. They must be planning another attack and Terri wanted to be ready to take them by surprise. The Mohican she'd just hit had fallen back and hit her head on the floor and looked to be out cold. That left two. One of them wasn't showing any fight at all, but the other one was twisting and turning, keeping out of Lori's reach, but looking ready to strike if she got the chance.

The tougher of the two women was still trying to throw punches at Lori, whilst shouting abuse at the other woman telling her to join in, which she eventually did, albeit reluctantly and with no real danger to Lori.

Lori stood her ground, fending them off quite easily and when she could, she'd try to catch them with a right hook. But she could feel her energy was dropping. She was tiring and if anyone else came to attack then she'd be back in trouble. At least knowing Terri hadn't gone far was a massive relief, especially as she knew she couldn't keep this pace up for too much longer.

Suddenly, there was another woman at the door. It was Morales.

"You two! Out now and take her with you," she barked.

The two women each took an arm as they dragged the Mohican out of the cell, leaving Morales alone with Garcia.

"Impressive, Garcia, very impressive. No one has been able to touch Rosa in the time she's been inside and you've done it twice now. Fair play to you, but it's just going to make it even more satisfying when I personally take you out."

Lori went into her fighting arc stance, side on, keeping light on her feet and her hands held ready to attack or defend. She was trying to breathe slowly, but she could feel the tiredness in her legs and knew she was going to struggle to put up any sort of fight against Morales, who was rested and fresh.

She thought about shouting out for Terri, but if

Morales was set on killing her here and now, then so be it. She'd give it everything she had to fight her off, but she knew deep down that she couldn't bring herself to endanger Terri. Losing her would be hard enough for Greg to bear, but the thought of him losing the two most important people in his life wasn't something she would ever be able to chance.

Then Morales was laughing at her.

"Oh, Inspectora Jefe! Did you think I was going to kill you now? That would be just too easy." She laughed again. "No, you will have to wait and see when I decide the time is right. It might be tomorrow, or maybe the day after. You'll have to wait and see now, won't you? But for now, why don't you get a good night's sleep, but not too good, hey? Maybe one of the guards might open your cell door for me in the night, Señora? How about that?"

"Why, why are you doing this? Just get it over with if that's what you want."

"Oh, it's not what I want, Garcia. It's what your friend, Diego, wants. He wants you to suffer because you murdered his brother."

Lori knew there was no point arguing the point that Alejandro Sanchez had caused his own death by raising a gun towards one of her team.

"You don't have to do this you know, Morales?"

"I'm sorry, what do you know about what I need to do, or not do?" snarled Morales.

For a moment, Lori saw the chink in Morales's armour. The tough out-facing look of a crime boss, but who was herself scared of Diego Sanchez and what he might do to her, or her family if she didn't obey him.

But then it was gone. Morales had regained control and her smile was cold as she said, "Good night and sweet dreams. Maybe you can dream about your boys? You should enjoy them whilst you can, Garcia, because you may not have many more nights left."

Morales turned and walked away, leaving Lori to catch her breath, the mention of her boys having hit her hard. Her breathing eased as she took double breaths to fill her lungs, and she started to check her body for any injuries. She flexed her knuckles. Her hands were blood stained and bruised, especially from when she broke Rosa's cheekbone because she'd hit Rosa really hard. But all in all, she thought, she was in pretty good shape overall and her hands were just about okay, hardened from years of practising on the punch bag her husband had bought their boys. She and the boys had used it for many years, sometimes as an outlet for them all to let out their grief over losing him after he was murdered by a crime gang. Grief management had later changed to improving fitness and fighting skills after she re-joined the police, and she had good cause to be grateful for Felipe having bought it all those years before.

Lori waited by the side of her bunk, ready in case Morales had lied and someone did come for her before the lock-down. There was a strange quiet descending over the module. Lori hoped that news that all hadn't gone to plan for Morales had reached the rest of the module and was causing its own confusion.

'Anything,' she thought. *'Anything to give me some sort of edge tomorrow.'*

She was still on high alert, but she found herself thinking about Felipe and couldn't help smiling at what he'd be thinking if he could see her now. One thing was for sure, she knew he'd want her to keep fighting and after Morales's warning, it looked like she would need to be ready to do exactly that at some stage tomorrow.

However, after what she did to Rosa's cheekbone, Lori thought she'd be surprised if Rosa made it back from the hospital ward and anyway, she'd probably need x-rays which might mean a trip to one of the local hospitals under guard.

That was one less of Morales's enforcers to worry about, which suited her down to the ground, although she hoped to God that Morales's threat to come in the night was just that, a threat, as she needed to get a good night's sleep.

As she heard one of the guards call out, "Lock up time, ladies!" Lori sat down on her bunk. She'd survived another day, but not just that. She now had Terri watching her back! She lay back on the bed and felt something surging through her body. She thought it might be the adrenalin from the fight, but no, it was something else, something she'd lost for a while. It was a sense of hope!

*****

45

It was seven o'clock the following morning and they'd met in a warehouse on an industrial estate, away from any unwanted prying eyes and ears at the police station.

DI Nino Castillo briefed Pérez and his team on the operation and told them to be ready to deploy sometime during the day. Once he'd finished, he handed over to Pérez to finalise the tactics in detail with his team and left them to sort out a recce of the sites Tommy and James had previously identified as local haunts for Ortiz.

Nino went and sat down next to Maggie Cruz and Penny Hastings who had both been listening to the briefing. He'd arranged for them to come so that Maggie would know exactly what Pérez and his team would be doing to protect her when she confronted Ortiz.

"Are you happy with all of what you've heard, Maggie?" he asked gently.

"Yes, Inspector, thank you. I just hope I can do a good job." She then excused herself and went to find the toilet.

Nino looked at Penny.

"How's she holding up?"

"She's getting very jittery and that's her third visit to the toilet. But as we said, Nino, in some ways that's possibly a good thing as I'm pretty sure he'd be suspicious if she was too cool and calm."

"And now she knows it's today, then hopefully she'll at least feel that it will all be over soon."

"Yes, at least this part of it," said Penny.

*****

James and Tommy had been watching Ortiz for a while now and had begun to see something of a pattern in his behaviour.

"I'll bet you a quid he goes to the same café as yesterday for some breakfast," said James.

"You're on!" said Tommy.

"Looks like we won't have long to wait to find out, Tommy. Standby, standby. Subject is out of the apartment on foot. He's wearing blue shorts, a white round neck t-shirt and sunglasses. They look like Aviators."

"Copied, James. Are you okay sticking with him for now?"

"Yes, yes."

"Good, let me know when you want to drop off as we've still got two of Pérez's team with us, Bravos 55 and 66. They're in a car and can deploy on foot as you need them."

"Will do, Tom."

"55 and 66 did you copy the last?"

"Si, si."

"My quid is looking safe. Subject is still heading towards the same café as usual. Plenty of cover from the morning commuters, so I'm happy to keep on him."

"Copied, James. I'm going to call it in as this looks like it might be a runner." He rang Greg. "We've got movement, Greg. It's the same café, same time. He's a creature of habit, so we're expecting him to stop at the tabac and pick up a paper to read."

"Okay, I'll ring Nino, so you can focus on Ortiz and then he can run it over the radio. You've got the police frequency locked in?"

"Yes, and we've comms checked it with the bravo guys we've got here. It's all good."

"Nice one, Tommy."

Anna looked at Greg. "We're good to go?"

"Yep, just ringing Nino."

*****

As they drove towards the café, Nino and Penny could sense the nerves were getting to Maggie Cruz.

"I'll be right alongside you, right up until the time you need to walk by him and pretend to recognise him," said Penny.

Maggie nodded, but she couldn't stop her hands from shaking. "And you've got men close by, Inspector?"

"Yes, Maggie. They will have you in their sight all of the time and they are all armed, so we will make sure you are perfectly safe."

Penny looked at him. She knew Nino meant well, but she'd heard those words before, many years ago, when she was being deployed on U/C jobs with MI6. She'd also been told she'd be 'perfectly safe,' but experience had then told her all too well that it was almost impossible to guarantee someone's safety, especially the person going undercover, or as in Cruz's case, when they were the one who was right at the forefront of the operation. It took Tommy's beautiful lilting Bajan accent, coming across Castillo's radio, to bring her back to the present.

"He's been into the tabac to get a paper and he's back out now and walking towards the café. No deviation and ETA is around three minutes.

"Sergeant Pérez, Alpha One, confirm you are in

position please," said Nino, knowing Pérez already was, but he hoped that Cruz hearing it across the radio would help to settle her.

"Si, si, Boss. We're all set up and we have eyes on the café."

"Okay, Maggie," said Nino. "We're all good. Now if you go with Penny, she'll take you to the start place. Just test your mic one last time when you get there okay? Penny will be able to hear you and can confirm with me that the device is working. You've got this, okay? And we'll see you soon back at the RV, the rendezvous point, Maggie."

She forced a smile and the two women got out of the car and started walking towards the small square. Penny kept talking slowly and gently to Maggie, but could tell she was growing ever more anxious the closer they got to the café.

"Say something, Maggie, as a final comms check."

"I'll be glad when this is over." She tried to grin.

"Yes, that came through loud and clear, Penny, thanks," said Nino.

"Everything is working perfectly, Maggie. It's time to do this."

Maggie suddenly stiffened. Her body reacting to the adrenalin that was pouring through her, and Penny saw Maggie's pupils widening as the hormone took effect, preparing her body for a fight or flight response.

"Breathe, Maggie, just breathe slowly like I showed you."

Maggie tried, but she could just feel her chest tightening. She started panting, gulping in air, her chest heaving under the strain.

Penny could see she was losing control and of the two possible actions Maggie's body was getting in readiness for, flight seemed the much more likely outcome.

"Nino," said Penny, quietly into her mic. "She's losing control. If he doesn't come soon, she's not going to be in any sort of state to even get near him, let alone confront him."

"Tommy, James, where is Ortiz now?"

"One minute, repeat, one minute," said James, who was now hanging back, but still had a good view of Ortiz.

The seconds ticked slowly by. Penny would have liked to have been looking around in the morning sunshine, as it flooded in over the top of the surrounding buildings to the beautiful little piazza. But instead, she was focused on the woman in front of her who was starting to shake from side to side.

"Alpha One, I have eyeball on the subject. He's carrying a paper and is about to sit down at a table outside the café," said Pérez.

"All copied, Alpha One," said Nino Castillo. "Penny, are we good to go? I need you to make the call on this and I'm happy to abort if your experience tells you that's the right call."

Greg and Anna were listening in to the radio transmissions.

"What do you think?" said Greg.

"If he's asking that question of Penny, I think he already knows the answer," said Anna.

And to confirm what Anna had just said they heard Penny respond over the radio.

"Stand down, stand down. We're returning to the RV point."

"Understood and confirmed. Thank you, Penny," said Nino.

"Back to square one?" said Greg. "Or have you got another idea?"

"Actually," said Anna, "I do."

*****

Maggie was in tears by the time they met back up with Nino Castillo.

"I'm so sorry, I'm so sorry. I wanted to help and I really thought I could do it. But just the thought of being near him again? I just couldn't."

Penny was doing her best to console her when she heard her phone ring. She looked at the screen and then mouthed the words, 'It's Anna,' to Nino and he took over trying to console Cruz.

"Good call, and the right call by the sound of it, Penny," said Anna.

"Thanks, I appreciate that, Anna. I know there was a lot riding on this, but there was no way she was going to stand up to him, let alone get him to talk."

"You absolutely did the right thing to pull it, especially because we haven't lost her as an option and besides, I've got another idea."

"Go on."

"She's definitely keen to help, isn't she?"

"Yes, very much so. What are you thinking?"

Anna then outlined a change in tack and after hearing what she'd said, Penny smiled.

"I'll leave the phone open on speaker phone so you can hear what we're saying, Anna." Penny looked across to Maggie. "Maggie, Anna has come up with another idea. But first, can I check. You do still want to help, don't you?" said Penny.

"Yes, but I don't think I can do it, not with Ortiz."

"Don't worry," said Penny. "Anna's come up with another way of doing this. Nino, you'd better listen to this as well, as we need your buy in again to make this happen."

As she watched her listen, Penny saw that it didn't take long for Maggie's breathing to slow as she started to relax.

"I can do that. I know I can face her."

"You're sure, Maggie?" said Penny.

"Yes, I am." They all detected a touch of defiance in her voice.

"Nino?" said Penny.

"If you can get her to talk, Maggie, then this could really blow everything apart and it might be enough to convince Comisario Gutierrez to open up Lori's case again."

It was a different Maggie Cruz who was now sitting before them. The young lawyer was back in control of her emotions and ready to put on a performance with the woman who was responsible for getting Jaime Ortiz to drug and gang rape her.

"We'll need you to still wear a recording device and you'll probably have to do it in her office." Nino paused, "That means we wouldn't be able to have anyone as close to you as we did today." He waited for his words to sink in. "You do understand that, don't you, Maggie?"

Cruz nodded.

"If you can keep Ortiz from getting anywhere close to Lopez's office, Inspector, then I know I can do this."

"Anna," said Penny, "we're back on!"

*****

Greg had booked a call into the prison to speak to Terri.

"How's it going?"

As she spoke, Greg had to listen hard to the thickly disguised accent Terri was using, that is until she suddenly changed.

"Hi Dad! I'm alone now. Jeez, it's been tough hanging on to that bloody accent!"

"It's good to hear you, Terri, but tell me, how are you and have you been able to make contact with Lori yet?"

"I'm good. I had no issues with the process like Lori had. It was a different crew who were on. So it all went smoothly. There was only one hiccup. I wasn't put in the same cell as Lori."

"Is that a problem?" said Greg.

"Actually no, and in fact, it's worked out for the better as I'm now sharing a cell with Morales's main enforcer, a right charmer by the name of Rosa."

"You take extra care then, Terri. That's sailing very close to the wind, being in the proverbial lion's den with her."

"It is, but I've got a lot of info out of her, so it's been worth it. It's only been handbags at ten paces so far, and to be honest, Dad, Lori has done a bloody good job of fending them off on her own, however, Rosa has told me straight that Morales plans to kill Lori."

"Shit!"

"I know, so I hope you guys can make something happen so we can get her out of here soon, and I mean real soon, Dad."

"I know and we are trying, my girl. Now, I don't know how much time we've got on this call, so does Lori know you're in there?"

"She does and going by the way she put my new bestie, Rosa, back in the hospital wing last night with what sounded like a smashed cheekbone, I think it's really buoyed her up."

"Good for her!" said Greg.

"Yes, but now I've lost my snout so to speak, so I don't know when Morales is likely to strike, except that it is probably going to be sometime today, or maybe tomorrow."

"Are you going to be able to manage this, or do we need to try something else?"

"Like what, Dad? We already know that we haven't got any sort of credible case to take to the prison governor to get her protected and there's no point her moving prisons anyway, as it's likely it will just happen again, so at least we can control here to some extent. I think that if we can deal with Morales, then the rest of them in here will fold and Lori will be in a much safer position."

"Okay, that makes sense. Just to keep you up to date, we blew out on the plan to get Cruz to confront Ortiz. Long story, but essentially, she couldn't face it, so we pulled the plug. The good news is that Anna has come up with Plan B and that potentially may be even better. We're going for Hannah Lopez and using Cruz to try to get her to spill the proverbial beans."

"Okay, I like that and if I get a chance, I'll fill Lori in on what's happening. By the way, the promised easy access to phone calls? It seems it's not as easy as it apparently should be, so you may find you're told we're out exercising, or doing something if you call in."

"Why's that then?" asked Greg.

"Lazy guards who can't be arsed to come and find us and take us to the phone room."

"That's appalling, but okay, that's useful to know. In the meantime, my darling daughter, please take care in there and no heroics, you hear me?"

"Don't worry and Dad, I'm fine. Actually, I'm better than fine. I'm feeling more like me than I have in, well, let's just say in a while."

*****

46

Sam had picked up one of the national papers on the way to Greg's hotel.

"Have you seen this!" said Sam.

"Not the papers, but I didn't need to. It's all over the morning TV news."

"Wow," said Sam. "If that doesn't put the cat amongst the pigeons then I don't know what will."

"Kat and Bella have really gone to town on the whole thing, including how Lori has been falsely accused and imprisoned. The TV stations have got crews camped outside the police headquarters and one of them has just door stepped Gutierrez as he left his hotel. God knows how they knew where he was staying!"

Sam grinned.

"You told them?" said Greg.

"I texted Bella Santos after I followed the Comisario last night and clocked where he was staying. Seemed only fair that he got just a little taste of the crap that Lori's been having to cope with. Did he say anything?"

"No, he's just gone 'no comment,' which didn't looked great and so it looks like the wolf pack sense there's another story still to be told and they aren't going to let go until they find it."

Sam finished reading the newspaper article.

"They've not held back regarding the witness intimidation about the brake deaths, have they?"

"No, and look." Greg pointed to the TV screen that showed TV crews were now gathering outside the Lopez HQ. "I don't suppose Manny, or Hannah, are going to be happy about this either."

*****

"I thought you said you had both reporters under control! I mean, have you seen this!" Hannah Lopez yelled.

She had the news on the TV screen in her office and she was looking out of the window as first two, then three and then more vans emblazoned with TV station logos on the sides arrived and started setting up outside the front of the Lopez headquarters.

Jaime Ortiz had rarely, if ever, seen Hannah Lopez as angry as this. Saliva was literally flying from her mouth as she spat the words out.

"What do you want me to do?" he said.

"Nothing, just nothing. If you do anything now, it will just reinforce the Press's view that we must be guilty. So do nothing, got it!"

It was the way she spoke to him, more than what she said that most annoyed him. Despite all the charm she could use to wheedle him around her little finger, he knew the bottom line. He was nothing to her, at least nothing more than an employee to do her dirty work for her.

He didn't acknowledge her or say anything. He just got up and started to walk out of her office.

"Where are you going? Stop right there and damn well tell me where you're going!"

"Why? Why do you care where I'm going? You've made it abundantly clear that you don't want me to do anything and you've also been quite specific in telling me what you think of me."

"What do you mean, 'what I think of you'? What do you think I mean?"

He could see she was barely able to control her anger.

"I'm just a pawn to you, and Manny for that matter. I always have been. I see that now. I didn't mind so much when it was your father, but you! I thought you might have …" His words trailed off.

She realised what he was getting at and she scoffed at him.

"What? Did you really think I had feelings for you? Why would you ever think that? You were a convenient shag, Jaime, that's all, so get over it and help me figure out what we're going to do."

He'd known in his heart what she was going to say, but it still stung.

"I'm sorry, did you just say 'we' somewhere in all of that? You want me to help you after what you've just said?"

"Aren't you forgetting that my father and I have made you a very wealthy man, Jaime? Without us, you'd be nothing."

"No, Hannah, let's be straight here. Without your father, I'd be nothing. But don't forget that doing what I did also made your father a very wealthy man. So, without you? That's a different story altogether and yes, you're right, there is no 'we', because as far as I'm concerned, from now on, you're on your own."

He turned and walked out of the door, leaving Hannah Lopez with her mouth wide open.

"Is she free now, Señor Ortiz?" asked Juanita, Lopez's PA.

"For the time being," he replied, which brought a look of confusion to the PA's face, who got up and went and knocked gently on the open door.

"I've got Reception saying there's five, possibly

six journalists wanting to get your response to the newspaper article. What do you want me to tell them?"

"Tell them 'No comment,' then get me the Head of Legal and Frankie Rodriguez on the phone as soon as you can. And Juanita! Get me a portable shredder and make it a good one!"

*****

Ortiz had no intention of walking out of the front door of the Lopez offices, but with no rear access, he knew he'd still have to run the gauntlet of TV cameras as he drove out.

After getting in his car, he pulled his collar up around his neck and put on a peaked cap and sunglasses. He drove slowly towards the front gates with the car's front sun visors down and whilst keeping his head as low as possible. Then timing his exit through the electronic gates perfectly, he accelerated hard past the waiting TV crews and headed towards Palma.

James and his two GEO helpers, Bravos 55 and 66, were safely parked up out of sight waiting for Ortiz to leave. They saw him come through the main gates and then kept their distance as they followed him back towards the city.

James called up on his radio.

"Tommy, we've got Ortiz back in his car and he's heading towards the city. Judging by the speed he drove out, it looks like he's not a happy bunny. Plus there's a whole pack of TV crews outside of the Lopez HQ. Did we know about that?"

"It's just come in, James," said Tommy, who had just arrived at Greg's hotel meeting room and seen what was playing out on the morning TV news. "It looks like the shit has hit the fan, so stay with Ortiz if you can, at least for the time being."

"Yes, yes, no problem."

Tommy turned to Greg.

"Boss, I'll keep James on Ortiz until you tell me otherwise. Presumably this may change things with your Plan B, Anna?"

"Maybe, but only because we may not physically be able to get Maggie in to see Hannah Lopez now, as she's probably put the shutters up. But it's interesting that Ortiz may have gone off in a bit of a huff. I wonder what's happened there?"

"A woman's scorn, possibly?" said Anna.

"Maybe," said Greg.

"Can we get to Lopez another way?" said Sam. "Get her out of her office on some pretence?"

"It would have to be a hell of a pretence!" said Greg, but then he smiled.

"What?" said Anna.

"Where's Manny's villa?"

"It's up in the hills, just above Palma."

"I think we should get a call into Hannah to say her father has a visitor, one Maggie Cruz," said Greg.

"Do you think Maggie will do that? See Old Man Lopez?" said Sam.

"She won't have to. We just need her to look as though she's been to see him," said Greg.

"Not sure I follow where you're going with this, but I'm sure you'll explain in due course," said Sam.

"I will, so let's get this going. Anna, can you please ring Nino and get him to come here as a matter of urgency. I need him to sanction this because of the wire."

"Right away, but who is the wire for?"

"Still Maggie. Oh, I nearly forgot," said Greg. "Can he lend Penny one of his team's unmarked cars? One that doesn't look like a police car."

"Shouldn't be a problem. Then what?" said Anna.

"Tell Penny to take Maggie to Lopez's villa."

"Okay…"

"I'll need to know the moment she's in sight of the main gates, but no closer than say 200-300 yards. At that stage Penny needs to get out and get Maggie to drive up to the entrance and make it look like she's just leaving the Lopez villa. Is that clear?"

"Yes, got it," said Anna.

"So, it will look like Maggie has just come from seeing Manny? You're going to suck Lopez in," said Sam.

"Exactly," said Greg.

"And catch her with her guard down," said Anna, with a wry smile.

"Let's see if it works!" said Greg.

*****

DI Nino Castillo's phone was ringing, again. So far, he'd ignored the calls, but they were stacking up on his missed calls list. He knew it was Comisario Gutierrez, but he'd thought it better to not have to answer any questions about what he had been doing with the 3R team.

"Boss," said Pérez. "You'd better see this."

He passed him an iPad.

"Oh, Lord," said Nino, when he saw the news and the storyline from Kat and Bella.

"It gets better, Boss, wait for the bit about the Comisario."

Nino couldn't help but laugh when he saw the images of the TV crews with Gutierrez outside of his hotel.

"I guess that's why he's been ringing me then. Ah, here he is again. Perhaps I'd better answer this one."

He flicked at the screen of his phone.

"Comisario, I'm sorry, I can see you've been trying to call me, but my battery was flat. What can I do for you?"

Nino saw Pérez trying to suppress a laugh and wagged his finger at him to keep quiet.

"Have you see the news, Castillo?"

"No, Señor," he lied.

"Well, make sure you do! It's all over the Press that Garcia has been set up and the Lopez brake deaths investigation has been compromised."

"I did tell you there was nothing in it, Boss, that Lori, I mean Inspectora Jefe Garcia was innocent, but as I recall you wouldn't…"

"Shut up, Castillo and listen. Or rather shut up and tell me what you think has happened and if there is anything in what you say that I might just believe, then I promise you, I will move heaven and earth to get this sorted."

He'd heard the Comisario had a gruff nature but underneath it all, he was essentially a good old-fashioned copper, who was firm, but fair and he could ask nothing less of the man if he was going to be open to what he was about to tell him.

"Can you meet me at the Born Hotel?"

"In the Carrere de Sant Jaume 3?"

"That's the one, Comisario. In ten minutes? There's someone I'd like you to meet."

*****

"Penny, what's going on now? I thought we were going to the Lopez HQ to see her?"

"Change of plan, Maggie, because of what's broken on the TV with Kat and Bella's story."

"So where are we going?"

"Manny Lopez's villa."

"I'm not sure I can face…"

Penny stopped her.

"It's okay. You won't be meeting him. We're just setting it up to make it look like you've been to see him."

"But why?"

"Maggie, it's a bit of subterfuge. We want Hannah to

see you and think you've just been to see her father."

Maggie then twigged what was going on. "And she'll want to know what I've been to see him about."

"Yes, at least that's what we hope."

"And if she doesn't?" asked Maggie.

"Then you go for her with all you've got, Maggie. Whichever way it goes, Lopez will either try to blank you altogether, and deny all knowledge of what you're talking about, or she'll look to pin everything on Jaime Ortiz and if she does that? Then drive it home hard."

"Because you're going to use it to get him to bring both Manny and Hannah down."

"That's the plan. Think you can do that?"

Cruz didn't hesitate.

"You're damn right I can. After all, the bitch was the reason Ortiz put me through what he did."

Penny waited to see if there were any tears, brought on by the woman's horrific memories, but this time there were none. Cruz was calm and in control. She was going to get her revenge, if that's what it was, but in her own way, by drawing the evidence out of the accused in the same way she'd been doing for years every time she stood up in a court of law.

*****

47

Greg was more than a little surprised when he saw who had followed DI Nino Castillo and Sergeant Fernando Pérez into the hotel meeting room.

"Greg," said Nino, "this is Comisario Juan Gutierrez."

"Encantado, Señor Chambers, my name is…"

"I know who you are, Señor. Now tell me, what brings you here today?" said Greg, coldly.

"Greg, he's here to listen."

"Go on then, Comisario, why has it taken a press article and presumably, a lot of unwanted media attention for you to suddenly be willing to consider that there is a different side to this thing?"

"Greg.." said Nino, trying to ease the situation.

The Comisario knew that if what Castillo had told him was true, then he would have no choice but to eat a fair chunk of humble pie, both to this man and to DI Castillo, but most of all to Lori Garcia. But all that was a long way off, as it would take a lot to convince him that there had been a miscarriage of justice.

"It's okay, Inspector. Let's be clear here, Señor Chambers. At Inspector Castillo's suggestion I've come here to listen and if, and only if, I think there are other factors to be considered, then I will re-open my investigation into the bribery allegations against Lori Garcia. But please be under no illusion that I'll need a lot of convincing."

"Fair enough. At least we both know where we stand. So maybe we had better get on with it."

Greg had wanted to say, *'get on with doing your job for you.'* But that would have been unfair against Nino and his team with all they'd done so far, going way beyond the line of expected loyalty to Lori, so he let it go.

Between them, Greg, Sam and Anna talked through what had happened so far. For the most part Gutierrez just listened, but occasionally he'd interrupt to ask a question, or clarify a point. He raised his eyebrows and looked directly at Nino when Greg mentioned the team members who had taken annual leave and then helped with the surveillance on Ortiz.

"You knew about this, Inspector?"

"Look, Comisario, if you're going to do anything about any discipline charges, then can you please just wait until we've finished what we're trying to do?" said Nino.

Gutierrez nodded and continued listening until Greg, after a deep breath, as he wasn't a hundred percent sure he should tell the man, told him about Terri.

There was the barest of reactions, but they all saw a look of disbelief on his face.

"Are you going to tell me how you have managed to get a woman, you say it's your daughter?"

"Yes, she's my daughter."

"My half-sister," chipped in Sam, adding to the look of bewilderment of Gutierrez's face.

"….how you got your daughter, and your half-sister, into a state penitentiary?"

"Probably best we don't give you the detail, suffice it to say that they are connected to your Intelligence

Service."

"And presumably that is because of the tragic death of Cesar Mendez?" said Gutierrez.

Greg nodded. Perhaps it was his turn to acknowledge that the Comisario may be more aware of the bigger picture than he might have given him credit for.

"Why did you feel the need to put someone into the prison?"

"Do you recall the murder of a British citizen during last year? He was shot dead here in Palma by Diego Sanchez," said Greg.

"Yes, it was Garcia who handled the investigation and she broke up the Sanchez crime gang. It was a brilliant outcome, but one that is sadly held in some doubt now because of the allegations against her."

"Comisario, Nino here, is putting his trust in you by bringing you here. That trust is, something that, and I have to be honest with you here, is something I do not yet share, although I'm willing to be convinced otherwise. Therefore, perhaps the fact that Diego Sanchez has ordered a hit through Valeria Morales on Lori may be something to help you reconsider that she is not the guilty party here."

"But why haven't you told the prison authorities this?"

"And what? Let them move Lori off the island to another prison, where she will be even more vulnerable," interjected Sam.

"But what about getting her put in solitary?" said Gutierrez.

"Comisario, Lori has already told us that Morales controls a number of the guards in the prison, either through coercion and blackmail, or money for them to turn a blind eye, so why on earth do you think solitary confinement is going to give her any sort of protection."

"We need to get her out of there and get her out now!" said Gutierrez.

It wasn't just Greg who was surprised by Gutierrez's outburst.

"What? You don't think I care about the threat to life of a police officer? I don't care if she's guilty or not, Señor. She still deserves to be protected. Castillo help Señor Chambers, or should I say, continue to help him if any way you can and leave me to deal with the threat in the prison."

"What are you going to do, Boss?" asked Nino.

"If we don't want to move Garcia, then I can get Morales out of there."

Greg was the first to speak.

"If you can do that, Comisario, then that would be great, because we think Morales might be planning to do something sometime today, as Lori had a run in with some of her enforcers last night."

"Is she okay?"

Greg saw the concern on Gutierrez's face. Maybe he had misjudged him.

"Yes, she's fine, but the others aren't. Lori's tough and can handle herself, Comisario, but sooner or later someone is going to get a lucky strike in on her and if it's with a weapon then she could be in serious trouble."

Greg saw the look of relief on the man's face.

"Boss, can I ask? Are you beginning to think Lori might have been set-up?" asked Nino.

"Let's just say, Inspector, that I'm more open to the idea than I thought I might be."

Greg shook his hand.

"Thank you for listening."

"There's a long way to go, Señor Chambers, but for now, the priority must be Inspectora Jefe Garcia's safety. Inspector Castillo will keep me posted but now,

I need to make some urgent calls, because we all know how bloody slow and bureaucratic the prison service administrative function can be."

*****

"Greg, we've been past the villa and checked out the front. There's a whole load of CCTV cameras along the perimeter fence, but we're parked out of sight, about 200 yards away," said Penny.

"Good, I'll put the call in now, or rather Anna will, as we need it to be in Mallorquin."

Anna made the call through to Lopez's mobile phone on the number Maggie had given them.

"Yes, what is it?" A terse voice answered.

"Señorita Lopez? I'm calling about your father, he's been taken a little unwell and is asking for you."

"Oh my god! Is he okay? What's happened? Is the doctor there?"

Anna smiled at the reaction she was getting.

"Si, si, we have the doctor here and we're monitoring your father's heart. We're doing some checks, but his breathing is very heavy and laboured and we're not yet clear what brought this on."

"Did this just suddenly happen?" yelled Lopez. "You're supposed to be giving him twenty four hour constant attention, so you must know what happened!"

Greg, Nino and Sam were all listening on speaker phone and Greg gave a thumbs up to Anna. The call was having the desired effect.

"I am so sorry, Señorita, but your father told us to leave when he had a visitor. It was after they went that he became unwell."

She straight away jumped to conclusions, thinking it was Ortiz. He must have gone to tell her father what had happened and to lay all the blame on her.

"Was it a man?"

"No, Señorita, it was a woman. I don't know who she was as none of us had seen her before."

"Didn't you get a name? Or what did she look like?"

Lopez was bursting. *'Why the hell didn't they know who it was? Surely, they must have some protocol to know who was coming to see her father, or if not, then they damn well should have!'*

"I don't know if we got a name, let me check."

Anna left her hanging for just long enough to raise her agitation level even more.

"I'm afraid we didn't, Señorita, but one of the team says they think they heard your father call her 'Maggie.'"

Hannah Lopez felt an involuntary twitch as her stress level went through the roof.

"Juanita! Get my car brought around to the front. Now!"

*****

48

Nino Castillo left Pérez to deploy his team accordingly to cover the anticipated interaction by Maggie Cruz and Hannah Lopez.

Pérez had positioned his team inside a mile radius of the Lopez villa. Alphas 22 and 33, in an unmarked 150 mph Skoda Octavia vRS, had quickly reached the location and parked up in a secluded spot just south of the villa even before Lopez had accelerated hard out of the Lopez HQ gates, scattering the waiting group of reporters in the process.

The GEO team motorcyclist, call sign Charlie Four, was on the outer radius, waiting hidden behind a parked up HGV wagon, but with a clear view of the passing traffic.

"Charlie Four to Control," called up Juan 'Cecil' Moriarty.

"Go ahead, Cecil," said Pérez from his Control Car, half a mile north of the Lopez villa.

"Sarge, just seen a dark blue BMW 8 series fly by at speed. Female driver, looks like Lopez."

"Gracias, Charlie Four."

"Got her!" said Nino, who was sat with Pérez.

Pérez flicked his radio mic open.

"Control to Penny. We've sighted Lopez in a dark blue BMW 8 series. She's one mile out heading towards you at speed. Please move into position."

"Yes, Control, all received. One last test. Are you picking this up?"

Pérez looked over his shoulder to Alpha 88, Juan Flores, who was sat behind him monitoring the recording device Maggie Cruz was wearing. Flores gave him a thumbs up and a grin.

"You're loud and clear, Penny. Time to roll," said Pérez.

Penny turned to Cruz and squeezed her hand.

"Come on, time for you to get some justice, Maggie Cruz. Drive to the front gates and make it look like you've just left the villa. You've got this."

Maggie swallowed hard as she nodded. Penny got out of the car and quickly made her way to some trees, where she had some good cover. She then watched as Cruz drove up to the main gates and then manoeuvred the car, making it appear as though she had just left the villa.

It seemed like an age to Maggie before she saw the BMW approaching. She recognised the driver. It was Hannah Lopez and when she saw Maggie, Lopez seemed to accelerate straight at her, making Maggie wince and brace herself for a collision.

At the last minute, just as Maggie had starting instinctively to turn away in her seat, she heard tyres squealing and the smell of burning brakes as the BMW screeched to a halt right in front of her.

Maggie saw the BMW's driver's door fly open and suddenly there was Hannah Lopez screaming obscenities at her. She didn't know why, but she just sat there, unfazed by Lopez and with a growing sense of calm and control, the same feeling she would get before she went into Court to defend a client.

She stepped out of the car and stood her ground, even as Lopez continued shouting at her.

"What are you doing here, Cruz?" demanded Hannah Lopez.

Nino and Pérez listened as Cruz played her part to perfection.

"I wanted your father to tell me to my face."

"Tell you what!" snapped Lopez.

"Why he told that monster Ortiz to do what he did to me!"

"You'd better shut up now, Maggie Cruz, before I release that video, and you wouldn't want that now, would you?"

"I don't care, do you hear me? I don't bloody care any more. I just wanted your father to tell me why!"

"And did he?" snarled Lopez. "Because I'd be very surprised if he did, you stupid bitch, because it was me who told Ortiz to do it."

Cruz knew she had her, but she needed to get Lopez to open up even more.

"Do you know what he did to me? And I mean, do you know exactly what that bastard did to me?" She was shouting at Lopez now.

"What? That it wasn't just him who raped you?" Lopez had a look on her face that made Cruz shiver. "Well, you're not the only one to have seen the video, Maggie." She was grinning at Cruz, but it was a cruel, heartless look. "I told him I needed you to never ever want that video to be seen by anyone, so I think getting those other three guys to give you a damn good ride really did the trick. It looked like they did a pretty good job on you too, but of course you wouldn't have known that, would you, sweetie? Not after Ortiz had slipped you a little something. What was it now, Rohypnol?"

"I hate him and the others for what they did to me, but I hate you even more! How could you let him do this to me? And it isn't just me, is it? I know how you work, Hannah Lopez! Christ, you're some evil bitch and how the hell did you get that police officer locked up?"

"She should have kept her nose out of our business. Just like those interfering journalists! My father ran The Foundation perfectly well for almost fifty years until Eduardo bloody Ramírez got a pang of conscience. Damn near killed my father, so Eduardo had to go, but then his son joined in asking too many questions as well!"

"Are you quite sane, Lopez? You kill off two members of your own organisation and go around threatening the brake death witnesses and anyone who gets in your way for that matter. You really are some piece of work!"

"Careful, Maggie," muttered Nino, as he listened. "You're pushing too hard."

And Cruz realised too late that she'd made a critical error, because Lopez's expression changed in an instant and she got the full impact.

"Oh my god, Maggie, I don't know what I'm saying. I was just so wound up worrying about my father because he's been so unwell and now there's been all this appalling press intrusion. I'll tell you now. I never wanted any part of this and I told my father that from the start, but it was Ortiz all along. Can't you see? He wants to take over everything when my father dies, so he did the same to me. Raped me and said he'd tell my father I was a slut and a whore, so he could persuade him to give him the company. And, and," Lopez was sobbing now. "It was his idea to gang rape you! To compromise you. I'm so sorry Maggie, that's why I was coming here to warn you not to see my father because Ortiz would then release the film he's got of me and…," she sobbed again, "… my father would never be able to handle that. It would kill him!"

Cruz looked at her, incredulous. Staggered at the performance this woman was putting on. She couldn't think of any words to say and was relieved when she saw Penny walking out from the trees and then two GEO cars approaching fast before they stopped, blocking off any possible exit for Lopez's BMW.

"Who are you?" Lopez said. Her demeanour had changed again. Wary, on her guard.

"DI Castillo, GEO."

The sobbing started again.

"I'm so pleased you're here, Inspector. Maggie and I need to report something to you. But it's very sensitive, so can we please go somewhere quiet?"

"Yes, of course and just so you know, Hannah Lopez, I'm arresting you on suspicion of conspiracy to murder, conspiracy to rape, bribery and corruption of public officials, blackmail of Señora Cruz here, witness intimidation of all of the witnesses in the Lopez Autoparts brake death trial and," he paused, "well, that should be sufficient for the time being." He cautioned her and motioned to Pérez to handcuff her.

"But I'm innocent! I'm a victim, like her." But she was losing control again and the savagery they'd heard before was quickly returning to Lopez's voice.

Nino looked at her.

"One piece of advice. Keep the play acting for court, as I think you're going to need it. Put her in the car, Sergeant and take her to headquarters whilst I go and arrest her father."

*****

"Maggie, you were amazing. I didn't need headphones to hear what was going on, I could hear everything from where I was," said Penny.

"Thanks, but I nearly made a mess of things when I went after her a bit and she sussed what was happening. I was just so angry!"

"But don't worry, because I think you'd got enough by then to nail her," said Penny.

"And she really shook me when she said those things," said Maggie quietly, reliving the moment as another shiver ran through her body.

"It's okay, it's over now."

"But I'll have to go to court, won't I?"

"That's not for me to say, but let me ask you, what do you think you should do, Maggie?"

Cruz looked at her. She'd been trying to forget it had ever happened, but then it had always been hanging over her and then when Lopez threatened her, she'd given up Mendez and now he was dead.

"I need to do it, don't I?" she said softly.

Although Penny could hardly hear what Maggie had said, the tears in her eyes gave it away.

Then Nino stepped forward.

"You did so well, Maggie! Well done and there will be a lot of victims thanking you for your bravery and for stepping up to the plate. What you've done is to open up this entire thing and now we can finally move against these people, with something concrete to go on."

"Come on, let's get you back to the hotel to see the others," said Penny.

"You think they'll still want to see me? You know, after what I did?"

"I think you've gone a long way to redeeming yourself, Maggie, especially when you've managed to bring Lori Garcia into the frame with Lopez as well."

For the first time in a long while Maggie Cruz felt the weight lift from her shoulders and she almost felt like the person she used to be, before she had met Jaime Ortiz.

*****

By the following morning word had got around that

today was the day Morales was going to take out the bent cop. Lori could sense the tension and anticipation growing inside the cell block even before the cell doors electronically opened.

As she left her cell to go to breakfast, she hoped to see Terri, because she'd already seen who the morning guard team were and that had done nothing to ease her feeling of trepidation that the day ahead was going to be a tough one, and one that she might not make it through!

Making her way towards the food hall, Lori saw her. Even without her long blonde hair, she could tell it was Terri by the way she was standing. Just seeing her smile was enough to help Lori start breathing a little easier. She wasn't alone!

But she'd need to keep her guard up, as she had no idea when the attack might come. Although the fact that she'd made it to breakfast in one piece suggested that it might be in the exercise yard where things were going to hot up again.

*****

Comisario Gutierrez had personally taken the judge's order to the prison to get Garcia released on bail.

"I'll need to refer this to the Governor, Señor," said the prison officer.

"It's Comisario," said Gutierrez gruffly, "and the Governor's expecting me. I phoned him on my way here."

"Please wait here, Comisario."

"I will, but please be quick. This woman's life may be in danger."

"This is a prison, Señor, we have guards watching the inmates all the time."

"You are either very stupid, or you are complicit in what is about to happen. Get me the Governor now!" demanded Gutierrez.

*****

49

The mid-morning call sounded and Lori, together with the rest of the inmates made their way to the exercise yard. She saw Valeria Morales strutting around. The woman was clearly enjoying the moment. This was her theatre and there was no doubt in Lori's mind that Morales intended to make this a spectacle to enhance her reputation.

Morales was smiling and chatting with the two guards on duty. They were the same ones who had hosed Lori down and now they were standing by the doors to the yard, so it was clear to Lori that Morales had them in her pocket and they were there to block off any possible escape.

Lori was keeping her distance and watching Morales's every move. She knew the woman would be far too savvy to carry a weapon until the very last moment, so she was ready when she saw Morales move alongside another inmate, a 'carrier,' and Lori caught a glimpse of a blade being pressed into Morales's palm.

It would be something that had started life as a non-threatening, blunt edged tool, maybe a toothbrush or a food hall utensil, which had since been honed into a killing blade.

Morales checked the cutting edge and nodded with

satisfaction. She didn't need anyone's help to do this. There was a reason why she was in control of what went on in the prison and it wasn't just because she happened to head up a major crime gang on the outside. As many had found to their cost, Valeria Morales was the toughest fighter of anyone in there, and she'd previously shown little or no mercy to anyone who had offered any sort of challenge to her.

Terri held back, just behind the crowd that was gathering around Morales, and watched her make her move as she started walking towards Lori. Terri needed to make sure she wasn't going to get boxed in when things kicked off, but she also had to keep her eyes peeled for a clear pathway to get through the mass of people before her in case things got out of hand and Lori needed help.

Lori had wondered about just telling the guards she didn't feel well and was going to stay in her cell. But the threat from Morales wasn't going to go away and although she'd been lucky so far, with the two clumsy attacks on her in the cramped conditions of the cell, she decided she might as well manage the 'when and where' it happened if she could.

She called out, "You ready, Morales? You've got your little audience, but do you really think you can take me?"

Morales smiled. This woman was a hell of a lot braver than most she had gone up against and not just brave, Garcia had shown she could really handle herself. Rosa was testament to that.

"Brave words, Inspectora Jefe, brave words. But you have no friends in here. None of your GEO to come to your aid."

"You really think I'll need help against you, Morales?" mocked Lori.

Then, having decided she wasn't going to wait to be

attacked, Lori quickly darted forward as she was still talking, catching Morales off her guard as she landed a sharp right jab on her chin, and drawing blood from the woman's mouth.

'Nice one, Lori,' thought Terri.

Morales stopped and put her finger to her lip and then looked at the blood, before licking the rest of the blood away from her lip.

"Nice. But let's see how you go on against this," and she pulled the blade from her back pocket, bringing a few grunts of approval from the watching crowd.

"Keep the noise down," called out one of the guards, anxious that it would draw attention to the CCTV operators.

Morales was quick and feigned one way and then the other, slashing out at first at Lori's face and then at her arms. Lori instinctively crossed her arms together in an 'X' shape to block the blade but still felt the pain as it cut deep into her right arm.

Knowing she couldn't take too many slashing wounds to her arms, as sooner or later she'd feel the effects of the blood loss, Lori took a few steps back and quickly yanked off her prison top, bringing whistles of approval from some of the crowd.

She twisted the top into a makeshift defensive weapon giving herself something to try to ward Morales off with and she flicked it hard at Morales, catching her on the side of the head, but it only stung her, rather than cause any hurt.

Lori tried again, to keep Morales out of range with her blade, but the problem was that once she'd flicked the top, it lost all its energy. Then if she didn't twist it back into something that half-looked like a rope, it had little or no impact.

Already both women were starting to breathe more heavily, and Lori knew she needed to stay light on her feet to be able to find time and space to re-twist her makeshift 'rope' back into position in readiness to flick it towards Morales.

The problem was that this was giving Morales opportunities to get in close to Lori and she was starting to cause even more damage with the blade, catching Lori both on her arms and once across her back.

Lori changed tack and next time she managed to fend off an attack by stretching out her top with her two hands in front of face, but that meant she couldn't re-load the tension in it, giving Morales the advantage.

As she slashed first one way and then other in quick succession, the backward slash almost caught Lori full across the face. She just managed to tilt her head at the last moment and the blade hit her side on, rather than blade first, so she felt the impact of Morales's fist more than the blade.

"Do her, do her!" The crowd was shouting now, getting more and more agitated, wanting blood.

Terri was getting concerned that two of the crowd in particular seemed to be getting too close to the action. Whilst Lori was holding up pretty well against Morales, if the others steamrollered her, she'd quickly be in real trouble.

Deciding that now was not the time to give anyone a chance, as she couldn't risk the rest of the crowd ganging up against them, Terri stepped in behind one of the two agitators. A quick glance around and whilst the others were wrapped up in the fight, Terri whispered to the woman, "Can I have a quick word, amiga?"

The woman looked at her.

"What?"

"Over here." Terri flicked her eyes towards the nearby wall, then as the woman came in close and without any warning, Terri punched her hard in the stomach and then again in the head knocking her out cold, before lowering her to the floor and propping her up against the wall.

As Terri slipped back into the crowd, the other agitator eyed her suspiciously.

"Where's Maria?"

"Over there," said Terri, flicking a thumb towards the wall. "Said she wasn't feeling well."

The woman went to look for Maria who was still slumped unconscious against the wall. Terri followed her and as the other woman bent down to check Maria, Terri slammed her fist down hard into the middle of her back. She dropped onto all fours, stunned by the force of the blow. She lifted her head as she tried to get up, only for it to come into range of Terri's right knee who smashed it into the side of the woman's head, sending her sprawling to the floor on top of Maria.

'Two down.'

As Terri moved back into the crowd, it was evident they were getting restless. Lori was gaining in confidence and wasn't just fending off Morales, but was now getting a few well struck jabs in of her own. They weren't enough to take Morales down, but they were still sufficiently stinging to make the gang leader think twice about coming forward.

The problem was, this wasn't like a boxing match, where you got to have a brief rest every three minutes. Both women were tiring and despite Lori's efforts, Terri was starting to worry that Morales might get through with a serious strike with one of her increasingly wild slashing attacks.

And if that didn't happen, then the crowd might take things into their own hands as they were getting closer and closer to the two women, with some of them trying to complete a circle around them. Terri eased herself forward to get in besides the women who getting closest to Lori's back.

'It's time to come out of the closet,' she thought.

"I'm behind you. Got you covered."

Lori heard the Australian accent and even manged a grin as Morales threw another lunging slash towards her.

"Gracias, amiga. Can you cover me whilst I finish this off?"

"Yes, no problem."

The woman next to Terri looked at her, confused, as she'd last heard this woman talking with a heavy Mediterranean accent.

Terri grinned at her. "Confused? I know." Then she hit her with a flying forearm smash that threw the woman's head back with blood pouring from her nose.

"Back away. Now, Señoras!" yelled Terri, stepping back slightly to give herself some space as another woman came at her. She ducked under the woman's clumsy attack and then threw an arcing right hook that landed squarely on the woman's jaw, dropping her like a stone. "I said, back away!"

A couple more went to move forward, but then seeing no one was going with them, they started shifted backwards.

Morales saw what had happened.

"Ah, so you do have a friend then, Garcia? How nice for you." She smiled at Terri. "Police?"

"Not me, no," said Terri, with a laugh.

"Well, I'll get to you, whoever you are, in just a moment…"

But the moment didn't come as Lori gambled, risking another cut on her arms, where the blood was now seeping quite heavily. She rushed at Morales, with her arms crossed in front of her face. Running straight at her, her arms caught Morales hard under the chin and knocked her flying backwards.

Morales hit the floor, dropping the blade which flew off to the side, where Terri quickly picked it up and pocketed it.

Lori wanted to get on top of Morales to pin her down, but the other woman was too quick and was back up on her feet and now it was her turn to run at Lori. She careered into her, taking both women to the floor. Morales was the first to react, rolling over on top of Lori and managing to pin her down and get in some solid right and left punches before Lori could get her arms up to protect herself.

Terri went to help, but suddenly found four women right in front of her. Blocking her way.

"Not this time, Raptis, or whoever you are?" said one of them.

Terri couldn't leave Lori pinned down, so she rushed the four of them, but two of them caught her and held her back as one of the women stared punching her. She was taking punches to the stomach and head. She was okay, but the women holding her were strong and she couldn't shift free.

She looked across at Lori. Morales's punches were getting through Lori's defences. How much more of this could she take?"

*****

"Comisario Gutierrez. Sorry to have kept you, I was..."

"I don't care what you were doing! Where are they? Where's Garcia and Morales?" demanded Gutierrez.

The prison governor looked at his watch.

"They'll be in the exercise yard, but as I said to you on the phone, we have guards out there, so nothing will happen to her."

"You're either a fool or you're in her pay as well. Take me to the exercise yard now! And you'd better get another team of guards there too."

The governor went to protest, but saw the look on the police officer's face and shouted out a few instructions and then said, "This way."

The two guards on the door to the exercise yard saw the prison governor through the door window. He was with another man they didn't recognise, together with some of the reception team. The governor flashed his name badge at the electronic door lock and waved the two guards out of the way.

"Get in there and break it all up. Sound the alarm and get everyone back in their cells. Now!"

The reception guards moved in swiftly to break up the crowd and the inmates who'd been hitting Terri quickly backed off, trying to slip away into the rest of the crowd.

Morales was pulled off Garcia and held by two of the guards.

"Take her to solitary. I'll deal with her later," said the Governor.

Gutierrez gently helped Lori up off the ground. Seeing she'd lost her top and was just in her bra, he shouted at one of the guards, "You! Get her a blanket, or a new top. And get some bandages too."

"Lori, are you okay?"

"I am now. How did you...?"

"Know to come?" said Gutierrez. "Your Señor Chambers and DI Castillo are very persuasive. Come on, we need to get those injuries treated."

Lori let out a deep breath, a shudder went through her whole body as exhaustion flooded over her as she realised how close she'd been to losing against Morales.

She looked around for Terri and managed a smile when she saw her. They both stood there, blood glistening on their faces and Lori's arms dripping blood from the slash wounds.

"Thank you," said Lori softly.

Terri smiled. She didn't need to say anything, but instead she hugged her and then held Lori in a tight embrace, relieved that they were both still alive.

*****

50

Nino Castillo spoke into the intercom at the entrance gates to Manny Lopez's villa. Moments later the electronic gates started to open and Pérez eased the car through the gates and up the long drive to the front of the villa.

A man was waiting for them.

"Señor Lopez is very ill and cannot see you."

"Is he conscious?"

"Well, yes."

"Then he's fit enough to see me. Besides, I haven't got much to say to him."

"You can't come in. Not unless you've got a warrant," smirked the security man.

"Got a law degree, have you?" said Pérez pushing past him. "But I guess not, as otherwise you'd know we don't need a warrant to enter a property to make an arrest."

"But you can't arrest him!"

"What? Are you going to stop us?"

Pérez turned and fronted the man out. He saw the man start to try to block him and didn't hesitate, moving in quickly and grabbing the man's arm and yanking it hard, bringing out a yell a pain and forcing him to his knees, where he handcuffed him.

"Watch him," Pérez said to Flores.

Nino and Pérez went in through the door and were met by a nurse.

"What's going on?"

"DI Castillo, GEO." He showed his identity badge. "Where is Lopez?"

She motioned for them to follow him.

"You can see him, but he's very weak, so you can't move him."

"That won't be necessary, I just need to speak to him for a moment. Is he sufficiently well enough for that? Nurse, it's important."

The nurse looked unsure. "I should phone his daughter."

"That won't be possible. She is already under arrest."

"I see. Then yes, he is well enough, but just for a couple of minutes. As I said, he is very weak."

"What's going on out there!" A voice said from the next room.

"Doesn't sound that weak to me," said Pérez.

"Señor Manny Lopez, I'm DI Nino Castillo."

"What do you want? You can't just come barging in here! If you don't get out of my office now, I'll sue the arse off the lot of you."

"Let's start with what I want, shall we, Señor?"

Lopez heard the tone in Castillo's voice. There was no apprehension or even a sign of any uncertainty.

"Manny Lopez, I'm arresting you on suspicion of murder, corruption, witness intimidation and as head of Lopez Autoparts, corporate manslaughter."

"You've got nothing. You're just fishing!" snarled Lopez. "Nurse, call my daughter please."

"She won't be returning your call, Lopez. She's already in custody for the same things as you, plus conspiracy to rape."

"Rape, what are you talking about man?"

"The gang rape of Maggie Cruz."

The look on Lopez's face when he heard Cruz's name was enough for Castillo to know he'd definitely scored a point.

"Yes, Lopez. Maggie Cruz, who your boy Jaime Ortiz gang raped under your daughter's direction. But now we've got her and other witnesses who are now willing to come forward. So that glass pyramid you built on fear and coercion? Well, it's about to come crashing down on you, Señor."

"You've got nothing, nothing, you hear!" repeated Lopez, but this time Castillo saw the first signs of uncertainty.

"Nurse, nurse, get my lawyer on the phone. Do it now!"

"You are of course, allowed access to a legal representative and in view of the current state of your health I am now bailing you to attend a police station in a week's time. If you are still not fit enough then, I shall arrange to extend the bail date. Do you understand?"

"Once my lawyers get on this, you won't ever get me into a police station!"

"Don't think for one moment, Lopez that I don't know what you'll try to do to delay things, but don't forget I have your daughter and very soon we'll have Ortiz in custody, so as for you? Well, from what we hear it's your daughter who runs things now, so she's the one I'm going to make sure gets locked up for a long time, a very long time."

Nino let the words sink in and watched as the man who had built Lopez Autoparts into a multi-million euro business, as well as fronting the Foundation for the best part of fifty years, took in what he'd just said.

"Inspector," said Lopez after a few moments, "I think I would like to make a voluntary statement."

*****

51

Greg held Lori close. The relief flooding through him that she was safe and, except for some nasty slash wounds to both her arms and the heavy bruising around her face, she wasn't too seriously harmed.

"I'm okay, I'm okay," said Lori, the tears she'd been holding back finally starting to flow. "If it hadn't have been for Terri…" her words faded and he felt her body twitch.

Terri, who also had two black eyes and had taken a lot of bruising punches to her body, hugged them both.

"I was only there as a bit of moral support, Lori," she grinned. "I reckon you'd have been okay without me."

Both women knew better. It had been a close run thing and Gutierrez turning up when he did had prevented either of them being more badly injured, or worse.

"It's good to have you back, Boss," said Nino.

"It's good to be back, Nino," she smiled, "and I think I've got to thank both of you," she looked at Greg and Nino, "for persuading the Comisario to come and rescue me."

"It should be me thanking them, Inspectora Jefe," said Gutierrez, with a grimace.

"It's Lori, okay? No hard feelings. You were just…."

"Doing my job? Maybe, but perhaps I should have looked a little bit closer."

He saw the expression on both Greg's and Nino's faces and held his hands up.

"You're right. I'm sorry, I should have looked a damn sight closer."

"Okay, I think we should move on," said Nino. "So, Boss, we've got Hannah Lopez in custody and I've arrested and bailed Manny Lopez. He's too sick to bring down to the station and no, there's no play acting going on. But what he has done is make a voluntary statement."

That got everyone's attention in the room.

"Is he taking it all on his head?" said Greg.

"Effectively yes," said Nino.

"What are you going to do now?" said Gutierrez.

"Boss?" Nino looked at Lori.

She smiled.

"The Comisario is asking you, Nino. You've got this and you don't need your Inspectora Jefe sticking her oar in, especially when she's officially signed off on sick leave."

"You're on sick leave?" said Greg. "When did that happen?"

"As of a minute ago," grinned Lori, knowing that Nino had the investigation well under control.

Nino flushed with pride, then looked around him as everyone waited for him to speak, to decide what was going to happen next.

"We arrest Ortiz. Have we got contact with Sam?"

"Yes," said Anna. "He's with Tommy and James, they're sitting up on Ortiz's apartment. Shall I get him on the phone?"

"Please, Anna."

"Sam?"

"Is everyone okay, Nino?"

"Yes, Sam, Lori and Terri are here, but before you speak to them, I need you to confirm that you've still got eyeball on Ortiz's flat."

"Yes, yes. No movement since we brought him back here."

"Good. I'm sending Pérez down with a team to pick him up, so stay there and guide him in. If he comes out before they get there, then do not engage, just follow. Is that clear Sam?"

"Yes, yes."

"Good luck with that," Greg whispered to Anna, whose look suggested she knew exactly what he meant.

*****

Ten missed calls from Manny Lopez and all because Ortiz had been bristling with anger after seeing Hannah and had turned his phone off. But it was still no excuse for missing his boss's calls and Ortiz knew it.

He phoned him back.

"Jaime, at last. Where've you been? I've been calling you and calling you!"

"Sorry, Boss, I was… I had my phone off. What's up?"

"Hannah's been arrested and so have I."

"What!"

"Yes, but I've been released on bail because, well, because it seems I'm too sick to even be arrested properly."

Ortiz heard Lopez laughing, but there was no humour in the old man's laugh, just more of an acceptance that he really was very ill.

"What do you need me to do, Boss?"

"I need you to disappear, Jaime. You should have plenty of money, so get out of Palma and don't come back, you hear?"

"I don't understand. What about you and Hannah?"

"You can't help me now, son and I've told the police

that it's all down to me. Everything. I told them I forced you to do it, and that Hannah had no knowledge of what I was doing."

"Did they believe you?"

"No, of course they didn't," he laughed. "They're not that stupid, but that's not the point. The fact is that they might not look a gift horse in the mouth, as proving anything against Hannah may be difficult and if they can't find you, then they might just settle for me."

"I don't know what to say, Boss. I don't want to just leave you here, not after everything you've done for me."

"Listen, Jaime, do as I say, this one last time. Disappear. I'm not going to be here that much longer anyway, not according to the doctors, who despite the fact that I pay them a lot of money, still only give me bad news. I've got months, possibly just weeks, so maybe I won't even give the police the satisfaction to get me into a court room."

Jaime took a deep breathe in. "Boss, you're sure that's what you want me to do?"

"Positive. Get out of there now. I don't know how much time you've got!"

*****

"Tommy, I think we've got movement. The lights have just gone out in the apartment," said James.

"Sam, did you copy that? What do you want us to do?"

"Shit" said Sam.

"Martínez to Pérez?" Sam called up on the frequency the GEO were using.

"Please don't tell me you've got movement, Sam? We're still eight minutes away."

"Sorry to be the bringer of bad news then," said Sam.

"Sam from Nino. Do not engage, Sam. We know how

dangerous this guy can be and he could well be armed."

"I know, but…."

"No buts!" said Nino. "Do not engage, I repeat, do not engage."

Greg looked at Anna. The worry on both their faces clear to see. Whilst Sam had been a highly trained police firearms officer in his time, Jaime Ortiz was a cold-blooded killer. Greg moved quietly away from the rest of the group and made a call. No one, except Anna, noticed him. Then when he came back into the middle of the room, she looked at him questioningly, trying to read what he had done.

Greg then said to Nino, "May I?"

Nino nodded. "Please."

"Sam, it's Greg. I concur with Nino on this one. You, I repeat you, are not to engage. Please confirm."

"Thanks, Greg, that's appreciated." said Nino.

They waited for Sam's response and Nino blew out his cheeks in relief when he heard Sam say, "Confirmed and understood."

*****

Sam was left wondering what the hell was going on, then he heard Tommy calling him on his 3R comms radio.

"Sam from Tommy."

"Yes, yes, Tommy. Did you get the last from Greg? We are not to engage. Repeat, we are not to engage."

Tommy had been with Greg Chambers for as long as 3R had been in existence and knew his boss better than most.

"Sam, what exactly did Greg say to you?"

Sam thought for a moment.

"He said, 'I am not to engage,'" Sam said slowly.

"Agreed," said Tommy. "You, Sam, are not to engage. James, are you ready?"

"Moving in now, Tom," replied James, who had

taken the call from Greg and was already preparing himself to take on Ortiz.

"James?" said Sam.

"It's okay, Sam, I've got this, mate."

Encouraged to join the SAS by his mentor Simon Barnes, James Porter had served for ten years before following him into the private sector, where he joined 3R International on Simon's recommendation and had since already proved himself a worthy addition to the team.

"Anything you need me to do, James?" said Tommy.

"Talk me in and then just be ready to move in on my shout."

"Copied that."

Sam and Tommy watched from their hidden positions, as James moved on foot towards Ortiz's SEAT Cupra, where he crouched down behind it and waited.

"Subject is leaving the front entrance to the apartment, James. Heading towards the Cupra. He will be with you in 5-4-3-2-1.

*****

52

"Contact," said Tommy, as he saw James step out behind Ortiz as he was opening the driver's door. He slammed Ortiz hard in the back, catching his head on the top edge of the door. But Ortiz didn't seem to feel any pain and he spun around, reaching inside his left jacket pocket.

"Possible gun, James!" radioed Tommy.

James kicked out at Ortiz's legs, trying to take him to the ground, but Ortiz was strong and somehow kept his stance. However, he was sufficiently off-balance for James to get a punch in, hitting Ortiz hard in the kidneys and he dropped the gun, which went clattering to the floor.

Ortiz fought hard to catch his breath and thrashed out at James, somehow catching him high up on the forehead. No real damage done, but it was a reminder to James, as if he needed one, that Ortiz wasn't going to be an easy take down.

Both men were eyeing the gun. It was about three yards or more away from them, but to get to it would require either man to run the gauntlet of being attacked by the other before they reached it.

As they vied for position, it occurred to Ortiz that whoever this man was, he hadn't made any attempt to arrest him.

'So, if you're not the police?' Ortiz thought. *'Then who are you?'* He tried talking to the man, to get him off his guard.

"Who are you and more importantly, what do you want?" said Ortiz.

James wasn't falling for any of Ortiz's distraction tactics and kept moving, making sure he didn't get any closer to where the gun lay.

"Let's just say I'm a friend of Lori Garcia."

"Shouldn't you be arresting me then?"

"Who said anything about me being in the police?"

As he spoke, James feigned a left jab and quickly followed it up with a vicious right hook that Ortiz only just saw coming at the last moment. He ducked, but it still caught him on his left ear, leaving him with the sensation of a dull, rolling noise bouncing around inside his head, but after he ducked he kept rolling, getting closer and closer to the gun.

'Got it!' Ortiz said to himself.

James knew he had to take cover and quickly! He ran as fast as he could, past the SEAT and past some more parked cars.

"James?" called Tommy.

"He's got the gun."

"Where are you, Pérez?" said Sam on the police radio frequency.

"I'm here. You can tell me later why you engaged with Ortiz, but for now, back off and let me do my job."

"Understood," said Sam.

"Ortiz!" yelled Pérez. "Armed police! Stand still and drop the gun."

Ortiz stood his ground, but didn't drop the gun.

"Look about you, Ortiz. You're surrounded. Put it down, now!"

"Or what?" snarled Ortiz.

"If you make any move to raise that gun or if you try to leave then I will stop you."

"Brave words when you're surrounded by your mates."

Pérez tried a different tack. "Look, this doesn't have to end badly. You can walk out of here and give your side of the story." "Walk away from what? This isn't even my gun, it's his." Ortiz pointed towards James Porter, who looked at Pérez and shook his head.

"But you can walk away. I mean, that Hannah Lopez is a real piece of work. But I expect you know that already?"

"Shut your mouth. You don't know anything about her!"

"I know what I heard her say and she's really dumped on you, big time!" Pérez saw a look of growing confusion appearing on Ortiz's face. "She's told our boss that everything was down to you. She even said you raped her, like you did with the Cruz woman."

"I didn't," Ortiz said quietly.

Pérez knew he had to tread carefully, but this was an opportunity to de-escalate the situation that he couldn't let pass. If he could just get Ortiz to cooperate.

"What? Rape both women, or was it just Maggie Cruz?"

"I know what you're trying to do," said Ortiz. "And to be fair, it's not a bad attempt." A thin smile crossing his lips.

"I'm not lying here, Ortiz. I can get the audio sent to me so you can hear for yourself."

Sam was texting Nino already and moments later Pérez heard a ping on his phone.

"Sam to Pérez. That's the link, amigo."

"Gracias. Bravos 22 and 33, cover me, guys."

"Si, si," said Bravo 22.

The two Bravo officers regripped and re-focused

their H&K semi-automatic rifles, leaving Ortiz to look down at their red dot aimpoints on his chest.

"Oritz, I'm getting my phone out, okay?"

Keeping his eyes fixed squarely on Ortiz, Pérez slowly slid his hand up to the breast pocket of his body armour and carefully lifted his phone out with two fingers.

"Listen to this."

Pérez had to look away from Ortiz to work the phone, a danger moment, but it passed without issue and as he pushed the arrow on the phone screen Ortiz heard her voice.

Hannah Lopez was crucifying him. Laying everything on him, just as the cop had said.

'Could it be a fake? But there was no way they could have put this together so quickly.'

Ortiz looked down at the red dots again and smiled. Pérez breathed in. This wasn't looking good.

"Ortiz, I only played this to you to let you know I was telling the truth. She's not worth it, man. Talk to us. We know it was her and her old man who were running things."

Ortiz was still smiling and Pérez realised the situation was in serious danger of going 'pear-shaped' as Ortiz seemed to be pushing them towards a 'suicide by cop,' an acknowledged suicide strategy where a person knows how firearms police will react if they are provoked into a life-threatening situation.

"Ortiz," Pérez tried again. "Drop it. Drop the gun. Let's do this another way."

"I'm not sure you're really giving me much of an option are you..," Ortiz looked at the chevrons on Pérez's epaulettes, "...Sergeant?"

"Well, there's one way I really don't want this to go, Ortiz."

"I have a similar view, Sergeant, namely going to

prison and I have no intention of doing that."

Ortiz saw the police officers stiffen slightly. He'd given them a red flag. He wasn't going to come quietly. Now all they had to decide was whether he was going to open fire on them and try and take as many with him as he could before they shot him or, whether he'd bring his gun up, as though to fire it, in order to force the police to shoot him.

"Castillo to Pérez?" Nino called up on his police radio, to ensure his transmission was digitally recorded and would therefore provide clear support to his firearms team in the inevitable inquiry of what looked increasingly likely to be a police shooting.

"Yes, Boss."

"Sam has been giving me a running dialogue. I gather that Ortiz appears intent on pushing you towards a potentially fatal engagement and it sounds like you're doing your very best to stop him. To confirm, you have my authority and full support to use the appropriate level of force, including lethal force if required, to prevent harm, or injury to the public, the police and if possible, to Jaime Ortiz."

"Understood, Boss and gracias."

Pérez hoped to God that this didn't end in a fatal shooting, but if required to do so, then he knew he would shoot to stop Ortiz if he had no other choice. But he was going to try one last thing. He slipped his phone back into his pocket and re-sighted his H&K MP5 on Ortiz. Then he clicked his radio mic to open, "Bravo 22 and 33? Move to your less lethal option, your Tasers and fire on my word."

"Si, si, Sarge," both officers responded, and switched from their H&K semi-automatics to Tasers, the electroshock weapons with a range of twenty-one feet, and capable of discharging a five second shock of 50,000 volts through two darts attached to insulated wire.

"Sergeant?" said Ortiz. "I'm not going to allow you to take me to prison. Do you understand? Stand your men down and I suggest you get these people well away from here."

Pérez had seen a number of people come out of their villas and apartments to see what was going on and despite them being urged back inside by some of his team, together with the 3R guys, some were still out in the road or on their balconies, possibly mistaking this for a scene out of a TV series that was being filmed.

But it wasn't, and although Pérez was aware of the potential for the public to be caught in any subsequent cross-fire, he just felt there was something about the way Ortiz was looking and talking that indicated the man wasn't about to open fire on the police, or the public for that matter.

"Look, like I said, we can talk this through. Put your side across."

"Sadly, Sergeant, whether or not it was Hannah Lopez, or her father, who directed me to do the things I may have done for them and the Palma Foundation for the past twenty years, almost matters not. But if it helps? Then, yes, it was her father, Manny, who set up the way the Foundation was run and we didn't take any crap from anyone. As for Hannah, I knew I was never going to be good enough for her, but I certainly didn't rape her as she suggests. But," Ortiz paused, "there were certain things I did in accordance with her direct orders. Things which you might wish to record via your radio?"

"Go on," said Pérez, opening his radio mic to transmit.

"It was Hannah Lopez, and not her father, who told me to get rid of both Eduardo and Marcos Ramírez and if she tries to wriggle out of it, she made it perfectly clear that she meant permanently. She was also the one who wanted the witnesses in the brake death litigation case silenced and I know that because Manny, Señor Lopez, was surprised when I told him what she'd instructed me to do. You get all that, Sergeant?"

Ortiz sneered when he said the word *'Sergeant'* and before Pérez, or any of his team, could react he'd flicked the barrel of his gun up under his chin and pulled the trigger.

There were screams and gasps from the public, with some of them diving for cover at the sound of the gunshot. Ortiz was dead by the time he hit the floor, although his body still twitched involuntarily for moments after.

Pérez was the first to react.

"Man down. It's Ortiz. He's taken his own life. No other shots fired and no other injuries."

*****

53

There was the usual debrief following the day's events, including the news that there would be a formal review of the police firearms team and the circumstances that led to Ortiz taking his own life.

However, Nino Castillo still had an investigation to manage because with his boss, Inspectora Jefe Lori Garcia, now on sick leave, he knew he needed to take the lead.

His priority was Hannah Lopez, who was in custody and therefore on a 24 hour custody clock. If he wasn't able to charge her within the first 24 hours then she would have to be released, or, brought before a judge to request a further detention in custody for up to 72 hours. Then if he still didn't have sufficient evidence to charge her, Lopez would have to go back before a judge to determine if there was a need to further detain her up to a maximum of 15 days.

Although he hadn't yet had the results of the state pathologist's examination of Eduardo Ramírez's exhumed body, Nino knew he had less of an issue in producing a convincing prosecution file to support two charges of conspiracy to murder in relation to both Eduardo and his son, Marcos.

However, it was the extent of the corruption

involved in the Palma Foundation that was giving him much more of a headache. The fact that Hannah and Manny Lopez were both being represented by Frankie Rodriguez didn't help. He'd considered arguing that there was a conflict of interest, not just because Rodriguez's father, Juan, was a joint founder of the Foundation, but also because the Rodriguez family law practice were representing both members of the Lopez family.

However, he decided, after much debate with the GEO's own legal team, that suggesting that one of the most respected legal families in Spain may be compromised would be a hard battle to win and if anything, it would more than likely detract from the prosecution case against the Lopez family and their running of the Palma Foundation.

The subsequent interviews Nino undertook with Hannah Lopez gave him nothing, except to provide further evidence of the lengths she was prepared to go to lay the blame at anyone's door, bar her own.

Her claims that Eduardo had somehow taken his own life and that Marcos had deliberately crashed his car in another apparent suicide, were laughable. But the fact they required Nino's investigation team to ensure they had covered every aspect of her wild allegations from the defence left Lori to wait anxiously for Nino's return from a meeting with the state prosecutor.

As he came through into her office she smiled.

"Welcome back, Boss," he grinned.

She knew it had been two weeks of hard slog for him and his team whilst she had been away on sick leave, and she could see the strain on his face.

"Don't hold me in suspense, Nino! Did you get it?"

He held up a handful of papers.

"Two counts of conspiracy to murder and authority

to seek a further remand in custody whilst we continue to investigate the witness intimidation in the brake death case."

"Yes!" cried Lori, punching the air. "That's brilliant, well done."

It was high praise indeed from the woman who had become such a close friend and from whom he'd learned so much.

*****

Greg had given back the meeting room, but he still had his room in the Hotel Born and Lori had spent most of the following two weeks she'd been on sick leave there with him.

Although she had been officially released from prison and all charges withdrawn on a Judge's order, Greg was still worried about her, about the impact of the attacks she'd been subjected to on the inside, even though she had tried to reassure him.

"Honestly, I'm okay, Greg. I was only in there for a couple of days and I had Terri in there towards the end, so she was watching my back."

"But..."

"Stop worrying about me," she said, gently kissing him. "I'm okay and that's all thanks to you, Anna and Terri. In fact, everyone who helped. So trust me when I say it's time to move on."

"As long as..."

"I am. Come on, let's go and see the others."

*****

Terri was back to her usual blonde hair colour when she, her father, Greg, and Sam all next met up with Anna at her villa the following day, together with Lori and Nino.

The conversation amongst them quickly ran through what Nino and Lori were able to tell them about the case, without breaching any confidentiality.

Lori also mentioned she had received a personal call from the President.

"I suppose he didn't have to call me, but it was nice to get it and it was also useful to hear what he had to say about the Foundation," said Lori.

The others waited for her to continue.

"We need to remember the Palma Foundation is a big deal, both in terms of its economic influence, but also politically, especially because of the impact of three of the four founder member organisations that now employ tens of thousands of people between them."

"So, the Foundation will continue, but now definitely as a force for good, whereas, Lopez Autoparts is no more. Is that right?" said Sam.

"Yes, although it wasn't said explicitly, however, I think this is where the President might have had something to do with what's happening. It seems he's on very good terms with the chairmen of the two major shareholders who instigated a buyout and rebranding of Lopez Autoparts."

"So, no redundancies?"

"Or lost voters," grinned Nino.

"Politics and policing crossing over then?" said Sam.

"Yes," said Lori. "I can't say I'm completely happy about it, and Kat Reyes certainly isn't, especially because I was told in no uncertain terms by the State Prosecutor, that Manny Lopez was to be the prime offender, with the daughter, Hannah, being treated as an accessory."

Sam had to smile. "So that's why there's been nothing major coming out in the media about Hannah?"

"Exactly," said Lori. "Kat was given the exclusive and persuaded to limit her attention to Manny, which to be fair, she accepted, because in reality she had plenty of evidence against him, but most of what she had against Hannah was speculation and circumstantial."

"And the President is happy?"

"Oh yes, especially as he hinted to the fact that Juan Rodriguez would be stepping back from political life."

"Ha, we're back to politics!" laughed Greg, before he frowned. "What about Maggie Cruz? What's going to happen to her? She is, after all, partly responsible for the death of Cesar Mendez."

"Not in the public interest to pursue a prosecution," said Lori.

"You happy with that?" Greg looked at her, doubtfully.

"She was a bit player who got caught up in it. Given what she went through with Ortiz and then the fact she helped bring the whole pack of cards down by getting Hannah Lopez on record? Yes, I'm okay with her getting a second chance."

"Me, too," said Terri. "After all, she did come good for us, guys, so why not give her a break? But what about the Foundation? Will they be prosecuted in any way? Corporately, I mean."

"No, and I'm okay with that. The Ramírez family trust is back in charge, with Christina, the mother as Chair, and Rafa is running the day to day business."

"I think we've all come to realise that Rafa Ramírez isn't just the playboy he allowed the media to think he was," said Anna.

"No, that's for sure and I've met him a couple times since and he's a really good guy. I think he and his mother will get the Foundation back on the straight and narrow, especially with the new blood they're getting in." Sam looked at his mother.

"Anna?" said Lori.

"I've been invited to join the new Board."

"That's excellent, Anna," said Greg.

"It was very kind of Christina and Rafa to ask."

"By the way, Lori," said Sam, "did you have any luck with the ledger that Manny was supposed to have kept?"

"No, but Nino, you tell them."

"We think Hannah got rid of it. I spoke to her PA and she remembers Lopez asking for a shredder around the time that Kat Reyes's article broke in the press," said Nino.

"That has presumably buried a lot of her father's secrets then?" said Sam.

"You're right I think, Sam. There's a lot we're never going to know, as the latest on Manny Lopez is that he's only got weeks, possibly days to go."

"It's still a really good result, Nino," said Lori. "Without your pressing they'd have literally got away with murder, including Cesar Mendez's."

"I agree," said Sam. "It's a bloody great result given what, and who, you were up against."

"Yes, I know," said Lori, "and I can take the fact that Hannah is getting off pretty lightly. That said, we've still got a lot to do, starting with the prison, what with Valeria Morales trying to finish me off for Sanchez and then there's the whole corruption thing with the guards, but Nino has all of that in hand with Comisario Gutierrez, haven't you?"

Nino nodded.

"You've really stepped up into your role, amigo," said Sam.

"Gracias, Sam."

"What about Pérez? How's he doing?" said Sam.

Because of the circumstances, Ortiz's suicide was still being classified as a police firearms shooting, even though no police officer had actually discharged their weapon.

"He really appreciated your call, Sam," said Lori.

"We all know he did everything he could to bring it home peacefully, but you still don't know which way someone else might view it in the cold hard light of day."

"That's true, Lori. Anyway, I'm glad the call helped. I was just trying to give him some extra support. Now what about you? Greg says you're feeling good and your injuries are healing?"

Lori showed them her arms. She still had plasters across some of the cuts.

"They're on the mend, thanks. I'm not sure if I was just lucky, but none of them went so deep as to cause lasting tissue damage."

"Terri was pretty impressed, Lori, with how you dealt with things in there," said Sam.

"What are you saying, Bro?" said Terri coming in late to the conversation.

"Just saying how impressed you were with Lori's street fighting."

"Better than yours, you mean? When you ran into that guy in Puerto Pollensa," she teased. "You know? When I had to come and rescue you."

Sam laughed.

"My sister's right, although she does love telling this story, but to be fair, I was getting my arse well and truly kicked and she did indeed rescue me."

"And you're taking some more time off, Lori?" said Anna.

"Just a few more days. I want to go and see my boys. So, Nino's in charge and I understand he's close to recruiting a new member to the GEO. Isn't that right, Nino?"

"Yes, we're opening up a satellite office in the Balearics, with Comisario Gutierrez's support."

"Interesting," said Sam.

"And I think you may know the officer who is

transferring across to us," said Nino, with a grin.

Sam looked at him and Anna saw her son was blushing.

"Sam?" she said.

"I'm assuming Nino means Detective Delgado?" said Sam.

"Since when have you called Sofi, Detective Delgado," said Terri, with a wide grin across her face. "Something going on is there?"

"Well, all I can say is that Sofi was a little reluctant when I first mentioned joining the GEO, as she thought it would mean a transfer to Madrid," said Nino.

"Look…" spluttered Sam, his face going even redder before his mother, Anna, gave him a hug.

"Mate, it's okay," laughed Terri, grabbing him affectionately around his middle. "We're just joshing with you. But it's about time too though, so just make sure you don't mess this one up alright?"

"I'll try not to," said Sam, with a sheepish grin.

*****

After Lori and Nino had left them, as they had work to do back at police headquarters, the rest of the 3R team sat out on Anna's terrace having coffee.

"Okay, what now, my intrepid team?" said Greg.

"Back to work I reckon, Dad," said Terri.

"Yes, I've got a meeting with Martin Carruthers and Lucas Iglesias. Lucas wants to introduce him to the person who helped put Terri's back story together," said Anna.

"Interesting, and that reminds me," said Greg, standing up getting ready to go. "James has asked for a period of unpaid leave. I told him that I thought it would be okay, Terri, but said I'd check in with you, seeing as you're the boss."

"I can help out if you need an extra pair of hands," said Sam.

"Sure, I don't see any problem," said Terri.

"Good, I'll let him know," said Greg.

Terri suddenly looked first at her father, and then at Sam.

"Why does he want the unpaid leave?"

Sam looked deep into his coffee cup. He wanted Greg to answer his daughter.

"Sorry, Terri, what did you say?" said Greg, as though he hadn't heard her.

"I said," Terri slowly responded, her lips tightening. "Why does James want the unpaid leave?"

"Oh, some family business, or something," said Greg vaguely.

This time Terri's voice was harder and more direct.

"His mother's dead and he's estranged from his father. Stop bullshitting me, Dad! What the hell's going on?"

Greg looked at Sam and then to Anna, before turning back to his daughter.

"He's got a lead on Diego Sanchez."

THE END

*****

BOOK FIVE

The 3R team will be back!

Keep up to date with what's happening by joining
The 3R International Facebook group
It's free to join!

You can also follow me on Instagram
the_mallorcan_bookseller

LIST OF CHARACTERS

Main 3R and GEO team (surname alphabetical order)

Terri Anderson – daughter of Greg Chambers. Brought up in Australia with her mother, she is a former Australian Army combat soldier and now the 3R Operations Director
Simon Barnes – now deceased, killed by Diego Sanchez. He was ex- SAS & worked for 3R International. He had only recently become Terri Anderson's partner.
Nino Castillo – GEO officer.
Greg Chambers – Founder of 3R International consultancy. Ex-MI6. Father to Terri and biological father to Sam.
Lori Garcia – GEO police officer, girlfriend of Greg Chambers.
Penny Hastings – ex MI6, now with 3R International
Anna Martínez – ex-MI6, mother of Sam, now part time with 3R and a consultant to MI6
Sam Martínez – son of Anna Martínez after her short relationship with Greg Chambers. An ex DCI, Metropolitan Police, he is now works with 3R International
Sergeant Fernando Pérez – GEO tactical firearms supervisor
James Porter – ex SAS, recruited into 3R by Simon Barnes.
Tommy Williams – ex-para. Longest serving member with 3R International

Palma Foundation (surname alphabetical order)

Manny Lopez – founder member, CEO of Lopez Autoparts
Hannah Luisa Lopez – daughter of Manny, CEO of Lopez Autoparts and the Foundation
Enrique Fernandez – founder member, CEO Enfern Hotels
Eduardo Ramírez – founder member, deceased, previously CEO CDM (Catering & Distribution) Ltd

Christina Ramírez – wife of Eduardo, shareholder of CDM Ltd
Marcos Ramírez – son of Eduardo and Christina, deceased.
Rafa Ramírez – son of Eduardo and Christina, ocean environmentalist
José Rodriguez – founder member, Lawyer
Francisco (Frankie) Rodriguez – son of José, Lawyer

Secondary (first name - alphabetical order)

Aina Vila (real person) – family owner of Coral Bar Restaurant, Port de Pollensa
Andres Gelabert (real person) – owner of Bodegas Angel, a vineyard in Santa Maria del Camí, in the Binissalem wine region
Angelina – nurse to Manny Lopez
Anna Dominguez – cover name for Anna Martínez's role as Lori's Madrid lawyer
Arlo – journalist friend of Kat Reyes
Cesar Mendez – CNI Intelligence officer
Chief Inspector Flores – Lori Garcia's boss at GEO
Dani - Custody Assistant
Diego Sanchez – youngest and surviving son of Alberto Sanchez, crime gang boss. Currently on the run after he shot and murdered Simon Barnes.
Detective Sergeant Vega – interviewing officer
Hugo – the bully at Jaime's city school
Isabella (Bella) Santos – local reporter
José Verdi – Chair of the Classic Car Rally Organising Committee
Juan Gutierrez – Head of Balearics CID
Juan Moreno – an IT specialist for Jaime Ortiz
Juanita – PA to Hannah Lopez
Kat Reyes – freelance journalist
Lisa Green – friend of Terri (featured in the Pollensa Connection)
Lucas Iglesias – retired Spanish Intelligence Service

Margarita "Maggie" Cruz – lawyer and friend of Sofi Delgado
Martin Carruthers – MI6, London
Miquel Bosch Abadal (real person) – owner of Contrabando Tapas Bar, Llucmajor
Miriam - part of the Contrabando team
Pablo Hernandez – Anti-Corruption Prosecutor, friend of Francisco (Frankie) Rodriguez
Paula (real person) – manager, Bar 13%, Palma
Detective Pedro Romero – Police officer on temporary attachment to CID
Rafa Ramírez – younger brother of Marcos
Rosa – prison inmate, enforcer for Morales
Señora Diaz – Jaime Ortiz's school teacher
Valeria Morales – Crime Boss, prison inmate

THE PALMA FOUNDATION LOCATION TOUR

As with all my books, and because of the interest it has generated with my readers, I have again included a list of the key places within the storyline should you be in Mallorca and wish to visit them.

Both Miquel at Contrabando and Aina at Bar Coral in Puerto Pollensa will be delighted to see you - and Aina even has some hardback copies of the books, just incase your Kindle breaks down whilst you're on holiday!

Mallorca
Contrabando Tapas Restaurant, Llucmajor
(Contact: Miquel)

Restaurante Bar Coral, Puerto Pollensa
(Contact: Aina and all her family)

Bodegas Angel (vineyard open for visits - best to book - and sales back to the UK/Europe), Ctra Santa Maria-Sencelles km, Santa Maria del Cami.
(Contact: Andres Gelabert)

Cappuccino Grand Cafe Borne, Plaza Juan Carlos 1, Palma

Bar 13% Vinos Tapas Bistro, Carrer de Sant Feliu, Palma
(Contact: Paula)

Centro Penitenciario de Mallorca, adjacent to Ma11 just before it joins Ma20 (they aren't open for tourist visits!)

Police Headquarters
Carrer de Simo Ballester, Palma (it's just off the Avinguda de l'Argentina, one of the city inner-ring roads)

Belver Castle, Palma.
It's high above the city and accessible by car or it's a very steep walk up some steps, but you get amazing views of the Bay of Palma and the castle itself is a really good visit (there is a charge)

London

Enoteca da Luca, St Paul's, (Italian Restaurant), 20-21, Watling Street, EC4M 9BR
(Contact: Matt)

THE 3R INTERNATIONAL SERIES

An exciting action crime series set primarily on the beautiful island of Mallorca, featuring the 3R International team, where Greg, Anna, Sam and Terri find themselves drawn into complex crime adventures where danger is never very far away.

The Mallorcan Bookseller

Book One

"Is Anna in?" It took just three words to change his life. Sam Martínez, a London detective, is put on sick leave suffering with PTSD resulting from a firearms incident that went wrong and his best friend was shot. Going home to Mallorca, where he grew up, he helps out in the family bookshop. But before long, he finds himself caught up with helping a family friend who has fallen prey to an IT scam. When another scam victim is murdered, he joins forces with the tough Spanish detective investigating criminal gangs on the island and a former spy to find those responsible for a complex web of crime and violence. Sam finds he has to learn to play by a new set of rules and a different type of justice when he goes up against the ruthless boss of an Armenian organised crime gang.

The Pollensa Connection

Book Two

Lily Green is scared stiff. Kidnapped after she leaves her work in Pollensa, Mallorca, she doesn't know why this has happened and even when drugged and interrogated, she still has no idea what they want from her.

When her grandparents ask for their help, Anna and Sam Martínez start to look into Lily's disappearance. Together with the rest of the team, they soon realise there's a lot more at stake when they find themselves pitched against Sir Charles Groom, the CEO of a corporate giant and Oleg Makarovich, a ruthless Russian billionaire, in a 'deniable' operation sanctioned by MI6.

What does Lily know and how is it linked to a shopping centre collapse in London and a multi-million pound money laundering operation? The more the team discover about The Pollensa Connection, the wider the net extends, leading to far greater danger for everyone concerned.

The Soller Solution

Book Three
Back for the third time in the 3R series, the team have to deal with three seemingly unconnected coincidences as they answer a call for help from Sam's old boss.

When Sam Martínez gets a call from Tony Theakston, he's at the hospital waiting on news about Terri, his half-sister. So the timing isn't great, but when Tony says it's urgent, Sam listens and eventually he and Greg agree to help try to prevent the theft of a €10 million picture.

What starts as a favour to his old boss, to try to stop an art thief holding an international art gallery to ransom, soon turns into a far more complex affair, involving a multi-millionaire security systems designer, one of Sam's old adversaries and a Spanish organised crime gang, where the stakes become increasingly more dangerous for everyone concerned.

The Palma Foundation

ACKNOWLEDGEMENT

This book would not have been possible without the help and encouragement of my wife, Julie, but it is also the motivation I have had from the amazing reception of the first three books in the series that I must thank you, my readers.

Little did I know when I started that my writing would lead me to connect with so many people and this in turn would bring too many happy experiences for me to mention here, but the ones in particular that stand out are my friends Miquel at Contrabando Tapas Bar in Llucmajor and Aina and her family at Restaurante Bar Coral in Puerto Pollensa and Andres Gelabert of Bodegas Angel vineyard in Santa Maria del Camí, who bring a little bit of real life to the storyline with the cameos they each play.

I must also mention all my new friends within the Writers and Readers of the Balearics Facebook group, who regularly meet up in Palma de Mallorca, and have made me feel so welcome when I've been able to get to one of the meetings.

Once again, I have had the fantastic help of my review team, Chris Back, Julie Davies, Caroline Green, Shonagh MacMaster, David Parker, Maureen Webb and Alan Young - thank you so much again guys for all you do for me.

REVIEWS

Reviews and feedback are the life blood of all of us authors. So, finding out what you thought of my book is really important to me.

If you have purchased this through Amazon, then please may I ask you to take a moment to leave a review for me on their website.

The more (hopefully) good reviews a book gets, the better the chances are for Amazon to promote the book when readers are searching for new titles, so please help me to attract new audiences with a positive review of what you liked about this book.

If there is anything you wish to send to me personally, be it inaccuracies, typos, or just to tell me you liked the book, then please email direct on petedavies01@hotmail.co.uk

And I am usually in Mallorca 2-3 times a year, so let me know when you're over there as I often meet up with my readers at Restaurante Bar Coral in Puerto Pollensa. Thanks again, Pete